THE GALAXY IS OURS

A Superhero Epic

JAIME MERA

Dedication

I dedicate this book to my beloved children, and extended family of friends. In the world of science fiction, the most amazing stories of aliens, monstrous creatures, villains, heroes, people as yourselves, or spirits can come to life. Nations can battle nations, planets can conquer planets, governments can strengthen or oppress the weak, and stars can destroy or give birth to new life. A single person can change the outcome of many or many can change a person, but in all of this life and death drama, only a hero can change a galaxy.

Published books:

A Superhero Epic Series

Creator (2004, 2014)

He is Known as Ego (2006, 2014)

Guild Without a Name (2014)

The Galaxy is Ours (2014)

Non-Fiction

Jesus and the Paint on the Wall, What Do People Live For? (2012)

Preface

--- ✤ ---

The planet Moridan was in chaos having to plead for help, suffering from the Gillithe rampage of destruction in the Corima sector of space, known to Earthlings as the 30 degree outer rim of the Scutum-Centaurus Arm of the Milky Way Galaxy. The Argonian Empire had protected them for over a millennium introducing them to the space age a century ago, but they were on the outskirts of the empire's boundary spanning the majority of the entire galaxy. Moridanians had requested expansion into the Gillithe trade routes but political and economic agendas on both sides opened them up to piracy and treachery. The race was young, but their technology was vast with the help of the Argonians. They had colonized all habitable planets and satellites in their solar system, but were running out of livable space. The trade routes would allow them to expand in mass numbers instead of depending on small colonizing entities.

In the first decade of using the trade routes, many ships fell victim to pirates and heavy tolls enforced by the Gillithe regime. It was a case of suppression which didn't fare well for the Moridan government and colonies. Argonian negotiators were forced to leave the area, but the old Argonian treaty with Moridan kept the Gillithe regime from completely taking control of the sector with their dictatorial government and splintered factions. The Argonian monitors sent word to the royal family, but the problem was that even though faster than light (FTL) travel was available to the Argonians, they were stretched out to the limit with war on three fronts taxing their resources and military might.

The Moridanian fate was not the first time a race was in the brink of disaster, but it was the first time billions of living beings were being killed or oppressed for the sake of undermining the Argonian proclamations for freedom and peace in the galaxy.

The Argonian royal family and their allies agreed to face the problems with policing up the boundaries by creating a Galactic Guard force. It was their sole purpose to fix disputes, neutralize hostile forces, and even declare war in the name of the empire. It was a task which only the strongest and most loyal of super beings could accomplish for the empire. Queen Omia decreed that the Guards would not be of Argonian origin alone, and must be elected for their courage, integrity, power, and pursuit for justice. It was an undertaking which no one had done before, and was to be headed by Princess Navia Yalu, eldest niece of the Queen, and ruler of the Dothoria realm. Queen Omia had no direct off spring or husband, and Princess Navia was next in line for the throne if the queen died without a direct offspring, a king, or a suitable replacement host. Many races and planets had beings of great power, but it wasn't just about power, it was about diplomacy and the Queen trusted her niece to personally lead the critical mission. The princess sent emissaries and scouts to find candidates and confirm their right to be a Galactic Guardian. Time was running out as messages from Moridan came in with a call for reinforcements as the undesired war was being lost.

Many candidates were considered, but since time was a factor in selection, Princess Navia decided to select the initial guards with the trust of her scouts' investigations and recommendations. Once the royal family and parliament members got wind of her decision, the reputation and confidence of the Princess and Queen Omia were at stake. But, the Queen was not moved by the opinions of parliament, and gave Princess Navia full support to include an armada for Navia's personal use. The armada was gathered from the reserve forces, which the princess preferred because most of the ships and crew were veterans of past wars and operations. It was a race against time for every peace abiding being in the galaxy as guardians are informed and recruited into the greatest influential force in the Argonian empire.

This story does not start here however. This story begins aboard a courageous Earth space station caught in the middle of World War III. The International Space Station: a beacon of hope for a future in space, and a new era for Earth was now traveling in low orbit at over four thousand miles per second being witness to massive South American military forces simultaneously overrunning four continents in a matter of days without strong opposition. Colonel Brian Cornelius, US astronaut and commander, along with Cosmonaut Lieutenant Colonel Milan Golubova, communications specialist, monitored open radio traffic which the South American space fleet allowed to be received by the station. In less than six days, the military might of North America, Europe, and Asia had been neutralized. The only pocket of major resistance was in the Middle East and North Africa; however, reports indicated that they too had fallen to Estabon Ramirez's 10th Armor Legion a few hours ago. Superhumans were nowhere to be seen except in bits of radio traffic, more like rumors of superhumans, who were also being defeated by the South Americans. Australia seemed to have been doing nothing about the South American invasion. Both men aboard the station could only guess as to what would happen once the two military powers, or superhumans with power to destroy the Earth collided.

List of Characters

Lord Klakin — Leader of the Galactic Guardians (born on the planet Ios)

Lady Cerimon — Galactic Guardian (born on the planet Jahnuny)

Lord Hellfire (Rick Alexander) — Galactic Guardian and Member of Energy, Fire and Light (EFL) superhero group in New York

Lord Medroc (Patrick Lawrence) — Galactic Guardian (born in Seattle, WA)

Lord Morinar (Fedar Emsky) — Galactic Guardian (born in Arsk, Russia)

Lord Sedric — Galactic Guardian (born on the planet Tir Goth)

Lord Quatris (Scott Emerson) — Galactic Guardian and Leader of EFL

Lord Axer — Galactic Guardian (born on the planet Argonia)

Lady Kara — Galactic Guardian (born on the planet Shimoor)

Lord Paldez — Galactic Guardian (born on the planet Argonia)

Lady Sinop — Galactic Guardian (born on the planet Rasdal)

Lady Hebshilon — Klakin's mother and Special Envoy for Queen Omia

Larissa Emsky — Fedar Emsky's mother (born in Perm, Russia)

Princess Navia Yalu — Princess of Dothoria, the largest realm in the Argonian Empire

Queen Omia — Sole ruler and queen of the Argonian Empire

Sorthan — Emissary for Queen Omia and Princess Navia, in Kron sector of the Argonian Empire

Urhimia — Emissary for Queen Omia and Princess Navia, in Rim sector of the Argonian Empire

The Galaxy is Ours, A Superhero Epic

Yohania — Emissary for Queen Omia and Princess Navia, in Hith sector of the Argonian Empire, second in command of the starship Lardose

Elexsuia Peli Lanta — Second in command of Princess Navia's flagship

Joldar Crom — Argonian Royal Soothsayer for the Queen

Loar Crom — Argonian Royal Soothsayer for HRH Toluvis

Lieutenant Rudez — Argonian telepath of the House of Cammeth

Prince Hethos — Argonian Prince of the House of Cammeth

Her Royal Highness Toluvis Cammeth — Ruler of the House of Cammeth

Queen Neeva / Susan M. Goodman / Pandora — New Queen of the Argonian Empire and member of the Eternal Champions

King Etron / John Goodman / Mindseye — New King of the Argonian Empire and member of the Eternal Champions

Captain Allina — Captain of the lead scout ship Teldious

Admiral Frouls Lek — Admiral of the Royal 7th Pylaxian Space Fleet

Feesel — Drakon, mercenary

Hamiftar — Drakon, space suit engineer

Kormath Sittar — Faction Leader of Drakon spies

Emperor Tiaxtee — Ruler of the Pylaxian Empire

Emperor Zuphra — Ruler of the Sitherian Empire

Vox'wer — Celestial Seer spirit, planet destroyer

Colonel Peter Cornelius — US Astronaut and ISS commander

Lieutenant Colonel Milan Golubova — Russian Cosmonaut and communications specialist on the ISS

Joshua Marks — All powerful superhuman

Richard Octavian / Creator — Leader of the Eternal Champions

Elizabeth A. Octavian / Isis — Member of the Eternal Champions

Larcis G. Draven / Night — Member of the Eternal Champions

Erica — Member of the Eternal Champions (Super Artificial Intelligence computer)

Battle Fortress Lardose — Lady Hebshilon's flag ship

Star Destroyer Darhim — Commander Sorthan's scout ship

Star Destroyer Gurgus — Cerimon's flagship in the Colax sector of space

Star Destroyer Hydrex — Commander Urhimia's scout ship

Star Destroyer Volatis — King Etron's secondary flag ship

UFF Andromeda –South American Space Fleet Flagship

UFC Antares – South American Space Cruiser, Battleship class

Kiex – Pylaxian language

Vorlin, or Du Los – Universal languages used in the Milky Way Galaxy

Races

Argonian — Origin – Argonia	**Kelos** — Origin – Kel
Baxcion — Origin – Ios	**Moridanian** — Origin – Moridan
Drakon — Origin – Lyra sector of space	
Earthling — Origin – Earth	**Pylaxian** — Origin – Plax
Gillithe — Origin – Tarthillia	**Seer** (Crestin) — from dwarf galaxy
Goth — Origin – Tir Goth	**Sitherian** — Origin – Cros Asviel
Keelin — Origin – Jahnuny	**Wordian** — Origin – Cameil

Hutor, Quilar, and Morthemar — Argonian bloodlines, most royal bloodline traits come from the Quilar.

Contents

Chapter One

--- ❋ ---

The Guardians

The International Space Station, 241 miles above India, 2016

The Earth's surface was dark with extremely small lights indicative of the presence of humans living out the day in the early morning of the night. Colonel Cornelius looked out through a circular window the size of a basketball, wondering what was happening back on Earth. The South American armies where not destroying any civilian areas, property, even military installations which didn't present themselves as major threats. Early reports indicated all short range and long range nuclear capabilities were destroyed within the first hour of the South American space fleet launching into orbit. Eduardo Ramirez's declaration of war and call for surrender was broadcasted globally on all known open frequencies and in over 700 languages. It was made clear that South America was going to take over the planet to create one government and one global nation. Peter's heart was in conflict over many things. His country was being invaded and there was nothing he could do about it. His family was down there without him, and even though he knew the South Americans were not tyrants or blood thirsty, people would and have been killed already due to this invasion. For a third world war it was very low in casualties so far, but more would die before peace was actually realized. As he looked out beyond into the dark horizon and blackness of space, the station's electrical power went out. Peter looked around for signs of backups firing up, but there were none.

"Milan, what's going on?" Peter yelled across two modules/compartments.

The station was normally occupied by six to ten astronauts but in the wake of the invasion, the station was allowed to evacuate to minimal manning. The station was no threat to the military forces; however, South America and mission control thought it in the best interest for the astronauts to be on land instead of space for the time being. Two volunteer astronauts were kept on board to ensure the station didn't decay into the Earth's atmosphere. The station had been in orbit for over thirteen years and it seemed unlikely that it would fall out of the sky, but today was a day many people never wanted to see or imagined.

"Commander, we've lost everything, nothing electrical works!" Milan's mild St. Petersburg accent resounded back through the dark modules.

Milan feverishly touched the electronics and consoles he was so familiar with feeling his way towards wiring and backup batteries. Dim lighting from the window portals finally allowed his eyes to adjust, but the darkness kept him from seeing the internals of the consoles and batteries he was able to open. He tried his pen light but it too had no power. "Commander, nothing's working." He sadly and softly said in deep thought.

A green light shone inside his module as Peter entered the compartment with a Chemlight in his hand. "Good thing for non electrical backups." Peter slightly smiled, and tossed a stick towards Milan.

The chem-stick darted straight through the zero gravity environment into Milan's waiting palm.

They surveyed the equipment with dismay as if an electromagnetic pulse had destroyed everything to include battery backups. But that was almost an impossibility since their equipment was constructed to handle very strong EMPs, and it didn't explain the severe drain of energy from batteries or lack of power from the solar panels.

"There is a little power in the energy cell." Milan stated as the men were trying to figure out what had happened.

Before Peter could respond, a very bright green light entered the station's windows. The brightness easily overshadowed the two chemlights. Both men propelled themselves to the nearest window. They crowded the portal seeing the atmosphere covered by an opaque bright green aura. The Earth seemed to be encased in an energy field which barely engulfed the station.

Peter estimated that they were maybe a few miles or so

from coming into contact with the green field. He was severely troubled, but his face only showed mild concern. "We need to get power before we hit that thing."

Milan thought for a second. "Commander, we might be able to put together battery cells from other modules to get enough power for the radio and send a Mayday."

The station's orbit would decay in time, but the danger was not falling through the atmosphere and burning up, the immediate danger was going into an unknown energy field that might destroy the station on contact. The decay for several miles would be an hour or six. Peter thought about what Milan suggested and understood that the only ones who would most likely be hearing their radio broadcast or would be in a position to help them was the South American space fleet.

Peter relaxed a little. "Yeah, they're in a higher orbit so maybe they don't have the problems we do and can help us… How many cells do we need?"

"Six more cells should do it." Milan confidently replied.

"Let's get moving then."

The two men quickly gathered six battery cells and electronic accessories to link them together. Milan yelled out other materials for them to gather as they moved around the station. The cells were created to generate power over time if the power source from the solar panels failed. It wasn't a large amount of power, but combined with other cells it could be used to power a critical component. Unfortunately, the cells were severely drained of energy and the amount of energy was barely enough to power the radio.

They broadcasted a Mayday for several minutes but the cells were taxed too much. The men put on skin suits and prepared for the worst which would be freezing to death if the green energy field didn't kill them. Each module was supposed to be self sufficient, but when all fail safes were not working, it didn't matter since they would not be able to maintain a safe internal temperature, waste disposal system, or breathable atmosphere. It was twenty minutes later when the radio was operational again with power. They sent out a Mayday again but there was no response as the cells died once again. Both men continued to strategize other options, but there were none. They could only hope the South American space fleet was fully operational and able to save them.

The station's orbit was not decaying as expected, and the green force field seemed to be a few hundred meters from them. Peter and Milan both calculated the decay and were sure the station was not suppose to be falling that quickly. It finally dawned on Peter that maybe the field was getting bigger and moving closer to the station, not the station to the Earth.

Milan was looking out of the portal and a figure of a head appeared in front of it. He jumped back and even Peter was startled when his attention was placed on the window. But their shock turned to joy as they recognized the superhuman on the other side of the window as Quatris, leader of EFL, Energy Fire and Light, a superhero group stationed in New York.

Quatris' eyes and hair were glowing white. A black skin

tight mask covered his forehead, nose, and cheeks. He had a pure black outfit with a white star design on his chest, with extending white lines into his hands and feet. A dark field, more like a shadow entered the module where the window and Quatris was at. Quatris seemed to walk into the module by stepping through the sphere of darkness. The darkness went away, Quatris' eyes stopped glowing white and the green light from the force field below and chem lights returned the module to its unusual state of illumination.

"Colonel Cornelius and Lt. Commander Golubova I presume." Quatris said.

"Yes, how did you know?" Milan suspiciously asked.

"The Antares told me, once they heard your Mayday. But we don't have time to chat right now. Hold on to my hands and I'll fly you out to safety." Quatris commanded, and extended his hands, palms upward, out to the two men."

The astronauts grabbed Quatris' hands and a black energy like ball engulfed the three men. They moved through the module and into space. The space station quickly disappeared from sight as Quatris flew out towards the UFF Andromeda with his two guests. Peter wondered why Quatris didn't just push the station into a higher orbit, but that would not solve the energy problem; so he presumed that the fate of the station was sealed for destruction. The South American fleet flagship was four thousand miles in orbit from Earth. Its structure was an elongated triangular design, and completely black. The internal red and blue lights and landing guiding lights gave it an elegant look in the blackness of space and brilliance from the green field. It was roughly less than two miles long, three forth of a mile wide, and a quarter of a mile in height. Twenty nozzle like closed apertures on the rear of the ship were not being used at the moment, but it was very likely that their primary creation was for traveling long distances through space, not just the initial gravitational escape into Earth's orbit.

Quatris flew the thousands of miles in less than a minute. He entered the South American spaceship as if he were a regular crew member. They bypassed the landing dock and entered a transfer chamber, making it safe for the two humans to breathe the ship's artificial atmosphere. The men were met by a medical team, and a security escort.

A telepath was also present and explained what was happening to the Earth and the situation all life forms on the planet were in. The green force field was a weapon created by the Australians with alien technology. It was causing the climate to rise exponentially, and kept anything outside of the field from seeing the surface of the planet. It effectively neutralized the South American space fleet's space advantage and most of their air power. All living organisms would die of heat and lack of sunlight in less than a few days at best estimates.

The reality of the destructive intentions by Australia was very hard to accept, and if it wasn't for the presence of Quatris they would not have believed the information the South American telepath was telling them. South America started the war in order to get their space fleet into orbit, before the Australians could initiate their doomsday weapon. Steps were being taken to defeat the Australians and their alien technology by both South America and superhumans.

The meeting was short with the medical team and telepath. The ship was on high alert and they were told to stay with Quatris for now. Peter and Milan stayed with Quatris as he viewed Earth from an observatory room. The Andromeda, under the command of Eduardo Ramerize, ordered the fleet to increase their orbit by two thousand miles, and be prepared to fight a possible alien attack from outer space.

Peter and Milan had many questions that the telepath didn't expound on or knew. Quatris seemed to be in deep thought as he simply watched the Earth and the uncertain future.

"Why aren't you going down there and saving Earth?" Milan asked out of anger.

Quatris smiled and explained that the human race was at a turning point, not just for the inhabitants on the planet itself, but on an intergalactic scale. They had no idea how much power he and other superhumans wielded, but it was not his sole position to save the day on every occasion. Creator had explained it clearly and united the superhumans to currently fight the threat. It was not his time to act, so instead he told the brave astronauts the importance of what was really going on. He sat back on a lounge seat and started to tell them a tale of a far away empire called the Argonian Empire, ruled by a great queen. His story telling mesmerized the men as he spoke of the Galactic Guardians from the past and how Earth became a planet of great importance.

Nostha Plateau of the Tropical Belt, Planet Ios, 2001

An eight foot tall humanoid and reptilian figure crouched down on the tall grassy ground alert to all his surroundings. The odor of blood and animal flesh went through his nostrils being only a mile from a fresh kill of Marboo, a type of Earth antelope. His reptilian head had no hair, and nostrils were similar to a human nose, but had internal flaps which could instantly plug up the holes. His jaw and mouth extended outward like an ape, with sharp tiger like teeth. His eyes were wide like a snake with eye brows made of hundreds of very thin splinters of silicon cartilage. His skin was not smooth like a snake, but rugged with many small glasslike scales. His five foot long tail was eight inches thick at its base ending at a point on the other end, used for balancing his body when moving at high speeds. He was a predator, looking for another predator named a Liku.

The Liku were super fast large warm blooded quadruped hunters. Their bodies were covered with strong bone scales, but were very stealthy as natural oils and hairs kept them from rubbing together roughly. The scales were not for fighting other animals, but more for not sustaining injuries as they ran over eighty miles per hour through plants and terrain which would easily cut them to shreds without their special skin. Their heads were slender with an eagle beak like mouth. They had four ears, but were hidden by their bone scales. Their long tails had poisonous spikes, to include small four inch leg spikes. They were very slender and grew to be as long as twenty feet from the end of tail to beak. They were the deadliest predators in the tropical belt, but they only naturally procreated once or twice in their life time.

Young Liku were killed by the lead male bulls, when food was short or they felt threatened by too many up and runners for their position. It was a balance in the ecology which ensured survival for the species and other animals.

The Liku were now the hunted by a race called Baxcion, a mixture of reptilian, aquatic and mammalian characteristics into one humanoid formed being, from birth throughout their life span of a few hundred years. It was ironic that this particular Baxcion was not afraid of the Liku, since the Liku almost exterminated the Baxcion race while in the tropical belt of Ios. The migration to colder climates in the past centuries kept the Baxcion race alive, and in many ways made them stronger. Even then, the Liku were not to be played with being more dangerous than a charging lion or the most venomous of snakes, but this particular Baxcion was an exception to the rule being immune to the deadly poisons of the tropical belt and was much more lethal to his surroundings than his enemies. He was far stronger, faster, and smarter than any Baxcion on the planet. He was an outcast in his world and in many ways an alien in a world that had a balance of nature which he defied. The Baxcion was an advance race with languages and technology to some degree, but they were best described as a druid class with nature focused culture and ideology. It was this common way of thought which kept them grounded and never using their intelligence for space exploration. The technology was all nature based with great strides into medicine, communication, and forces of nature like energy, wind, heat, and gravity. The major metropolitans of the world were interconnected with vast transit systems using magnetism and heat conduction. Their communication technology gave them access to inter planetary races, but they made their intentions clear that they would not pursue space travel unless their planet was in an immediate global state of crisis. In addition, they made a proclamation of non-intrusion so that visits, media, and communication with outsiders were strictly monitored or prohibited. The great span of tropical rain forest surrounding the planet, known as the Tropical Belt, was made into a wildlife preserve to maintain balance and to advance medical research. The longevity of the race was due primarily to advancements in medicine, but what they did not expect was uncontrolled variations and adaptations in the gene pool.

Baxcion babies were born with physical irregularities, super intelligence, and mentally enhanced senses. There was a dark time in Baxcion history as many Baxcion were executed, or surgically altered to eliminate their special abilities. As knowledge of other worlds filtered down to the citizens, Baxcions were allowed to leave the planet as exiles, instead of facing execution.

Unfortunately, leaving the planet was not an option in the infancy of this Baxcion's past. His name was Klakin, who went into exile by default due to his parent's actions. It was an attempt to keep him alive as his parents escaped into the Tropical Belt many decades ago. Klakin was raised from infancy by his parents who taught him everything about the world he was thrown out of, and other worlds he only dreamt of among the stars covering the night sky every day. He was a genius and very strong, but his unique abilities didn't prevent his father from dying under the talons of the Liku. He and his mother lived in the tropical belt in relative peace and ease after Klakin staked out his territory covering a fifty mile radius around their underground home.

Many years passed until Klakin and his mother finally made interstellar communication with the nearest space faring race. There was a chance that communication outside of the planet would target them as a nuisance to the Baxcion united government, but they cared nothing about the government and the world it suppressed. They had lived in the tropical belt for decades without governmental interference or interest, probably because the government didn't see their existence and passiveness as a threat to the regime.

Klakin could talk to someone outside of a world that didn't shun him; unfortunately, the people on the other end did not have an incentive to go into a planet which was under stellar proclamation for seclusion. However, an Argonian scout was led to Klakin primarily through the interplanetary blogs and stories of a Baxcion who lived in the tropical belt of Ios. Normally, it was no major accomplishment for someone living in the wilderness of a planet, but the Tropical Belt of Ios was famous for its lethality, and it was not a matter to ignore as Argonians were known for their attention to detail, leaving no stone unturned.

Klakin's black oval eyelids blinked several times as a thin layer of clear silicon mesh protected his pupils. The Liku were intruding into his staked boundary, but now they were scattering, and running away from him. He looked up to see four bright blue lights descending on his location. He knew it was not an aircraft used in the major cities, and concluded that it was an alien craft of some sort. He felt defenseless out in the middle of the tall grass with no substantial cover nearby for several miles. His reptilian looking tail slowly swayed back and forth as he zoomed in on the lights with his eagle like vision. The outside of his skin was covered with very fine scales, and resembled reptilian features, but like the Liku, the scales were made of tempered silicon, almost like glass. The light which hit his body mixed with a complex circulatory system of pigments allowing his skin to mimic his surroundings. He was not transparent, but would put the best chameleon on Earth to shame. Klakin saw the exhaust of ion emitters with a circular base. The ship was probably spherical in design and used ion propulsion by the lack of loud sound, but it didn't make sense, since crafts like these were outlawed having thought to be damaging to the planet's atmosphere. The tropical belt was also a restricted area and crafts were not allowed to enter it within a twenty mile altitude. The ship was not here with the government's permission and in his heart Klakin was happy, knowing that not everyone followed the government's tyrannical laws.

Klakin jumped and sprinted south over 150 mph, quickly passing the fleeing Liku. The ship pursued with ease coming directly twenty meters above him. Klakin stopped in his tracks once he heard the ship call out to him in the Argonian language.

"We come in peace to request your help." A female voice said.

Klakin was familiar with the Argonian language, but he had only heard it in audio and video recordings, and his mother and father who spoke it to him as part of instructions.

He looked up at the ship which had also stopped moving and hovered above him. "What do you want from me?'" He said a little broken trying to recall certain words. He was semi-fluent in hearing and reading Argonian, but not in speaking it.

"Please allow us to land so we can come out and speak with you."

"Come." Klakin replied, his voice was very deep, but also very vivid to comprehend.

The ship moved forty feet to the side and landed on top of the grass burning circles at the touchdown points with four metallic pole shaped leg extensions, keeping the hull fifteen feet off the ground. The ship was saucer in design reaching a height of ten meters and about forty meters in diameter. A sliding square door opened along the underside and a suited figure in Argonian attire floated down on the tall grass. The low humming noise of the ship stopped as the engines were turned off or placed on idle. The Argonian suit was plain in design which resembled a military flight suit except it was semi glossy as if made of black aluminum foil. The female had no helmet on. Her crystal, and bright green colored eyeballs, along with silver skin quickly gave away her Argonian features. Her hair was silky reddish silver rolled up and bundled to the back of her head. She was short to him, maybe 70 inches tall. It was clear to Klakin that she was from the sub race known as Quilar.

The Argonians were three races in one, sub divided into the Hutor, Quilar, and Morthemar races. There were no major differences in DNA, but it was enough to separate the races. The immunity system and physical characteristics were somewhat different between races, but what united them all was that they all had a biological link which allowed them to naturally procreate among all three sub races. The dominate genes or natural selection took hold of the final offspring, which did cause problems in the past over a millennium ago, but the intermixing of the three races united it into what is known to the galaxy as the Argonian race. The royal family was predominately of Quilar descendants, but it didn't matter to too many people except those who knew the difference. Klakin had been taught well and understood that this alien in front of him was likely from a royal bloodline. The royal family was known to have special mental powers and could control energy to include antimatter. So, it was rumored, but how else could they have ruled for so long. Klakin's lungs expanded in excitement as thoughts raced in his mind. He had already logically figured out thousands of reasons why this alien was specifically in front of him, but the most important one to him was the high probability that he and his mother would not be stuck on this planet much longer.

"I am Klakin." He introduced himself before the Argonian said anything.

"I am Yohania, emissary to Queen Omia and Princess Navia, rulers of the Argonian Empire. I have come here on a mission to find heroes who are willing to fight to save the galaxy." Yohania's voice was rough, but feminine still. It sounded different in Ios' atmosphere than from the inside of the ship which was very rich in oxygen.

"I will go with you on one condition." Klakin replied knowing that this was a rare chance in a life time to be able to leave the world which he loved but hated at the same time. There was no future where he dwelt and in his heart there was a hope that space was where he could make a difference for himself and others.

Yohania looked at him, almost surprised that he would volunteer without questions or allowing her to explain the entire story. Her empathic senses took a few seconds to kick in, sensing that he was excited and truthful. "What is your condition?"

"I will only go with you if you get my mother off this planet right now and find a place where she can live in safety." Klakin said standing erect with his arms crossed.

"Done. Follow me and I will explain what you volunteered for." Yohania smiled inside with relief that his recruitment was so easy. She had been monitoring Klakin from orbit and knew he was unique with powers that fitted the profile Princess Navia demanded. What she didn't know was his character, but being near him, her empathy senses told her he was the kind of hero the princess asked for.

Klakin stood there for a few seconds, almost in shock as he realized that he and his mother were really going to get off the planet very shortly. He quickly came to his senses, unfolded his arms and swiftly walked into the field of light and energy where Yohania was awaiting him. They both floated up into the ship as the entrance automatically enlarged to accommodate both beings.

Ten minutes later, Klakin's mother, Hebshilon, was brought aboard the scout probe. She was in awe to see the Argonian and hear what was in store for them. She and Klakin saw their home disappear as the craft flew off, with no regrets or desire to return. The ship quickly made it into orbit, easily defeating any detection systems used by the ruling united government. Both Baxcion were surprised to see that the ship they were in flew behind Ios' smallest moon revealing Yohania's main ship, the Lardose. The shiny sea blue starship de-cloaked exposing its two and a half mile long super structure. It was of an elongated triangular design with what seemed like two cylinder shaped boosters on the bottom and two on top of the main fuselage. There was a bay entrance on top of the ship which opened up and swallowed the scout ship. The starship was a heavy military battle fortress and part of Princess Navia's armada. It was an older version of the starships fighting in the Void, a sector of space between the Milky Way galaxy and the Canis Major Dwarf galaxy, but there were modifications and unique advantages that the ship had which included a cloaking system that used less energy. The drawback was that the energy source was an old style fusion reactor which ran all shield systems. The weapon systems were crude in accuracy, but much more destructive. The crew was well trained and experienced, but due to the emergency mission many needed supplies and technical issues onboard were in repair or being produced. It would take several weeks for all food processers to be able to supply a well balanced spread of food, otherwise everyone had to settle with nutrition mixes and liquid proteinotic enzyme capsules. Many shuttles were being constructed or updated. The weapon systems were systematically being upgraded with electron generators increasing accuracy and sustainability. The main engines were already upgraded, but there was much work to be done in engineering and life support systems upgrades. There were always upgrades being done, and secret equipment projects were being lead by the Lardose special engineering section.

Princess Navia received the first report of a recruit which

met her standards. She was over 30,000 light years away, but commanded they rendezvous so she could personally meet this Baxcion which her emissary found. It was no coincidental finding and Navia would make sure Klakin knew what was at stake.

The meeting would take place in three weeks, in which time Klakin and Hebshilon caught up with current events on the galaxy. Both mother and son were amazed to see worlds which didn't resemble their own to include worlds they thought they knew about. The Argonian telepaths made it very easy for them to learn quickly, but it also placed a heavy strain on Hebshilon's mind. She requested to stop using the telepath's help after a few days and was content on the knowledge she had already gleamed to start her new life. It took them several more days to adjust to the high oxygen rich atmosphere in the ship, even though the Argonians didn't need oxygen to survive, consideration was given to other races in the ship. In some sections of the ship oxygen levels were very low or nonexistent to accommodate passengers and safety measures to prevent combustible compounds from creating a fire or explosions.

The ship came out of hyperspace two light years from the rendezvous point. They scanned the area for any anomalies twenty light years out, and Yohania commanded they wait decloaked for the Princess. An hour later, Princess Navia's flagship was detected a quarter of a light year away as they also decloaked. The flagship was saucer in design 1,000 meters in diameter and 250 meters at its apex. The surface was flat black and smooth with no running lights. There seemed to be no engine exhaust ports, but moving dark gray discolorations around the rim of the disk suggested emissions from the rim propelled the ship as desired. Several hundred bubble-like weapon turrets surrounded the body on top and underneath. It was not the largest or strongest of ships, but it had the most advanced defensive countermeasures, makeup of materials, and force fields. The flagship at the time was one of four ships which were specifically created for the royal family.

The two ships stayed ten hundred meters apart as Princess Navia's shuttle transported her into the Lardose. Klakin and Yohania awaited the princess in the landing bay which could store forty small shuttles. There were only eight shuttles thou, and room was intentionally made to facilitate the Princess's arrival. The shuttle eased into the locking platform, while guards ensured the bay was secure and clear of unauthorized personnel. The shuttle side door opened and a charcoal chrome black metallic ramp extended down to the platform.

Princess Navia emerged out of the shuttle. Her sun tanned skin was similar to human texture and pigment, which was a characteristic of a Morthemar, even though she was of Quilar origin. The natural long silver hair and crystal green eyeballs were trademarks of the royal family. She was slender, but not fragile at all as her special ability was to be able to instantly regenerate her body at will. Her mental abilities also rivaled any royal family member or soothsayer. She was the eldest of princesses or princes in the family having lived over 743 years. Queen Omia was the eldest of all the royal family having ruled for over a 1,100 years. Two kings had died, one of old age, and the other in war, but she hadn't remarried since Princess Navia came of age and status. Princess Navia's gray flight suit was lightly armored with shiny sapphire two inch plates covering the entire suit. She wore a slim titanium colored metallic crown around her head, but it served a dual purpose by proclaiming her royal status, and enhanced her mental senses.

An entourage of five people followed Princess Navia comprising of four guards and a soothsayer. The imperial guards carried heavy assault rifles and armor suits. The soothsayer was lightly protected with her black emerald cloak and a thick long silver staff. They all stopped at the edge of the ramp as Princess Navia stood directly in front of Klakin and Yohania. Princess Navia stood six feet tall, but Klakin's height of almost eight feet outdid everyone in the area. Klakin stood relaxed to include his tail which was coiled behind him but seemed to be almost lifted off the floor.

"You must be Klakin from the planet Ios?" the princess said perfectly in the Baxcion language, her voice very mature and soothing.

Klakin and Yohania knelt on one knee. Klakin was familiar with Argonian protocol, simple show of respect, and knew his general role as a Galactic Guardian, but he was not prepared to hear the princess speak to him in his native tongue.

"I am he, your highness." Klakin replied.

"Indeed, rise, and walk with me. Both of you." Princess Navia said and slowly walked to the middle of the bay away from the shuttle and entourage.

"I hear your mother is here on board the Lardose." Princess Navia said.

"Yes, your highness, she is."

"So why is she not here with us?" Navia turned towards Yohania.

"She is not here because she didn't want to be a burden to the mission." Klakin answered.

"Nonsense, she is not a burden, she was an inspiration to you in your youth, and so she shall be now." Navia countered and looked at Yohania.

"I will get her your Eminence." Yohania replied in Argonian and quickly left them, only being fluent in hearing and understanding the Baxcion language.

Klakin looked down at the Princess almost mesmerized by her majestic poise and peering eyes. "Your highness, I am sorry, I should have insisted my mother be here." Klakin said taking on all the blame.

"You can address me as princess. I am not the queen, and every time I hear Your Highness I feel like I'm above a princess. But don't apologize, Yohania knows that I value family and should have insisted Hebshilon be here." Navia politely declined his apology.

"Yohania did strongly insist my mother be here, but I commanded her not to force my mother. It was a decision my mother wanted, and I was not about to argue with her over such a minor matter." Klakin replied looking down into her eyes.

Navia smiled. Many people didn't contradict her trend of thought often and it was a relief to see that the Guardian in front of her was not afraid to speak his mind in a very tactful and honorable way. "To you it might be a minor matter, but to me it is not. Hebshilon is an honored guest, if it wasn't for her you would not be here. The Galactic Guardians will change the face of the galaxy with septillions of lives seeing peace and living in happiness. You do not fully understand the destiny which you are a part of, but I intend to let you and your mother see. In the meantime, tell me about your world."

Klakin was extremely humbled by her insight and demeanor. "Princess, I have only experienced the harsh and beautiful tropical world of Ios. My parents fled into the Tropical Belt when I was an infant. There they raised me in an underground home my father created. I have experienced the cold, but that was in a simulation chamber. I was twenty years of age when my father died from a pack of beasts name Liku. Most of the vegetation is sickening to the stomach or deadly, but very beautiful to behold with many colors and shapes. The orange sun shines on the water making it look like a deep blue color, and is very relaxing." Klakin paused trying to see if the Princess was attentive to his rambling.

Princess Navia was very attentive and motioned Klakin to continue with a nod and slight smile.

Klakin spoke of the many things he loved about his planet, and kept the things he hated out of the conversation or briefly summarized them as not wanting to give them importance to his memory or others attention.

The entourage stood at a distance as Yohania escorted Hebshilon out towards Klakin and Princess Navia.

Hebshilon's appearance changed the conversation to her with Princess Navia giving her a warm welcome and thank you for honoring her with Hebshilon's presence.

Hebshilon was almost speechless to see Navia's expression of gratitude for many things she had not yet done. As far as she was concerned she was going to pick a planet of her choice to settle down in and live out the rest of her life. Princess Navia made it sound like she was the defender of the galaxy just like her son.

Hebshilon was seven feet tall and very slender. She didn't have the special powers her son had, but she was Baxcion and surviving in the Tropical Belt of Ios made her very strong and fast, physically and mentally. Both Klakin and Hebshilon were naturally blending in with their surrounding, so they seemed to be dark grayish in color same as the bay platform and distant walls.

Princess Navia spoke to Hebshilon and Klakin for a short while about how they were treated so far in the starship. Then she requested that Yohania show her where Klakin's quarter was. The imperial guards and soothsayer followed the four once they started to leave the landing bay.

Princess Navia was very general in her conversation with her guests, but once they arrived in front of Klakin's quarter, she motioned for everyone to stay outside while she, Klakin, and Hebshilon went inside.

The living quarter was very spacious and compatible with Klakin's physical and mental needs, to include an extensive interactive three dimensional library. Princess Navia was pleased with the arrangements, because this told her that her wishes were being met. The suite was normally used for royal family and distinguished dignitaries, and as Princess Navia wished, Klakin was a distinguished member of what she called a Galactic Guardian.

Klakin and Hebshilon were both cautious and knew that them being alone with the Princess was a very rare thing. "I am here to ensure Queen Omia's intent is fully accomplished, so please bear with me. I need to mentally explain everything about your importance to the galaxy. I know you had problems with the telepaths, but I am not like the telepaths, you will be well." Princess Navia explained to both but mainly looked at Hebshilon.

"I understand." Hebshilon replied and they all sat down on the large chairs provided for Klakin at a table near his computer console.

"Do we do this one at a time?" Klakin asked knowing that when the telepaths helped him learn, they had to focus only on him.

"No, it is not necessary. I will be projecting thoughts into both your minds. I will make sure you remember all that is projected." Princess Navia extended both hands out so that she could touch them both before starting.

Hebshilon was hesitant, but Klakin softly grabbed her hand reassuring her it would be fine. Her black eyes looked at his son with pride. She extended her hand and grabbed Princess Navia's hand. Princess Navia's hand was warm and cool at the same time sending a soothing cool tingle of energy along Hebshilon's arm and entire body.

Soon, both Baxcion were in a trance. They saw Princess Navia's face and heard a narration of the past. Visions of the empire prior to Queen Omia explained how the empire was established. Most incidents were honorable, but some of the conquests were done out of greed for power and treachery. Queen Omia made sure such activities were stomped out and expanded the empire's power with alliances to include technological initiatives for other races across the galaxy, improving their technology and knowledge of space. Some advanced races opposed the initiatives, but Queen Omia was firm in her decision for the benefit of the race and protection of worlds that were vulnerable to alien conquest. The younger worlds with low technology were monitored and covertly assisted. Worlds that made it to space exploration without destroying themselves, were allowed to join the empire only if parliament agreed to an alliance.

There were six races in opposition to the empire. The separation of distance and conflicting agendas kept enemy forces from uniting and severely damaging the Argonian Empire. The visions of all the opposing races and events which led them to fight against the empire passed through their minds. Visions of the future showed Klakin, Hebshilon, and many other people in the middle of a great war. It was the first time Klakin saw an Earthling, several Earthlings, who fought by his side. They displayed great power fighting starships singlehandedly. The future of the Galactic Guardians was flashed before them and then they understood that what they did mattered for thousands of worlds, to include the Baxcion immigrates who lived beyond Ios among the stars. Queen Omia was concerned that the royal family was in danger from within the family who were siding with the Pylaxian Empire, the strongest of their foes. Pylaxians were bio-energy silicon based beings who fed on pure elements and most carbon based life forms, but they also used up resources like locust and deemed their right to live above all other forms of life. The Argonian Empire, enforcing peace around the universe, was their biggest threat to live without restraint, undermining their rule of a twenty thousand light year section of the galaxy they controlled. The Argonian Empire was peace abiding and not territory or power hungry which was one main reason the empire didn't invade and wipeout the Pylaxians. As long as the Pylaxians didn't start forcing their might onto other races, they would be left alone to live as other races. The images and imprinted knowledge seemed like a very quick, but extremely vivid dream. Klakin and Hebshilon came out of the mental trance. They felt well rested, remembered everything they saw and heard in their minds, but they had no clue how much time had elapsed while in the room with the princess.

Navia looked at both of them. "That didn't hurt did it?"

"No it didn't" Hebshilon said in Argonian.

"I do not have the powers that the other guardians have, why me?" Klakin asked knowing he could not start a fire without an ignition device and had to use a weapon to shoot things.

"Klakin, Klakin. You are the most important of the guardians. You are leader of the guardians. It is your leadership which will make a difference, not just your physical abilities."

Navia said softly. "My trust is in you. What you command in the name of the queen will be honored by her and me."

"I don't know if you should place such great responsibility on me. I am only a Baxcion who just wanted to get out of a deadly jungle." Klakin said looking at both the princess and his mom.

"Both of you are so humble, and that is why I am making you in charge. Your intelligence and love for each other tells me you will do what is right, and that is all the queen and I ask of you." Princess Navia said as she stood up.

"What exactly am I in charge of?" Hebshilon asked.

"The armada the Queen gave me. You will support the guardians and only I or the Queen can counterman your orders to the armada." Navia said.

"Don't you need the armada?" Hebshilon replied.

"No, I have seven fleets in my realm. And I also have to run my realm, therefore leaving you to the empire and your destiny."

The three left Klakin's quarters and returned to the shuttle bay. Princess Navia ordered Yohania to place her on the ship's intercom system, before she boarded the shuttle. "In accordance to royal decree from Queen Omia, Lord Klakin is leader of the Galactic Guardians, and Lady Hebshilon is Commander of the Galactic armada effective now until Queen Omia says otherwise. All Argonians and allies will treat Lord Klakin and Lady Hebshilon with highest status in all the Empire. No one is above them except for Queen Omia and me. The ship's recorder will inform the entire imperial realm of this order." Navia said as the decree was announced throughout the ship.

Klakin's keen sense of smell and attention told him the soothsayer was not pleased with the news and probably was not the only one in the empire with like feelings. As far as anyone was concerned, he was the third most powerful person in the empire now. Klakin didn't really know what to make of the soothsayer, because she seemed to be in her own little world. He knew they had powers to see the future, but that was not it. If she did see the future, then she would have known that he was going to be exalted above everyone else. Or maybe she only pretended to see the future, or was limited in what she saw. Whatever the case, Princess Navia either saw the future herself, the Queen gave her the visions, or a strong soothsayer gave her the visions of a possible future. Princess Navia's soothsayer should not have been surprised with the information; unless the future could be changed as Princess Navia might have done just now. This gave Klakin hope that not all the bad things he saw in the future visions were fixed in time, but it also allowed for good things not to go as predicted. It was up to him to do his best, as would his mother which was his inspiration to never give up.

He wondered if anyone else had noticed the soothsayer's extremely subtle reaction, but probably not since she was in the back and no one seemed to pay too much attention to her. He kept it to himself, but would tell his mom later in private. He was sure many people would oppose him, but maybe more towards Hebshilon being a commander of two fleets, especially since she didn't have the practical experience of being a commander; but Navia had taken care of that. He and Hebshilon knew everything there was to know about space fleet combat, engineering, communications, navigation, details about the enemy, and planetary invasion. Time would prove their competency, but time was not on their side. The Moridanians were on the brink of being destroyed and Klakin had to assemble the guardians as quickly as possible.

Once Princess Navia's shuttle left the ship, Klakin commanded that they depart to Earth. Hebshilon agreed allowing Klakin to find the guardians while she researched what to do with the rest of the armada, who were at the time scattered in a 90,000 light year span of space. Hebshilon thought carefully and knew that soon she could and would task a large part of the armada to wage war with the Gillithe and hopefully stop the bloodshed.

Yohania was informed that another guardian had been recruited in the Kron sector of space, but the details were vague since interstellar communication with that sector was very difficult due to several clustered quasars. The Lardose instantly headed towards Earth at maximum speed, while they communicated with Princess Navia's emissary, Urhimia, who was already in the Rim sector of space which Earth occupied.

Citadel of Ankis, Planet Tir Goth, Kron Sector of Space

The great prophecy of old was a way of life and absolute truth on the planet Tir Goth. The inhabitants, known as Goth, were a race of warriors, but no ordinary warriors. They were specifically bred to enhance their special powers, which placed them among the strongest single race in comparison to others in the galaxy. There were however, exceptions and it was in this particular time of coming that prophets spoke of and was confirmed by the arrival of the Argonian star destroyer, Darhim, and the Queen's emissary. A great tournament was conducted every ten years to find the most powerful fighter on the planet. There were two previous champions alive to battle on this special day, along with thousands of preliminary finalists leading to the tournament. The Citadel of Ankis was a two mile long stadium built to withstand the extreme damaging forces used by the Goth warriors. Large force fields, reinforced grounded safety seats, and light body armor protected the spectators down to the children.

The Goth were a proud people displaying their natural features which included steel like skin, glowing hair, illuminated eyes, or glowing auras around their bodies. Other than those obvious features, they were very similar to humans with a wide variety of facial and body characteristics. They mastered the disciplines of hand to hand combat, energy control, and mental domination. It was this type of visual display of power which gave the stadium a radiance of light as the contestants lined up in the opening ceremony. The Argonians had arrived twenty minutes ago, but the ship stayed ten miles inside the atmosphere as if prepared to fight other starships, and only the envoy, Sorthan, entered the stadium. The president of Tir Goth received Sorthan, and announced the start of the tournament. The planet was in the alliance, but not in parliament. This meant that the inhabitants of the planet Tir Goth were space faring with a very high level of technology, but elected to be neutral. They would be protected by the Argonian Empire and in return the Goth would fight for the Empire within five thousand light years of the planet. The treaty was created five centuries ago which Queen Omia personally negotiated. Many races avoided Tir Goth, knowing that it would be suicidal to fight a planet full of powerful beings that feared no one. A large portion of the population didn't need a ship to travel into space, but they still had a large space fleet which could be used to help the Argonians if ever needed. There was controversy from the beginning of the treaty, because as a race of super beings they did not need protection from the empire. The irony was that they were warriors but rarely ever left into deep space, so they competed against themselves when there were no enemies to fight. Many villainous or fearful people considered this as a blessing, because the Goth would not have much opposition if they desired to conquer any planet they wanted outside of the five thousand light year range. Whatever the reason, the Argonian Empire had a strong ally in the Goth, and in these critical times, they were going to help build the Galactic Guard force.

The matches were about to start as the world watched in person and on live video. Sorthan was seated next to the President in the presidential box. He was slightly shorter than six feet, but was very stocky and muscular. His skin was a very dark tan pigment, and his eyes were like topaz crystals. His hair was shiny black as were his glassy like black fingernails. He scanned the lineup of warriors in the competition and stands with his specialized vision. Energy levels were primarily highest in the lineup of contestants, with a few exceptions like the president and a hand full of spectators. The levels were about even among the lineup, and Sorthan was confident that the person or people he was looking for were among the contestants and not in the audience. He was amazed to see so many people with bio-energy levels almost as high as the royal family members. The energy levels for the contestants were higher than that of the royal family, which gave Sorthan comfort to know that they were on his side.

The first twenty matches simultaneously started without delay. Each match took place in an area of a ten meter circle and lasted until the opponent was knocked out, forfeited, or lost ten points. Points were lost when a damaging blow was physically taken. This meant that the damage had bypassed the defenses of the opponent to include any regeneration abilities. Any negative spike in energy level would indicate such damage. Sorthan thought they were using mechanical sensors to gage the levels, but soon saw that the machinery sensors were a backup as the judges naturally saw the levels and ruled on the matches expertly. He thought he was unique and he was right if he compared himself with the rest of the galaxy but not with the inhabitants of Tir Goth. Sorthan was once again surprised to see the energy levels increase a hundred fold as the contestants fought. The hand to hand matches were specific and demonstrated skill, speed, combative reflexes, and ability to take damage. Only the top twenty finalists were going to be able to fight full out; the preliminary matches were conducted to weed out the weaker warriors so there was a less of a chance for someone getting killed. Each warrior got three matches and would have to win two out of three in order to advance. The next set of matches had the same rules, except that the warriors would have to win all three matches to advance. In a matter of an hour almost 2,000 contestants were dwindled down to 400 warriors.

There was a transition phase that took about thirty minutes where ten fighting platforms the size of one half football fields covered center stage. The warriors were allowed to use power projections and defensive energy manipulation powers. This changed the energy levels to which Sorthan had only seen in starship battles. Sorthan saw many hopefuls but it was still too early to tell who would win or who would meet the Queen's standards. According to Princess Navia's guidance, the winner was not automatically Guardian material, he had to look beyond and pay attention to the person's character. There were about fifty female warriors, but only a handful seemed like they were going to make it to the last twenty. The bouts were exciting and some a little frightening as practically steel like bones were broken or losers were commonly taken off the platforms unconscious. Each platform had a light blue force field which kept the energy projections from hitting innocent targets. Warriors were given three chances and had to win two matches to advance. If a warrior lost the first two matches, he would fight a third match in the hope of eliminating a possible contender. Once the number of contestants went down to 150, another set of matches was started again. Once again the warriors would have to win three out of three matches. The warriors fought two set of matches coming down to the remaining eighteen. The competition was fierce as both previous champions had already been eliminated in the last set of matches.

Sorthan thought they would give the warriors a break for the next set of matches, but they didn't stop progress. The time allotted for recovery was minimal and a very closely monitored factor since endurance was a favored quality in a warrior. Nine of the ten platforms were connected together to create three large platforms roughly a hundred meter by seventy-five meter rectangles. The platforms were lifted twenty feet into the air so the majority of spectators could better see the combat at eye level. Three warriors were positioned on each platform, and the rules were simple, the warrior left standing on each platform was to advance. They were allowed to fly, but not beyond a hundred meters straight up or they would be disqualified. If they were pushed beyond that point they would be allowed to re-enter combat. The boundary of the platforms were enclosed by an almost invisible force field which some of the warriors used to smash their opponents into.

After the first match three warriors were left standing. Forlax, Jinjo, and Sedric. All seemed equal in power, but Jinjo and Sedric distinguished themselves for fighting both opponents at the same time with the quickest two times resulting in knockouts. The next nine warriors quickly took their positions and in a matter of a few minutes, three warriors were left standing, Handar, Dylon, and Wiquel. Sorthan was witnessing a special time of fortune and glory. Not even in Goth history had there been such a display of pure power as if each warrior was a starship shooting antimatter bolts at each other, energy bolts which would be sufficient to destroy cities in a matter of minutes. Two force fields failed and the backup force fields had to keep the energy projections from hitting the audience, but only cheers where heard as the seeming deadly blasts were absorbed by the fields ten feet in front of spectators.

"That was close." President Krachithous said excitedly to Sorthan.

"Do you think it is safe if they continue this way?" Sorthan asked almost naively.

President Krachithous looked at him as if wondering if Sorthan was joking, but he only smiled. "You might be right. We will need to put up two more force fields for the next twenty five matches. Sadus, tell them to add two more force fields!" Krachithous instructed his personal aide.

The crowd was roaring, cheering for their favorite fighters while the three platforms were disassembled and reconnected into one large 200 by 200 meter square platform. The restructuring of the platform took less than ten minutes and a lineup of who were first was created by the scoring system figured out by the fastest times and number of total wins. The lowest scorers were allowed to go last. It was a one on one match with no holding back of power. The ceiling was two hundred meters and a knockout or forfeit was required. Jinjo and Wiquel were the first ones up. The matching was simple; each warrior would have the chance to fight all the remaining finalists, so the warrior with the most wins of a maximum of five wins out of five matches would be winner. There was a possibility that two or three warriors would get four wins each and then there would be a tie breaker, but that would be determined if it happened.

Jinjo won the first match. Sedric and Forlax fought next with Sedric being victor. The warriors were evenly paired up, but there was a difference after the sixth match when the stronger of the six were paired up with the weaker ones. Wiquel instantly knocked out Handar with a close hand attack which was a very impressive feat because the two started out a hundred fifty meters apart. The speed in which the female warrior came next to Handar was mind boggling taking Handar by complete surprise not giving him enough time to react. The entire match lasted less than a second giving her the fastest win ever in tournament history. The stadium throbbed with slamming stomping feet and waling cheers by the audience.

The attractive long greenish yellow haired warrior flew to the side line with pride as Sedric and Jinjo gave her approving nods and congratulations, while the other contestants were awe stricken.

Almost everyone in the audience had to see the replay in slow motion to witness and appreciate the win. The cameras were still a little too slow to capture the speed of Wiquel, with maybe only Sedric, Jinjo, and Forlax being able to keep up with the action.

By the end of twenty matches Sedric and Jinjo had four wins each. Forlax and Wiquel had three wins each, but that didn't matter because the matchup between Sedric and Jinjo would determine the tournament champion.

The final match between Sedric and Jinjo started without delay. The speed and power which the two warriors demonstrated far exceeded anyone's expectations or dreams. The cameras could not keep up with their close hand to hand combat which lasted for several minutes, and then the combat changed to distant combat. Each warrior couldn't get an advantage fighting close up, so they shot at each other with energy beams hoping they could penetrate the other's personal force fields. Both warriors glowed bright white as they increased their power levels beyond any starship Sorthan had seen in his life time. He was worried that they would blow up the entire stadium and kill everyone in the process. The force fields were doing their job and four out of the five fields were brought down. Sedric changed his tactics and pretended to fire his bolts from his hands, but instantly flew behind Jinjo and attempted to hit him in the back with a quick kick to the head. The attempt was commendable and probably would have worked but Jinjo was just as fast as Sedric and flew out of leg range, turned and shot Sedric at point blank range. The blast hit Sedric, but his energy field took the blow and he countered with his own energy attack which he spread out so Jinjo couldn't dodge it. The attack hit Jinjo and temporarily stunned him, but brought down the last force field protecting the audience.

Sedric was about to blast Jinjo another time, but stopped himself and went in for a physical contact knockout. Jinjo recovered and instantly shot Sedric with all he had not realizing that the force fields protecting the audience were down. Sedric knew that if he dodged the attack the energy blast could hit the audience and kill someone, so he stood there and took the full blast in the chest. His personal energy field was weaken but not taken down. The fifty meter knockback of the blast caused him to barely fall off the edge of the platform, before the referee called for a stop in the match. Both warriors stopped fighting waiting to get a ruling since the force fields had been taken down and there were no safety features strong enough to allow them to continue.

The stadium was in an uproar the likes which no World Cup or Super Bowl could duplicate. President Krachithous was speaking to the judges through his ear piece. Sorthan could hear the conversation with ease, and wanted to step in, but waited for the right moment.

"So you are telling me that all the force field generators are blown?" President Krachithous sadly asked.

"Yes Sir." replied the lead engineer who was linked to the conference call with the judges and President.

"Okay judges, who won?" the president wanted an answer.

"Mr. President, both men were still able and ready to continue the fight. If they don't keep fighting until one stands we will have to call it a draw. But many people will not like that." The head judge stated.

"Well this is why I am president. Okay, what if they fight in space?"

There was mumbling in the background as the judges contemplated the question. "Mr. President, may I suggest something?" Sorthan spoke to the president, with the judges hearing what he asked through the president's microphone.

President Krachithous looked at Sorthan with interest. "You may Ambassador Sorthan."

"I have chosen the guardian already, which is Sedric. However, you must find the one winner. They can fight in space, and if Sedric wins, it will be that much easier for the people to accept his departure from your planet while Jinjo takes on the role of planetary spokesperson and runner up champion, but if Jinjo wins, you can declare him as your planet's champion of which Queen Omia requested he stay and train future guardians.

Whichever way you want to advertise it; you have your honored champion who will be an inspiration to your people and the Queen has her Guardian who will protect the galaxy from the dark war to come."

President Krachithous respected the Argonians and their elite, but Sorthan he respected the most. Princess Navia was a very wise ruler and Sorthan was handpicked by her for many reasons, and it showed by the wisdom and majestic persona he projected. "I like that idea. But tell me, why Sedric, I thought the queen wanted only the strongest?"

"Sedric backed off once the force fields went down, he could have won I think, but thought more of the people than himself. He is the strongest, inside and out." Sorthan explained.

"Interesting, you saw the energy levels?" President Krachithous was being impressed the more he learned about this Argonian emissary.

"Yes, Mr. President, I did." Sorthan simply answered.

"To space it is. Announce it and get video crews and judges up there. If the crowd wants to follow they need to stay at least three miles away. Make sure we have the lineup protecting the audience just in case." President Krachithous commanded.

The announcement was made and almost the entire audience started to fly into orbit. The only ones that remained in the stadium were the families with small children and those that were content with seeing the final battle on a live video screen.

Sorthan quickly called for his shuttle and ordered the Star Destroyer Darhim to move into outer space and monitor the match from a distance. The shuttle arrived and Sorthan boarded the craft quickly pursuing the President and his entourage of over two hundred thousand Goth. Sorthan was astonished to see that the Goth who were not in the stadium had flown out to see the spectacle wanting to see with their own eyes the terrific combat that they had first elected not to attend because of the sold out seats, but now that there was no seating limit; the excitement was too much to ignore after seeing what had already happened.

Thirty minutes later, the camera crews were in position about five thousand miles from the planet's surface. Tir Goth was a medium size planet with a circumference of twenty-eight thousand miles and a population of only three billion Goth. Sorthan knew that maybe four billion more Goth were living outside of the planet and many of the lineup contestants had trained in space, other planets, or moons. He was sure that more than ninety percent of the entire Goth population was watching the telecast, as were many enemies who wanted to spy on them and the Argonians.

Sedric and Jinjo were allotted three miles in all directions to fight, but each knew that the farther they were from each other the probability of hitting their target was decreased greatly even if they did spread their energy attacks. Missing was a waste of energy which in a long battle could easily cause them to lose the final match. They had mental powers like limited telepathy and mind control but they were experienced and strong enough not to be taken down by such mental powers. It was a test of pure energy, speed, and skill that would determine the final outcome.

They started out two hundred meters apart. There was no sound as Sorthan watched on from his scout ship and on video. The news commentators were giving a play by play narration which seemed weird because the first one to attack was Jinjo sending out a barrage of energy bolts at Sedric, but no sound could be heard.

"Wow, Jinjo missed Sedric with a hundred energy blasts. Sedric is flying above Jinjo. They are maneuvering into better positions. Wow, Sedric fires and misses. Jinjo retaliates. He misses and Sedric charges Jinjo! Did you see that? What just happened? Sedric wins! Jinjo was stunned somehow and Sedric blasted him from behind, skillfully knocking him out." The commentator yelled in disbelief.

Sedric had flown straight into Jinjo expanding his personal force field three times the size covering an area of ten feet radius just as he came a few meters from Jinjo. Jinjo would have normally dodged Sedric but he did not expect to hit Sedric's force field. It disoriented him for a second, long enough for Sedric to blast him at full power with an energy beam coming out of Sedric's hands. A bright white flash of light hit Jinjo in the back and he was thrown hundreds of meters into space unconscious, and continued to speed away from Sedric. The lack of gravity didn't slow down his momentum, but Jinjo was stopped in space by one of the referees. Thousands of people cheered basically to themselves as nothing could be heard in the void of space. There were however, cheers being heard over the commentators and people still in the stadium as Sedric was declared winner in all planetary broadcasts.

Sedric was seventy-four inches tall with extremely well defined muscles. His excellent physique personified the perfect human specimen even though he was not human. His hair was gold blonde in color and came down to his shoulders. His eyes were emerald green and skin was light flesh tone in color. He wore his distinct family dueling suit. It was black with silver linings exposing his forearms. It was specially created with materials that had reflective radiation properties. It was not really for combat itself, it was so that any harmful radiation would not be stuck to the clothing and therefore present a danger to other life forms that got close to him. Sedric's natural makeup rejected all harmful energy particles, and it included ingestion of such particles. He could literary go into a radioactive environment and not become radioactive like most objects or living beings.

They all flew back down to the Citadel of Ankis where the presentation was made in honor of Sedric and Jinjo the runner up. Sorthan was enjoying the moment like everyone else, but he knew that time was ticking and they would need to depart as soon as possible. He spoke to President Krachithous about the urgency of the situation, but Krachithous told him not to worry, and after the video shoot, Sedric would be all his.

Sorthan waited patiently for an hour before the President, Sedric and a few of Sedric's closest friends and family were escorted to a private room. It was no surprise to Sorthan that Jinjo and Wiquel were among the eight friends present. The interaction between all of the people in front of him was very warm and cheerful, unlike most warrior minded races that were sometimes too competitive or self centered for their own good.

President Krachithous informally introduced Sorthan to the group and Sedric.

Sorthan started by asking that what was said in the room must be kept in confidence. "The Queen has decreed a galactic guard force be created to fight in the dark war to come. Lord Sedric will be one of those Galactic Guardians; however, the Queen asks, when the time comes, for volunteers of all Goth to fight alongside the Argonians. I do not know why the Queen has placed such a strong emphasis on this request but it will be up to you all in this room to prepare for the future. You are the strongest of your race and with the president's resources and influence, I am sure you can prepare as the Queen asks."

The twelve people in the room were quiet for a moment not sure if they should speak or do something. Jinjo was a tall Goth with gray shiny long hair and had a strong square facial bone structure. His voice was very refined and masculine. "Ambassador Sorthan, we are Goth and know we were called to fight for our families. A few thousand years ago we almost killed ourselves by civil war and petty greed. We have come such a long way, and it's time we show the universe who we are." Jinjo stated.

"We fight for Queen Omia, because she has kept her word. Your enemies are our enemies. The Goth will be ready. Sedric here is the youngest champion to ever win the tournament and will continue to make our people proud." President Krachithous assured him, and motioned to Sedric to say something before he left their presence.

"Thank you Mr. President, and thank you all, mom, uncle Bantic. My friends. I will not let you down." Sedric said as he moved in front of his mom, uncle, and then his friends.

They all said their farewells with joy and some tears. Sedric and Sorthan were about to leave when Sedric stopped him at the exit. "Oh, I almost forgot. Can I take my ship?"

Sorthan looked at him a little puzzled. "We have many ships you can pick from if you really want a ship. Not that you really need one."

"This is no ordinary ship. I built it." Sedric joyfully said.

A harsh grumble came from behind Sedric. "You what?" Wiquel asked hearing the conversation.

"Well, I got some help." Sedric grinned, a little embarrassed for taking all the credit.

Sorthan had been astonished too many times today, so he didn't try to argue the point and played along. "Okay, take me to your ship."

"Oh, you can tell the shuttle to go back alone. I will take you to the destroyer in my ship." Sedric suggested.

They left the room and went out to the open area of the stadium. There were still many people celebrating, and the crowd exploded with cheers as they saw Sedric and Sorthan flying away in Sedric's yellow spherical force field. In a matter of ten minutes they traveled a few hundred miles and entered Sedric's work hangar. Wiquel and Kithorian followed them and landed next to the pair.

Sedric's ship was roughly sixty meters in length and looked like a fat SR-71 Blackbird, with two booster engines, but the wings were thin only at the outer rims. The base of the wings to the fuselage was almost as thick as the body. It had fins but was shorter and used only for in atmospheres if at all. The ship was silver and almost transparent mimicking its surrounding of the hangar. It didn't have wheels for landing gear, but instead had a tripod type of alloy legs the size of a few feet thick keeping the body of the ship from touching the ground. It had some characteristics of Argonian ship technology, and the skin resembled the Queen's own flagship, but the engines were definitely alien even to Sorthan.

"Is this shipped cloaked?" Sorthan asked seeing that it was very hard to see, almost like a clear glass ship and the inside was empty.

"Nah, if it were cloaked you wouldn't be able to see it, smell it, hear it, or touch it." Sedric replied.

"What, you mean it can cloak and you can't touch it?" Sorthan asked with a surprised look on his face which he never expressed since his arrival.

Sedric looked at Wiquel behind Sorthan and then up to the hangar ceiling as if in thought and he asked himself and Sorthan. "Well, it can cloak, and you can't see it and all, but if you can't touch it then why would it need to be cloaked? Yeah, you're right it can be touched."

Sorthan seemed confused now. "And I thought you Argonians had a sense of humor." Sedric laughed and positioned himself to the left front of the ship.

"Only when we throw planets into black holes." Sorthan's

mood changed to seriousness.

Sedric stopped in this tracks with wide eyes in disbelief. "You can do that?"

Sorthan stared into Sedric's eyes and smiled. "Nah, just playing with you."

The two laughed. "For a second there I thought we were the only ones that could do that." Wiquel chimed in.

Sorthan paused for a second only to see Sedric laugh some more when he noticed Sorthan almost falling for the false comment.

"Ramp and open." Sedric said still laughing and a ramp came out of the ship near the front and extended down to the ground. The ramp was an inch thick and was made of energy, even though it looked like a metallic ramp. "Mr. Sorthan, it will be a pleasure to introduce you to Ship."

"I put everything you need in the database this morning." Wiquel said.

Sedric smiled. "Thank you." They hugged like brother and sister.

Sedric led Sorthan up the ramp. Both men walked through the wall of the ship where there was an energy portal created by the ship a few feet before they touched the fuselage.

Sorthan saw the level of technology used in this ship was equal if not better than Argonian technology. The inside was spacious for such a small ship, maybe able to fit twenty people cramped in. There were twelve seats to include the pilot and copilot seats. A navigation, scanners and communications, weapons, and defenses console. It was not a starship configuration bridge, but it seemed like it could do what starship bridges did in combat and out of combat. There was an area in the rear for sleeping and storage which allowed comfortable living space for four extra passengers.

"Have a seat" Sedric sat down in the pilot's seat and motioned Sorthan to sit in the co-pilot's seat.

The hangar bay doors were open. "Taxi out." Sedric said and the ship automatically retracted the landing legs, and floated outside at a slow jogging speed. Sedric punched in a few instructions into the AI computer. "Mr. Sorthan you might want to tell your ship that we are coming and have them open their bay doors for us."

"Shouldn't we get closer; we're still on the ground?" Sorthan replied.

"Not for long." Sedric smiled and placed his hand on a glassy blue sphere connected to the side of the seat.

In an instant the ground which Sorthan could see from the front three dimensional windows disappeared and in two seconds they were in outer space. There was a two G-force sensation, and a humming noise of the engines in the back, but aside from that they were at the Darhim before Sorthan could start his hail to the star destroyer.

"Did we go FTL (faster than light travel) from the surface?" Sorthan asked understanding that any ship attempting FTL from a stand still inside an atmosphere with a moderate gravity faced being destroyed by its own inner makeup of propulsion system. The particles and physical design of the engine along with gravitational fields could disrupt ion and antimatter activators to overload and blow up the ship. In addition, there was no ship he knew this small that could go FTL or have a cloaking system that was comparable to the royal starships. This was a ship that would revolutionize Argonian technology, and it would be up to the Queen to get permission for this ship to be studied.

"So, can I bring her along with me?" Sedric asked, seeing Sorthan's topaz eyes in bewilderment as they flew into the Darhim's shuttle bay.

Sorthan looked around the inside of the ship again with his head in awe thinking of this unique ship and the Galactic Guardian sitting at his side.

"Lord Sedric, I wouldn't have it any other way."

Chapter Two

--- ⚜ ---

Earthlings

Sirenevyy bul'var, Moscow , 2001

Rain drops continued to fall from the tree leaves onto the ground and sidewalk. The long winter was over for now, but the temperature was still keeping many people indoors or heavily clothed. Many children and young people spent time outside as the school year ended and vacation was the focus for many families. The economy was on an up rise, but it was slow and many vacations were local or focused on visiting family.

Fedar Emsky was a young lad graduating high school with honors and a full scholarship to the Moscow Institute of Physics and Technology. He was excited and sad watching the scenery from the train as it took him to his parent's home. His curly sandy blonde hair was flattening on one side by the pillow his head had been resting on for the past hour. He was doing great in school with the highest scores ever recorded, but it bored him, and mostly importantly his father was very ill. He was happy knowing that his parents' wish for him to get an education was being met, but at the same time he was just living with no sense of future, and no control of what happened at home while he was away. Most college students didn't know what they wanted in life, and it wasn't until many years of trial and error that they finally find meaning in life or at least a worthwhile goal to strive for.

Fedar knew what his parents wanted for him, and his heart wanted that to because he did love school, but life to him seemed more than getting a good job and making a family. He had special powers which his parents didn't know about but, he was afraid they would not understand him especially since his parents were in the middle of a crisis. According to the news, he would be classified as a superhuman, should he tell anyone what he could do. There were very few superhumans who were out spoken; in particular, a new superhero group called Energy Fire and Light. In Russia, they were hated not because they were superhumans, more because they were Americans who fought for the American way of life. At least that was the thinking of the older generation. His generation did not have bad ideas of America, in fact, there were many young people idolizing the English and American culture, to include many political views. Many things had changed in the last decade, and many more were changing every day.

The United States and Russia were no longer the only two great super powers. South America and Australia had come up out of nowhere to claim the status of super powers less than a decade ago when he was still in junior high school. Yes, the world was changing and Fedar felt there was something special in store for him, far beyond his studies or his beloved country. But for an instant, he forgot about everything and considered just staying home and looking after his parents.

Fedar's train arrived at the Arsk Train Station, 550 miles east of Moscow, in the afternoon. His mother, Larissa, was there waiting for him. It was a joyous time as they reunited for the first time in almost a year. The time was cut short as Fedar asked about dad. His father was in the hospital recovering from complications to his second treatment in the fight against lung cancer. The cancer had spread extensively and the doctors gave him no more than a few months to live. His parents didn't tell him about the cancer when he started school, but his father's health was deteriorating so much they could not keep Fedar in the dark.

The visit turned dark as Fedar arrived to see his father's last few days on Earth. His father died in agony and with all Fedar's powers, he couldn't save him, or relieve his father's pain. Fedar stayed with Larissa for the duration of the summer, contemplating if he should tell her about his powers and look after her.

The night air was cold as he stood outside of his mother's house staring at the stars. Larissa was in her mid fifties, but she was not the bread winner and would struggle in caring for herself. He thought about maybe using his powers to get money and set her up for the rest of her life. He could fly and displace his body to go great distances, but what could he do with those powers? He could possibly tutor for income, but it was not enough for his mom's needs. He was very bright and had learned four languages on his own, but what could he do with a degree he didn't have to include a steady job.

His body was changing which was weird for him since about six months ago he didn't get hungry, have to eat, urinate, or defecate. He could hold his breath for several hours and his skin was super resistant to heat or cold. In fact, the night cold air felt cool but he knew it was forty degrees Fahrenheit. He hadn't sweat in over eight months no matter how much he tried to exert himself. He could sprint at full speed for thirty minutes before he started to get a little tired. Sometimes he wished he had been left back in school so that he could have become a super star athlete before he went into college. However, the government was looking for superhumans, so maybe it was a good idea he hadn't given himself away. He thought about maybe stealing money, but he was not a theft and his mom wouldn't want him to live a life as a villain. He had to make a decision to take care of his mother or go back to school and hope things at home got better on their own.

He went back inside and told Larissa that he would look for a job locally and maybe try to attend a local school. She would not hear of it, and urged him to go back to school in Moscow. After a minor argument he promised he would follow her wishes, but in his heart he was going to figure out how to get his mom a better life.

Fedar finally went to sleep, but it was a restless slumber as he found himself jumping out of his bed by a nightmare where he saw a spaceship with many lights, like in the old movies, come down on his house. He teleported to Larissa's room, but she wasn't there. He saw the multiple lights light up the inside of the house as if the sun were in the house itself. A loud engine noise could be heard outside as he teleported all around the rooms in the house finding it abandoned. He teleported outside on the street but there were no other houses or cars, just his house and a long street. The noise from the spaceship stopped, but the wind blew dust everywhere. A female alien stood ten meters from Fedar. She wore a ruby red gown adorned with various gems. Her feminine face was of dark African pigment, with light topaz illuminated eyes. Her slender body and quartz glittering long hair was mesmerizing to behold.

"Do not fear Fedar. I am Urhimia, emissary for Queen Omia and Princess Navia, rulers of the Argonian Empire. I am here to ask your help to save the galaxy from a dark war to come. If you allow me, I will explain everything to you in your mind." Urhimia spoke in Russian, but it seemed like she didn't speak at all.

"Where's my mother?" Fedar commanded to know.

"She is sleeping, just like you are sleeping. I have come into your mind, to communicate with you instead of actually bringing the spaceship for everyone to see over your home."

"So all of this is a dream?"

"It's an illusion, not a dream. You're awake." Urhimia's voice was very similar to his mother's voice.

Fedar thought about what Urhimia had said. "So if I let you come into my mind, you will be able to mind control me or something?"

"No, it doesn't work that way. If you let me go into your

mind, I can show you things without you overriding the visions with your own thoughts or memories. The illusion you see right now is not perfect and cannot hurt you." Urhimia explained,

Fedar thought carefully and remembered that he saw the spaceship in the sky for a brief moment while he was still in his room and understood what she was talking about when she said the illusion was not perfect.

"Alright, I will allow you to enter my mind." Fedar said.

In a matter of a few minutes, Princess Navia's explanation for appointment of Guardians, his role as a Guardian, who the Argonians were, and the foretold future was imbedded into his mind. Urhimia narrated the messages and concluded the illusion. "There are many questions which you might have so if you can fly to where my ship is currently located. You can better see for yourself the truth of what I said."

Fedar knew that the ship had landed about sixty miles to the southeast. All of the sudden he was in his dark room lying in bed. Fedar sat up wondering if he was crazy or something, but the memories of everything he had just experienced was very vivid. He felt a connection to Urhimia still and knew she was waiting for him. He teleported outside still in his sleeping clothes; a pair of shorts and T-shirt. The neighborhood was there as a few hours ago, and all was quiet with everyone seeming to be sleeping. He flew toward the spaceship and teleported intermittently every hundred meters or so depending on how far he could see or sense. He made it to the ship in a few minutes moving faster than the speed of sound, but there was no sonic boom. Teleportation was the main source of speed and not his physical flight ability so there was no breakage of air beyond the speed of sound. Fedar saw a vision of Urhimia inside of the ship, and in an instant he teleported in front of her.

Urhimia spoke to Fedar in his mind as she answered all of his questions. Larissa was the topic of a long discussion, primarily whether she would fare better if she was taken into space with Fedar, or if it would be better for her to stay on Earth. They would ask Larissa what she wanted to do, and that would determine if she would be taken into space or be given enough money to support her until Fedar returned.

Fedar was anxious not knowing how his mom would take the news, but Urhimia assured him that Larissa would be okay. Fedar went back home and changed into warmer clothes. He gently woke up Larissa and explained as best he could what had happened with the alien contact. Fortunately for Fedar, Urhimia intervened when Larissa thought Fedar was making things up in a childish attempt to stay with her. Larissa put on warm clothes and Fedar took her to the ship. She was stunned with all the things that his son was capable of doing, and the entire alien situation. Urhimia calmed her nerves and explained everything to her in a matter of minutes. Larissa thought about things carefully, and told Fedar to go with the Argonian and she would stay at home. Urhimia would provide her with thirty million rubles, which she could use little by little as not to attract attention to herself, but yet giving her a comfortable life style. Urhimia also assured her that someone would watch over her, and if she changed her mind she was always welcome to go into space.

Fedar spent one day arranging his withdrawal from the

university, and setting up Larissa in a new home in Kazan. Urhimia used the day to contact her next two Guardians, which was not quite as easy to do since they were both known superheroes, Quatris and Hellfire, who also had made contact with the Remarn race in the Orion constellation a year ago. Granted the contact was not a pleasant one, but the fact that they were not strangers to alien life forms to include the Argonian existence was a plus. Her communication plea for help from the EFL group in New York was received but no reply was returned.

Urhimia's main ship, the Hydrex, received a subspace transmission from the Battle Fortress Lardose informing them that Lord Klakin and Lady Hebshilon would be there within six hours. Urhimia was a little confused as to why Quatris and Hellfire had not replied, but that was something she would find out once Fedar was ready to leave, hopefully before the Lardose arrived to the dark side of the moon. Fedar still had to finalize legal matters with the property and a fake internet job for Larissa.

The Lardose arrived as scheduled, but Urhimia was still working things out for Fedar on Earth in the scout ship. Klakin transferred to the Hydrex, and Hebshilon departed with the Lardose to gather the armada. Klakin came prepared as he ordered the Hydrex to reposition itself on the dark side of Earth four thousand miles from the surface. The Argonian scanners searched for the four Guardians he was expecting to see there. Klakin told Urhimia to stay with Fedar for as long as he needed. He would contact the other three Guardians.

Klakin directed the ship's communication's officer to find a direct channel to the EFL computer. He knew that Quatris and

Hellfire may not be responding because the message Urhimia sent was from the surface of Russia. His ship was in space, but it would be easier for him to talk to the EFL AI and it would relay the information he wanted to the two superheroes. It wasn't long before Bob, the EFL AI, replied to Klakin's hail and plea for help. The discussion was short, and a quick response by the superheroes was given. Quatris and Hellfire flew up to the ship's location fifteen minutes later. Klakin and two Argonian translators met them in the shuttle bay. Klakin spoke English, courtesy of Princess Navia, but the two translators were there for the heroes to use initially before they were instructed on the few universal languages used by the empire. Computerized translators were used by many races, but telepathic instruction on the universal languages was best for what was expected of the Galactic Guardians. Universal translators were slow and sometimes didn't translate the proper verbiage or gestures implied by speakers. The royal family members were all fluent in the universal languages, and most were fluent in over sixty specific languages or forms of communication. Granted, a handful of the royal family members were strong telepaths, but even they could audibly speak a few hundred languages.

Quatris and Hellfire entered the Hydrex's shuttle bay wearing their superhero costumes. Quatris had a pure black outfit with a white star design on his chest, with extending white lines into his hands and feet. Both men wore skin tight masks, exposing their mouths, and Quatris' black eyes and Hellfire's blue glowing eyes displayed anti-matter energy and fire emissions. Hellfire's costume was dark blue with a yellow and red fire design extending from the waist running through the center of the chest to the forearms. They radiated very high energy levels as they entered the bay, but their levels went down to almost nonexistent when they stopped flying, landing in front of Klakin. No one on the ship could have known that except maybe the operator of the ships scanners, but it was evident to Klakin by the magnificently electrifying auras of the two men he felt underneath his skin by his specialized sensors.

"Welcome Quatris, Hellfire." Klakin said in English.

"Hello, Klakin." Quatris extended his hand. "You sure are taller in person than in video." Quatris said.

Klakin was familiar with Earth customs and shook both men's hands.

"We are running out of time and I need to know if you two will accept the appointments as a Galactic Guardian?" Klakin got to the point.

"We're here aren't we?" Hellfire replied.

"Yes, we will, but only for a temporary time. Our wives will not like taking care of the Earth all by themselves for a very long time." Quatris said as a matter of fact.

"I don't know how long it will take to police up the borders, but hopefully not too long. But, we are still two Guardians short, one here on Earth, and another one on the planet Jahnuny." Klakin explained.

"Who is the one here on Earth?" Hellfire asked.

"There are actually two others on Earth, but Fedar Emsky has already been recruited. He is settling his mother in a new home before he leaves. The other is Patrick Lawrence, who lives in a place called Seattle. It would help if you two could recruit him." Klakin said hoping they would be able to help him out.

"There are other very powerful superhumans on Earth, what makes these two guys special?" Quatris asked.

"They are powerful in their own way, but the Argonians can see the future and they are the ones I saw, to include you two." Klakin simply explained.

"Really?" Quatris said with doubt on his face.

"How do you know they aren't lying to you?" Hellfire asked.

"I don't, but it's highly not likely that Princess Navia would lie to me, even though I do not fully believe that they know the future; it will be up to us to make our own destiny." Klakin logically replied.

"So how do we see this future you claim to have seen?" Quatris asked.

"I don't know yet. I have to wait for Yahimia to return from the surface of the planet to see if she can show you. I understand that you two are very resistant to mental probes. Oh I forgot, excuse me, but these two Argonian soldiers here will be your translators until you have learned the universal languages." Klakin said and motioned to the two translators with his hand.

"I am Drekar." The taller of the two male soldiers said.

"And I am Corgan." The other male soldier said.

They were in body armor as if going into combat, but

without weapons. It was the normal attire aboard the space ships in case there was a space battle, which was likely in view of the ship's current mission and Captain's command. It was normal procedure for the ship to go into general alert when in planetary orbit, near stars, or near alien ships. The two heroes didn't really think too much about the choice of clothing in the spaceship, because they were expecting astronaut suits of some type. The battle armor seemed more like armor combat suits used by the Special Investigation Agency, or South American soldiers without their helmets back on Earth.

"Who knows the most English?" Hellfire asked desiring to be able to communicate technological and medical words and ideas.

"I am, Lord Hellfire." Drekar replied.

"Good. I will stay here with Drekar, and Quatris will go get the Guardian in Seattle." Hellfire said, waiting for a response from Quatris or Klakin.

"That sounds good to me. So, what's this person's address again?" Quatris said.

"We had his location programmed in this wrist device as you would call it." Klakin handed Quatris a wristwatch looking device with a small one inch touch video screen.

"Neat." Quatris said looking at the device noticing that it was capable of other features to include keeping the time, and a compass. "Does this thing act like a phone?"

"Yes it does. You can contact a spaceship up to a light year away." Klakin explained knowing that it was considered revolutionary on Earth.

"Okay, just wanted to know. I will be back in a few." Quatris said and flew away next to a bay exit door. The door opened and he flew through a force field screen out into space with the door closing behind him.

Klakin was a little confused by the figure of speech Quatris used. 'A few what?' He thought to himself. He noticed that Hellfire seemed to be okay with the expression and just played along. Maybe later he would be able to understand this Earthling way of speaking, even though he knew the language, he didn't know the many cultures and jargon which were very numerous within one planet.

Port Orchard Bay, Seattle, Washington

Patrick Lawrence listened to his walkman as his stocked boxes on a shipping platelet. He was looking forward to spending the next few weeks in Paris, London, and Madrid for a long Christmas vacation. He could have been working in the world of fashion with his very handsome, tall, and alluring stature, but he hated working with a lot of people who didn't interest him. His black hair was always perfect, never getting oily, and grew maybe half a centimeter a year. He lived his life in the low and middle class neighborhoods and liked being with down to Earth people. He knew he was different as a child and understood that he was a superhuman in his teenage years. He was an orphan with his single mother dying giving birth, but grew up in a caring foster family who raised him with love which he emulated. Sadly, the family separated by divorce and he came of age where he left as well. He kept in touch with his foster mom and dad on a semiannual basis, with them living across the country. He could have made up an excuse to visit them often, but he had his own life and goals to achieve. They were not earth shattering goals, like saving the world from imminent disaster, but he did help anyone he could.

He worked odd jobs which gave him the flexibility to travel without asking permission, and they sometimes gave him a high income. His latest temporary job was working as a factory loader. It paid a decent income which he used to pay his very few bills. He rarely ate and only turned on the electricity for people when he had company. He only used the bathroom to take a shower and the AC and heater to keep the room he rented from smelling stale. Half of the income he made went to charity, and the rest was well managed into savings. He spent many vacations around the world and helped the needy on long weekends, or specific times of the year.

Patrick was super fast, strong, invulnerable to human weapons of mass destruction, could fly faster than supersonic jets, survive in a space environment, and see twenty times better than an eagle. All of these abilities could not have prepared him to see Quatris fly down from the sky and into the warehouse. His antimatter aura slightly pushed a fully loaded palette which was rapped with plastic, a few inches. The sixty workers in the warehouse were filled with mixed feelings. Some were scared from the surprising entrance, mildly startled, awed by seeing the legendary hero in front of them, and one was fearful that he was there to hurt someone or save them from an unseen disaster.

"Patrick Lawrence! Your presence is requested! I'm here to offer you a job!" Quatris yelled in the middle of the warehouse floor.

"I'm Patrick!" Patrick stopped stacking boxes and walked towards Quatris.

Quatris waited for Patrick to come within arm's reach of him. "You're needed to save the universe. Will you accept this responsibility?"

"What makes you think I can help?"

"I didn't pick you sonny, I'm just the messenger. So you might want to hold on to me." Quatris extended his hand for Patrick to grab.

"What about work?"

"Who's in charge here?

"Quatris yelled.

"I am." One of the floor supervisors said as a crowd was gathering around the two men.

Quatris punched in a number on his newly acquired wristwatch. "Bob, I need you to make sure all of Patrick Lawrence's living expenses are taken care of until we return. Also, compensate the Mitter Company for whatever they ask." Quatris looked at the supervisor. "What's your name?"

"Peter Janson."

"Did you get that?" Quatris asked the AI.

"Got it boss." Bob replied.

"Okay, let's go." Quatris grabbed Patrick and dark energy enveloped both men. They flew outside and then straight up. A few sonic booms in the distance shook the warehouse and surrounding counties.

Patrick and Quatris were soon aboard the Star Destroyer Hydrex. Patrick was also resistant to mental probes so all four Guardians waited for Urhimia. It was not long before Urhimia's scout ship entered the shuttle bay and introductions were made. Urhimia was able to mentally instruct the four willing Earthlings in the universal languages and what they were expected to do as Galactic Guardians. It took her one on one sessions, but she managed to give them what they needed.

Klakin immediately ordered the star destroyer to head to Moridan at maximum speed. The Earth names would not be fitting their stature so Patrick's Guardian name was officially changed to Lord Medroc and Fedar's Guardian name would be Lord Morinar. Quatris and Hellfire kept their superhero names, not wanting to change their reputations on Earth and off planet. Klakin agreed and insisted they learn about each other's powers and train as a group before they arrived in the Corima sector of space. It would take two months before they arrived, and according to reports Lord Sedric and another Guardian named Lady Cerimon would be there two weeks earlier.

There were a total of seven Galactic Guardians as foretold by the queen and princess. Klakin was not totally convinced that what they were about to do was fixed in destiny, so he started to research the history and current activities of the soothsayers and royal family. Klakin had experience with censored information on Ios, and didn't trust anyone, even the royal family. He respected the Princess and the Queen from what he knew first hand, but even then he would have to do his own research and get hard facts, because it was not his nature to trust what people told him. He figured out the computer systems and had to find new data sources that had all the secrets about the soothsayers and royal family. This meant he would have to get access without anyone knowing, or hack into systems acting as a hacker and not himself. The chances of any incriminating data being stored by the royal family or soothsayers were very low, but it wouldn't be if the data came from a neutral party or enemy. Klakin thought about a plan to get such information if it existed, but first he would have to see which Guardian he could trust before put the plan into action.

The unclassified information on the royal family and soothsayers was positive, but it left many questions. Queen Omia had a soothsayer with her all the time, but it was rumored that she could tell the future without the use of a soothsayer. Klakin surmised that the queen used the soothsayer to confirm her predictions or just to keep an eye on the soothsayer community. Whatever the case, he remembered everything there was to know about the soothsayers and the royal family in a matter of a week. To his relief, the Earthlings had already shown him signs of great loyalty and desire for justice. They were also very resistant to mental manipulation which made them good choices if he wanted them to keep a secret. In the end, his duty was to the queen and the princess. He would have to keep whatever he found in the best interest of them and for the good of the galaxy, which meant he would decide what information to release to his fellow guardians.

The training in the ship's combat simulator was used by him to see the Guardians in action, but more importantly, their character in combat and after combat. The combat simulation started well, but was abruptly stopped when the force fields used in the room couldn't contain Quatris, Hellfire's or Medroc's energy blasts. Hellfire's scientific skills helped in fixing the problem, but it was a partial fix. Quatris being the most powerful would have to use no more than a tenth of his full power to keep from bringing down the force fields. The other two would also have to severely tapper their energy output as well. In the end, they at least became very comfortable in coordinating attacks and covering for each other. It helped greatly that Quatris and Hellfire were already experienced fighting as a team. Medroc and Morinar were novice, but learned quickly. Morinar didn't have the great damaging energy attacks, but he did have the ability to teleport all over the place. He was given an Argonian top of the line heavy plasma rifle which he used to attack targets at crazy point blank ranges and angles. It was sort of comical on how Morinar teleported around and shot at the three other guardians, like Peter Pan flying around trying to shoot plastic pellets at three M1 Abrams tanks. Morinar would yell out, "Die scum, Meet your maker", or similar emote type of sayings in Russian and English before he shot each opponent.

Normally, Quatris would get annoyed with such foolish talk during combat, but it made him laugh more than angered him. Quatris knew he could take out Morinar anytime he wanted, but Morinar's comical antics was very entertaining as he let

Hellfire or Medroc knock him out several times with an area effect energy explosion.

In the control room, one of the Argonian technicians made a comment that the Guardians were not taking things seriously, but Klakin quickly corrected him telling him that it was better that they live life with joy, than die with regrets. The technician didn't know what to make of Klakin's words, but he kept his opinions to himself afterwards seeing that Klakin was taking things very seriously. The team spent two weeks in simulations and tested their knowledge of aliens, the Moridanians, and Gillithe. Hellfire and Medroc were able to improve the communication systems which would be used in space. The only real technical communication system available was a wristwatch with text ability in a space environment and the normal audio and video in an atmosphere. Klakin and Morinar were the only two Guardians who needed to wear modified space suits in order to be functional in the void of space. By the end of four weeks, all five Guardians had become good friends and their knowledge of the galaxy was far greater than any Argonian would have thought possible for what was considered a low race in a gene pool of the galaxy. The only two Guardians that most Argonians would consider their equal would have been Sedric and Cerimon simply because they came from highly advanced technological worlds. Queen Omia and Princess Navia knew that the origins of the Guardians would be a source of controversy, but they also knew that the Earthlings had more power and potential which the galaxy was yet to witness.

Chapter Three

--- ⚜ ---

Only the Beginning of War

Cormia Sector, Two Parsecs from Moridan, (Earth time 2002)

Humongous polymorphic first stellated dodecahedrons mines spanned the wormhole gateway. Unmarked mining vessels finished releasing the last layer of space mines trying to disrupt space operations in Moridan's trade routes. The wormhole was crude but an efficient method of stellar travel for ships without quantum ion or antimatter accelerator engines. The advanced top of the line engine type allowed for ships to focus on the ship's shields which kept the ship from being destroyed in FTL travel while moving through different gravitational fields from planets, stars, and entities like black holes. In essence, the ships that used wormholes were the slower, weaker, and smaller non military space vessels which needed to use worn holes to go faster. If the supply ships didn't use the wormholes, they would be in space a lot longer and were easy targets out in deep space. The alternative response was not to travel to Moridan, but there were a few who dared to risk their lives to save a planet or at least attain great wealth from those who paid for overpriced scarce resources.

Gillithe starships had diverted almost all of the Moridanian military to protect Moridan which left the trade routes open to outside attack and piracy. An incoming ship was detected by one of the lead minelayer vessel. It alerted the other four vessels and armed the antimatter mines, as the five vessels prepared to leave the area.

"Captain, I have a contact at 349Q3. Wait, it's gone." The acquisition officer on board the vessel reported detecting a faint energy pulse in the distance opposite the wormhole in the general line of travel they were about to go.

The Drakon Captain looked at the main screen seeing nothing but space and a computer generated red dot which flickered for a moment and then vanished. "Raise shields and prepare for FTL."

Drakons were very tall mammalian creatures with four arm-like appendages. Their outer skin was very rough made of dead cellulose fibers. Their bodies were very similar to human anatomy except for the extra limbs, vastly stronger organs and bone structure. The hair coming out of the cracks of the skin were like plant fibers giving most of the Drakon's entire body a brownish to bright green complexion. Their eyes were larger than human eyes and had inner transparent eye lids to protect against ultraviolet rays.

The Captain's face showed no fear, but he was confused as to what to do next. The energy pulse was not a malfunction in the ship's sensors and there were no energy sources nearby besides the wormhole, so it had to be a cloaked ship. The problem was he didn't know how the cloaked ship was still evading their sensors so close to their location which would have at the very least showed some unusual energy patterns in an area of empty space. In addition, the pulse was a flicker so something came out of FTL still cloaked, which was impossible for large military cloaked ships to do without setting off more scanning information, even the Argonians.

"All ships, scatter and head home." The Captain ordered the other ships over their secure subspace frequency.

"Captain, we are being jammed!" The communications officer reported.

"What? How?" The Captain asked, but before he could say anymore, the ship's forward deflector force field completely collapsed from a direct hit of an antimatter torpedo. The ship's hull was disintegrated by the blast causing the front of the ship to almost implode. Sedric's ship appeared in front of the lead Drakon minelayer and shot another torpedo into the now defenseless vessel.

Lord Sedric and Lady Cerimon came out of Sedric's stealth ship as the second torpedo left the underside of the right engine. They flew in opposite directions attacking the other four Drakon ships. Their speed was astounding as they flew close to FTL speed taking the four minelayers by total surprise. Sedric saw that one of the vessels didn't have their force fields up to full power so he shot it first with an intense surge of energy coming out of his hand. The beam easily penetrated the hull of the ship and practically cut the four hundred meter ship in half.

Cerimon was sixty-five inches tall, but an enormous amount of energy emanated from her as she flew through the force field of the farthest Drakon space ship straight into the engineering room. She mentally knocked out the fourteen occupants in engineering with telekinesis, tore out the computer consoles, and flew off towards the bridge. The vessel was horseshoe in design and had two engineering sections, but disabling one section was good enough to keep the ship from going into FTL travel. As quickly as she had entered the ship and neutralized the engineers, she knocked out the crew in the bridge.

Sedric flew a strafing run by one of the fleeing minelayer ship. His initial energy blast brought the ship's force field down to almost nonexistent. Sedric's ship flew in front of him before he could blast the ship a second time. He assumed that the Drakon ship had hailed surrender, and his ship was telling him by getting in the way. The minelayer shut down its engines as Sedric flew after the last ship attempting to go into FTL travel. The ship jumped as Sedric blasted the rear force field with half his power penetrating the shield and engine exhaust emulator. The energy damage started a chain reaction and the ship blew up in mid jump causing the ship to seem like it partially blew up, disintegrated, and vanished at several areas of the ship from rear to front. The entire mine field blew up in a chain of sequenced commands from the minelayer ship Lady Cerimon had disabled. Cerimon had ordered the bridge weapons officer to blow up the mines. It resembled a chain of thousands of fireworks, except the works were fifty kiloton nuclear type explosions in the middle of space with the black background of the wormhole in the distance.

Sedric flew back towards his ship which was monitoring the activity on the surrendering minelayer ship. He flew inside with ease as the ship allowed him to enter through the force field and door skin. There was no one inside except him and the onboard AI, Ship.

"Status on the Drakon pirates?" Sedric said.

"They are waiting to be boarded." A very monotone young masculine voice came from the ship's surround sound system.

"We don't have time for this." Sedric said and concentrated on Lady Cerimon. 'Cerimon, can you come here and disable this ship in front of me so we can continue. I will try to get the incoming transport freight to tow these two ships to the nearest Moridan military vessel.' Sedric projected his thoughts as Cerimon facilitated the mental communication.

'On my way.' Cerimon replied.

"Ship, hail the incoming vessel. Alert them of the attempted mine field, and the two surrendering vessels. Tell them as per Argonian order; they will tow the two vessels. Also, patch me into the two Drakon vessels."

"Hailing Drakon vessels now." Ship replied.

"Drakon vessels, I am Lord Sedric, Galactic Guardian of the Argonian Empire. You will be towed to the nearest Moridan military vessel which will process you as their prisoners. However, you are my prisoner now until turned over to the Moridans. If you decide to escape from the towing transport, I will find you and will destroy you with no chance of a second surrender. Acknowledge."

There was a moment of silence as the two Captains and crews of the ships contemplated a response.

"Drakons have acknowledged to your terms." Ship said; as Lady Cerimon disabled the FTL and weapons systems of the second defeated minelayer.

A Noheevat freight spaceship squeezed through the wormhole without incident. It had a very long and well built hull maximizing cargo space and adaptability. The two mile long by seven hundred meter wide and seven hundred meter tall design made it look like a supersized futuristic oil tanker in space. It was primarily dark gray in color with many booster nozzles evenly spaced out every fifty meters. Large sections of the ship were capable of detaching and attaching from the base hull acting as mobile cargo crates when loading and off loading cargo. It was not a very fast ship with four moderate capacity engines which were used for travel and maintaining a strong fixed orbit around most planets.

The Noheevat ship hailed Sedric.

"We received your transmission. There are no Moridan vessels nearby. Can you escort us to Calis?" The captain of the freight asked.

"Negative. I will order a Moridanian ship to meet you within a few hours. If we don't get to Moridan, the war will end badly for you and your cargo."

"Understood, we will comply, Lord Sedric." The Noheevat

captain replied.

The Noheevat were cellulous based plant creatures of various sizes with very durable bodies, and had many plantlike limbs depending on the age and family lineage. Their bio waste and resources were a source of food and raw materials for many races which gave them a lucrative enterprise in trade and exporting. Their normal atmosphere was not compatible with most planets so they lived on their world and traded outside instead of inhabiting a customer's world. The captain knew they were taking a high risk of being killed, but the pay off was four times his annual salary due to the war between Moridan and Gillithe. The Guardians had saved his ship and cargo, so following Sedric's commands was the most prudent and courteous thing to do.

Sedric waited for Cerimon to return to the ship; plotting a route to the Moridan solar system. Secure subspace transmissions were indicating that the Moridan defensive line was penetrated and would completely collapse within the hour. They had arrived to the Corima sector six days early, with Klakin's group still two weeks out. It would be up to Sedric and Cerimon to stabilize things while the Star Destroyer Darhim arrived in six days and the Hydrex in fourteen. He was sure that he and Cerimon could take care of any opponent in many battles, but it was very hard to be at multiple locations at the same time. The Moridan system was very large with eighteen colonies and Moridan itself. Sedric had Ship monitor the transmissions carefully trying to determine the areas needing the most assistance. At this point in time, the main defensive line around Moridan needed saving.

Cerimon entered Sedric's ship without using the door and reported a situation update. "The crews will obey for now. Hopefully you scared them enough that they won't try to attack the Noheevat."

"Ship has their crew roster. I will hunt them down one by one if they don't. Okay it's time to go. Ship, max speed to Moridan." Sedric commanded.

"Affirmative." Ship replied.

The ship warped into FTL travel instantly. Cerimon sat down and looked at the incoming reports from military and commercial sources. "There are slightly over two hundred Gillithe vessels still in the fight." She said and reclined back on the seat.

"We need to find the command and control vessels, then the battle fortresses." Sedric strategized.

"What about the jammers?"

"Ship can take care of them." Sedric replied.

"Fourteen minutes twelve seconds until within scanning range." Ship reported.

"Ship, alert the Moridanians of our presence once we get within scanning range. Tell them to make a deliberate hole in the line. I will be waiting for the Gillithe there while Cerimon takes out their command center." Sedric instructed.

"Affirmative." Ship replied.

Sedric relaxed in the pilot seat and looked at Cerimon next to him. She was very beautiful for an alien. Born and raised on the planet Jahnuny, she was very young at the age of 87 Earth years. Her black short hair was made of fiber nylon atoms, but resembled silky strands of Angora rabbit hair. Her body features were the same as a Goth, Earthling, or Argonian, but her skin was riveted with microscopic particles of blue crystals which gave her a bright blue complexion to include her lips. Her elf like shaped ears and spider like eyes showed a sense of intellect, with a feminine facial structure enhancing her beauty. Sorthan had told him she was a rarity in her world because of her ability to use one hundred percent of her brain capacity, but her super flight and teleportation powers alone made her rare in any world. She wore a guardian uniform given to her by Sorthan which mirrored after Sedric's attire being engineered specifically for her body and special powers. Black and silver were the main colors which complemented her black hair and blue skin.

Sedric was not certain about Lady Cerimon's ability to be a guardian, but the first hour in the Darhim simulation battle room quickly convinced him that she was an equal. Sedric was a Goth and was taught not to underestimate your opponent, but she was not a Goth. It truly humbled him to see that Cerimon was rightfully a guardian being able to hold her own and knock him out with her mental powers.

The minutes passed by quickly as they saw a three dimensional battlefield map from the scanners projected out of the cockpit windows inward. The planet was being attacked from all angles with the command and control vessel near the smallest moon about 400,000 miles away. Moridan satellite defenses kept the penetration of the defensive line from being effective, but the Gillithe were positioning their battle fortresses near the penetration point and it wouldn't be long before the defensive laser satellites would be destroyed.

Sedric changed his mind after seeing the situation. "Ship, tell the Moridanians to focus their attacks on the surrounding ships to the northern and southern quadrants. They need to stay away from the battle fortresses. I will take care of them. While I do that, you take out their jammers to the rear. Cerimon, make sure the fortresses are ordered to enter the penetration as quickly as possible. That will get them all together near me." Sedric commanded.

"Are you sure you can take eight battle fortresses?" Cerimon said not really knowing the full extent of Sedric's energy powers.

"We'll find out." Sedric smiled and stood in front of the exit door. Cerimon followed him and in less than a minute the ship had positioned itself between the Gillithe fleet and Moridan's smallest moon.

Cerimon stared at Sedric seeing that he was ecstatic with anticipation. She was not sure if the warrior aspect of Sedric was coming out or if it was a playful youthful aspect of excitement, or both. What she admired the most was that he was surely at peace in the face of possible death. It inspired her and she also smiled as they both flew out of the ship to their intended targets.

Sedric bolted into position at multiple times the speed of light in the center of the penetration, forming a yellow force field around his body. The battle fortresses scanned the area, but they didn't see Sedric with their instruments. They warped at over fifty thousand miles per hour towards the penetration which was about five thousand miles in diameter. The formation was mismanaged with a basic free for all as the lead battle fortress was suppose to draw fire from the Moridan ships. The Moridan ships however, didn't reposition themselves to cover the penetration so the battle fortresses assumed there was no opposition and started to gaggle through the penetration trying to get through before the Moridan ships decided to react. The Gillithe battle fortresses were of an awkward pyramid design, but it suited the intent of the Gillithe which allowed for maximizing energy collection and their spiritual belief of energy and spiritual balance. The Gillithe race was bent on total equilibrium of energy, mind, and body. They were not great traders, but for some reason they were totally against the Moridanian activity in the trade routes. Many people would say the Gillithe gave Moridan access to the trade routes only to have an excuse to go to war with them and take control of the Moridan solar system. The Moridanians requested a truce at the start of the war, but it was rejected under the pretense of irreconcilable attacks on Gillithe ships and the Politon outpost which was backed up with very partial and questionable evidence. Whatever the case, Sedric and Cerimon were the first decisive Argonian response to a war where the Gillithe were not compromising on. The Guardians would stop the war by force now that a truce was declined and ignored several times.

Lady Cerimon flew quickly to the flagship ignoring the ship's shields and hull by materializing through with a form of teleportation or de-solidification ability. She entered the bridge and forcefully pushed everyone to the outer walls with her telekinesis. Half of the crew was instantly knocked out by the first attack, and the ones still conscious were flung around like rag dolls against the walls, ceiling, and floor until they lost consciousness. Cerimon looked around the bridge console controls and found the navigation section. She plotted a course straight into a barren area of the moon. She locked the computer and went directly to the communications console. She saw the reports by the lead attackers and typed in the command to converge on the penetration. She then disabled the comms system by instructing the ship's computer to run an intruder protocol which made the ship go into silent running and stopped all coordinating instructions to the fleet. She went to the navigation controls again and punched in maximum power to the engines. The ship didn't go into FTL travel because the computer would need the navigator's security code, but it did speed towards the surface of the moon at over 500,000 mph. Cerimon turned transparent and flew into space as the ship left her position and collided with the surface of the moon two thousand miles away. The very thin and weak atmosphere was not able to damage the ship before its shields and physical hull hit ground. There was a very large explosion and dark cloud of moon rocks and dust. Cerimon flew toward bright flashes in the distance as Sedric fought the battle fortresses in the penetrated defensive line.

Sedric's force field negated the ship's scanners so they basically came towards him without knowing he was there. Sedric played on this advantage as he flew underneath the two mile long fortress and shot it point blank with a tight beam penetrating the ship's shield and destroying a path six feet in diameter straight up through almost the entire ship. The energy did a lot of damage to the ship, but the vacuum created on all decks of the ship completely disrupted every ship system. It was unfortunate for the Gillithe that the bridge was in the upper center of the ship which Sedric inadvertently penetrated and destroyed with his energy attack. Sedric didn't know the full extent of the damage to the ship, but he assumed it was enough for his purpose as long as the fortress stopped in mid space and confused the follow on ships enough to slow down or stop.

The battle fortress instantly lost speed and rotated out of control like a dead stick on a running stream. Sedric flew straight towards the nearest fortress and attacked this one from above. He made it clear that he was there as a humongous energy bolt erupted out of both his hands. The battle fortress's shields were made to withstand nuclear explosive forces, but Sedric's energy bolts were more damaging than a ten megaton explosion. The four shields collapsed and a tenth of the ship was pulverized into nothingness. A chain reaction of explosions extended into the ship as it cracked into several gigantic pieces. The momentum of the ship through the void of space caused large damaged sections of the ship to expel tremendous amounts of atmosphere and freeze.

Sedric couldn't maintain the yellow force field around him cloaking him from their energy scanners, but he never intended to fight them behind camouflage which used up a lot of his own energy. He gambled that the battle fortresses would not figure out what was going on until he was able to destroy or disable maybe four of the eight ships. Two were destroyed, two more followed before he would have to worry about their weapons being used on him. The ships were roughly several thousands of miles apart, which made things harder for Sedric since traveling between ships made him vulnerable to attack. He wasn't sure if the weapons would do him any harm, but why take the chance. He flew as close as possible to the nearest ship four thousand miles away as it was heading towards him trying to follow the lead ships. They started to change course as Sedric was able to fly underneath and blast it like he did the first lead ship. He didn't hold back this time and the ship blew up from the inside. The engine reactor overloaded and Sedric felt the nuclear blast of the ship to include several large pieces of ship debris hitting him at thousands of miles per hour. He felt the heat and physical impact of ship material, but it only hurt as much as fifty paper planes being thrown at you from across a standard household room. He knew that his force field took the lethal damage, and what he felt was his force field mildly weakening. The weapons on the ships most likely would be stronger, but so far the technology of the Gillithe was not as formidable as Argonian military ships.

Sedric quickly flew away from the destroyed ship and focused on the next fortress. They had changed course and started evasive maneuvers trying to get some distance from the three destroyed ships to their front and at the same time avoiding the Moridan fleet. They were in a bottle neck, and didn't have many options. The captain must have decided to seek better luck against the Moridan fleet as the ship flew max speed away from the center of the penetration point where Sedric was at. Sedric saw their trajectory and bypassed the fourth ship by shooting it with max power and spread his beam so not to miss. The fourth fortress failed to withstand Sedric's damaging attack, but it didn't blow up or break apart like the other three fortresses. He spotted the fifth and sixth ships in line and strafed the fifth ship with an energy blast. He didn't worry about destroying it; he simply wanted to get its attention. He flew almost on top of the sixth ship and shot it with an energy blast. He was too close to the ship to use maximum strength but it was strong enough for two shields to collapse. The fifth ship maneuvered closer to him, which was exactly what he wanted. He shot at the fifth fortress a good distance away. The beam missed by a mile. Sedric started to feel tired and was trying to get his second wind.

The fortress shot at him but he hugged the sixth fortress as he dodged the attacks so part of the salvo of plasma energy bolts from the fifth fortress hit the sixth fortress with weakened shields. The plasma ate the hull like a super acid and destroyed a large portion of the sixth fortress from the inside out. Sedric flew quickly to within five hundred meters of the fifth fortress. Their short range weapon system countermeasures shot at him but missed as he agilely moved faster than any single seat fighter ship. He blasted the ship with intense energy penetrating the shield. He noticed that it was a little harder to penetrate the shield, probably because they had diverted more power to the shields, but it was useless as the ship suffered critical damage to its main engine and plasma generators.

The seventh and eighth fortresses were reversing their course and attempting to retreat. Two hundred smaller ships comprising of cruisers, deckers, and drop ships cluttered their escape route. Sedric had his second wind now and turned on the afterburners dashing towards the last two battle fortresses. He came within two hundred meters of each fortress and blasted them in sequence destroying their force fields and crippling them so they couldn't escape or use their weapons with any significant effect.

Sedric's ship had destroyed the ten spaceship jammers but didn't join the fight in attacking the cruisers. Lady Cerimon arrived as Sedric focused his attention to the remaining battle cruisers and deckers. Deckers were a mixture of gunship weaponry and assault assets specific for boarding and conquering other spaceships, military installations, and battle stations. The Moridanians closed the penetration with twenty able cruisers, but they didn't join the battle being preoccupied with salvaging the few Gillithe survivors from the fortresses. Sedric easily crippled every ship within two miles of his circling flight path. Many missiles and plasma beams overwhelmed an area of over 20,000 square miles trying to stop Sedric's one man assault. Lady Cerimon stayed in the perimeter of the main concentration of ships as not to get in Sedric's way. Ships started to disperse in all directions as the Moridan ships enveloped the remnants of the Gillithe fleet.

Sedric was finally exhausted after destroying over a hundred ships and deflecting over twenty missile attacks which came within a hundred meters from him. He didn't know how many ships the Gillithe had in their entire space fleet, but he knew that losing eight battle fortresses and two hundred or so smaller spaceships was a large dent in their space arsenal. The only reason Sedric really stopped destroying Gillithe ships was for that fact that Moridanians were accepting prisoners and mixing in with the Gillithe ships. He dared not fire on more Gillithe ships and commit fratricide on the first battle of his job as a Guardian. It wasn't long before Sedric's ship flew next to him and decloaked. Sedric entered the empty ship and sat down in the pilot's seat getting an update on what was going on in the aftermath of the battle. Lady Cerimon was aboard the Moridanian flagship coordinating a readjustment to the planet's defenses. The Gillithe had communicated a surrender before Sedric and Cerimon had destroyed a quarter of fleet, but Ship knew that both Guardians didn't have a way of knowing and probably would not have honored the request in light of past behavior by the Gillithe. Ship knew that Sedric and Cerimon were making a statement which all other races would come to accept as truth. The Guardians were not playing around and they were willing to fight unto the last ship or opposition was stamped out.

Sorthan informed Sedric and Cerimon well on their expected duty which Queen Omia desired. The prisoners and wounded were taken to the planet. Sedric and Cerimon helped in neutralizing dangerous debris which could have a chance of falling into Moridan's atmosphere. Sedric ordered the Moridans to dispatch six cruisers to get the two Drakon minelayers which the Noheevat were holding. There were a handful of Gillithe ships that retreated and escaped capture, so there was a chance and fear of Gillithe retaliation for the lost fleet. Sedric and Cerimon thought differently, and told the Moridan command to resupply, take care of their wounded, and repair what they could. They assured them protection and instructed they let ships and people rest while they awaited the arrival of more Argonian reinforcements. The Moridan high command was surprised to hear that the Argonian Empire was sending such a powerful asset to their rescue, and wholeheartedly welcomed the needed assistance. Once the defensive line was cleared and stabilized,

Sedric and Cerimon waited in Sedric's ship for the rest of the Guardians.

A few days passed by until Sorthan and the Darhim arrived in orbit around Moridan. The Star Destroyer was an impressive sight compared to the Moridan ships, but it was more what it represented being more powerful than any Gillithe Battle Fortress and a symbol of an Argonian promise to protect them from alien conquest. Sorthan and all the crew of the Darhim were extremely impressed by Sedric's and Cerimon's decisive win over the Gillithe fleet. It was the first time single beings were able to go head to head with many starships of moderate technology and firepower. Communication with Klakin and the rest of the Guardians was achieved without interference and orders were given to assemble at Moridan.

A week passed until Lady Hebshilon and a fleet of twenty star destroyers and forty cruiser class Argonian ships arrived. The Hydrex arrived a few days later, and all the Guardians finally met each other aboard the Lardose, Hebshilon's flagship.

The Lardose's battle room had a large forty foot by forty foot conference style footprint. There were thirteen seats facing each other in a circular pattern but no table. The ceiling was high up to twenty feet with a large eight foot dome light blue fixture in the center. The table which normally would have been present was sunk flush with the floor to allow the members to see each other and any 3D holograms presented by the speaker or briefer. Lord Klakin addressed the Guardians, his mother, the three Argonian emissaries, and the president and vice president of Moridan. An entourage of twenty people waited outside of the battle room, most were there for the Moridan dignitaries, but in the twenty were six Argonian body guards for Hebshilon and the three emissaries.

"It has come to my understanding that the Gillithe invasion was planned over a year ago. Gillithe will more than likely attempt to surrender before any significant military force is at the Gillithe home world of Tarthillia. I believe there is more to this war than what can be seen. Two star destroyers and twelve cruisers will stay around Moridan until Gillithe is under complete control by us. Thanks to Lord Sedric and Lady Cerimon, we know that Drakons are involved, which is not unexpected, but their actions were far beyond piracy. Gillithe had the war won, but it seems they wanted Argonian intervention. Whatever the reason, we will find out why. The rest of the fleet will go to Tarthillia and destroy any significant military force they have. Are there any questions?" Klakin stated.

"Lord Klakin, we want to once again extend our gratitude for your gracious help and wish we could do more, but we do not like the idea of burdening you with having to put fourteen of your ships around our planet." President Oskimarc said.

Klakin smiled but it was very faint as his reptilian mouth was not constructed to curve like human lips. "We understand your concern Mr. President, but it is not a burden and needs to be done for the sake of you and other trade ships in the area. The cruisers will escort ships in and out of the trade route wormholes. They will also assist you in rebuilding your military. We have engineering and technical support teams moving to your damaged ships and even your future ship companies so that you will be able to protect yourselves better. The ships are projected to be with you for about six months if not less depending on your progress." Klakin replied.

President Oskimarc stared at Klakin and then at the rest of the Guardians and Argonians.

"If you should wish to have the ships stay longer with you, I will arrange a new relief of ships for another six months." Lady Hebshilon added.

The President and Vice President were both surprised and humbled with thankful appreciation. "Thank you." President Oskimarc said, with Vice President Kiolo echoing the thank you.

"You're very welcome… If there is nothing else, we need to make preparations, so if you would be so kind Mr. President, Commander Yohania will escort you and Vice President Kiolo back to your shuttle." Hebshilon stated, and they all stood up and slightly bowed their heads as a way of bidding farewell to the two leaders of Moridan.

Once the President and Vice President left the room, all remaining members sat back down except for Klakin. The lighting in the room dimmed, and a colorful 3D hologram of the Gillithe solar system appeared in the center of where the table would normally be erected. Klakin walked in the midst of the 3D hologram and pointed out Tarthillia, the Gillithe home world. The planet increased in size as the hologram zoomed in to display what Klakin was briefing.

"The Gillithe star system is comprised of fourteen planets, of which four are inhabited, primarily by Gillithe settlers and military personnel. The blue ring seen here is a planetary defense grid, supposedly able to neutralize a Beta class Star Destroyer. It is not confirmed that they have this technology; however, it is not inconceivable. Lady Hebshilon believes that it is newly acquired technology from one of our foes."

"Lord Klakin, the battle fortresses that I destroyed didn't seem like they could give an Argonian Star Destroyer any competition. So, why would they have a defense system that is more advanced than their space fleet?" Sedric interrupted.

"Good question." Klakin replied and motioned for his mother to answer the question.

"The Gillithe fleet is thought to be over eight hundred spaceships strong. They didn't send their entire space arsenal of fleets to Moridan because they didn't want to leave Tarthillia open to attack. In addition, my intelligence analysts say their modern space fleet is staying near the planet. They are either staying out of the war in order to surprise whoever tries to attack them, or they had the intent of fighting the Argonian Empire with the new ships from the start. What they sent here was only the weaker ships. Fortunately for Moridan and the empire, no one was expecting us to be able to destroy the attacking fleet so quickly and easily." Hebshilon explained.

"Well, it seems all we need to do now is go in there and wipe them out." Lord Quatris interrupted with a smile.

"I agree, and disagree at the same time." Klakin interjected. "You, Hellfire, Sedric, and Medroc could go in there by yourselves and destroy the entire fleet even with their advanced technological boost; but we need to find out who gave them the illogical idea to start a war with us, and why. As you can see, the defense grid is made to fight against star destroyers, but they are not ready for a cloaked ship that is smaller than a standard shuttle. They are also not expecting a seven person team to infiltrate and get the information we need before we destroy their space fleet."

"So what are we suppose to do once we infiltrate?" Lord Morinar asked with a very faint Russian accent.

"The key is to get Lady Cerimon close enough to the right people who know what is really going on. Chances are that most of the populace is only following orders from the top, and even then not all high ranking personal may know all the secrets we are trying to find out." Klakin replied.

"What if there are no secrets and they simply wanted to take over stuff for the hell of it?" Lord Hellfire asked.

The four humans knew what Hellfire meant with his question, but the others were a little confused. "I don't understand what hell has to do with them?" Klakin replied.

Hellfire smiled. "Hell is a metaphor of things gone into chaos. So what I meant was just maybe they wanted to take over property because they simply wanted to and disrupt the peace in the process."

"Yeah, they wanted to scratch a nonexistent itch in their behind." Lord Medroc joked.

Quatris wanted to laugh out loud, but kept his composure. "Okay guys, that's enough. Excuse us, but what if we find out that someone else is behind all of this drama. Do we go after them too?"

"I like you Earthlings. You are very interesting." Klakin stated and pointed at the Chancellor's palace as the 3D hologram zoomed into the palace grounds, and the Chancellor, leader of the Gillithe regime. "We will deal with whatever we find even if we have to take the galaxy apart. This is only the beginning of war, and the first thing we need to be concerned about is finding the Chancellor. He will be the one who knows more or less what is really going on."

"This all sounds great and all, but there is something that needs to be fixed before we go in there spying and blowing things up." Sedric stated as everyone's attention turned toward him.

"Go on Lord Sedric." Klakin requested.

"Since I never had to talk to anyone while I was flying around space all by myself, it didn't matter, but now that we are going to be shooting at things as a group I think we should be able to talk with one another. If I hadn't got tired and the Moridan ships had not got in my way, I would have destroyed the entire Gillithe fleet. So, would it be possible to create something so we can communicate with each other while outside of a spaceship?" Sedric asked.

"I don't know if that would be possible unless we make a helmet for everyone to wear." Commander Sorthan interjected.

"The helmets will take up too much space away from our skins, which will be destroyed by our energies, so they won't work for Quatris, myself, and probably also Sedric and Medroc. I might be able to fashion a small mouth and ear piece which will be able to withstand our own individual energies." Hellfire said.

"Ship might be able to help you Lord Hellfire." Sedric said.

"Me too." Morinar happily added.

"How long will it take to get to the Gillithe star system?" Hellfire asked.

"At the star destroyer's maximum speed, it will take three days." Hebshilon answered.

"So, a little more than a day in my ship." Sedric said.

"Are the materials and resources available on your scout ship?" Klakin asked.

"I don't really know, I didn't create the replicators so I guess I can ask Ship." Sedric said not really knowing everything his ship could do since a major part of the ship was created by Wiquel who was back in Tir Goth.

"Okay, well Sedric and I can find out after this meeting." Hellfire stated.

"Lady Cerimon is the only one that can get the information from the Chancellor without him deceiving us. I propose that Lady Cerimon and Lord Morinar infiltrate the palace, get the information, and if possible take the Chancellor prisoner as a means to finalize the end of the war. Quatris, Hellfire, and Sedric will take out the fleet. Medroc will support Morinar and Cerimon if they need the firepower." Klakin continued his briefing.

Everyone approved the overall plan, and the Guardians went to Sedric's ship, while Hebshilon and the emissaries stayed in the conference room preparing to speak with all ship captains over the assignments for the next several weeks. Lady Hebshilon wanted to make sure things seemed like they were preparing to fortify the borders instead of attacking Tarthillia. Most of her ships would be follow-on forces after the Guardians destroyed the opposition, so it was simple to maintain good operational security. The only leaks if any would be through the Presidency entourage or well placed spies in the Argonian side, which would have been extremely difficult to do since the Argonians under her command were extremely loyal to the Queen. But, for all her precautions, Hebshilon knew and considered forces beyond her experience which pointed to super beings capable of knowing things without resorting to cloak and dagger techniques or spies. However, she also knew that well performed counterintelligence and operational security would keep many friendly and innocent people from being killed. To many Argonians, war seemed to be a way of life, but to Hebshilon it was her first war and her son was leading it by her side. Time would tell if Princess Navia's faith was well placed.

Chapter Four

--- ⚜ ---

The Gillithe

<u>Orbit around Tarthillia, Corima Sector of Space (Earth time 2002)</u>

The Gillithe high command was convening an emergency telecom meeting through a battle station ten thousand miles from Tarthillia. The Gillithe crew moved around the station frantically trying not to upset the commanders of each section. Subspace secure communications patched into distant locations in the middle of space. The planet seemed to be on high alert as word was passed down that they would be under attack by the Argonian Empire within the next few days. There were no details, but it sounded like an entire fleet would be invading their solar system. Admiral Telk spoke to twenty five captains instructing them to stay four parsecs away until they were called upon. The defensive ring was active and would repel most of the Argonian fleet before they would be used to crush the invaders. Precautions were taken to ensure secrecy of their activity, but they were vainly ignorant of the surveillance conducted by Klakin and Medroc.

Sedric's ship was hovering a few meters from the station, making sure they didn't touch the defensive force field or place themselves in the maximum sensor waves from the station, which started about twenty meters from the surface of the station. Sedric's ship was longer than twenty meters but it hugged the station length wise. The height of the ship was slightly beyond twenty meters but it was not the major part of the fuselage which helped in not revealing the ship. Sedric and Hellfire told Klakin that the Gillithe sensors would not be able to detect the ship while cloaked even in the sensor's maximum strength, but he didn't want to take any chances. Cerimon and Morinar listened in as Klakin and Medroc talked about possible locations for the ships out in space waiting to ambush the Argonian attackers. Quatris, Hellfire, and Sedric likewise waited two light years away for word of where the Gillithe fleet was at. Sedric was cloaking their presence and high energy levels with his unique energy bubble as they relaxed and floated in deep space ignoring the absolute vacuum of air, and tremendously cold temperatures. It took a while before Klakin and his team agreed that the fleet or fleets were dispersed in deep space in the direction of the Untary Quasar. There was a lot of empty space to search even if they knew the direction and general distance, but it was a start and Cerimon would be able to get details once the Chancellor was kidnapped.

The team concentrated on finding the Chancellor and confirming his identity. Cerimon looked deep into several minds in the station from a distance, which didn't reveal much except that the Chancellor was scheduled to address the world on a telecast within the next few days, but the details were not in the minds of any of the people on the station. Medroc suggested she enter the station and create an illusion so no one would know that she was using the station's scanners to find the Chancellor. It would have been a great plan except that Cerimon didn't have the skill or power to create such illusions, but the suggestion gave her another idea. She could enter the station in an unoccupied area where she could patch in directly into the computer. Getting into the computer was not the great idea; it was getting the science officer to come to her in the secluded room and having him bypass the DNA security features the computer would require for using the station's equipment. Cerimon had the power and skill to mind control one to two beings long enough for them to get the information they needed. The plan seemed sound, but Klakin pointed out that the officer would know that he was mind controlled and be missed if he was knocked out or put in a storage compartment. This small problem meant that they would have to go and kidnap the Chancellor immediately after finding him, no matter where he was and then get word out to Quatris and his team on the exact location of the ambushing fleet.

There were still many other problems on top of problems. The combat strength and technology of the fleet or fleets were unknown. The Gillithe were collectively taking a humongous and deadly risk in getting the Argonian Empire involved, unless they had someone else who supported their efforts, or thought they could win a war against the Empire. No one expected the Argonian response with the creation of the Guardians and their seemingly decisive victory in the defense of Moridan. The Argonian military strength had not diminished from the already committed fronts, so whoever would have benefited from the movement of military forces didn't. If the situation was suppose to cause economical, social, or political changes in the Empire or other regions of space, then Klakin, Hebshilon, and all of her intelligence advisors couldn't piece it all together.

Cerimon and Morinar rehearsed the infiltration, actions onboard the station, and ex-filtration. Medroc and Klakin had strategized possible actions in case they were found out, what they would do if military forces were diverted against them, and what to do once they found the Chancellor. Luckily for the team, Ship was capable of flying the ship as any intuitive pilot, allowing all the guardians to perform more actions besides piloting a ship. However, Klakin was a quick learner and knew Ship's controls in case they had to fly the ship manually. Klakin would be directing the actions of individuals from the ship, allowing Medroc to leave the ship and support Cerimon and Morinar once they went after the Chancellor.

An hour passed by as Cerimon and Morinar initiated their infiltration. Morinar wore a modified Argonian space suit, but it was not distinctive to reveal the maker. It did show the trademark colors of the Guardians. His helmet was uniquely made for him to keep an internal atmosphere around his face. If there were a puncture in his suit it would not suck out the atmosphere unless it was in the face area. He could withstand the extreme temperatures for a short period, long enough for him to patch up the suit if he needed. He didn't need to breathe for a very long time, and the suit worked like an underwater re-breather, except it was exponentially much smaller and more efficient. The skin tight suit allowed him to move easily and use his teleportation powers to encompass an area a few feet all around him. It was a skill which Lady Cerimon was able to evoke inside of him during the time it took for them to leave Moridan.

Morinar hugged Cerimon and they teleported into the room she had designated. It was easier for him to teleport to points he could see or knew distinctly were they there, so with close examination of what the ship's sensors saw, he could teleport accordingly. In a fraction of a second both of them were in the auxiliary bridge. Their almost transparent figures moved slightly above the floor and then they both materialized into a solid state. Cerimon flew the entire time touching as less as possible. Morinar did the same and stayed close to her looking out for anyone who might surprise them, or anything out of the ordinary. Cerimon closed her eyes and scanned for the science officer's mind. She found him with ease being familiar with his brainwave patterns. The science officers were dual trained in using the scanners and reported all detailed results to the captain or commander in charge. Several technicians were specifically trained in using the scanners which duties were performed during routine operations and in combat. Getting one of these technicians to use the scanners would draw attention since the computer and the technician on duty would know or be missed if Cerimon were to take one of them to perform the scan for the Chancellor. The science officer used the scanners at random times, and he would not be missed as much as the personnel who were supposed to be sitting in the bridge or in the crew quarters area. Cerimon concentrated and instructed Commander Rillon to go to the auxiliary bridge. Commander Rillon promptly arrived to the auxiliary bridge with a relaxed face as if he were going to perform an inspection on equipment.

Morinar looked uncertain at the Commander. "Are you sure he will do your every bidding?"

"Yes, I am. Are you?" Cerimon replied.

"Well I don't know how you are supposed to look like when you're being mind controlled, so no I'm not."

"Don't worry Morinar, I'm in control." Cerimon said as Commander Rillon sat down at the scanner console and started scanning for the Chancellor without being audibly instructed to do so.

The two Guardians looked at the information Commander Rillon was gathering. Morinar knew that once the information was obtained, he would have to teleport Cerimon and Medroc to the Chancellor's location. Klakin decided on bringing Commander Rillon into Sedric's ship where they could keep him unconscious and not worry about him being found by one of the crew. Morinar was prepared to do all of the teleportation tasks, and was somewhat anxious never really having the opportunity to teleport from an orbit to a planet. He had teleported for a distance of three hundred miles in one teleport before, but he didn't know the limits of his power as he would have to cover about five thousand miles from the station to the surface of the planet with the least amount of dematerializing as possible. Materializing and dematerializing with two extra people used up a lot of his energy so the least amount of times he would have to teleport, the better it was for him. His anxiety was tempered by Klakin's trust in his abilities having been given many pep talks while in and out of the training sessions after leaving Earth. The alien experience was somewhat unnerving as everything he was taught about the world to include science facts were not all true. Travel faster than the speed of light was taught to have been an impossible feat according to Einstein. He couldn't time the speed of his teleportation, but he was somewhat sure it was not faster than light. He heard of other superhumans in the world, but he never thought that humans like Quatris and Hellfire could fly faster than the speed of light in a void of space. Most of the laws of the universe were not captured by man's logical reasoning or ideological imagination, and the alien reality simply contradicted his ingrained human teachings.

Commander Rillon located the Chancellor's body. His unique DNA, personal security, and type of commutation activity around him were easily captured by the station's multiplex hyper wave radio scanners. Ship could have scanned the area, but it would have given away their location emanating active energy waves. The Chancellor was in a fortified underground installation at the moment in case the planet came under attack. Morinar tried to see the details of the location, but there was too much information to remember. Cerimon saw his frustration and mentally imprinted him with the information. Morinar knew exactly where the Chancellor was and grabbed Cerimon and Commander Rillon.

A second later, the three were on Sedric's ship. "The Chancellor is at coordinate: 67.8 longitude 305.2 latitude negative 1560 ft. Are we ready to go?" Morinar said and asked.

"Not yet." Medroc replied and placed his hand on Commander Rillon's forehead. A flash of light and static energy knocked out the commander. Rillon fell backwards on one of the passenger seats. Medroc and Cerimon strapped the commander to the seat while Klakin waited patiently at Ship's scanner and communications console.

"We're ready now." Medroc said, and then Morinar and Cerimon hugged him.

The three Guardians saw Tarthillia's atmosphere for a brief second only to find themselves inside the Chancellor's chambers in a blink of an eye. Their ghostly bodies felt weightless for a brief moment as Morinar made sure none of them were going to materialize inside any solid objects. They materialized and Medroc walked towards the Chancellor who was completely taken by surprise and momentarily thought the room was haunted. Medroc saw that the Chancellor was about to speak and instantly he was behind him holding his hand tightly around the Chancellor's mouth. Cerimon took control of his mind and they all teleported back to where Ship was supposed to be. To everyone's surprise and the Chancellor's fatal predicament, they were five thousand miles in orbit but no space station or Sedric's ship.

Morinar quickly teleported down into the atmosphere where the Chancellor was able to breathe. They floated there as Morinar explained.

"Hmm, did the ship move?" Morinar asked.

"Of course. It was moving thousands of miles per second like all satellites do when they are going around a planet. You must be accustomed to ground level speeds as the planet rotates" Medroc said.

"Well I need line of sight then if it is constantly moving that fast." Morinar said.

"Cerimon, find Klakin's general direction and guide Morinar to him." Medroc ordered.

Cerimon scanned for Klakin's thoughts. She pointed into the sky and Morinar teleported several times before he saw the station and then where Ship was supposedly at when they last left the ship. All four people were in a tight bundle as they dispersed except for Morinar and the Chancellor. They all materialized within the ship's passenger/cargo hold in the middle of the fuselage. Cerimon was in constant control of the Chancellor's mind as they sat facing each other. Morinar removed his helmet and sat in the copilot seat monitoring any Gillithe activity which indicated they had found out that the science officer was missing or that the Chancellor was kidnapped. He was going through the motions as Ship was already monitoring and would have told the group any important updates to the mission, but it gave him a sense of accomplishment by doing something besides idly waiting for the next task. It wasn't long before he had the idea to see if Ship or he could create a display in his helmet which helped him see where ships were at. He didn't have to see the ship with telescopic vision or anything like that, all he needed was a direction and distance indicator. He might not be able to see other ships with his eyes, but it would help if he could at least see general location and speeds of objects in the vastness of space so that the missed teleportation incident didn't reoccur and possibility get someone else hurt or killed.

As Morinar pondered on his possible invention, Cerimon

spoke to the Chancellor and probed his mind. The Chancellor was forthcoming with no ability or advanced skills in protecting himself from mental domination or scans. Cerimon was extremely powerful and skillful in her abilities so she was able to retrieve the information she was looking for, but there were unexpected complications.

"There are two fleets at these two coordinates." Cerimon moved to the navigator console which was where the copilot seat was and leaned over Morinar, typing in the coordinates.

"Very good. Ship, transmit the locations to Quatris." Klakin ordered.

"But there is a problem. It seems the Chancellor has been consorting with Drakon mercenaries." Cerimon interjected.

The Drakon race was extremely vast in number, but they were nomads, dispersed among the galaxy, with no real world of their own. They were also splintered into many factions. There were peaceful factions, and very hostile factions which fought for the side which they thought would benefit them the most. Among those extremes, there were Drakons who had ideologies which allied themselves with Argonian enemies. Cerimon was sure it was one of these well placed emissaries who coached and purposely convinced the Chancellor and other leaders to go to war with the Moridanians and the Argonian Empire. The Drakons alone would not have the resources or the desire to get the Gillithe into a war, so the problem was they still didn't know who was running the show. The only way to find out seemed to mentally probe the people who were pulling the strings or the specific Drakon agents involved. The only link they had to the people behind the scene was a memory of the Drakon, named Thowl, which Cerimon would share with the others, but it was unlikely they would find him any time soon.

"Are these the people who tried to lay mines in the trade route?" Medroc asked being familiar with the Drakon race through the telepathic teaching sessions and story of Sedric's rescue of the Noheevat.

"They are different, but they both give the Drakon race a bad reputation." Klakin replied. "Many are loners and work in small cells. They are attracted to conflicts and assemble because of the situation, not because they are working together."

"I don't buy that malarkey. Someone took a bunch of flies and let them loose on a pile of dung." Morinar joked.

Klakin understood that Morinar didn't agree with his statement, but the joke and metaphor went over his head.

Cerimon however, did understand the joke having mentally mended with the four Earthlings in the past and smiled. "Morinar is correct. The Drakon were gathered together and let loose to start this war and fuel it." Cerimon explained.

Klakin thought about the concept for a moment. "If this is true; how do we find these people who masterminded this war?"

"Let's focus on ending this war for good." Medroc suggested instead of strategizing over this new development.

"You're right. Quatris should have the coordinates soon. I suggest we take down this defensive belt, and hit the planet from within the defensive grid." Klakin said.

"According to reports and what I learned from the Chancellor. There are key personnel on the outlining stations that know how the defense grid works. If I can see what one of them knows; we can attack any weakness in the belt." Cerimon stated.

"What do we do with these two?" Medroc asked referring to Commander Rillon and the Chancellor.

"They stay here. Cerimon, can you keep them unconscious for a few hours?" Klakin asked.

"For maybe an hour, but it would be easier just to blindfold them, gag them, and bind them to the chairs." Cerimon stated.

"Sounds like a plan to me." Medroc said and started to strap the Chancellor to the last passenger seat in the rear of the ship. The commander was already strapped to another seat, but he wasn't gagged or blindfolded. Morinar and Cerimon assisted in securing the two prisoners.

"Okay that will work. Ship, tell Quatris to start the attack whenever they're ready, and let him know to come to our aid once they're done." Klakin commanded.

"Affirmative." Ship replied.

"You're pretty sure they will complete their mission before we do?" Cerimon asked.

"Quatris, Hellfire, and Sedric can destroy the solar system in less than twenty minutes, if it wasn't for the amount of time it takes them to travel the distance between planets." Klakin said knowing that without restraint those three Guardians could effectively produce enough firepower to resemble a solar flare engulfing a planet, if not more. Hellfire, Sedric, and potentially Medroc were about even when it came to their energy levels, but Hellfire's physical molecular structure allowed him to withstand more damage than all the Guardians. Quatris was in a league of his own when it came to energy levels, because of his special antimatter manipulation abilities, he was able to emit destructive energies that mimicked a one hundred mega ton nuclear explosion with one shot. It was sort of ironic, because he had never been on the receiving end of his own destructive attacks, and there was a chance he could hurt or kill himself if he were to somehow shoot himself with his own energy blasts at maximum strength. They were powerful indeed, and Klakin was happy to know they were compassionate and on the side of truth and justice.

"What we need to do is make sure we don't get into each other's way. Cerimon, you will need to find those key personnel; and Medroc, you will need to distract them by disabling or destroying the inner stations and any reinforcement ships." Klakin explained.

"What do I do?" Morinar asked.

"You stay with me, and be ready to back up Cerimon or Medroc." Klakin instructed.

Morinar looked at Cerimon and Medroc, and then smiled with pride. "Well if you two need my help, things must be really bad."

Medroc returned the smile, "You backing use up, hmm; I wouldn't have it any other way."

Ship had identified two key personnel which were luckily on the same station orbiting the moon of Tarthillia called Aeriok. Aeriok was the largest of the four satellites around Tarthillia, slightly smaller than the size of Earth. Aeriok had a small atmosphere but what made it very valuable to the Gillithe was that is supplied raw materials for the creation of super conductors and chromium alloys used to diffuse energy particles. The raw material was like a treasure planetoid for the Argonians or any other race with the technology to create the advanced chromium metals and poly-carbon insulators. Klakin had considered the implications of this resource which would fall into Argonian hands once the war was over. Many races would claim that the Argonians went to war only because of the resources, and not the treaty with the Moridanians. Klakin didn't care what people thought, but it wasn't up to him to decide or care, his concern was what Queen Omia would think of the situation. He considered maybe suggesting they put a strong military presence and mine the materials for a span of a decade. During that time, the Gillithe would be allowed to recover and grow under the supervision of the Argonian and Unification Council of Planets. The council would monitor the plant's social, political, moral, and idealistic status and tendencies. It would be their recommendations which would give the resource rights back to the Moridanian and Gillithe regimes. In the end, the resource would be a barter tool for the Gillithe and Moridanians since Argonians and other allied races would pay a lot of money for the mined materials even after a decade of mining by the Argonians.

"Okay, here are your targets." Klakin pointed at the two targets which Cerimon and Medroc needed to focus on.

"Just say the word." Medroc replied ready to fly towards the southern orbital path of the largest defensive battle station twenty thousand miles from Tarthillia.

"Ready." Cerimon said.

"Go, now." Klakin commanded.

The two Guardians flew out of the ship and at almost light speed they left Ship and the Gillithe station without triggering the Gillithe sensors.

"Ship, monitor the planet surface for any unusual energy spikes or buildup once Medroc attacks." Klakin directed.

"Affirmative." Ship's slightly robotic male voice replied.

Deep Space, one and a half parsec from Tarthillia

Quatris, Sedric, and Hellfire received Ship's subspace directional transmission at the same time. There was a minute time difference from where they were to Ship, so they knew that Klakin and his group were probably already committed to their actions.

Quatris looked at his Argonian lit up wristwatch which pointed to the two locations of the fleets. "I will take the fleet on the left, you two can take the one on the right." Quatris said through his new mouth and nose piece, and flew off towards his target.

"Roger." Hellfire replied and also bolted towards the targeted fleet.

Sedric flew next to Hellfire soaring through space multiple

times the speed of light. "Who or what's Roger?"

Sedric could hear Quatris laughing in the background as Hellfire explained. "Roger is another word for I understand or affirmative."

"I see." Sedric replied, "Are there any other sayings I should know about?"

"Yes, Wilco, means I will comply, and twenty means location." Hellfire said. "There are more, but that is all you need to know for now."

"I will need to look up these special words later, thanks." Sedric replied and focused his attention to the Gillithe fleet he could distinctly make out which was still half a light year away.

Sedric, like Quatris, Hellfire, Medroc, and Cerimon had telescopic multiwave vision and could easily see trillions of miles in several spectrums of light waves, which gave them the ability to travel at FTL speeds and avoid from inadvertently hitting harmful objects at those great speeds. It was no coincidence that they had these powers; the Guardians were chosen for their powers which complimented each other. There were beings in the galaxy that had the power to travel beyond the speed of light, but they were limited to the distance of their vision or perception. Otherwise they would die or be injured from colliding with unseen or unperceived objects in the path of travel through space.

Sedric was highly impressed by Quatris and Hellfire's flight speed as he vaguely strained to keep up with their pace. The fleet was not the normal make up of pyramid shaped battle fortresses, but more of a juggernaut design with three elongated cylinders connected together side by side. They were roughly two to three miles long and had two upper decks on top of each cylinder. The escort ships and cruisers were tailored after the modern Argonian ships, but it was clear that they were not Argonian. The protruding turrets and skeleton frames on the surface of the ships were not perfectly smooth like Argonian ships. The shield system for modern Argonian ships used the smoothness of the outer skin to displace or collect energy as desired for defense against multiple energy wave lengths and physical attacks like missiles. The Chromium alloy technology allowed for more efficient usage of space within the ship and requiring less materials in thickness, so they didn't have bugling areas or framing which was a trademark in modern Argonian ships. Sedric's ship was smooth, but didn't use Chromium alloys; instead his ship used Palladium/Titanium interwoven and layered alloy base materials which were almost impossible to create if it wasn't for him and his friends who engineered it by trying to improve the existing Goth space technology.

Sedric told Hellfire he would start on the left and work his way to the right. Hellfire broke off towards the right side of the fleet. Sedric came up on top of an unsuspecting large ship and blasted it with all his power. The energy blast tore through the entire ship and continued beyond, hitting a cruiser a hundred miles away. The bolt was as large as an average sized pharmacy store by the time it hit the cruiser which blew up like a miniature super nova. The guts of the battle fortress also blew up with two very large white flashes of light almost blinding an outside viewer from seeing it get cracked and broken up into thousands of pieces in all directions. Sedric saw that the Gillithe ships seemed to be stronger than the ones he had destroyed, but not by much as he was accustomed to fighting spaceships by now knowing the exact amount of energy to use to converse energy and be effective against them at the same time. It was far easier than fighting other Goth who could withstand most of his initial attacks, but it was not as enjoyable since he liked challenging fights.

Hellfire flew likewise on the opposite side of the fleet area which covered an area of about 40,000 miles with over 200 ships, dispersed as a collective group, taking on a battle fortress with blue beam of light energy instead of fire; coming out of both his hands at the speed of light. The fire beams cut through the battle fortress like hot knives through butter. The Gillithe weapons fired at Hellfire, but their slow missiles and plasma beams only annoyed him like a buzzing Nat. Hellfire flew from ship to ship destroying whatever crossed his path without mercy.

Sedric likewise flew for all the large ships, numbering in the dozens. The fleet was in complete chaos trying to figure out what was going on or trying to get a lock on Sedric and Hellfire with their weapon systems. Sedric didn't try to use any strategy this time, and flew at and shot at anything which hadn't already exploded.

The fleet which Quatris chose was in worst predicaments. Quatris flew to the top edge of the fleet and made a straight route through the middle of the fleet. He slowed his speed as to not bypass ships as he shot his energy bolts. Spheres of black, white, red, and pink energy blasted out of his hands as he constantly twirled 360 degrees and shot one energy ball towards each ship within 30,000 miles of his moving position. The energy balls were no more than hand sized when they left Quatris' palms, but they grew to the size of a half mile, 10,000 miles out, so that the farthest ship was engulfed by a one and a half mile diameter long sphere of antimatter energy. It was weaker than the energy balls closer to Quatris' position, but it was strong enough to completely destroy the Gillithe ships' shields and physical structures. The antimatter energy seemed to capitalize on the law of entropy and a closed system as it made contact with the shields causing a chain reaction at the molecular level that made each ship seem to blow up like a miniature nuclear explosion. Quatris flew and swirled around like a rotating sprinkler leaving a cluster of flashing lights and cloud of massive utter destruction in his wake. The antimatter explosions kept the ships from producing nuclear reactions with radiation emissions. There were no broken pieces of ship, just gaseous and tiny ionized melted particles of debris. The Gillithe reaction was very slow and no ship escaped Quatris' destructive attack as he made it to the other end of where the fleet once existed in less than a minute.

Quatris was exhausted from his mission, and could hardly speak as he looked down from where he came, to see if he missed anyone.

Sedric and Hellfire were still fighting the remains of the Gillithe second modern fleet while Quatris visually confirmed there were no survivors among the fleet of over four hundred starships.

"You guys okay there?" Quatris weakly asked.

"Yea, I'm good." Hellfire replied a few seconds later.

"Me too. What about you?" Sedric also replied with a few seconds delay being half a light year away.

"I'm done, but if you don't need me, I'm just going to float here and take five." Quatris said happy to hear he didn't have to do anything now that he had depleted almost all his energy and needed to recover.

"Take five?" Sedric asked, thinking it was another codeword and had to do something similar to a location, but his thoughts were mainly on the first part of Quatris' statement. 'He's done. Wow, that was fast, and the entire fleet. I still have like forty ships to go on half the fleet.' Sedric thought as he flew after and blasted the smaller remaining cruiser type vessels.

"It means he's taking five minutes to rest and relax." Hellfire explained.

"Oh, thanks." Sedric replied.

It didn't take long for the remaining Gillithe ships to be destroyed with a few sitting idle in space thinking their pleas for surrender would be heard and granted. The truth was they might have been granted, but Hellfire and Sedric couldn't hear any subspace communications by them since they were on a different and secure channel once combat started. The individualized earphones and microphone head pieces were not capable of scanning for and monitoring millions of single and multiplex hopping subspace frequencies. There was a universal clear frequency, but it was not monitored by them since there was always some form of static from distant chatter across the stars, so the default setting was to have that frequency disabled when in combat, so as not to have a constant hot microphone sound ringing in their ears.

Sedric finished with his last ship and flew towards Hellfire. Hellfire was flying through space almost leaving a blue light trail behind him. Sedric noticed that Hellfire's personal force field wasn't a force field like his. It was an aura of fire which surrounded Hellfire's body causing massive damage to anything he touched. He flew through the ship's hull with ease, his body getting bright blue as he burned through the ship and then his body went back to normal with his damage field disappearing when he was finished. Hellfire stopped as he approached the last ship and left it alone, maybe hoping they would be witnesses to the power of the Guardians and deter anyone thinking they could defy the empire by force. Sedric flew next to him. There was massive ship debris scattered over the battlefield, but Sedric and Hellfire could see there were no steady active energy levels, except from the last surviving ship. Whatever survivors there might be among the debris they would soon die in the emptiness of space, if the last Gillithe ship didn't feel like rescuing their own people.

"What took you so long?" Sedric smiled but it couldn't be seen since his mouth was covered by the mouth piece.

There was no reply from Hellfire as he pointed to his ear and talked in space with his mouth exposed to the environment, but no sound could be heard. Sedric saw that Hellfire's mouth and nose piece were gone. Sedric gave Hellfire the sign for okay with his hand telling Hellfire he understood that he couldn't speak and hear him. Hellfire pointed into space where Quatris was supposed to be. Sedric nodded and they flew to link up with

Quatris.

"Quatris, Hellfire lost his mouth and earpiece." Sedric reported to Quatris as they quickly approached his location.

Quatris floated in the darkness of space with his eyes closed, but opened them once he felt Hellfire's and Sedric's energy approaching. "Hmm, he must have burned it off with his fire shield."

Sedric and Hellfire appeared in front of Quatris as if they teleported, slowing down and stopping on a dime. "We can get him a spare later, but what do we do now?" Sedric asked, but was looking at the complete absence of wreckage. Quatris had vaporized the fleet, and Sedric was awed with deep respect for this Earthling who seemed to have no equal.

"Tell Klakin we're on our way back and that Hellfire has no comms." Quatris said and pointed towards Tarthillia.

Hellfire tapped Quatris's shoulder to get his attention and said okay.

"Hellfire said okay." Quatris told Sedric.

"What, how do you know?"

"We had this problem a long time ago, so we learned to talk to each other and read each other lips. So, anyways, let's go." Quatris said with a weary voice.

Sedric smiled seeing that the two made an excellent team and had much to offer the other guardians when it came to teamwork dynamics and practices.

The three Guardians warped though space to assist Klakin and his group.

Station 22, orbit around Aeriok, Tarthillia's largest moon

Lady Cerimon flew into the station's communication node. She felt a tingle of energy throughout her body as she passed the station's force field. The station was different than the one closer to the planet. This one was newer and much bigger. The schematics which Ship recovered showed her where the communication nodes were, but they didn't reveal any major technological advancement. The force field around the station seemed stronger, and working on a different energy wave length because it did slightly affect her body while her molecules were separated and vibrating allowing her to phase through just about any material or energy barriers. It didn't matter that she felt it at this point though because she was inside and could leave anytime she wished.

The station was on alert with a low humming ring coming out of the ceiling speakers. Cerimon was not invisible and the station detected her but failed to shoot her before she entered; probably because they were not prepared for a person flying through space without warning and bypassing the force fields. There were three Gillithe operators at their stations who jumped up out of their seats in complete surprise. They knew the station was under attack, but the sudden appearance of the intruder in front of them made them forget about their communications job. Cerimon tossed two of the operators against the wall with her telekinesis, and entered the mind of the smaller female of the three. Cerimon paralyzed the operator's body so she couldn't use her legs and arms. The operator fell back down on her seat and witnessed Cerimon sit next to her as her coworkers were tossed around the small round into unconsciousness.

"Locate General Pathron and monitor his any messages he is currently having." Cerimon ordered the operator as her fingers quickly manipulated the console station in front of her.

"Yes, Ma'am." The operator replied and also input information into her console.

Cerimon monitored any communications from the direction of the modern fleets, and Medroc's targets. She patiently waited for the operator to find the general and report his activates.

"Ma'am, General Pathron is in the war room, but is not linked to any communication devices at this time."

"Thank you, now go to sleep." Cerimon said.

The operator placed her head on the console and fell into a very deep sleep, ignoring the alarms and sounds around her.

Cerimon heard a few distress calls from the Gillithe fleets, but they were soon silent.

Cerimon focused her telepathy on General Pathron in the war room. She went deep into his mind and searched for weaknesses in the defense grid. The general was a very complex male, but his excellent memory helped in revealing what she was looking for. The grid was made up of one hundred sixty thousand micro phased probes. They were each the size of a football field, and scattered in a hemisphere pattern protecting the planet from whatever direction they chose. The probes were very large and unconventional as compared to standard satellite defense systems. Most of their mass was used to house and create the cloaking device making them invisible to the Argonian sensors. If a ship approached a probe it would move out of the way depending on its defensive settings. The probes themselves didn't emit energy for its detection system. It relied on the stations closer to the grid which emitted subspace light waves; this assured the probe would be cloaked instead of emitting energy waves and its location. Like Earth's radars, wave emissions would reflect back to the stations, but it was mainly intended for the probes so they would be aware of any objects in space which the stations relayed to them. Sedric's ship bypassed the grid because nothing detected it, and the probes didn't activate. Space is large and it was by probability that Ship didn't collide with a probe, both being cloaked. The probes were designed to use neutron particle accelerators coupled with a plasma beam. The particle beam weapon was suppose to penetrate the enemy vessel while the plasma beam entered the penetration point and destroyed the vessel from the inside. This was new technology, even for the Argonians, but the plasma damage would not be sufficient enough to destroy an Argonian destroyer which was very well compartmented unless it hit the ship in vital areas in the engines or weapon systems. The probes were cloaked which gave them the element of surprise and also the advantage of getting a clear shot into the engine vital spots. The weapon system vital areas were too small to hit intentionally, so the engines were the prime targets configured into the probe targeting systems.

Cerimon was satisfied with the information and she mentally shocked the general's mind; who fell unconscious on the floor. She concentrated on Klakin's and Medroc's minds and mentally spoke to them. 'If you take out the stations around Aeriok up to the fourth quadrant of Tarthillia, the defense grid will not be able to detect any movement by a ship or object. There is a code system which relocates the probes to move the grid, but they are controlled from the planet surface through relays. There is no self destruct command, but there is a maintenance command which takes a probe out of cloak.' Cerimon explained.

'Good, find the maintenance codes for all the probes and wait for Medroc to take out the stations. Quatris and his team are on their way here.' Klakin directed.

'I'm already hitting the stations.' Medroc replied.

'Understood, I'll be ready.' Cerimon replied, and looked at the operator next to her. Cerimon mentally revived her and took control of her mind again.

"Find the maintenance codes for the probes in the defense grid, and be prepared to transmit them to all the probes." Cerimon ordered the operator into action.

"Yes, Ma'am." The operator replied, and diligently went about decoding old transmissions which had the code information during a recent maintenance ticket.

Cerimon sensed four Gillithe security soldiers approaching her location. Their thoughts betrayed them as they prepared to assault the room by force. "Quickly, lay down on the floor." she ordered the operator and ran to the wall besides the entry way door.

The Soldiers wearing body armor overrode the electronic doors and opened them quickly, throwing in two small grenades of some sort. The grenades soared through the air like racquetballs which hit an invisible wall only to return back towards the soldiers in the hall way. Two bright flashes and sound of thunder erupted from the hallway as one Soldier was violently thrown into the communication node by the concussion of the grenades. Cerimon jumped in front of the now open entrance and grabbed all four Soldiers with her telekinesis, flinging them up into the ceiling and back down to the hard floor several times until all were unconscious. She grabbed the soldier in the room and tossed him outside with the other three. She then mentally forced the doors closed and told the operator to continue with her work.

Medroc was destroying the fifteenth station's communication dish with red energy beams which came out of the palm of his hands. He had completely destroyed the first two stations, but it took too long, so he changed tactics and only went for the communication dishes instead of the entire station. He really didn't know how many stations existed in the area Cerimon mentioned, and it was possible he might have missed one in such a large area, but he would find out as he approached Aeriok. The moon was large and he would have to make one or two orbits to ensure stations were not hidden by the moon's physical mass. The Gillithe were mobilized from the Aeriok moon base, but it was too slow and weak to hamper Medroc's swift attacks.

Cerimon monitored Medroc's progress but then realized he was quickly coming towards her location. She instantly focused on Medroc's mind. 'Medroc, skip this station. I need it to tell the probes to de-cloak!'

Medroc was about to slice the dish in half, but pulled his attack barely missing the dish and causing the station's shield to buckle under the extreme energy spike.

Cerimon looked down at the console seeing it blink on and off a few times, but to her relief it was still operational. "Be ready to send the codes."

"Ready, Ma'am." The operator replied.

'Medroc, let me know when you are finished.'

'Yes, Ma'am.' Medroc replied.

Medroc flew two times around Aeriok and found two other smaller stations. He quickly disabled their comms, but then he looked carefully at the moon base which had launched fighters in his direction. The fighters were too slow and his light speed flight kept them far away from him, but he had to get a little closer to the moon base to make sure they didn't have any communication systems that were used as backup for the stations.

Medroc stopped five hundred miles above the moon base and saw three communication dishes. He flew down and quickly destroyed them. The moon base shot lasers at him, but they seemed only to make Medroc angry as they burnt very small holes and large dark blotches on his uniform which resisted most of the attacks. Medroc felt like he had entered a tanning booth set on maximum without the pleasantries of a host with a welcome and body message. Medroc saw four laser accelerators and shot them with wide beams of energy. His red beams seemed to carve out house sized sections of the mile long moon base, creating large explosions roughly at each corner of the base.

"Medroc to Cerimon. I think I'm done." Medroc said through his mouthpiece com link and flew around looking for more stations.

"Understood." Cerimon replied.

"Send the code now." Cerimon ordered the communications operator.

The code went out to the probes, and the probes started to de-cloak as quickly as the transmission was received.

"Quatris, probes are de-cloaked, you can take them out now." Cerimon said over her comlink, then flew outside to disable the station's communication dish.

"Roger." Quatris replied a few seconds later.

The three guardians flew towards the now visible cube shaped probes equally spaced in a twenty thousand mile hemisphere and maybe ten probes deep.

Quatris told Hellfire what was going on, and then put his mouth piece back on. "Sedric, I will take the outer rim in a circular pattern and work my way inward. You and Hellfire take the center and go clockwise working your way out."

"Are you rested enough?" Sedric asked noting Quatris' lack of enthusiasm.

"Yeah, I ate my Wheaties this morning." Quatris said and flew off to the outer rim.

"Whatever that is, it sounds good." Sedric replied and bolted for what seemed like the center of the grid.

Hellfire and Sedric quickly destroyed the probes in the center area, but the probes didn't passively wait to be attacked. The probes which blew up emitted scanner waves which the working probes detected. They fired at the last position of the where Hellfire or Sedric flew, but missed by several hundred meters.

Quatris on the outer rim was gradually disintegrating probes, but it was slower than the combined efforts of Sedric and Hellfire. He was still recovering from destroying the Gillithe fleet and had to stop his attacks for a brief moment. The three eventually met in mid space several minutes later. The defense grid would have inflicted substantial damage to the Argonian armada; coupled with the two Gillithe fleets, it was conceivable that the Gillithe would have decisively won against Moridan and the expected Argonian reinforcements, but the precision and power of the Guardians changed the war and future of the Gillithe.

Klakin sent a message to Hebshilon reporting their mission was completed. Klakin kept Ship positioned next to the station as Medroc and Cerimon took complete control of the station. Morinar teleported Klakin into the station; where Klakin video broadcasted the Guardian declaration of conquest to all the solar system.

"People of Tarthillia and allies, your entire armada, defense grid, and outer stations have been destroyed. I am Lord Klakin, Leader of the Galactic Guardians in the Argonian Empire.

Your hostile and illegal actions have forced us to render your military helpless and your planet is now property of Argonia. Under treaties of galactic peace enforced by the United Galactic Council, your right to interplanetary expansion and trade has been revoked. You are ordered to stand down your planetary defense forces and conduct rescue and recovery operations on stations and Gillithe survivors in deep space. Argonian starships are prepared to assist your efforts. You will convene all of your planetary representatives and leaders in front of the Chancellor's palace in two hours. If you do not comply, your planet will be decimated and your race will be scattered across the galaxy never to return to Tarthillia." Klakin announced with his reptilian facial features revealing no emotional feelings.

Chapter Five

--- ⚜ ---

Outpost Var 115

Royal Palace and Command Central, Tarthillia

The Gillithe people powered down all weapon systems and assembled as instructed hoping to appease the Argonian fleet and Guardians now in orbit around Tarthillia. Fifty-four representatives, six generals, seven parliament leaders and the Chancellor who was the last one to arrive, waited outside on the palace grounds. An Argonian advance detachment had placed chairs and tables along with security and media coverage. The detachment was a thousand strong, with a large footprint so that long range hostile attempts to disrupt the meeting wouldn't occur. Klakin was not about to take any chances on Moridan, Drakon, Gillithe, or any other sabotage towards a peace treaty and Guardian diplomacy.

Klakin, Hebshilon, Morinar, and Cerimon traveled to the meeting in Hebshilon's shuttle. The other Guardians flew down to the palace arriving there before the shuttle and attracting much attention by the Gillithe attendees. It was the first time they had ever seen any being fly through the sky without the use of technology. The fragmented reports of beings flying through space and destroying their space assets were confirmed by the presence of the four Guardians who sat at the main table conversing with each other as if the war never happened and they were there for a press conference. Hellfire and Quatris didn't have their half mask costume, with their heads exposed showing their true human features and identities. Quatris liked the look and had suggested to Hellfire that when they return to Earth, they would make it known to the world who they were; getting rid of their secret identities. Their eyes glowed as they were constantly at the ready for combat. Sedric's eyes glowed yellow, Quatris' eyes glowed white, and Hellfire's eyes glowed a bright fire blue. Medroc's eyes didn't glow but he was fully aware of his environment. He casually scanned the area seeing through objects with his enray vision. It was a form of x-ray vision, but more precise and non evasive. He could distinguish the makeup of materials to include very tiny air particles. He could see wind currents if he concentrated enough on the small particles, and even though the Argonian detachment had scanned for bombs, biological and chemical weapons, Medroc looked systematically around. Medroc was always weary in unfamiliar environments and didn't know how well the Argonians were in securing an area. All that needed to happen was someone to set off or lobe a nuke into or near the meeting and kill many people. He was certain Sedric could protect people with his force field who couldn't survive such an explosion, but Sedric could only protect the few hundred people in an area no larger than fifty meters square.

Sedric was telling the group about Tir Goth and his friends while Medroc looked far out twenty miles into the horizon. He knew Ship and other Argonian spaceships were also scanning for missiles or weapon platforms around the palace. But, it comforted him to know he scanned the area for himself. Everything seemed well, as Hebshilon's shuttle landed a hundred meters from the tables without tossing up ground debris or making more noise than a Cessna taxing on a runway. The Argonian security guards were evenly scattered around the Gillithe representatives. The Chancellor and his top officials sat at a rectangular table facing the four Guardians ten meters away as Lady Hebshilon and her entourage exited the shuttle down the craft's ramp. A trumpet six chime sound announced the presence of leaders with a verbal announcement by an Argonian male orator. "Behold, Lord Klakin, leader of the Galactic Guardians, and Lady Hebshilon, leader of the Guardian Armada!"

Klakin sat in the center of the long rectangular table where Quatris and his group were at. Lady Hebshilon sat to his left. Sedric left of her, and Morinar and Cerimon left of them. Quatris, Hellfire, and Medroc sat to the right of Klakin. Commander Yohania sat to the right of Medroc. All attendees were instructed to stand as Klakin took his seat. The audio visual personnel were prepared to amplify the voices of anyone speaking for all to hear, which included a live broadcast to the planets Tarthillia, Moridan, and Argonia.

"This meeting has come to order." Klakin introduced each Guardian by name from right to left. "In accordance with the rules of war and galactic Treaty of Corimar, the Gillithe will comply with absolute control of government and planet to the

Argonian Empire. Moridan is given rights over resources and compensation in form of credits. The Gillithe population will focus on economic growth and education. All military personal will be disbanded and work for social reform. The joint Argonian and Moridanian security forces will maintain law and order along with recruited Gillithe police forces. The Gillithe have attempted to enforce their will on the Moridanians, and its allies. The attempt has failed and the will of Argonia will be enforced on the losers. Peace has always been the intent of the Argonian Empire, and so the will of the empire is a focus on peace. The education of your people will be just that, peace and equality. We know of the Drakon influence on your decisions to attack Moridan, but rest assured, your associates will be hunted down and justice will be administered. Your intent was to exterminate the Moridanian people, and anyone who came to stop this war. You attacked and accepted no surrender or prisoners. We are not here to justify ours or your actions. The war is over and time has come to live free and in peace. The time for killing is over, you must look forward and in time hopefully everyone can forgive each other for the lost of love ones. Are there any comments anyone wants to say at this time?" Klakin asked knowing this was the first time in Argonian history that any proclamation of unconditional surrender was opened up with a two way conversation.

There were mumbles in the crowd as many were surprised that they were allowed a chance to speak. No representative spoke however, fearing the previously established Gillithe government, or they really hadn't thought about what to ask, or say.

"The Chancellor is no longer in control and is demoted to the status of representative of the Palace district. Do not be afraid or shy to speak your minds." Klakin said.

"Lord Klakin, who will be our leader?" One of the representatives asked after raising his hand.

"One of your own will be chosen, within the next few hours. Some of you will be replaced, but your faith in rebuilding will be your strength to become a new people who will be honored and praised across the galaxy." Klakin stated.

The Chancellor kept quiet, but Cerimon knew why as did Klakin. Cerimon had probed deep into his mind and knew he was conflicted with many things he was told by the Drakon emissary and other political advisors. He was very ambitious and to his faults he thought it was the right thing to do by attacking Moridan, especially since the new technology would guarantee success. But the war had turned into an uncontrollable animal which included a type of genocide he didn't see until it was too late. His position as Chancellor gave him allies, but also enemies now that his leadership was to blame for the defeat or lost of Gillithe lives. His moral good intentions were for the people, which is why Klakin decided to keep him in a leadership position.

"Lord Klakin, how long will we be ruled by the Empire?" The Head of Commerce asked.

"The Empire will have ten years resource rights, and your government will be ruled for at least eight years, depending on the progress of the reforms and the people's willingness to live in peace with the Moridanians. The Argonian directors which will be with your leader and representatives will make that determination."

"I have a question!" One of the representatives in the back row loudly announced.

Everyone seemed to turn their heads in his direction. "What gives you the right to kill every man and woman in our space fleets?" The man's tone of voice indicated anger and a great lost, possibly family, spouse, or extended family.

"I can answer that one." Quatris stated. "I could simply say that whoever has the power has the right to do what they like, but I will put it this way. Lethal force is met by lethal force, and since my powers work on antimatter principles, it destroys all that it touches. Your planet could have been obliterated, but yet you were spared not because you have a right to live, but because we had the power to let you live."

"I said we would not talk back and forth justifying ours or your actions. We do feel pain for so many people, dying on both sides, but be it known that the Guardians will maintain the peace across the galaxy even if we have to kill living beings." Klakin interrupted.

"Lord Klakin, do you speak for the Queen?" The Chancellor asked seeing that there were many of his people who didn't understand that Klakin spoke for the Queen.

"Yes, I do, and as such, you have my word that the Gillithe will not be mistreated. Moridanians will comply with the treaty and both of you will assist each other in raising your orphan children and single parent families due to the war. There will be peace and each of you will learn to live in peace." Klakin replied.

The audience was silent, contemplating what was said.

"All representatives will file through our processing center, and meet with your directors. If you have any other questions, please ask the directors. This meeting is now adjourned." Klakin concluded the Guardian portion of the meeting. Klakin had ordered telepaths to scan the representatives while in the meeting and processing phase looking for uncooperative Gillithe and finding that one effective leader who would propel the peace efforts and also maintain a unified Gillithe group whom they were likely to follow.

Everyone stood up as the Guardians left the table and headed towards Hebshilon's shuttle. Klakin looked at Cerimon and nodded approval. They all entered the shuttle and huddled together.

"Well that was the first time I saw a press conference in a war treaty." Morinar said.

"It was necessary for the people to see our intentions." Klakin said.

"The Gillithe people or other people?" Quatris asked knowing the audience was the galaxy.

"You are correct Lord Quatris. We have great power, and the beings we will meet in the future must know that they are not doomed; this will make them more likely to surrender or side with us. The ones behind this master plan of causing wars must also know that we mean business." Klakin said.

"So what now?" Medroc asked knowing that they were still in the dark as to who was behind the war making.

"Lady Cerimon." Klakin motioned.

"The Drakon emissaries retreated through an outpost in the Raelin Sector. The faction is from Lorli, so if we can track down this lead, we might be able to find this Drakon, or at least find out who the employer is with other clues we might find." Cerimon said.

"You sly dragon you." Morinar smirked. "You knew that someone would think of the Drakons once you mentioned them. You had Cerimon scan for their thoughts. And you didn't tell us."

"That's' why he's leader." Hellfire stated.

"So where to?" Medroc asked.

"Outpost Var 115." Cerimon replied.

"Where's that?" Medroc asked.

"It's in quadrant KSL489905. Two hundred three Earth light years from here." Hebshilon answered while she pointed at a navigation screen on the wall of the shuttlecraft.

"We take Ship, infiltrate the outpost and find out where this Drakon went to. Lady Hebshilon will assemble the rest of the armada minus the detachment to Moridan and Tarthillia, in the Bir sector." Klakin said.

"It might be best if we don't all go together. Maybe I should stay with the Lardose and assist the armada with whatever we run into." Quatris said.

"I agree, but take Morinar with you as well." Klakin replied.

"Sounds good to me." Morinar said.

"By the look of our success, why doesn't the queen order us to finish the war in the Void?" Medroc asked.

"I don't think anyone really expected the Guardians to be so powerful, but I suspect the Princess knew we will be more effective the more we work together and since we are able to administer Argonian justice we are best serving their purpose by acting on their behalf in other parts of the galaxy." Hebshilon answered.

"The war in the Void is lasting a lot longer than expected, so don't rule it out; we can still be diverted to assist them." Klakin pointed out.

The shuttle landed in the landing bay of the Battle Fortress Lardose while Hellfire and Sedric figured out how to improve the mouthpiece comlinks. There was no getting around the comlink from being destroyed by Hellfire's fire shield or Sedric's quantum field, so the only solution was for them not to use those particular abilities, while the other guardians carried two or three extra comlinks in case any comlink did inadvertently get damaged or destroyed.

Quatris and Morinar stayed with Hebshilon as the other Guardians went into Ship who was waiting for them in the shuttle bay, and warped out of Tarthillia's orbit.

Medroc sat in the co-pilot seat while the rest sat in the back seats strategizing and learning all they could about outpost Var 115. The outpost was in a neutral area where all forms of beings were allowed to travel through. There was a military/police force which kept the peace on the outpost. Privately owned unauthorized governmental weapons were not allowed past the processing stations. Four space stations processed people where they were given access to the outpost situated on a small planetoid seven thousand miles in circumference. Unauthorized ships were not allowed to land on the planetoid and people were transported to the outpost by commuter shuttles. The outpost was more than a trading post, it was a point of communication and liaison between all sort of ideologies, people, and business. It was of no major strategic or economical value; however, it survived many hostile excursions in the surrounding star systems because it had a neutral benefit for all that came near it. Most people wanting to disappear used its neutrality and heavy population of mixed races to find cover before secretly leaving. There were inside connections and outside connections. The smugglers on the inside, no matter how good they were, would not be able to cover all their tracks, but it helped that the local police force impeded outside investigations like any Argonian authority trying to track down suspects. Criminals were a different story and any authority outside of the outpost would be given full cooperation in tracking acknowledged criminals; however, the outpost had the option to accept or not accept the claim that a criminal was a criminal. The requesting authorities would have to show proof of a crime in accordance with galactic law and not just the local laws of a nation, planet or colony.

Klakin explained this to the group after reading what Ship had downloaded from the Lardose's computer, so it was decided that they would infiltrate undercover and not let the locals know they were there by authority of the Argonian Empire or anyone else. It was also a mute point because the only one that might have a traveling galactic passport was Cerimon who had traveled by spaceship in her surrounding star systems. Passports were created for all the members, which was only a start in a data based system used by most regions in the galaxy. The passports were only useful if services or access was required to certain areas like this particular outpost which was not under direct Argonian control. Otherwise, passports were not needed and their identities as Guardians, already in the Argonian data system, was the only thing helpful but not needed to act on the empire's behalf. But, Klakin said undercover, so the created passports had to be credible, with accurate fictitious information for their system to accept it as a valid passport.

Many races had telepaths to some degree and even though many were not anywhere close to being as powerful as the Argonian telepaths or Cerimon, the group could not rely on Cerimon scanning hundreds to several thousands of people in the outpost. There was also a possibility that her scans could be detected by a moderately strong telepath and be reported to the authorities. She could walk around and passively read surface thoughts but that would likely not reveal anything of importance, because even if the person who knew who and where the Drakon emissary was at; surface thoughts wouldn't reveal that information. They needed to gather intelligence the old fashion way, by face to face interactions for leads, and by getting access to the rosters of people who were or had traveled through the stations and outpost.

The data part was relatively easy since Cerimon could access the passwords by targeting key personnel like the immigrations security leaders, and Ship could get close enough so they could physically access the data servers. Klakin and Cerimon would get the access codes and pin point the server conduits, while Hellfire, Sedric, and Medroc scouted the stations and outpost by asking around and trying to make contacts with knowledgeable people.

They arrived to the outpost within a day and waited several thousand miles from the space stations getting a feel for the type of traffic coming in and out of the area. It seemed very busy as three spaceships arrived within a six hour period. Most of the ships were not large industrial cargo ships associated with outposts, but instead were commercial alien cargo ships carrying roughly one to three hundred passengers. The ships were each directed to dock with a space station. The stations could accommodate four large cargo ships at one time, but each station was given one ship to process as to not stress out one station, and also not keep people waiting in line for the immigration personnel to clear them to stay on the station for re-boarding or proceeding to the outpost.

There was a repair facility on the planetoid which was not on the outpost foundation. Gravity was close to three fourth that of Earth so parts of ships and stations were repaired in the facility and sent up to the recipients with relative ease. An orbital ship repair facility was between the third and fourth space station, but it was only used in emergencies or times when someone was willing to pay outrageous prices to fix a damaged ship without having to wait extra time while repairs were made on the surface of the planetoid. Space repairs were considered moderately risky and resource intensive since the personnel conducting the repairs had to repair things in a space environment as opposed to a controlled environment on the surface of a planet or in a ship's landing bay.

The Argonians had routinely created humongous space repair facilities which averaged four miles long and could be enclosed with a gaseous atmosphere. Their large military ships were repaired quickly with the advantage of zero gravity and atmosphere control, but it was still resource intensive in getting the atmosphere and temperature stabilized once the damaged or outdated ship entered the facility. This allowed the workers to use lighter space suits and didn't require them to worry about running out of air since they could breathe the atmosphere with safety filtering masks. Unlike most races, the Argonians had the resources and technology most races didn't have or needed for practical purposes in high technological and massive constructions. The Argonian Empire was in the business of creating large high tech military spaceships while most other races were not.

Klakin ordered Ship to park next to the ship repair facility after he, Cerimon, Medroc, and Hellfire were dropped off in the space stations. Ship stopped at Station One where Cerimon and Klakin transferred to the station. The two hugged Sedric and his energy field allowed them to fly into the station undetected. The station was very large, three miles long, with many rooms and corners in the station which allowed Sedric to drop them off without someone visually noticing them. Sedric flew back to Ship and likewise assisted Hellfire and Medroc to their respective stations. Sedric flew into his station last and Ship flew to his standby location monitoring their activities. Klakin and Cerimon wore attire similar to their respective planets with Baxcion trademarks for Klakin; and Jahnuny for Cerimon and Sedric.

Everyone else wore attire similar to traveling merchants from the Caspian star clusters. Nothing fancy, but not poor either. If their covers were to work they had to look the part of being able to pay large amounts of credits and not attract attention at the same time.

It took about three hours for all of them to clear the station's immigration process which included an intensive weapons check. This check took forty-five minutes which searched for biologically time released weapons stored within or on the person. There were DNA scanners, but they were for crude identification purposes to detect shape shifters, unlike a blood exam down to the molecular structure could uncover the fact that they were very powerful beings; to include origins. The taking of blood in accordance to galaxy law was an invasion of privacy without consent. It was not like blood couldn't be taken by force or by non evasive means, but it was a courtesy for all races so that there wouldn't be hostile disputes over the issue. It was an eye for an eye trend of thought which kept people from performing or ignoring certain laws; the extraction of blood only with consent being one of those laws which most races agreed upon. Consent being that the person agreed; and was not under criminal investigation and been deemed exam able by a court justice order.

The fact that Earthlings were not space faring should have been a red flag to the outpost authorities, but it was also not a big issue since humans were not a significant race to be concerned about. New races were identified in the stations every few decades, but they only cataloged the information for legal and outpost purposes as future reference to maintain situational awareness should a medical need require a particular race to stop an epidemic or death of a injured person. The races which brought up major concern were Pylaxian, Sitherian, and Argonian royal blood. Pylaxians and Sitherians were usually accompanied by death and destruction. None had set foot in a station or the outpost, but both their identities were well known to the surrounding star systems and travelers. Royal Argonian blood was usually accompanied by a large military presence which disrupted operations in the stations and outpost. They never had a Goth or Earthling in their midst, but it was ironic because they saw that the two Earthlings and one Goth were different, and they didn't know exactly what to classify them. The computer system automatically classified them as Primary Kelos for the humans and Primary Keelin for Sedric. The computer matched the closest DNA makeup which was firmly established in the database to their current makeup. Primary meant that the origin was not complete and there was a very minuet mutation from that specific race. To Sedric, it only showed him that the Keelin race which was Cerimon's race was the Goth's closest DNA relative, if not Goth. The Kelos race was also closest to human DNA which most genealogists would agree with if they visited the Kelos star system and examined the inhabitants who were physically identical to human Earthlings.

Medroc and Hellfire didn't know why they were given those race designations, and were not questioned about them, but to Ship's credit, the race embedded in their passports reflected this possibility of a computer matchup due to a DNA scan. Sedric knew what had happened and thought about what Medroc or Hellfire might be doing if the misguided computer didn't match up their DNAs as expected. But, his thoughts turned positive as his race was matched as expected so he assumed Medroc's and Hellfire's race matchup would also be alright.

The three mile square shaped stations were highly automated and traveling aliens were not allowed to stay in them for more than six hours. They would have to board a ship or commute to the outpost. If they boarded a ship and returned, they would have to go through the screening process again which took time and almost all travelers preferred to wait on the outpost if they were waiting longer than six hours for an outgoing ship. The outpost was very large and could house a million beings but the authorities limited permanent residence to a hundred sixty thousand; and temporary residence to two hundred thousand. All other personnel had a maximum of one hundred twenty days with four approved extensions. The average monthly population of the outpost was half a million beings.

There were ambassadors on the outpost for many political reasons, but for the authorities it helped in keeping the peace. Ambassadors on the outpost kept races with military might and governments linked like an invisible alliance. The Argonians had an ambassador in the outpost, but Klakin would only use him as a last resort for information. Their presence alone was like the queen visiting, but it was good that their reputation had not gotten to the outpost. In time, it was likely that visual recognition protocols would identify them to the outpost authorities, but not yet. Klakin knew this once he and Cerimon were cleared. His broadcasted speech from Tarthillia would not get to the outpost for maybe a month; he hoped. It all depended on the station's and outpost communication filters and if the travelers placed importance on the information they were spreading. The authorities would have to intentionally order a facial recognition analysis be conducted for their database to be populated. There were too many beings on stellar news broadcasts, and the computers were not going to automatically and instantly analyze every face that was received on millions of subspace frequencies.

In time the computers would analyze the images, but it was put on a priority default setting which took several weeks depending on what was going on with the activities of the population. Non residents were constantly tracked by a micro tracker on a wristband and by facial recognition. Cameras were placed in all public areas, in most domiciles, and at every entry way with a door or passage. If the face didn't match the locator wristband, the person would be hunted down and arrested, deported from the outpost and in many circumstances, not be allowed to return for many years topped off with a heavy fine. The locator and facial recognition procedure kept people from committing crimes and running around without any accountability.

There was also a slight chance that a traveler might recognize him or the other guardians, but Klakin would worry about that if it happened. Cerimon and Klakin looked for the immigration supervisor, and once Klakin gave Cerimon the all clear, she specifically scanned his mind. The security codes were changed once a week, but there was a problem. Even with the security codes, the hacker would have to perform a facial recognition search for the Drakon emissary without attracting attention. Ship might be able to do it, but Cerimon couldn't project her mind into Ship to show him what the Drakon looked like. Hellfire had sketched the Drakon's face very well after

Cerimon projected the image into their memories, so it was all Ship had to work with. Not that the sketch was not good enough for the computer system to get a match, but since the sketch was not an actual picture or video, the outpost computer might alert someone else for verification of the recognition order.

Cerimon mentally gave all the information she had scanned to Klakin. After a few minutes, Klakin decided to continue to the outpost, find the person in charge of the outpost security investigations department and get him to authorize the search. Cerimon agreed and they both went into the first available commuter shuttle.

Hellfire, Medroc, and Sedric looked for the Drakon emissary, but they were looking for a needle in a haystack, that was probably not there anymore. The Gillithe had lost the war, and the emissary knew he had to get as far away from Tarthillia as possible or at least away from anyone wanting to kill him to get rid of loose ends. Klakin was hoping the Drakon emissary would not be killed, but he was expecting an honorable foe or an egotistical one. Hellfire and Quatris had their doubts knowing the way human criminal minds worked, and if an Earthling were in charge he would have killed the emissary, anyone near him and his whole family as the price for failure.

Cerimon was certain she could get what they needed with the emissary or not, she just needed to be exposed to the right people. To her, it was a matter of time as the Guardians had the resources to travel the star systems and get that exposure. The group collectively felt strongly that if it was a conspiracy, it was a large one and not isolated to the Corimar sector of space.

The five guardians had planned a meeting point five hours after Klakin and Cerimon were first dropped off in Station One. Hellfire, Sedric, and Medroc met early near the meeting point in an open market center. They had a little more than an hour before meeting Klakin and Cerimon who were nowhere near them. Medroc scanned for them but couldn't see them. They didn't take the comlinks because they would have alerted the authorities something was wrong. Phones were available, and they bought five, but what good were they to Klakin and Cerimon if they didn't have them on their person at the time. They sat in an open eating area. The Outpost bluish glass alloy dome a mile high was a marvel to see. Medroc and Hellfire enjoyed the view of a futuristic looking city like if they were in the middle of a mixture of a Star Wars and Star Trek dimension. The dome was for climate and weather control, but it also served the purpose of keeping everyone inside the Outpost territory and protected from the harsh atmosphere. Wanderers outside the dome would be exposed to extreme desert and arctic environments, but the dome also prevented people from using the planetoid as a hideout or haven for criminal purposes. It was possible to go outside of the fifteen mile long outpost dome, but it would have to be approved by the authorities.

"You two need to relax and wait, they still have sixty-four minutes." Hellfire said in the galactic universal language for that quadrant of the galaxy.

"You know, we could go talk to those Drakon down by the bridge. They are carrying concealed weapons." Medroc said, easily spotting the polychromic alloys in the weapons through their clothing. The alloys would have been spotted in the station screening so they were smuggled into the outpost or the Drakon were undercover police.

"Really, you can see that?" Sedric asked Medroc.

"Yeah, they have some kind of small energy weapons. Are Drakons able to be policemen?" Medroc asked.

"I don't think so. I don't think the outpost has undercover officers, especially Drakon." Hellfire said.

All three men could see the two Drakon waiting by a bridge overlooking a river which ran through the market place about three hundred meters away. "And what do we ask them?" Hellfire asked.

"We can ask them if they know where we can go gambling and work the conversation to who they are. Once Cerimon arrives we can hunt them down and get more info." Medroc suggested.

"That sounds okay to me, but why don't we just get them into an alley and beat the information from them?" Sedric said thinking they were being too passive, especially on people who shouldn't be carrying weapons.

"Or, we can just keep an eye on them, follow them if we have to, and get Cerimon to scan them when she gets here." Hellfire said.

"We could, but I like my idea better." Sedric replied.

"Well that means my idea is in the middle. Come on Sedric." Medroc said and got up from his seat.

"So you two aren't going to listen to me?" Hellfire asked

sarcastically.

"I don't think so boss man." Sedric replied with human jargon he had been studying, and followed Medroc.

Hellfire stayed seated and smiled. "It's your funeral, but take me off your cell phone contacts before you get to the bridge." He had been used to Quatris doing some outrageous things especially when it came to talking to the press. Each Guardian was an equal and if one of them wanted to act in an immoral fashion, he would step in, but if they wanted to do something which would get themselves into trouble, well – he had warned them. There was a very small possibility that the mission might be compromised, but it really wasn't a matter of a mission success or failure. To Hellfire, it was a learning process and this mission was a search for information. Information which would in one shape or form would not disappear forever or be linked to only one lead in an outpost in the middle of basically nowhere. The learning came in the form of group dynamics and growing up. Both Sedric and Medroc were young, and inexperienced, they needed to learn the hard way if they didn't want to learn things the easy way.

Hellfire kept a watch on the four men. He could read their lips and gestures as long as he knew the language and they stayed in his line of sight. His hearing was very good, but not good enough to ease drop on their conversation, especially with the noise of conversing people, cooking, music, and advertising all around him.

Medroc approached the two Drakon who didn't pay attention to him until Medroc and Sedric were within ten feet of them. There was light traffic on the twenty foot long bridge. The

Drakon men were standing ten feet from the base of the bridge on the far side next to the river. When Medroc and Sedric made the corner and started to walk towards the Drakon, they were put on their guard. One Drakon looked around as if trying to locate any surveillance or other people looking in their direction. The tallest of the Drakon stared down Medroc who was about a foot shorter. Sedric was also dwarfed by the large Drakon, but Drakons seemed short being compared to Klakin who was two feet taller than all the Guardians.

"Excuse me Sir, but my friend and I are trying to find a good casino. I was told Drakons were known for their gaming spirit, and maybe you might know this area." Medroc stated.

"We don't gamble and don't know of such a place. You might want to talk to the tourist center." The shorter Drakon replied.

"Really, I was sure all Drakons gamble. I mean you two don't seem like scenery watchers, I mean you're standing here by the river looking in all directions." Medroc countered.

"We don't like being in the middle of passing crowds, so leave us alone before I call the police." The tall Drakon threaten.

"There's no need to get hostile, we just wanted to ask you gentlemen simple questions thinking you were street smart. But you are getting to be very rude." Sedric stated while standing within arm's reach of both Drakon.

"We told you to leave us alone." The smaller Drakon said and tried to push Sedric with all four hands.

Sedric wasn't heavy, but he easily saw what was coming

and planted himself in position with his flight and energy abilities defying any lateral or horizontal movement. He grabbed the Drakon's left lower wrist and twisted it slightly in a mercy angle. His grip and strength was more than the Drakon could bare and he instantly fell to one knee. "That is not very friendly of you. Perhaps I should ask you in a different way. What are you two really doing here?" Sedric squeezed the man's wrist with bone crushing pressure.

The tall Drakon went for his weapon, but Medroc was following every move he was making. Medroc shifted his entire body forward and grabbed the weapon from the outside of the Drakon's clothes and ripped it away from the Drakon before he could touch the weapon. The speed in which Medroc had moved and taken the weapon away from the Drakon was faster than a blink of an eye. The Drakons were completely dumbfounded, but nothing stopped the taller Drakon from trying to sprint away.

Medroc didn't think the Drakon would be foolish enough to attract more attention so in his disbelief, he watched the Drakon run into a crowd of people and a few tables knocking people and food to the ground in his attempt to flee. Medoc came to his senses, ran after him and tackled him down to the ground. Most of the crowd scattered with a handful of women screaming, but there were a few people staying at a distance trying to see what was happening. Medroc grabbed the Drakon by one of his four arms and dragged him back to Sedric's location. People kept out of Medroc's way, and there was one Felorian man who was approaching Medroc, perhaps attempting to ask what was going on, but he quickly turned about as three one foot long hover cameras swooped over their position. Each hover camera had four circular enclosed metallic rotors which provided its lift/hover capability. The center of the hover camera contained an air inductor and video camera. The inductor was used to propel the hover camera at speeds faster than a Formula 1 race car. The three cameras spread out one hovering ten feet over Sedric, the second over Medroc, and the third stayed in between the two cameras. "You will stay where you are. Security officers are on their way to your location. Cooperate and you will not be harmed." Commands echoed out of the hover cameras.

The commands were not automated and came from a person on the other end, in control of the cameras. "See what you two did?" Sedric said as Medroc came within six feet from the two.

"Release your prisoners immediately. All four of you will comply and sit on the ground with legs crossed and hands on your head."

Medroc let go of his Drakon captive. The Drakon sprinted away once again, but one of the hover cameras followed him like a bee around honey. Medroc saw the security officers closing in on their location. There were twenty officers plus converging on their location by foot and probably more soon by air. "Well, maybe we should have waited." Medroc grinned and stood there with his hands to his side instead of sitting.

"Don't worry; I won't let you run off." Sedric said and slammed the Drakon chest down on the ground. Sedric sat down on top of him. The Drakon felt Sedric weighing over four hundred pounds as Sedric used his abilities to keep the Drakon from getting up and also running like his partner.

"So what do you think will happen to us?" Sedric asked, but was not too concerned because his mind had already figured out an escape plan.

"Don't know. But I'm sure they will have some explaining to do once they find the concealed weapons." Medroc replied as he saw the fleeing Drakon get tackled by four security officers two meters away behind an alley way.

"And how do we explain we knew they had those weapons?" Sedric asked.

"Let me think about that one." Medroc said as eight security officers came ten meters from the group with weapons drawn.

"You have been instructed to sit on the ground!" One of the security officers shouted.

Sedric quickly stood up, and a security officer shot him with what seemed to be a Taser round; without the wire system. The round mushroomed before hitting Sedric and the energy it discharged was instantly eaten up by Sedric's personal force field. Sedric gave the officer a death stare as if he was crazy for shooting him, then turned his head towards Medroc.

"Well I'll be back while you think about it." Sedric said. His entire body glowed a yellowish color from his force field, and he shot straight up into the air at hypersonic speed, but didn't create any sonic booms. Sedric flew past the doom in less than a few seconds and disappeared from everyone's view once he started flying but stopped fifty miles above the outpost. His force field prevented anyone from detecting him with machinery, but he knew Medroc and Hellfire could see him so far away and through the dome shield.

Two dozen security officers surrounded Medroc and the now submissive Drakon, but almost all were looking around for the glowing man who disappeared. There were a few guards who could swear they saw him going straight up at the dome, but it was speculation as they were not keen or quick enough to track Sedric's exact movement. "Geez, thanks for having my back." Medroc joked, knowing it was something he wished he could do and had not thought of it first. Yeah, he could fly away too, but he couldn't pass the dome without breaking it since he didn't have the power to pass through the doom like Morinar, Sedric, or Cerimon. Medroc sat down slowly as not to cause anymore unnecessary reactions from the officers, and then he looked for Hellfire. Hellfire was still sitting at the same table and had not moved an inch. Medroc saw him grinning and nodding his head but he didn't know if it was due to disappointment or righteous ridicule. The officers cuffed the two men, and transported the three perps towards their nearest detention center. Hellfire didn't follow and patiently waited for Cerimon and Klakin.

Sedric flew down to within three miles from the dome and peered through the clear doom with his telescopic vision. He could make out what was happening in the area he was last at and located Hellfire. He floated in mid air and waited for Hellfire to make his move. Hellfire didn't do anything except drink his beverage and Sedric finally concluded that Hellfire was going to wait for Cerimon and Klakin. Medroc was being escorted away, but Sedric didn't know what to do next, now that he had placed himself on a fugitive list of the security outpost. Sedric wore the identity bracelet, but was sure that as long as his force field was active, it couldn't be used to track his location inside or outside of the dome.

Sedric looked out towards the surrounding terrain beyond the dome. It was barren rolling desert with many rock features all around for many miles with a barren high mountain range in the east. He was certain that the outpost had a way to travel outside of the dome, which meant anyone wanting to hide could do so outside of the dome or somewhere in the dome which evaded the cameras. He knew from experience that in almost all civilizations, there were communities living in the shadows. The underground civilization would have access to both areas in and outside of the dome. He thought about flying around the dome looking for any signs of intelligent life. It was a long shot, but he could contact those in the underground to get back into the dome and hopefully help in the investigation to find the Drakon emissary. He didn't want to fly back inside the dome, because he would have to evade every camera which seemed too much of a hassle for him to do. He finally conceded to wait for Klakin to meet Hellfire. Once Cerimon was there he might be able to communicate with her and Klakin could tell him what he should do. He got into this situation by not being a team player and just maybe Hellfire was right after all. He only hoped that Hellfire had kept an eye on him and knew that he was floating above the dome as they both waited on Klakin and Cerimon.

It was less than half an hour when Klakin and Cerimon came into the market area near Hellfire. Sedric could see them join Hellfire, but it was a brief meeting and Sedric saw in his mind the image of Cerimon. "You know Klakin is not happy about this."

"Yes, I figured as much. What does he want me to do now that I'm outside of the dome?" Sedric thought out loud.

"He says for you to stay outside of the dome, but track us. When we find the emissary you can fly down to us and take him to Ship. We will have to clear up this diplomatic mess you and Medroc have created, afterwards." Cerimon stated.

"Okay, but can you tell Klakin I'm sorry."

"You can tell him yourself later." Cerimon's thoughts stopped coming into Sedric's mind.

Chapter Six

--- ❋ ---

The Underground

Medroc sat inside the back of a security transport. It was very large and was designed to accommodate creatures of various sizes up to fifteen feet long with a tall. There was an over abundant amount of room as he faced the two Drakon prisoners on the far side of the ground transport. The hand and leg cuffs were very sturdy but he doubted they could keep him from escaping. If he couldn't break them with sheer strength, he was sure he could vaporize them with his energy powers. But what then? His best bet was to drag out his identity and mission as much as possible if not forever, allowing the others time to complete their objectives. Then it dawned on him. Well this was a situation, but he could take advantage of it since he now had the undivided attention of the two Drakon in front of him.

"Hey, you two there. I might be able to get you out of this mess if you're willing to work with me."

"And what can you do?" the shorter Drakon asked. His tone of voice was not aggressive or heavy as before, but was tapered down to a kind of a disbelieving attitude.

"Well, you two didn't do anything bad enough to warrant imprisonment, so they will at the very worst just band you from entering the outpost for many years. What would you say if I could offer you another place to do business or even live better than you are currently?"

"You know that they are recording everything we say and do?" The taller Drakon interjected.

"Really?" Medroc looked around for the cameras thinking about those people on television who are drunk in the back of a squad car being videotaped and incriminating themselves on the way to jail by saying they were not drinking and driving. There were two cameras installed inside the forward wall with a one-way transparent alloy which kept the cameras hidden. Medroc could see the microphone connections to the cameras and one on the ceiling of the compartment. "Oh I see."

Medroc innocently pointed with his hands and fingers in the direction of the cameras. An invisible energy wave pierced the transparent alloy and camera lenses. The cameras melded along with the two microphones. Medroc then likewise destroyed the microphone on the ceiling. "My name is Medoc, the cameras and microphones have been destroyed. We don't have much time. If I get you two out of here, and you show me where I can find a certain Drakon male who recently visited Tarthillia, I can get you a profitable job working for the Council Alliance."

The Drakons seemed confused by his proposal. The Drakons were a nomadic race for the most part, and this alien in front of them had no knowledge of who they were, their past, and what if any information they could give him. The Council Alliance was a conglomeration of many races across the galaxy and it was very unlikely they would employ a Drakon, let alone two Drakons on a permanent legal non-covert basis.

"Do you think he's crazy?" Hamiftar, the smaller Drakon asked, his companion.

The taller Drakon stared at Medroc. "Who are you to have such authority or ability?"

Medroc had thought about what he would say before his proposal, but now he was having second thoughts. If he did tell the truth and they didn't accept his offer, then he would be labeled as a crazy and go to the detention cell with security using his claims as part of the investigation, or they might believe him and then he would be okay. At least that was how Medroc reasoned.

"I am someone how has direct access to, and authority from Queen Omia of the Argonian Empire. So do you accept?" Medroc said as serious as he could be.

"We accept, but how are we going to get out of here and away from the police?" Feesel, the taller Drakon replied.

"Easy." Medroc said and a section of the cuffs on his wrists disintegrated as if a tight beam of acid ate away at them. Medroc's energy beam was intermittently seen as he cut the cuffs on his ankles, and immediately he expertly cut off all six cuffs from both Drakons. Feesel and Hamiftar glanced at each other and then stared at Medroc and then their cuffs and chains on the vehicle floor. "So do we open the locked door and jump out while the transport is in motion?" Feesel asked.

"Now, we wait."

"Wait for what?" Hamiftar asked.

The transport quickly stopped. Either, they had stopped at a stop light which didn't exist, they were at their location, or the guards were responding to the lack of video feed from the interior cameras. Medroc was hoping for the guards investigating the camera outage, and it was visually confirmed when he saw the two guards driving the transport come to the rear with their weapons drawn and an escort vehicle stopping and unloading their occupants to assist the two transport guards. There were a total of six security guards at the back of the transport getting ready to open the rear doors.

"Stay seated, and hold on to something." Medroc commanded and flew up onto the ceiling of the transport spread eagle with this head facing towards the front of the vehicle. He lifted the transport without making a hole on the ceiling, and flew off a mile away leaving the security guards speechless. Medroc could see the multiple cameras in the area and found a secluded area where only one camera covered, and wasn't open to many witnesses. He landed the transport and quickly shot a very tight laser beam from his hand through the transport wall and destroyed the camera. He stood on the floor and cut the lock on the doors with another tight laser beam around the border of the doors, opening the rear of the transport. The three men stepped outside onto an alley way.

"Okay, I just need to know where to go from here." Medroc asked.

"Where are we?" Feesel asked.

"Near the Broker District." Hamiftar answered.

Feesel looked around the alley more intently. "Are you sure?"

"We're running out of time." Medroc interrupted and cut off his identity wristband. "Hold your identity bands out in the open."

The two men did as instructed and Medroc cut the bands off with his finger as a tight laser beam melted through the band but not their rough skin. The two men walked around looking for something.

"Is everything alright?" Medroc asked.

"It's alright. We go in there." Hamiftar pointed at a sewage duct double the size of a standard sized manhole, which was in front of the transport facing the interior of the alley. It was an access entrance to the sewers, which was electronically locked. Hamiftar placed his right upper forearm along side of the door scanner and the duct entrance doors unlocked.

Medroc focused his vision on Hamiftar's forearm and saw a small microchip. It was so small he missed it when he roughly scanned the two men. He must have had the chip implanted once he was within the dome, otherwise it would have been spotted by the space stations' scanners. It was also possible that the Drakons had connections and bypassed the station scanners, but not likely.

Hamiftar led the three into the sewers. Medroc could see through ground and metal, but his vision was limited to several hundred meters in dense areas of corridors. They traveled quickly through a thousand meters of tunnel, and headed downward. Medroc noticed that there were cameras in the upper levels of the sewer system, but they weren't working or had been bypassed. Cameras were nowhere to be seen the deeper they went into the lower section of the sewers. The corridors were very dark and contained dull lighting in some sections. The Drakons could see in the dark, probably better than predator cats in Africa, which also made sense why there were no cameras in the lower levels. Spending resources to have cameras specially designed and maintained to monitor practically empty corridors was something the authorities didn't want to bother with. It would be easier to deal with the underworld leaders, than to try to control everything that lived on the planetoid. They came to a section of a corridor in the middle of nowhere and stopped. Hamiftar placed two hands on the back of his head as if he were under arrest. Feesel followed suit and they both stared at the wall. Medroc could see a hidden camera on the side of wall and a hidden passageway with a concealed doorway acting as the wall. Feesel looked at Medroc, as did Hamiftar motioning him to imitate them, assuming that Medroc could see them in the dark having followed them this far. Medroc turned in the same direction of the camera and door, and then placed his hands behind his head. "So how long do we have to stay here posing in the dark?" Medroc jested.

"They're making sure you are not a spy and are on the run." Hamiftar explained.

"What makes you think that I can't be a spy, planted with you two on the run as a cover?" Medroc countered.

"The authorities aren't that smart, and by the things you can do, it's probably true that you work with the Argonians." Feesel said.

"You sure put a lot of trust in people." Medroc replied.

"People think us Drakon are without honor, but I gave you my word by accepting your offer." Feesel stated as the concealed wall opened up for the three men. The hydraulic system was underneath the four foot thick stone door.

The three men entered the passageway and the stone door closed behind them. The corridor sloped down and curved to the right. It was wide enough for two Drakon to fit side by side. Medroc could see that the corridor stopped curving after walking six hundred meters. It straightened up and opened up for a fifty meter stretch. There were two intersecting corridors attracted to the open area, possibly used as in infill or exfiltration route from an ambush position of the open area. There was no one in ambush, so Medroc knew they were expected. They continued straight for another five hundred meters and came upon a heavy duty metallic door, opened only from the inside.

Outpost Var 115 Market Square

Cerimon sat at the table next to Hellfire. Klakin didn't sit since none of the seats were large enough to accommodate him.

There were seats that were big enough, but he didn't want to get one a good distance away, so he squatted in position next to Hellfire. "Where's everyone?" Cerimon asked in English.

"Medroc is under arrest heading to jail, and Sedric is a fugitive floating in the air outside the dome three miles up." Hellfire casually explained.

Cerimon thought he was joking for a second, but Klakin knew better. "Link us together so we can see what happened." Klakin ordered.

Cerimon mentally linked the three together and they saw and heard exactly what Hellfire remembered and experienced.

"Contact Sedric and tell him to stay outside and follow us. Once we find the emissary he can come to us, and take him to Ship." Klakin instructed.

Cerimon stayed quiet for several seconds, "He understands and will be waiting for our signal."

Klakin looked down at Hellfire even though he had squatted; he was still over a foot taller than Hellfire in a sitting position. "Hopefully they will learn their lesson, and we can be more effective next time." He glanced at Cerimon. "Okay, tell them everything."

Cerimon mentally linked to Sedric and Hellfire and projected the memory of their exploits at the security command center. Cerimon and Klakin were able to get one of the security investigators for missing persons to look for the Drakon emissary on their recognition database. The emissary never left the station, but his presence was not seen in the outpost for over two days.

Either the emissary was dead, in hiding, or left the outpost with another name and face. They had an address to a temporary residence used by many travelers in the Night District, a community of short term hotel type of establishments.

The three Guardians left the market eatery and headed straight to the hotel the emissary should have been staying. Sedric followed their every move high above the dome. Cerimon would keep him updated of what was going on if they entered a building or went out of line of sight for more than fifteen minutes. Hellfire gave Cerimon and Klakin their temporary cell phones for use in the dome and space stations. The phones could be resold to the Var 115 vendors at a heavily reduced price depending on their condition, but like most things in the outpost, temporary services and fast food was the focal point for most transactions with passing travelers.

"Cerimon, scan a high ranking security officer when you get a chance, I want to know if there are any reports of Medroc." Klakin said in English as they walked towards the Night District. There were no privately owned vehicles except for the ambassadors' and high officials' vehicles. The primary mode of transportation was by rail trams, buses, and moving sidewalks. The buses were like trains with three cars and ran on electricity. The Night District was about three miles away, but the next bus stop to that location was half a mile away, so that was where they were headed on the moving sidewalk. Cerimon scanned a security official she had previously scanned in command central from a distance of five miles, and found out Medroc and the two Drakons with him had escaped while en route to Detention

Center Three. "You Earthlings must like getting into trouble." Cerimon said to Hellfire.

Hellfire looked at her and smiled. "Why, did Medroc make a prison break?"

"Yes." Cerimon looked at him coldly.

Hellfire smiled even more. "I'm sure he didn't plan it, but the Drakons are probably working with him now that they have a common goal."

"What goal is that?" Klakin asked.

"What most criminals do when they are being chased; run away."

Klakin almost formed a smirk with his lizard mouth but his chameleon reflexes easily covered it. "Who would think that such a person with the power of a starship would be on the run?"

"Yeah, Quatris would have taken command central by force, and be issuing orders by now." Hellfire laughed.

"That's not funny. We shouldn't be portraying ourselves as bullies." Cerimon rebuked him.

"I'm sorry, but I meant it knowing how Quatris and I think for the most part. We shouldn't have to doubt our intentions or actions when we have the authority and power, and then have to consider what the peanut gallery has to say or is thinking before we enforce our will. We serve the public back on Earth, but sometimes it is their best interest we serve, not their misguided, ignorant, or bias opinions."

"You humans are indeed very interesting." Klakin said

thinking of how closely this Earthling's ideology resembled that of Queen Omia and Princess Navia.

Cerimon sensed that their discussion in English was attracting the attention of nearby walkers on the moving sidewalk. They didn't know the language, but it was unfamiliar enough for them to wonder what the three must be talking about or where they came from.

'We are starting to attract attention with the people around us. I suggest we stop talking for a bit.' Cerimon mentally told the two men.

"Well this is our stop." Hellfire said in the universal Vorlin language. They stepped off the moving sidewalk and waited patiently at the bus stop.

Cerimon mentally told Sedric what had happened with Medroc while they waited.

Underground Complex beneath Outpost Var 115

The three fugitives didn't have to wait long before the metallic door locking bolts released and the opened inward. Medroc could see eight aliens, one Drakon, wearing normal attire as was usual within the dome surface, but these men carried heavy assault weapons. He saw them before the door opened but now he could see details and smell the better non sewer air escape from the new large room.

Weapons were not drawn on the men, but they were at the ready. "What's going on Feesel?" Carmock, the Drakon contact asked as he stood in front of Feesel.

"We never met the snitch. Medroc here and his friend interrupted the meeting. The police grabbed us, but Medroc broke us out of the police transport." Feesel explained, waiting for what Carmock had to say.

"Where's this friend you talked about?"

"He got away and is on the run like us."

"So what are you doing here?" Carmock asked.

"We can trust him." Feesel said, while Hamiftar nodded approval as well.

"You know the rules. You don't decide that." Carmock countered. "Secure him." He ordered the men behind him.

Feesel stepped in the way. "It's alright Feesel. I will go along peacefully." Medroc assured him.

Feesel looked at Medroc, then at Hamiftar, who motioned with his eyes towards Medroc indicating to follow Medroc's intentions.

Feesel backed off the men and let them shackle Medroc with cuffs. The men all went into another corridor which was surrounded by multiple infused alloys. Medroc could see the layers of different alloys, but there was a point where his vision couldn't penetrate the entire thickness of the walls with ease. In fact his vision was extremely limited by the new encasing materials used on the underground complex. He could see past one wall of the alloy, but not a second wall. They came up on a very large room the size of a factory floor several hundred meters square. He didn't see it earlier due to the encasing materials, and was impressed by the adaptations used by these people. It was hidden from the surface and starships using high tech scanners. He could see several hundred aliens, but they were not the outcasts or slumming inhabitants of most city streets. They were similar to the people on the surface dome. The only difference was most of them were carrying personal weapons and seemed to be working for the black market companies up top.

"Why do you people work in black market items and not in legitimate businesses on top?" Medroc asked the entire group of people surrounding him.

"You need to stop asking questions, if you know what's good for you." Carmock answered.

"The outpost imposes taxes, as all the other races, but there are items which are outlawed by the outpost, so we make and sell those items." Hamiftar answered as well, ignoring the angry stare from Carmock and one of his escorts, who at this point had been quiet the entire time.

"I see." Medroc said and smiled. "Well I hope to talk to your boss soon; I have a few ideas of my own about things you can sell under the table."

"And what are some of those ideas?" The quiet escort asked. He was indigenous from the outpost. The outpost was several hundred years old, created by the Wordian settlers. The Wordian race was similar to Earth's Germanic tribes, except the Wordians' skin color was primarily a light purple color and rough texture. Their eyes were multicolored with several shades of dark and bright color combinations. Their hair was thick with only dark colors in the gene pool.

"I was thinking of an underground database system to sell information to worlds with a demand for information. Or, a weapons factory." Medroc said knowing that his ideas were not new or practical to many degrees, but all he wanted was to get people talking around him. The spoken word of people told a story which Medroc was interested in. He could tell that this now talkative escort was someone important; otherwise Carmock would have told him to shut up too.

The escort seemed of adult age, but to Medroc in an alien environment, it didn't say much of anything since he thought Queen Omia and the Princess were in their late twenties. When he understood that they were over a thousand years old, he stopped trying to gage the exact age of all aliens.

"I don't think those are good ideas." The man replied.

"No, now that I think about it, you might be right. But what about an underground military base who helps mercenaries and spies." Medroc's eyes widen as if he just had a revolutionary idea.

"Carmock is right. You should just be quiet, if you know what is good for you." The man replied being somewhat aggressive towards Medroc's ignorance or deep insight in their operations within the complex.

"Well, I thought you would like to be on the winning team, that's all." Medroc commented.

"That's enough talking." Carmock loudly and quickly interrupted.

Many people working on the factory floor glanced at

Medroc, out of curiosity, maybe due to the ten man escort for one person who seemed to be nothing more than a normal looking Kelos male. They walked across the entire floor to the other side where they entered a hallway connecting to many hallways, storage rooms, office rooms and living facilities. Medroc could see clearly through these walls with a few minor areas that were internal to the complex. There seemed to be a sheet of the alloy material covering the entire upper complex to prevent scanners from above. Many people roamed the hallways and offices. They finally came to the destination Medroc was hoping to find.

Carmock introduced Medroc, Feesel, and Hamiftar to a distinguished man in a large command center. The Wordian seemed of older stock than the others around Medroc, and his hair was long and very black.

"Commander, we have the Kelos male who escaped from the dome police." Carmock stated. "This is Feesel, captain of the 6th Mercenary squad, and this is Hamiftar, an engineer."

"What is your name?" The Wordian asked, standing seven feet tall, and very bulky from neck to toe.

"I am Medroc."

"Where are you from?" The commander asked feeling that he was not Kelos.

"A planet called Earth."

The room of over thirty people seemed to be attentive to the conversation. "Earth you say." The commander said as he looked at a hologram in front of him which only he saw from his view point. "You are very far from your planet." He continued to question as he touched the hologram screen, looking up more information on Earth."

"I have come here to make a treaty with you and your people in the underground." Medroc said boldly.

"We are not at war with you. What kind of treaty are you talking about?"

"If you help me find a Drakon male who recently arrived from the planet of Tarthillia, I will ensure your operations here is not destroyed."

"It says here that Earthlings haven't traveled further than their own moon. How is it that you are here?"

"I am a Galactic Guardian of the Argonian Empire. Do you wish to discuss business or ask twenty questions?"

The workers in the room all ceased their duties and slowly backed away into the far corners of the room or left the room. The escort guards all trained their weapons on Medroc. Feesel was the only one standing next to Medroc, but he was visibility disturbed by Medroc's claim.

"Your weapons can't hurt me, and if I want to I would have already taken all of you prisoner or killed you, so please put those weapons away." Medroc calmly said staring straight into the commander's eyes.

The commander looked around at his followers. "Put the weapons away. Clear the room." The commander sat down at one of the many chairs and pulled up another chair in front of him. "Let's talk business."

An escort male gave the keys to the Medroc's shackles to Feesel. Feesel unlocked the shackles from Medroc's wrists and ankles. "I will stay with you if that's alright?" Feesel asked.

"Yes, you and Hamiftar are welcome to stay." Medroc said.

The silent escort also stayed and there were five people huddled together in a circle of chairs.

The chairs were very spacious and Medroc normally would have to manually adjust a chair to the right height, but these chairs had sensors on them and adjusted automatically to the person's height, girth, and weight.

"Medroc, this is my son, Alac. I'm Commander Gyung. I don't know who this Drakon is you are talking about. As you know, the Drakon people are scattered throughout the galaxy. If anyone knows it is the Drakons themselves."

"This particular Drakon may have gotten a hold of forged papers, a passport and changed his appearance. I know your underground has the ability to do these things. I met Feesel and Hamiftar in an attempt to get to someone with the resources to find out where this Drakon is." Medroc explained.

"Do you know this Drakon's name?" Hamiftar asked.

"No, but I know what he looks like, and that he left Tarthillia four days ago, and arrived here maybe a day or two ago. My friends are trying to track him down on the dome surface now."

"Tarthillia, why is that name familiar." Commander Gyung said.

"Isn't that the Gillithe home world?" Alac answered.

"Yes, it is, and we conquered it two days ago." Medroc said.

"Who are, we?" Hamiftar asked.

"Me and six others."

"Only seven of you?" Commander Gyung said in wonder.

"Medroc, we Drakons are numerous. We stay within our own circle of people. We can ask around, but not even other Drakons will cooperate with use if this Drakon is on the run." Feesel said.

"It is not a matter of friendly cooperation. We are on the hunt for this Drakon because he helped in starting and fueling a war with several worlds to include the Argonian Empire. We want his employer, and it is better that information be given to us, than us taking it by force. The other Guardians are not as patient as I am, so it I important that we here agree on a course of action before my friends decide your fate.

"So the other person with you at the market is another guardian?" Feesel asked, thinking about Sedric's willingness to use force and then ignore the police as if they were beneath him.

"Yes, he is a guardian and a Goth." Medroc stated hoping the Goth reputation would also fuel the urgency to cooperate to the fullest extent.

"We will help you Medroc." Commander Gyung said and looked at Feesel and Hamiftar. "I assume you two need a list of Drakons here in the underground?"

"That would be a good start, Commander." Feesel replied.

Night District, Outpost Var 115

Klakin led the way into the Starlight Hotel. Cerimon immediately probed the minds of the manager, attendants, and porters. She ended up mind controlling the manager and attendant so they would pull up all information on the Drakon emissary. The room was still being used by emissary under the name of, Rhyon Tilor. The people working there remember seeing him leave about two days ago, but never returning. They didn't recall the event if they consciously tried, but Cerimon was able to draw the memory no matter how subtle it was. The manager gave them the room swipe card and Klakin and Cerimon went up to the room. Hellfire stayed in the lobby in case the emissary showed.

Cerimon and Klakin entered the moderately furnished room with a separate entertainment area, making the room feel like if it were two rooms. It had a food dispenser which had not been used in several days. The non-disturb sign was turned on at the door, and it seemed the room had not been used in over several days. In fact the bed was not touched. Klakin could smell the scent of Rhyon, but it was faint enough to confirm that he had not been in the room for over two days. He could see no signs of any other person being with Rhyon, and thought about what else they could do to find him. There was a chance he would return, being that he had not checked out, but that was probably a ruse, and he would never be returning.

Cerimon scanned several adjacent rooms for any leads of Rhyon's activities, but nothing panned out. "I have nothing. What now?"

"We can try going to the last place a camera saw Mr. Tilor." Klakin suggested.

"Where's that?"

"Outside of the hotel." Klakin stated knowing that Cerimon would have to get the camera feed once again by mind controlling the security official in command central. She could easily do it, but it would take up more time than expected.

As they were going towards the elevator lift, Cerimon received a phone call, from an unregistered number.

"Hello."

"Hi Cerimon. Your presence is requested." Medroc's voice was cleared heard by Cerimon and Klakin's keen hearing.

"Where are you?"

"I'm deep inside the ground. Go to 2273 Hipler Street, and ask for the manager, Mr. Soso. He will lead you to me." Medroc instructed.

"We're on our way." Cerimon replied and mentally told Hellfire and Sedric what was going on.

Klakin ordered Sedric to go back to Ship and see if he could find anything out about Rhyon Tilor.

It wasn't long before the three guardians met up with Mr. Soso and they were led to an underground room several levels down. There, Medroc and his two companions were waiting. Medroc quickly told Cerimon to read his memories and relay them to the others. Feesel and Hamiftar helped in guiding the four guardians around introducing them to all the Drakon in the underground. Cerimon scanned all the Drakon and after a few hours found a lead to Rhyon. It was an alias, and the Drakon's real name was Oport. A new passport was created for him to include a new face. Oport departed the outpost not more than eight hours before they arrived to the star system. This meant that Oport had a fourteen hour head start.

Klakin ordered Sedric to bring Ship straight above them outside of the dome. Medroc told Commander Gyung if he needed any help he would be there for him as long as it was not harming other life forms. All he would have to do was communicate with the Argonian ambassador and a message would be sent to him. The four guardians, Feesel, and Hamiftar went to the surface in a park area. Sedric flew down through the dome and landed in the middle of the group. Medroc held Feesel and Hamiftar's wrists as a large yellow sphere engulfed the entire group and they all flew up outside of the dome and then each entered Ship one behind the other. Ship warped out of the sector in hot pursuit of the merchant ship which Rhyon had boarded.

Feesel and Hamiftar were in awe to the technology and abilities of these aliens. Klakin, Cerimon, and Medroc spoke to them to figure out where they could best serve the Empire and live a fulfilling lifestyle to include a retirement plan. They were Drakon, and solely working for the Argonian Empire was almost a betrayal of their oath as a Nomadic race. But that was just an excuse for the majority of Drakon to justify moving around and working for the highest paying employer. Many Drakon would have been content on finding a planet to settle in, but their reputation as a race didn't allow them to be left alone to progress. Many Drakon factions frowned on it and would attack their own people taking advantage of gaining power over a settlement few people supported. Argonian rule provided a means for mass settlement, but Drakons were unpredictable in very large numbers. Two Drakon working for the Guardians was an opportunity neither man wanted to pass on. Their questionable way of working and living was now in the past. They would have access to resources, and authority which placed them in high positions. Medroc's hunch about the men's favorable integrity was confirmed by Cerimon who scanned them with their permission. Feesel was a mercenary and knew Drakon tactics, many Drakon military leaders and units. Hamiftar was a space suit engineer and was knowledgeable in spaceship gadgetry. They were helping a smuggling company at the outpost, but never got their instructions due to Medroc's interference.

Feesel was sure that Rhyon was going to transfer to another ship in deep space, the possibility of that ship acting on the employer's behalf was very good, and there was a very slight chance it would be the employer, not wanting to have any more middle men. Feesel reasoned that Rhyon was not killed because he had something the employer wanted, something material or critical information.

Ship warped at maximum speed in accordance with the last given destination of the merchant ship. The ship didn't have to go there, and if they deviated from the logical route, then it would be very hard to locate the ship. Ship's sensors would be able to track the emissions of the ship once they were well out of common ship routes. Fortunately, the merchant ship was taking a very rare and dangerous route near the borders of two hostile sectors, which made it easier to track.

All of the guardians got along with their guests, and Medroc learned a lot from these mysterious Nomadic aliens. As Ship was speeding away towards the 98th quadrant of the Cameil sector, Klakin sent a message to Quatris. It was a short summary of their findings, but at the end of the message, Klakin asked Quatris to see if there was any way the forces in the void could be assisted. Klakin would have to wait a day for a reply, but was sure Quatris and Morinar wouldn't let him down half a galaxy away.

Chapter Seven

--- ❄ ---

Guardian Dominance

Star Fortress Lardose Bridge, Bir Sector of Space

The incoming message was taken by Quatris and Hebshilon in her quarters. Hebshilon was happy to see her son in so long a time. It was the first time he had been gone from her sight for more than a day since he was born. She knew he was strong and protected, but it was not a sense of worry or harm falling upon her son that stirred her heart, it was a motherly desire to be close to her one and only son. The encrypted directional message was not a recording but it was almost six hours old. The distance was great and the reply would take just about the same amount of time to return to Klakin. The message was to the point asking Quatris to look into possibly assisting the forces in the void with the help of the armada if need be. Klakin didn't want to go into why he wanted the forces relieved but it was probably a strategic move that Quatris understood full well. The war in the void was a montage of hit and run tactics using large scale forces. The Sitherian forces were in alliance with un-cataloged aliens from the Canis Major Dwarf galaxy. The massive amount of Argonian ships sent into the Void was a reaction due to the increased amount of raiders in the area which penetrated the borders and disappeared in the Void after destroying outposts, settlements, and/or reinforcements. The Argonians were in a protective stance along the border and even though they attempted to strike the large concentrations of hostile forces, the Sitherian forces dispersed and wore down the Argonian forces. There was no advancement or committed intention by the Sitherian and alien allies to cross over the borders and control the territory conquered.

Hebshilon was aware of Quatris' and Morinar's abilities, but she didn't really know Quatris' extreme limits. Quatris was happy to tell her what very few people knew. The energy a black hole or quasar produced fueled his powers. If he were near one of those, he wouldn't tire and his powers would multiply several times over. This was one reason he called himself Quatris, which also meant, man from hell. Quatris told her of a time when there was a villain who had the power to repulse energy to ultra high levels. The villain attacked their headquarters in New York, and attempted to use his antimatter energy against him. The plan only succeeded in destroying EFL Headquarters surface levels. Quatris used one of his moderately strong energy bolts on him which the villain reflected back at him. Quatris absorbed his own blast, but knew that if he used more, the Earth would be in jeopardy. He changed tactics and was able to get the villain to fight in outer space beyond the dark side of the moon. Quatris used his full power on the villain who wasn't able to reflect the full amount of the attack. The villain was disintegrated, and a very large section of the moon's surface was transformed into a layer of crystals. The villain did however reflect a large amount of energy back at Quatris. The ensuing power which he had to intentionally absorb was too much, but it didn't hurt him. Hellfire said it had to do with a portal or vortex which Quatris created in the absorption process that left it open and increased his powers and ability to take on the massive amounts of negative energies his body created. In an experiment, both of them went into space and found out that the proximity of a quasar, or black hole would make him stronger; or if he could attack himself with his own antimatter or negative energy, which would probably not happen in another million years.

Hebshilon was amazed to hear his tail, and a crazy idea came to her once Quatris had finished his story. "How close do you have to be to a black hole?"

"Depends on the intensity of the hole." Quatris replied trying to figure out what she was thinking.

"Does the gravity have something to do with you getting stronger?"

"Sort of. It causes my body to fight against the gravity pull which is trying to suck in energy. Since my powers work on what I call it: antimatter, negative energy, or entropy energy. I haven't figured out what it really is. Anyways, my body opens up a portal inside of me and I feed on that energy which also counters the effects of the black hole's Egrosphere."

"What happens if that portal inside of you is always open?"

"It's always open to some degree, but I think that if it is opened too much for too long, then I would have to get rid of the excess energy or I might... create a new big bang." Quatris said as if that were the first time he came up with that theory.

"What if there were black holes in the Void? Would you be able to hunt down and destroy every enemy military presence there?" Hebshilon asked.

"How big is this Void?"

"About forty thousand light years cubed."

"If it's that big, then there are probably a lot of black holes in that area. I might be able to hop from black hole to black hole gaining power, enough to do the mission and get me to the next black hole. But it would be easier if we can get the Sitherian to concentrate their forces as much as possible near a black hole. You can augment the Argonian fleets with the Armada and make it look like we are going to attack them in a flank. They will try to leave a decoy and move their forces away from that area." Quatris proposed.

"It's worth a try." Hebshilon confidently said.

"How long will it take us to get to the Void boundary?"

"If we start now; in a week, but the entire armada will not be there until another week."

"It's okay; tell the rest of the armada to head to the second location of unrest."

Hebshilon thought carefully. The second location of unrest was near the Pylaxian border. There were no hostile incursions, but reports were coming in that the Pylaxian forces were building up near the borders. It could have been a ploy to stress out the Argonian military or a posture ready to act if the war in the Void turned catastrophic for the Argonian Empire.

"I agree. Lord Morinar should go with a starship to lead the forces there." Hebshilon stated.

"Okay, let's get Morinar in here, and reply to this message." Quatris suggested.

Aboard Ship, Cameil Sector of Space

Sedric and Medroc sat behind the controls as Ship tracked the merchant ship's emissions. It wasn't a steady trail of ion particles or a disturbance in cosmic dust, but more of a cloud trail covering millions of miles wide, causing Ship to dance around in space like a wire guided missile making corrections every few seconds trying to get to its destination. The two men never seemed to sleep as well as Hellfire; in fact the three guardians didn't need to sleep at all. Hellfire reclined in his seat and closed his eyes only to relax and listen to his digital music playlist. Klakin slept in the weapons control seat knowing he would be needed to stay awake later. Feesel and Hamiftar spoke with Cerimon for several hours, but they ended up sleeping in the back, while Cerimon did research on the Drakon factions.

Kormath Sittar was the Drakon action leader for all spies, which was unique when compared to the Drakon faction architecture, nomadic lifestyle, and alliances. In many ways, it was very similar to an Earth assassin or thieve guild. The only major difference was that there were many guilds with many different guild leaders on Earth and in many other worlds, but the Drakon had placed all spies and assassins under one leader. This meant that Kormath was involved with Oport's mission, directly or indirectly, or Oport was acting outside of Kormath's authority. One way to make sure was to find Kormath and mentally getting the information on all Drakon spies and operations across the galaxy. No doubt he would be protected by physical and mental means. But at this point, she had the authority and ability to invade the privacy of any alien who stood in the way of galactic security and peace. She thought about her actions, and got angry but caught herself as she thought for a second that she was thinking like Quatris, Hellfire, and Sedric. They were either rubbing off on her, or maybe they were being more truthful with their role in the universe. Medroc, Morinar, and Klakin were more on the side of truth and justice, but they always tried the proper procedure first until it failed them, then they would use the: who has the bigger stick approach. She made a plan with Ship to submit her proposed mission to the group and see if that was an option they should pursue even after finding Oport.

Ship's scanners started to pick up stronger emissions and the rest of the crew was alerted. Everyone went to the front seats next to Sedric. A merchant ship was detected twenty light years to their front. There was another ship which was closing in on it, about thirty-five light years away. Ship couldn't get a lock on the second ship, but it was a large enough ship to use hyperdrive technology, meaning it didn't require a jump gate or wormhole to go FTL. The merchant ship was not moving and waiting in space as if broken down. There were no transmissions between the ships, but it was clear they both saw each other.

Ship easily covered the distance and stopped a few miles away from the merchant ship by the time the Pylaxian cruiser pulled alongside of the vessel. The two ships docked with each other. "Do we stop Oport from transferring, follow the cruiser, or take the cruiser with Oport in it?" Sedric asked.

"I say we take both ships prisoners, and not wait for the cruiser to get into Pylaxian space." Hellfire suggested.

Klakin agreed and ordered Cerimon and Medroc to enter the merchant ship's bridge and, Sedric and Hellfire would enter the Pylaxian cruiser. The Pylaxians were highly resistant to mental attacks or manipulation. Cerimon would be able to use her mind control or telekinesis to physically handle any one Pylaxian, but for a group of five or more, it would require more power which Sedric and Hellfire obtained.

There were very few people who had met a Pylaxian in person. The Pylaxian wore a body armor type of tunic which kept them from freezing or burning in open space. It was a covering similar to a nylon robe which kept people from seeing their true body form. It was rumored that they had tentacles or suctions where their mouth was normally positioned on a humanoid. They were thought to be bipedal but it was all speculation. Pylaxians were never captured in battle and there was a chance that the cruiser might attempt to self destruct, but Klakin was ready for that event. Ship hacked into the main computer system and disabled both ship's operational systems except for life support. This feat by Ship would normally be extremely difficult or impossible to do against a starship in the middle of battle or in red alert. But, Ship was no ordinary AI, and the ships were not expecting a hack while they opened up channels for the docking and transfer of information. The physical proximity of Ship also allowed for the hack since Cerimon was able to mentally read the merchant ship's crew and access codes. An innocent transmission by the merchant ship to the cruiser was in fact a loaded hack program created by Ship. There were counter measures established for such incidents, but they required manual input to some degree by the crew, who were at this time preoccupied.

Sedric and Hellfire flew out of Ship and passed through the force field and structure of the Pylaxian cruiser. Sedric's force bubble faded away as both men stood in the middle of a machinery room which they thought might be a bridge. Both men instantly split up and flew through the ship looking for engineering or the bridge. Hellfire used his fire shield to bypass walls and locked doors by burning through them. Sedric used his quantum field to repel any Pylaxian he encountered. The force used by his field was so great it crushed fixed furniture like a compactor in a junk yard, but was careful to not crush crew members.

Hellfire bypassed all Pylaxian personnel and focused on getting to the bridge. There were a few people who fired a sonic weapon of some sort at him, but it only made his skin tingle. He knew that if he were a normal human, his bones and flesh would have been shattered into thousands of particles or turned to mush. He took the time to quickly shoot a hand sized fireball at the weapons, burning the wielders and melting the weapons enough to make them useless. The Pylaxian language was based on an extensive range of sound frequencies and intensities. A universal translator was needed by many races in order to communicate with them. All the guardians wore universal translators implanted in their ears, which allowed them to understand unknown languages but it didn't allow them to speak to the alien who didn't understand their language. Hellfire would have understood what the Pylaxians were saying, but once again his fire shield destroyed the implant, so when he got to the bridge, and burned through the entrance the eight Pylaxian moved away, screaming it seemed, from him as if he were a deadly poisonous creature.

Hellfire looked for what seemed like the main computer console. A Pylaxian moved towards Hellfire, but stopped two meters from him and spoke. Hellfire looked at the alien and said in the universal language. "I don't understand what you are saying, so speak to me in Vorlin, or step back."

The console was state of the art, but it was meaningless to Hellfire as it was all written in gibberish.

Hellfire faced the Pylaxian who approached him. His or her robe was very colorful in desert camouflage patterns of black, silver, gold, and white. The head of the Pylaxian was similar to the upper portion of a prey mantis' head, and lower portion of a human skull. It was not the true skin, but a mask which covered the alien's fleshly features. The large eyes glowed violet. Hellfire could faintly smell unfamiliar odors in the room, but realized that the atmosphere was almost 100 percent nitrogen, and the odors were influenced by that fact.

"You must be the captain." Hellfire said and scrutinized

the people around him. They were staying at a distance, and the only one close to him was this Pylaxian.

Sedric entered the bridge and the crew members near the entrance quickly moved away from him.

"Who understands what I'm saying?" Hellfire asked hoping someone would respond and Sedric would let him know what was said.

A Pylaxian behind Hellfire replied.

"What did he say?" Hellfire asked.

"He said, he understands." Sedric answered.

Hellfire faced the Pylaxian, "Tell your captain, that you are not going to be harmed if you don't resist. The Drakon spy is under our control. Once you have been given control of your vessel, you will leave the area or be destroyed."

Sedric looked at the main screen. It was a blank dark green color as the ship's systems were still under Ship's control. "Ship, patch the universal translator through the intercom system so everyone can speak to each other." Sedric said on his comlink.

The Pylaxian captain was speaking as the universal translator came up on the cruiser's speakers, ship wide. "on this vessel is a violation of stellar treaty and you will surrender to us immediately."

Hellfire didn't need to hear the beginning of the speech to know the captain was quoting some law or agreement which was probably created many years before Earth was thought to be flat.

"You misunderstand Captain, we didn't ask permission to board this ship nor are we going to ask permission to leave. The Drakon emissary who boarded this ship or was about to board this ship is now our prisoner for crimes committed against the Empire, the Moridan people, and your treaty. Unless you want to claim that you were a part to a conspiracy to overthrow a world in protected Argonian space?" Hellfire's blue burning eyes stopped blazing and his normal blue eyes showed a patient wait for a reply.

The Captain motioned his head as if nodding, but kept silent.

"I didn't think so. I am Lord Hellfire; Galactic Guardian of the Argonian Empire, my fellow guardians bid you apologies for the damage to your ship and injured crew members. If you would all stay where you are, not touch any consoles, and wait for us to leave, we will get along just fine." Hellfire smiled in a non sarcastic way, ensuring his smile was received in a friendly manner. Not that a smile meant anything to the aliens, but it was an intended good gesture.

Sedric handed Hellfire a spare comlink. "Cerimon, what's the status on our new friend?" Hellfire asked, and motioned Sedric to cut off the universal translator.

"Unfortunately, he's dead." Cerimon replied.

"And how did that happen?"

"A guard shot him as he was boarding the cruiser."

"What did the guard have to say?" Hellfire asked in

English.

"It was a Pylaxian guard, and he was ordered to kill him if it seemed that he would fall into enemy hands."

"Does he know you scanned him?"

"Yes, I can't scan them without them not knowing."

Hellfire thought for a moment, as Sedric studied the Pylaxian in the bridge.

"Klakin, we are done here, I suggest Ship record everything that happened for later use." Hellfire reported.

"Understood. Ship's recording. Everyone, come back to Ship, bring Oport's body, and we'll be on our way." Klakin ordered.

Cerimon and Medroc returned to Ship, with Hellfire and Sedric being last to return. Klakin moved Ship several hundred miles away from the two spaceships. The merchant ship quickly continued to its intended location, while the Pylaxian cruiser retreated towards Pylaxian space.

Oport's body was scanned for electronic devices to include biological homing devices, and then placed in a cryogenic bag used for preserving corpses. They would need to take the body to an Argonian starship for an autopsy. Klakin and Hellfire were on the same sheet of music, as they knew that the Pylaxians were the ones instigating the insurrections, but it would not have been in their favor to inflate an intergalactic incident over a few Pylaxians who might have proof of such activities in their minds. It was likely the cruiser was given orders to retrieve Oport, but they didn't know why, which meant the crew of the cruiser would not be able to give them the information they wanted, but the data aspect of the Pylaxian activities was another matter. Ship was able to copy all the information he could about the Pylaxians, to include routine space operations. There was encrypted information which would take a while to decode, but it was a start. Goth AI technology was beyond Argonian or Pylaxian accomplishments and Ship was able to take secure information without leaving a trace. Klakin knew that the Pylaxian crew would be debriefed once they arrived at a space port or sooner, but they would not be sure if their computer system was fully compromised. Either way, the Pylaxians would now try to spy on the guardians if they weren't already trying to after Klakin's speech in Tarthillia. The guardians were in the process of intelligence gathering, and almost all of it so far pointed to the Pylaxian Empire.

Ship hyperjumped towards the Bir Sector of space, in order to link up with armada forces heading towards the Void.

The Void, sector Canis 2230

Quatris left the Lardose shuttle bay with a booster comlink able to communicate several hundred light years from a starship. Hebshilon ordered the armada ships and ships in the Void to get within docking distance. A telepath in each Armada ship would communicate all instructions to the captains. As far as the crews were concerned and in all subspace communication chatter, the Argonian effort was to spearhead an attack into the Void axis of sector 0010. The captains knew better and understood what the efforts were suppose to accomplish. If

Quatris were to come up on their communication's secure band, they were supposed to direct him towards the closest concentration of enemy forces. Quatris could see for many light years, but space was very large and what he needed was a location to go to instead of flying around like a chicken with its head cut off. The Argonian ships would help him get to his targets and he would do the rest.

Quatris flew straight to the first black hole at exponential amounts of light speed. As expected the entropy, negative energy, or antimatter inside of him grew several times over. His natural blonde hair, turned white and his eyes glowed pure white. The first targets were given to him before he left the Lardose, so he flew straight for the concentration of Sitherian ships three hundred light years away. The speed of his FTL was so ridiculously fast it seemed like he was teleporting across time and space covering the distance in less than a few minutes equating to twelve trillion miles a second. The concentration of forty-seven ships was no match for Quatris as his antimatter bolts disintegrated the starships without mercy. He flew off towards the next black hole, but before nearing it, he requested the next target. He knew that the areas near the border would be easy, but the areas away from the borders provided no targeting intelligence since the Argonian ships would not be able to monitor or scan so far into the Void. This meant he would have to hunt down ships as he hopped around the black holes. He didn't need to see the black holes, because he sensed their attraction if he concentrated enough. The strongest attraction was probably the closest black hole to him.

An Argonian ship replied with a direction and distance. He continued to the black hole and then to the next enemy target. Quatris was tireless and the process of destruction continued for an hour with a quarter of the Void clear of enemy forces. Hebshilon headed the spearhead into the Void, but it was not to purposely make contact with the enemy. It was to get closer to Quatris as he went in deeper into the Void. Many Argonian crewmembers aboard the Void ships and Hebshilon's armada ships were in complete awe as they heard word or saw with their own eyes on battle screens, the systematic disappearance of enemy vessels as if they were in a video game and Quatris was on god mode.

The speed and devastation which Quatris inflicted on the Sitherian and alien forces was so overwhelming that only five smaller class spaceships had survived the onslaught as Quatris was half way through the Void. Reporting of the extermination of ships was vague or exaggerated. There was confusion on most reports thinking that the Argonian fleet had a secret weapon and were moving without opposition. One ship continued to report correctly that a single super being resembling a bright star had destroyed their task force of eighty ships, but it was pushed aside by the other reports of the Argonian fleets on the move.

Hebshilon sat in the captain's chair in deep thought. Her heart was touched by the unyielding progress Quatris was performing. It was admiration of the human who was god like in power, but there was also deep conflict for her love of life. She didn't expect Quatris to be so efficient and fast. There were many people in the enemy ships who didn't get a chance to surrender and were following their duty for their world or a cause they thought to be noble. The Sitherian were not known to be honorable, but that didn't mean the Argonian Empire had to use like force. There was such a thing as fairness in her morals, but at the same time the forces which survived in the Void would be used to kill innocents in later battles. "What percentage of the Void is clear?" She asked calmly.

"Ma'am, reports indicate ninety-seven percent."

"How many ships and people is that?"

"Ma'am, over ten thousand ships; approximately 300,000 personnel." The science officer reported. "The majority of the forces were destroyed within the last thirty minutes. Instead of dispersing, the Sitherian tried to assemble for a counterattack. Lord Quatris has caused the ships surrounding the assembly point to disperse and are now retreating out of the Void."

"Tell the closest Argonian vessel near Lord Quatris to tell him to stop the attack and return to the Lardose. Then, instruct all ships to return to the border and await further orders." Hebshilon commanded, relieved that the killing and war was over.

"Yes, Ma'am." The communications officer complied.

The victory was bitter sweet as many lives were saved on the Argonian Empire's side, but the enemy suffered great loses of which they would blame solely on Quatris and the Guardians once the rumors were laid to rest. The Guardians had indeed made a profound statement to the inhabitants of two galaxies. Hebshilon knew that even within the Argonian realm there would be activists who would condemn their actions and if given the chance would support the very enemy whose goals were to kill or enslave them.

Quatris quickly returned to the Lardose. His arrival inside the shuttle bay was received with cheers and reverence. His eyes weren't glowing white, but his hair was now naturally white instead of blonde as if his hair strands were reborn or evolved into a higher state of existence. Hebshilon and Quatris spent an hour talking about the future, now that the war in the Void was over, and Klakin's request was achieved. To Hebshilon's comfort, Quatris admitted to not liking to destroy all those ships and people in them, but this war was not one sided and was started by the enemy. The expectation of dying had to be accepted, otherwise why start a war which involves killing and think you shouldn't be able to die. As Quatris put it, "They dug their own grave, I just covered it up."

The Argonian fleets in the borders were ordered to return to their normal sectors of patrol or back to Argonia. Klakin asked Hebshilon to meet them at the Pylaxian border where Morinar was at as time permitted. Hebshilon agreed and took the rest of the armada, eight hundred starships strong, to rendezvous with Klakin. It was not a military habit of moving mass numbers of starships around the galaxy for leisure, but it was for Hebshilon's desire who could take her armada escort anywhere she wanted. The show of force and authority to do so was her way of showing the galaxy that she was in command. Many people in Argonia would say it was a waste of resources and unnecessary time wasted for the space crews so far away from home, but in reality, many of the veteran Soldiers liked moving around space which exposed them to traveling adventures and action, rather than patrolling a sector of space and see nothing but cold empty space for months or years on end.

Hebshilon knew this and ordered a two week shore leave for all personnel after reaching the Pylaxian border outposts. It was uncommon for such activity at so large a scale which would normally place the minimal manning of starships vulnerable to military attack or covert operations, but she knew that the victory Quatris secured would keep any opportunist at bay for some time. In addition, the Guardians were once again assembled, and no force that she knew would dare attack the armada as long as the Guardians were in the vicinity.

Quatris was given the red carpet treatment by his fellow guardians as they all assembled in the Lardose conference/battle room. Klakin and Sedric were the most eager to hear from Quatris on how he wiped out the Sitherian and still unknown alien forces in the Void. Quatris described the ships used by the Sitherian, but it was unknown whether the ships were manned by Sitherian or alien crews. The ships were not the standard or older models of the Sitherian age, but were like the Gillithe ships, modernized by advanced possibly alien technology. Quatris was humble about his exploits which impressed Hellfire, knowing him for over a decade. Hellfire knew his true power, and it was a given that no one he knew could match it. He knew it, and most importantly, Quatris knew it. This truth made Quatris more secure in who he was and what he did. His heart was for truth and justice, tapered with love, a love which wanted to help the weak and helpless. Humans and aliens were to him not someone to rule, but someone to protect and if need be, at times enforce his own will on them for their own good and growth as a people and world.

Sedric saw Quatris as his hero and mentor. One day he would have such control and power. He was young and it was good to see that his efforts to have mental control, power, and vision were truly possible by the living example Quatris demonstrated.

Klakin was accepting and understanding to the moral implications of killing almost half a million living beings, but it was a mixed feeling, because a ten thousand plus strong mass of starships were not going to be used for friendly exploration. The fact that they were being used as a staging area or a distraction worried him. The Argonian Empire had close to fifteen thousand ships; half of those were smaller class starships. The Pylaxian Empire was also very large at the time of the last war over nine hundred years ago. The two hostile races had more numbers than the Argonians, but it was the Argonian technological superiority and allies which placed them at an advantage if both races went to war with the Argonians at the same time. Quatris alone was an unexpected game changer in the galactic scheme of power struggles. The other three energy projecting guardians had yet to show their true powers, and Klakin knew that the seven guardians were only the start. Princess Navia told him there were four other guardians to be recruited in the future, and peace would come to the galaxy for millions of years because of the guardians. He understood now how influential one guardian could be to the galaxy, how much more with eleven guardians. Klakin expressed his thoughts to the group once Quatris had finished answering questions by his friends.

Medroc was the first to make a comment. "It seems obvious to me that someone was trying to divide and conquer, but now that they have failed, they will try it in another different way."

"Maybe we should discuss what those other ways are?" Hellfire suggested.

"Well they waited eight hundred years to act. Why don't they wait another thousand and hope we're gone?" Medroc said.

"The Pylaxians can't sustain their empire for that long of a period according to the rate of their resource consumption. They will have to act soon to conquer some section of this galaxy, or another galaxy." Sedric replied having read up on much of the non-encrypted information Ship stole from the Pylaxian cruiser.

"They can try to divide the royal family and disband us." Cerimon stated.

"They could also destroy Argonia or some other critical planet and blame it on one of us." Morinar added.

"Well they could do many things. But I think what matters is that they know we'll be waiting for them." Quatris stated.

"I don't know if I can live a thousand years." Morinar countered.

Hellfire smiled. "You my young guardian are the most important of us all, so don't worry, you won't need to wait a thousand years."

"Yeah, everyone will ignore you thinking you're useless and you'll slip in before anyone knows it and take out the head honcho." Medroc joked.

Half the room laughed while the others smiled out of respect for the Earthlings and their humor.

Chapter Eight

--- ❋ ---

Before the Calm of Peace

T he emperor's palace was active as usual. Management of the empire and military routines on the grounds were the first order of business. The defeat of the Gillithe in the Moridan war, and Sitherian in the Void, placed the empire back on the drawing board. Emperor Tiaxtee sat on his throne viewing all the videos and data files the empire had acquired on the Galactic Guardians. All of his three hearts beat calmly as his eyes read the virtual screen in front of him; and he heard Admiral Frouls Lek, commander of the Royal 7th Pylaxian Space Fleet, give him a status on their new planet destroyer.

The Emperor was very tall for his race measuring above ten feet standing straight up on all four legs. He was over six hundred years old, but his physical and mental attributes were stronger than ever with the life expectancy of an average Pylaxian being less than a millennium. He didn't have a robe as did the crew of the Pylaxian cruiser. The silicon based body with very bright natural colors of his skin made him seem to be made of shiny plastic or metal. His entire body seemed half insect and half human. The chest and abdomen were human like with a horse like groin extending backwards a few feet to accommodate his four insect like legs. At the ends of the foot thick legs were small feet with three toes. The soles were rough and thick with metal like skin. His arms and hands were human in form but his hands had two opposable thumbs, instead of one. The bright colors of silver, whites, reds, and yellows were mixed together in short and long vertical stripes a centimeter in width all throughout his body except for his head and chest. His head was a shiny aqua blue with black markings similar to a lionfish. His chest was also designed like his head, but the stripes were larger and the aqua blue was replaced by a dark blue.

Admiral Lek's body was similar to that of his Emperor, but he was several feet shorter and the colors of his head and chest were a variety of dark yellow and black. Each Pylaxian was able to distinguish themselves by many features, but it was the colorful design of the head and chest which gave them their major physical descriptively unique features, as would facial features and hair on a person. Several admirals, commanders, and generals stood around the throne room floor facing the admiral's back, hearing the same report. None were wearing robes or masks, it was a show of non-hostile intentions before the Emperor and customary within the palace.

"Emperor, the Seer have confirmed their intentions to assimilate star systems in Colax space. But, as you can see, these Galactic Guardians have frightened the Sitherians. The Sitherians have stopped operations and request a meeting." Admiral Lek reported calmly.

"Am I to understand that the Seer are not going to let the Guardians change their time schedule?" The Emperor's heavy bass voice rang clearly.

"Vox'wer has assured me that nothing has changed."

Emperor Tiaxtee stopped viewing the video and turned his head towards the admiral. The Seer were indeed powerful celestial beings, but the power which Quatris displayed was beyond a Seer's ability to overcome. Tiaxtee was not fearful of Quatris, the Guardians, or the Argonians; and was above all else, fascinated by the Guardians and Argonians. They were not perfect and had great power, but everyone had a weakness and he would be the one to find it. "You are one of my most optimistic admirals and that is a good thing, but optimism alone doesn't guarantee victory."

"Sire, we have never seen a Seer get full."

"I have never seen a Seer try to eat a star all alone either. Its best we find out what the Guardians are capable of before we move into Colax. Tell Vox'wer to continue on his own; we will not move until they have secured the area."

"Sire! The Seer will see this as an act of weakness." General Irodax stepped forward.

"But we know otherwise, don't we general?" Tiaxtee replied, almost snapping at him, but there was a majestic aura about him that showed almost perfect emotional control.

"Yes my Emperor." The general stepped back knowing his place. The Emperor had been on the throne for centuries because of his fearless strength being unchallenged in physical and mental superiority.

The home planet of Plax was on the brink of starvation before the Emperor expanded the empire to the Sitherian borders and out to the Dwarf Galaxy. Everyone owed the Emperor for the salvation and leadership he brought and maintained. The Seer spirits became an ally to the Pylaxians only because of Tiaxtee's resolve. Vox'wer, the strongest of the Seer spirits, agreed upon a mutual exchange of food for both races. The food was primarily energy created by the planets and smaller stars for the Seer, but for the Pylaxians, it was the biological carbon based life forms, and minerals used to nourish their life force and advance their race in all forms of technology. The life forms inhabiting the star systems were according to their thought process at the bottom of the food chain. The Argonian Empire was for over several millenniums a big thorn in their side, but now that resources were being depleted, they had no choice but to invade Argonian protected space and fight the Empire until only one stood alone.

Tiaxtee wanted to see how the Seer and Guardians would interact. He would examine them both, and use this information to destroy the Guardians, and when the time was right, also destroy the Seer once the Argonian Empire was erased from the universe.

"Admiral Lek, one last thing before you leave. I want all the information you can get me on this planet Earth. And I want the best scout ship you have to find allies there."

"As you command, my Emperor." The admiral replied

and all the officials quickly left the throne room.

Emperor Tiaxtee raised his hand and summoned an imperial guard. One of the dozen guards in the room came within several feet of him and kneeled. The guards were wearing body armor which was covered by a Pylaxian space suit, or better known to other races as a robe covering and mask.

"Get me a secure line to the Sitherian high command."

"Yes, my Emperor." The imperial guard replied and rapidly left the room through another exit not used by the officials.

Battle Fortress Lardose Bridge, Pylaxian border

"Ma'am, Argonia is transmitting a message. It's from Queen Omia." The communications officer reported a little surprised that the queen herself was communicating with them so close to hostile borders.

"I'll take it in my quarters." Hebshilon said and walked out of the bridge and into her room which was twenty meters down the corridor.

The message was encrypted, but nonetheless it would definitely be intercepted by the Pylaxains. She didn't know what to think, if it was a simple greeting, top secret assignment, or what. Princess Navia was very inviting and straightforward, so she hoped Queen Omia was also, even though the message was ten hours old. She sat at her console and commanded the computer to open up the Queen's message.

"Greetings Lady Hebshilon. Princess Navia has told me so much about you and your son. I would like to meet you and the

Guardians at your earliest convenience. As you know, it is not safe for me to travel such a long distance and it would be easier for you to come to me. I and the Empire are grateful for your heroic accomplishments and look forward to our meeting. Your Queen."

The video of the queen showed her standing and Princess Navia by her side. The queen had very long blonde almost glowing hair; her skin was sliver to almost glasslike reflecting light and shadows at times when she slightly turned her head. Her facial features were very comely to behold, even for many different alien races. Her royal gown was like a pure white wedding dress filled with sparkling tiny emeralds. A necklace similar to the one Princess Navia had, held a single large emerald stone. The Queens eyes slowly shifted from clear white crystal to ruby red. Her lips were glossy ruby red, but it was not certain if it was makeup or her natural texture. She was standing at the time and the Princess next to her was an inch or two shorter.

Hebshilon knew Queen Omia from seeing her in the visions which Navia gave her, but this video message was like a verification of Omia's realness in her heart, not just her mind. She breathed deeply and thought of a reply.

"Reply follows… My Queen, I graciously thank you for your kind words. The armada has a few days left until shore leave is over. We will depart then and arrive in Argonia in six weeks. We are looking forward to meeting you and hope our voyage is uneventful. Lady Hebshilon. Send reply now." Hebshilon said, and the ship's computer instantly sent the encrypted reply.

Hebshilon touched an icon on her console. "Commander,

prepare the armada for travel with personnel on hand, we will all be moving out in two days once all crew members have returned from leave and are accounted for."

"Yes, Ma'am." Commander Yohania replied.

Hebshilon would tell the guardians the good news, but for now she would take a nap and enjoy her time of peace before people started running around getting ready for the long trip home.

A day passed and Pylaxian activity seemed to go back to normal along the border with many ships slowly leaving back into the heart of Pylaxian space, which Hebshilon sort of expected after the message from the queen. It was encrypted, but decodable with the right resources and time. The armada was leaving, so it was prudent on the Pylaxian side not to give the armada a reason to stay. Hebshilon wondered if they were reacting in response to the armada activity, the message, or perhaps orders from higher up the ladder.

The Guardians were honored and excited to go to Argonia and meet the Queen. It was a first for all of them and even though some had personally met world leaders in the past, the leader of a galactic empire was not something you get to do every day.

Medroc and Sedric stayed aboard Ship, while the other guardians mostly stayed aboard the Lardose. Ship was Sedric's second home away from Tir Goth, and Medroc was a welcomed guest as they used the time to become good friends. Medroc learned much from Sedric and Ship which made him put Tir

Goth on the top ten places he wanted to visit before the end of the year.

Hebshilon enjoyed her time with Klakin. She also took every opportunity to personally meet the crew of all the ships in her command. She was close to half way through the armada in the several months she had received her title. It was not normal practice, but Hebshilon and Klakin both moved around to other ships while in hyperspace almost the entire trip. Ship facilitated the movement of the ship to ship visits, which the slow shuttles couldn't accomplish without severe safety hazards while moving at over light speeds. Quatris and Cerimon spent their time roaming the battle fortress like a tourist and enjoying the leisure and entertainment areas for the crew to relax and socialize. Hellfire and Morinar were constantly in medical center, engineering, and the science laboratories studying all they could about the galaxy in general. The Argonian crewmembers working in the sections were very receptive to their presence which gave all of them a chance to learn from each other. Earthlings were a very unfamiliar race, since they weren't space faring, and this exposure to a new race was welcomed by the veteran crew. In addition, the Earthlings were Guardians, a title which was now the talk of the empire.

Six weeks later, the armada entered the Argonian star system. Hebshilon's popularity was coupled with admiration as the crews were able to meet her in person over those six weeks. Hebshilon ordered all but twenty ships to stay in the vicinity of the eighth planet, Sibos. She didn't want any perception that an eight hundred strong spaceship armada surrounding Argonia was a military display of defiance to the Argonian people on the planet, the Empire, or the Queen, even though the armada was technically the queen's property. She wasn't concerned about the negative opinions towards her, but she was mindful of any unnecessary negative opinions towards the queen or princess because of her actions.

Argonia was the seventh planet from an M-Class star, named Argon, with a twenty-two thousand mile circumference. The star system was at 306 degrees in the Orion Arm of the Milky Way Galaxy. It was far from the Void, and unfortunately for maintainers of the peace, far from all the major trouble spots in the galaxy. The planet had a stronger gravity than Earth, but its atmosphere was thicker and higher in high altitudes because of Argonian technological orbital atmospheric modulators. Climate control made the entire planet eco-friendly to all life forms while maintaining its own global ecological balance. The sky was pinkish and waters were almost crystal clear giving the oceans multiple colors mirroring the sea bottom of vegetation and sediment ground textures. It was large for its low population of four billion people, but that was due to the migration of people outside of the planet and governing bodies who limited residence as not to overpopulate the planet. Many citizens visited their home planet year round, and never complained that they were relocated outside of the planet many years before. The Empire was vast and Argonian homes were scattered among a third of the galaxy. Argonia had pure air and wonderful landscape, but so did other planets which Argonia colonized or cohabited with other races.

Cities were distributed evenly along the coastline, mountains, and plains. The makeup of twelve continents allowed for the royal family to dwell in their own continental regions, Princess Navia controlling the largest continent and realm named, Dothoria. Queen Omia's palace was in this same realm, but she governed no single continent, but the world as a whole to include the empire beyond the planet. Any disputes between realms were taken care of by the Queen, which she diligently performed without fail. The star system was protected by the Royal fleet whose sole purpose was to guard the fourteen planets around the star Argon.

Hebshilon's shuttle carrying all the Guardians was escorted by the Imperial Guards interceptors into the Queen's palace grounds, being setup to take dignitary space shuttles. The palace footprint measured seventeen kilometers in diameter. There were many right angles of building structures, but the dominating features were the symmetrical ellipses, ovals, and spheres made out of tempered silicon based glass and metals. There was plush green grass, small reddish trees, and flowers everywhere in the many courtyards surrounding the foundation. The group disembarked from their shuttle and was greeted with a hundred guards in a column formation.

Princess Navia stood in the middle of their intended path towards the palace entrance. Her very elegant white dress was covered with sparkling white diamonds even though it seemed to be made of linen by the way it moved on her body. Her entire body was covered by the gown except her hands, head, and neck area. Her crown and necklace were the only constant articles on her person that never changed. Hebshilon and Klakin walked side by side with the other guardians following behind them in pairs. They were outside and the circumstances didn't require they kneel, so they both greeted her and bowed at the waist once in front of the princess. There was room enough for two more people to get beside the couple before having to push the imperial guards out of their formation at attention. Sedric and Morinar behind Klakin both moved next to him and his mother and also bowed. The other four guardians in the back bowed as well.

Princess Navia scrutinized the Guardians she had not met in person. They all had energy vibrations flowing out of them except for Sedric. His life energy was lower than Hebshilon which intrigued her knowing he was Goth. It was not the time to talk about power, so she graciously noted the fact and welcomed all the Guardians by name. Each Guardian had their own opinion about the Princess, but a common feeling was her persona was very warm and joyful. Her majestic aura also added a sense of peace and strength at the same time.

The Princess escorted the group into the palace entrance, and a very long football field size oval chamber. The floor was glass like marble and gold cut into eight foot square tiles. Silver and sapphire crystal columns eight feet thick stretched across three deep all around the oval chamber. The entire ceiling was clear but in mid day slightly tinted crystal exposed the Argonian sky and clouds to the people inside ninety feet above them. It was likely that anyone outside of the palace couldn't see the inside with normal vision if they were flying above the grounds, due to a security or privacy film of some type on the glass ceiling.

Queen Omia was waiting for them standing in the center of the gorgeous room. Her emerald and light pink royal gown complimented the exposed silver skin on her forearms, face, and neck. Her blonde hair was rolled up this time and decorated with silver and gold hair pins. She wore a gold thin crown with twenty-four 5 carat round diamonds all the way around her head.

Joldar Crom, the Queen's royal soothsayer was behind her and to the left. He was short compared to the Queen and Princess, measuring little less than six feet tall. His skin was very dark, but there was a brightness about him as if he absorbed darkness and exchanged it with light. He was dressed in a light blue and silver embroidered cloak, like that worn by Celtic priests in medieval times. His bald head and aqua blue crystal eyeballs gave him the appearance of having wisdom or great knowledge.

The Queen overshadowed Joldar's aura as her pulsating aura was invisible to the naked eye, but could be felt from a distance in the minds and hearts of the people she encountered. It was a soothing but yet invigorating pulsing sensation that kept you wondering if it was corresponding with her heartbeat or your own. Sedric could see the power which all three emitted, the Queen's aura being the strongest, aside from Quatris, Hellfire, and Medroc. But he knew that gauging power levels was not a true indicator of what energy or capabilities a person had. In his world, he was taught to use the energy levels to get a basis of your opponent's potential, but never the true indicator since many very powerful Goth naturally masked their energy until they used it.

All of the Guardians made a semicircle around the Queen and bowed. Princess Navia didn't bow and walked up next to the queen and stood by her side as she introduced the invited guests.

Queen Omia gave them all salutations and introduced

Joldar. A large table for twenty people was setup near the edge of the room thirty meters from them. They all sat down at the table and conversed about all the events of the past four months. Each guardian was able to describe in detail about their history and home world. The Queen was very attentive to all of their stories. There was a time when Princess Navia asked specific questions about Tir Goth, which the queen saw as odd. Queen Omia knew that most of the questions Princess Navia asked, she already knew since Sorthan had shown both of them all that he had experienced while visiting Tir Goth and the recruitment of Sedric. Queen Omia added questions of her own to help out Navia, which was specific to Sedric and what his childhood was like. Queen Omia, Cerimon, and Hellfire were the only ones to notice that Princess Navia was clinging to every word Sedric said, and that Sedric enjoyed the attention. They didn't eat a meal, but were served an Argonian desert. Joldar stayed very quiet, until Medroc asked him how it was like to be a soothsayer. The reply was long winded and philosophical, but it was clear Joldar was not one to talk much having a curse of seeing the future many times over in a single day. After a few hours of conversing Queen Omia asked the guardians to stay in the palace for a day, before they went back out to space.

The group accepted, but Hebshilon requested that her armada be allowed to visit the nearest planet for half a day if they so wished. The queen had no objections and both the Queen and Princess escorted the guests around the palace. Joldar excused himself, while Queen Omia showed Hebshilon, Klakin, Quatris and Hellfire the north wing of the Palace. Princess Navia showed the rest of the guardians around the south wing of the palace. The intent was not to show them all that the palace had to offer, but it was for them to know more about each other. Princess Navia had mentally melded with Klakin and Hebshilon, plus she knew Quatris and Hellfire were the strongest of the Earthling guardians from reports, so Queen Omia wanted to get to know them personally first of all. Princess Navia also never personally met the rest of the guardians and was very interested in Medroc and Sedric who got themselves into trouble at Outpost Var 115.

It wasn't long before Princess Navia requested that Feesel and Hamiftar be sent to her palace so she could get them trained in becoming special operations officers, which was an Argonian way of saying, a top spy or consultant. The four guardians enjoyed Princess Navia's demeanor, knowledge, and humility. They had known the princess to be a very strong leader, but now they knew her to be an extremely loyal and trustworthy leader. Queen Omia had picked wisely in giving the princess power to rule if for some unforeseen reason, the queen died. The day grew late and they all ate dinner in a big banquet where many admirals, starship captains and officers, parliament officials, a few royal family members, and Hebshilon's top officers attended. The mood was very festive and enlightening for many Argonians who heard many things about the Guardians, but now they saw firsthand who they were and what they were like in a social setting. Klakin was the only one who even though he acted like it was a great party, knew and felt the eyes of the soothsayers or someone lingering in the shadows of the crowd.

He didn't sense Joldar as being opposed to them, but there was that old sense of anger or hate he had felt on the Lardose with Navia's soothsayer. The same soothsayer wasn't there but the same emotions were there in the air, so it was one or several people who had some sort of evil or negative intentions towards his mother or the guardians. Most people present were Argonians, with a few mixed races, primarily ambassadors from other worlds and parliament members. He tried to pinpoint the origins of the scents but there were too many people and a few scents he was not familiar with never being exposed to the new stimuli. Hebshilon noticed her son's distraction, but was not going to bring the subject out in public. Cerimon on the other hand saw Hebshilon's slight mood change and she mentally asked her what was wrong. Cerimon could try to link all the minds of the guardians together, but there were telepaths in the huge banquet hall strong enough to know a group mental link was being conducted, so Cerimon opted out of linking the group together and instead asked Klakin what was wrong after speaking with Hebshilon. Klakin explained and told her that she shouldn't do anything, and let him try to find the source of so much discontent. Cerimon agreed but struggled inside her heart, not being able to tell the rest of the guardians or at least tell Princess Navia, who she trusted, what had happened and was going on now. But it wasn't her place to divulge that sort of information without Klakin's or Hebshilon's permission. Klakin was leader and maybe mentally broadcasting information was not the best thing to do with royal family members and other telepaths in the area.

She decided to wait until later to press the issue if Klakin or Hebshilon insisted on keeping the fact that someone in the hall was full of bad intentions to themselves. She had lived most of her life without secrets because no one could keep them from her, and she knew very well that secrets most of the times were more trouble makers then peace makers.

Princess Navia's mater dean led the banquet with organized toasts, a selected opportune speech by the Moridan ambassador for the rescue of the Moridanians, and Prince Belock for the return of the fleets from the Void. Queen Omia was the last to make a scheduled speech which represented the empire's resolve for peace in the galaxy and honoring the guardians for their service. In the end, Queen Omia asked Klakin if he would like to say anything on behalf of the Guardians.

Klakin was not expecting to speak, but he knew that if he didn't his mother would do so out of courtesy for the group and audience. Besides, if his mom wouldn't speak chances were that one of the humans would, and who knew what could happen then. "We are honored by your words and have tried our best to fight for justice and peace. Many people have lost their lives and war is always an ugly reality with horrors none of us want to participate in or witness. This has not deterred us to fight with honor, power, and compassion. No one should fear us except those who do evil or have no regard for the freedoms of all beings to live in peace. There is still much to do and we will continue to protect the galaxy from all evil. Thank you very much once again for your hospitality and praises." Klakin spoke in an almost perfect Vorlin language.

Applauses were strongest from Hebshilon's officers, which only a few people with enhanced hearing noticed. Hebshilon being one of them, who appreciated it most of all knowing the officers under her command approved of her and the guardians.

The night went on with the guardians mingling with the crowd of a thousand aliens. Queen Omia departed to her sleep chamber several hours later so as to allow the guests an opportunity to leave at their leisure and not feel obligated to stay because she was there. Princess Navia, several armada officers, the Kimias Ambassador Eon, and the Guardians were left telling or hearing stories of exploits by Quatris and Hellfire back on Earth, and Ambassador Eon telling of the forming of the galactic parliament. Everyone knew the general history of the parliament, but the ambassador was over nine hundred years old and served as a starship first mate and captain in the ancient wars. His perspective was different than that of Princess Navia, who was as interested in his tail having heard it for the first time.

Ambassador Eon was very stocky and short measuring little less than five feet tall. He was from the Kimias star clusters close to what used to be controlled by the Sitherian Empire many centuries ago. His star system was on the frontlines for the Sitherian defeat, but as Eon told his story the audience got the hint that the Sitherians bred into the races before departing to their now relocated home in the out shirts of the Milky Way and Dwarf galaxies. Eon was very descriptive on the major battle for the sector near the Riso Quasar. The Sitherians had the advantage, until the Argonian Empire scout ships assisted them with intelligence and weapon upgrades. The use of fusion bombs on remotely guided shuttles changed the situation to some degree, but it was a covert mission of a few Soldiers who penetrated deep into the rear and destroyed high command to include most of the imperial hierarchy which turned the tide of the war. Queen Omia assembled allies to create the galactic parliament giving Argonian technology to hundreds of races, which ensured many star systems the ability to protect themselves to some degree, long enough for stronger allies to assist them. Ambassador Eon commented on how his people were saved by a race they hardly knew, and now a people few people knew about were saviors of many, referring to the Earthlings.

The Guardians took his tale to heart and were moved by his obvious emotional recollections of history. Princess Navia was very pleased to sense the compassionate emotions in the group, feeling confident that they were true heroes who wanted to protect all those they could.

The next day was a time for all the Guardians to roam the palace. Queen Omia spent most of the day in conferences which Hebshilon and Klakin attended as observers with the Queen's permission. Princess Navia spent a lot of time speaking with Medroc and Sedric. Sedric of course had more to say having traveled to several worlds for training to fight in the Goth tournament, while Medroc's life and childhood was simple and routine in Seattle and Dallas. Medroc didn't mind not having to talk much, he enjoyed paying attention to people, especially two aliens who were rich with knowledge and stories. He liked studying Sedric's and Princess Navia's different forms of speaking, interacting responses, mannerisms, and topics which were brought up. He noticed that the Princess and Sedric were attracted to each other, but wasn't sure if they both knew it, or if they did, they seemed to try to hide it by changing subjects every now and then. After an hour, Medroc made an excuse to leave the two alone saying Cerimon was calling him. Princess Navia and

Sedric spent many hours talking together with imperial guards at a distance. They both felt very comfortable with each other asking and answering very personal things. Before they parted, Navia mentally spoke to Sedric with his permission. The conversation lasted thirty minutes in the physical, but in their minds it lasted half a day. Their positions in the current situation didn't allow them to date or become close, so they agreed to continue a relationship in the future when they thought it proper. Before the mental conversation was over Sedric kissed the Princess who returned the mutual exchange.

Their parting was hard on them both, but they soon got back into the matters of galactic peace; Sedric with the Guardians and Navia with her duties as ruler of her realm. Reports of an alien entity in the Colax sector of space brought great concern to the intelligence community and parliament. The sector was almost ninety thousand light years away. Hebshilon suggested Klakin take half of the armada to investigate, while she patrolled the Pylaxian borders in case they acted up while he was so far away.

Klakin knew the armada was powerful, but he didn't like the idea of his mother galloping through space without one of the Guardians. Klakin asked for a volunteer, of which Hellfire took the task of aiding Hebshilon while they were gone.

Klakin's used the Star Destroyer Hydrex as his command ship and set off to the Colax sector of space that same day. Five weeks through the journey, reports came in to the armada that two star systems had disappeared. Klakin ordered Sedric and Quatris to take Ship and scout ahead of the armada. There were no visual reports of hostile forces in the sector, and any nearby ships who investigated were never heard from. Klakin hoped that Ship would be able to get in there and get good information as to what was happening in the sector before blindly committing four hundred starships into an unknown situation.

Cerimon stayed with Klakin, while Medroc and Morinar stayed aboard the rear star destroyer, Caplis. If the armada were surprise attacked or divided, the Guardians would be evenly distributed to react more efficiently. Ship stealthy entered the Colax sector six days before the armada's projected arrival. The Colax sector of space was five thousand by ten thousand light years in size. The Pylaxian and Sitherian empires were far from the sector, but it was on the outskirts of the galaxy and subject to invasion from other galaxies. The sector was quiet with a few civilizations still bond to their planets, actively broadcasting information into space. Similar to Earth's attempts to find life beyond their planets. The sector was large in part to the practically dead stars, and numerous nebulas that gave it its signature attributes. There was no sign of activity in the farthest area of the sector closest to the galaxy rim. The reports which came in several weeks ago mentioned coordinates, but according to Ship's data and reports, those star systems were not registering on his sensors.

"What do you think?" Sedric asked, the two men sitting in the pilot seats viewing the 3D map results of the long range scan.

"I think we should go here and look around." Quatris pointed at the far end of the sector where two star systems had vanished.

"Could they be cloaked?" Sedric suggested.

"Why would you want to cloak a solar system?"

"I don't know, just thinking if something is cloaked and we fly into it. It might hurt a bit." Sedric said wondering if Quatris would survive such an impact.

"Well, I think it would hurt them more than us." Quatris laughed as if he were indestructible.

"Ha, ha, ha, yeah besides the odds of two cloaked objects hitting each other in deep space are like me throwing a rock from here, it traveling to the nearest habitable planet, and hitting a little birdie on the head."

"If you put it that way, I guess we don't have to worry about colliding with a cloaked object."

"Good." Sedric said and edged his hand on the navigation sphere.

"Then again I can throw a rock pretty hard." Quatris smiled as they warped towards the designated spot he suggested.

Sedric and Quatris were very attentive to Ship's scanning limitations and knew that even with Ship analyzing the data instantly without missing a data bit, they might see something Ship didn't. Ship was an AI and could come up with theories or ideas, but the unknown was something that the biological emotional mind could understand better. The first star system was nowhere to be found. There were no asteroids, planets, the star, satellites… nothing. It was as if the entire area the star system occupied faded out of existence. The scanner did indicate a large amount of ionized particles as if a trillion ion propelled ships had passed through the system thousands of times over.

"Have you two ever seen anything like this before?" Quatris asked being in space for the second time and new to space anomalies.

"I am aware of planet and stars being destroyed, but there is always evidence of their existence." Ship replied.

"Yeah, I have blown up large moons, but could never turn them into anything smaller than houses." Sedric added having mentioned it before when he talked about his training sessions for the tournament.

"So it was something that sent the entire system into another plain of existence or it sucked up all the matter and energy in the system."

"It?" Sedric questioned.

"Yeah, whatever it is, man, monster, machine, or being, I will call it, IT." Quatris replied with an Earthling metaphor, but it went completely over Sedric's head.

"So how do we find IT, before the armada gets here?"

"May I suggest you look around the nearby star systems that are still registering on my sensors." Ship interjected.

"Do you have a lot of information on the missing systems?" Quatris asked.

"Affirmative, Lord Quatris." Ship replied.

"See if they have something in common. Maybe this thing

is only targeting certain star systems. If it is, we might be able to know what system is next." Quatris explained.

"And if there is no commonality?" Sedric asked.

"Then we better keep hunting and hope we stay upwind."

The nearby star system was young with very little life, and not capable of space travel. They spent several hours scanning as far as Ship could without actively announcing his presence or location. They moved from star system to star system. The six star systems near the two missing systems were normal. There was no major common thing about the two missing systems and the rest, except that the missing systems had interstellar capabilities and were farthest from all the rest with the Zymas nebula separating them. They had not traveled outside of their star systems, and the initial reports which had alerted them of the situation seemed to have come from the missing star systems. Ship analyzed the reports once again and concluded that the missing systems would not be able to send out the alarm. The interstellar worlds in the area had sent two ships to investigate, but that was over two weeks ago and without a response they didn't send out another ship.

They were on the way so the worlds would not be sending anymore ships. Several days passed with Ship skirting the entire half of the sector seeing nothing out of the norm.

To Klakin's discomfort, he brought in his entire force into the sector, but split it into four groups at the center of the sector. He convened a meeting with the group commanders, five captains from each group, the Guardians, and the top ten science officers.

The meeting started with the reports of the initial alarm. The originators of the message were in one of the star systems that had vanished. Sedric presented the findings they came up with before the armada arrived. The commanders and captains were mostly attentive to what was being said instead of suggesting their own theories as strategic conventional methods could not answer the mystery of the missing star systems. However, a humble captain, Captain Beth, asked if a reconnaissance of deep space was conducted out towards the Andromeda galaxy.

"The armada is here now, and our presence is known to everyone in the sector. However, we can take Ship in that direction maybe ten thousand light years and hopefully see if the thing which did this is hiding in empty space." Quatris suggested.

"My Lords. We haven't considered that there are four nebulas in the sector that can potentially be used to hide from us." Science officer Rolas interjected.

"Our sensors would have picked up a ship inside the nebulas. If it were cloaked the nebula would have disabled it or created a shadow." Science officer Ismoz countered.

"We are assuming that what we are looking for is a ship, and uses our cloaking technology. It could be a ship or ships like Lord Sedric's ship, or it could be a creature with signatures we haven't calibrated for." Science officer Rolas continued.

Ismoz kept silent and looked at her commander. "Can we send probes into the nebula looking for anything out of the norm?" Klakin asked.

"Ship's capability to stay invisible even in a nebula is

unique because of its size and I'm sure that whatever did this to the star systems is larger than a shuttle." Sedric interjected.

"May I recommend we send twenty-five ships to each nebula to probe them, Lord Sedric's ship can scout out into the deep, and the rest of the ships can position themselves between the nebulas and key locations?" Commander Blacq said.

Everyone looked around the group waiting for someone to add or counter Commander's Blacq's recommendation. "It seems we have a winner." Medroc said.

Everyone looked at him sort of confused. "That means each group will provide twenty-five ships to probe the nebulas. Group Commanders, I will expect your selections within the hour, and be prepared to move to your assigned locations to monitor anything out towards open space and within the existing systems." Klakin instructed.

The group disbanded and went about their assigned tasks.

Ship and Quatris were the first to leave the sector and into deep space. An hour later, one hundred starships positioned themselves around the four nebulas in the sector. There were two dark nebulas, a planetary nebula, and a diffused nebula on the far end of the sector towards the center of the galaxy.

The probes started on queue with three ships entering the nebulas from eight different cubic points and one ship stayed outside at the center apex to direct ships and receive data. The ships entering the nebulas would be blind to some degree, and had their sensors set for short range and at maximum power. The formation or deformation of the objects and particles in the nebulas made them unpredictable with very destructive and disruptive energies equivalent to stars. There were very few ships that could get within the outer most surface of stars in the mist of the corona and survive for only an hour depending on their shield matrix, and special life support systems specifically geared to perform such an act. They were few and obsolete, being the first star research pioneers, nicknamed Star Swimmers, proved too deadly and unproductive since modern scanners could explore the stars better than live probes. The same technology however, was used on Argonian military ships in the event they had to come close to a star's photosphere and atmospheres in an emergency or out of necessity. The nebulas were not as harsh as a star with solar flares, but dark nebulas were potentially entertaining a star in the making which presented itself with similar sporadic nuclear reactions or bursts of intense radiation, heat, and electromagnetic disturbances.

The Rhimas and Zymas dark nebulas were the largest of the four nebulas, measuring a trillion miles in length. The Imiter diffused nebula was half a trillion miles and the smallest was the Olymas planetary nebula only three-hundred thousand miles in diameter.

Almost immediately, each group lost communication with the ships monitoring their probes. Four ships reported that the entire probing units had moved in several hundred thousand miles and comms went dead. Before the Hydrex or any other ship could reply to the four group command ships, a distress came from two of them.

Klakin ordered all ships to converge on the two distress

calls, and told Medroc to see if he could investigate before the ships arrived.

Medroc quickly made it outside of the ship and warped towards the nearest command ship in distress. Medroc came within a light year of the Rhimas nebula, but the command and escort ships were nowhere to be seen with his superhuman vision. Medroc could sense an energy spike inside the rim of the nebula. It wasn't a steady flow of energy, more like a very short burst. His vision would be very limited inside the nebula, but he was sure it was reliable within close proximity of about twenty thousand miles to be able to distinguish the starship materials from other materials or energy. He entered the nebula, but quickly slowed down trying to adjust to the new environment. He sped back up as he noticed that the energy spike he had felt earlier was a good distance to his front. The amount of time that elapsed was short or so he thought as he flew forward sensing a large object to his front. He didn't see anything beyond fifty thousand miles, but he heard a strong rumbling sound like a thousand bass drums. It was space with no air, but the sound was not traveling through an atmosphere of gases or empty void; it was traveling through a mass of energy particles in the nebula. Medroc was sure it wasn't sound waves, but more like energy waves which his skin and body could feel, and for some reason it was so strong that it sounded like if it were in his ears. He flew faster but quickly stopped as the mass of a small planet size object came into his vision. He had stopped but the object was moving towards him.

A very loud rumble like thunder hit him without ebbing. He felt very weak as if his superhuman energy or life force was being sucked out of him. The sphere like object was too far away for him to distinguish physical features like a normal planet, but the silhouette of the object gave it the appearance of a planet. It was possible it could have been a space ship, but not likely since the only manmade space ship he knew resembling such a large object was the Death Star which was a science-fictional creation. The object was moving very fast for a planet and he could not sense any metallic properties which most spaceships possessed. But his main concern at the time was trying to overcome the nausea and weakness that had started once he felt/heard the rumbling.

The planet size object came closer until he was several thousand miles away. Now he could see a very large crater like opening a thousand miles in diameter in the center of the half rock and half living organism. At the center of the crater was a glowing light as if in the center of an active volcano. There was no atmosphere like on a normal planet, but the object seemed to have a clear glossy jelly like bubble covering it and a small gravitational pull. Medroc wasn't sure if it was like a protective covering similar to many ocean creatures on Earth. He wasn't sure if it would sting him, hurt him, or make him useless like a prey in a spider web, so he quickly turned around and flew as fast as he could in the opposite direction. He was very weak and the sound seemed to get louder the closer the creature got. To his dismay, he wasn't flying very fast, and the speed of the creature increased behind him and was quickly overtaking him.

Medroc calmed down and relaxed, focusing on tuning out the energy noise the creature was throwing at him. He sensed a little bit of energy return to him and he warped with all his might around to the back side of the creature roughly a twenty thousand mile trip in a few seconds. A flux of energy was slot in his direction resembling a very large energy beam, but it missed him as he warped out of the way. Medroc now knew that the energy spike he felt earlier was the energy beam he just evaded, lasting for only a few seconds. He could have blasted the creature from behind, but to what end? The creature was huge and he was still very weak, so his blast would be like shooting the Moon with a miniature nuke. He knew his limits and this was a time to retreat to fight another day. He warped out away from the creature as fast as he could through the nebula. He didn't know where he was headed, but was satisfied that it was away from the creature. The nebula was enormous and even though he was sure he was flying several hundred thousand miles per hour, it would take too long to find a way out of the nebula and report what he came across if he didn't go faster. He hadn't gone deep into the nebula, but maybe he was flying deeper now that he had lost his bearing.

The sound stopped, and the only energies he sensed were from the center area of the nebula. He stopped warping through space and concentrated on the center of the energy source. His strength was returning, and he could go FTL away from the energy source, but he would be flying blind into unknown space. It was not likely he would collide with anything inside or just outside of the nebula because of the vastness of space, but there was that small sense of self preservation or fear he had been taught on Earth which he had to overcome before deciding to warp blindly in any direction.

Medroc looked around him seeing only darkness as if he were in a murky ocean. 'If only the guys in Vegas could see me rolling dice' Medroc joked to himself and warped into FTL. In less than a minute he was out of the dark nebula, but he had no comms with anyone. The ear piece wasn't working, probably disabled by the creature. He scanned the area for any ships, looking at stars trying to figure out his location or at least a bearing towards the Hydrex. He tried to sense for energy levels from other ships, but the energy from the nebula flooded his senses even though it was very far away. Anger rose up in his chest; as he couldn't sense Sedric's power and the other two powerful guardians he could normally sense were not in the sector. He felt helpless and looking for any Argonian ship would be like finding a needle in a hay stack which would take too long for any warning or assistance to be effective.

He thought for a second, 'What would Chuck Norris do?' He knew that floating through space, even though it was at the speed of light, was not good enough. He wasn't able to sense Sedric's energy level, but maybe Sedric could sense his.

Medroc warped into FTL and every twenty seconds he would expel a burst of energy in all directions. He did fly in the direction of the Zymas Nebula which he assumed would be the location of the Hydrex since it was more or less center mass of all the nebulas. If for some miracle he would come across a starship that would work, but his main plan was hoping Sedric would sense his energy bursts and come to investigate. If all failed, maybe the creature would come out of the nebula and show its face. His normal energy levels were nowhere near that of a small star or large planet, but it was unique and Sedric should sense it.

Chapter Nine

--- ✻ ---

Peace at a Cost

The Hydrex was in a stationary position a light year away, trying to establish comms with any ship performing the recon of the star systems around the Zymas Nebula and probing groups. The subspace transmissions were leaving the ship but nothing was coming back, as if all transmissions were being sucked by the dark nebula. Sedric standing next to Klakin sensed a faint energy pulse. He almost instantly appeared behind one of the sensor operators. "Ensign, scan that sector of space." Sedric commanded and pointed at an area outside of the nebula towards deep space.

"Yes, Sir." The ensign complied and scanned the area as quickly and efficiently as possible.

"Look for energy emissions and find out what is causing them." Sedric elaborated on what he wanted done.

"What is it Sedric?" Klakin came up near him.

"I think it's Medroc. I feel his energy coming from that direction."

Klakin's reptilian face showed no surprise, but it was clear in his voice. "How is that possible?"

"Sir, there is an intermittent energy burst every twenty or so seconds, moving at approximately four times the speed of light. I cannot tell if it is artificial or biological." The ensign reported now knowing that he was looking for energy bursts possibly caused by Lord Medroc.

"I will go take a closer look." Sedric said, but waited for Klakin's approval.

"Take an extra comlink." Klakin stated.

Sedric quickly grabbed a spare comlink from the communications officer. His force field lit up around him and he flew through the ship's hull like a ghost, then out towards the energy spikes.

"Hail Lady Cerimon and Lord Morinar." Klakin ordered.

"Lady Cerimon and Lord Morinar have accepted the hail." The communications officer reported.

"Put them on the main screen."

Lady Cerimon appeared on half of the main screen while Lord Morinar on the other half. Each guardian was on separate starships being assigned each a nebula to oversee. "There has been no communication with the probing ships, but I sense a large distress as if they are dying or in great fear." Cerimon reported before Klakin could say anything.

"All ships battle stations. Retreat to these coordinates and regroup." Klakin commanded and keyed in a coordinate in his navigation captain's chair console.

"Lady Cerimon, I need you to scan this sector of space for Medroc." Klakin continued as he sent her the coordinates of where Sedric was heading.

"Sir! There are ships coming out of the Zymas Nebula." The lead scanning technician reported.

"On the main screen." Klakin commanded as he looked at the screen.

Seven ships were barely visible on the screen as one exploded like a bright star for a few seconds.

"What is that?" Klakin asked as several very large spherical objects appeared on the scanner array.

The science officer and his team frantically worked at their stations analyzing the data from the scanners. The rest of the crew scrambled into action as battle stations was announced on the intercom.

"Move into range and fire quantum sables until those things are destroyed." Klakin ordered navigation and weapons control. "All ships, protect the retreating vessels and destroy all unknowns coming out of the nebulas."

The Hydrex's main engines ignited into action and within a minute, they were in range of the now four moon size objects pursuing the fleeing six Argonian ships. The escort of four cruisers hundreds of thousands of miles apart from the Hydrex launched their sable weapons in unison with the destroyer. The colorful beams of bright blue light trailing capsulated quantum sable rounds traveled at over twenty times the speed of light hitting their targets with almost perfect precision. The constant barrage of a hundred rounds per ship seemed to look like the ships were firing laser beams, but the effect of the rounds was far from that of a light beam. A nuclear reaction occurred on impact, but the added introduction of quantum rounds into the area of the first impact exponentially increased the magnitude of the destruction of matter and redistribution of energy. All four Seer spirits were torn apart and collapsed from within as a very large portion of their bodies were disintegrated by energy which they were not expecting to encounter. Queen Omia had long since foreseen Hebshilon's armada as a top priority for weapons of mass destruction at levels which even the supposedly modern military could not accomplish. The Seer knew of the three Guardians with such energy powers, but this was different. The Argonian ships they were facing were far from weak. The remaining five fleeing ships turned about and fired their weapon systems at the threat, now that they were able to acquire targets and use the quantum rounds with Klakin's approval.

"Fleeing ships, do not engage. Retreat immediately." Klakin ordered once he noticed that the fleeing ships had turned about.

The Seer spirits burst into miniature exploding stars. Two of the fleeing ships were engulfed by the debris and took catastrophic damage. The other three also took damage but were able to get some distance away from the Seer spirits.

The crippled ships and dying enemy objects were a little

over half a light year from the nebula. Klakin looked at the battlefield screen. It depicted all the friendly and enemy objects in space, to include each location of the Guardians, expect for Medroc.

"Sir, the Nelus and Equilim have lost life support and request assistance." The communications officer reported.

Order the nearest four ships to conduct rescue operations and get the people out of the area immediately, evacuate the crippled ships and leave them there. "All ships, maintain battle stations. We don't know how many more of those things are in the nebulas.

"Commander Lim. I hope you can tell me what those things are?" Klakin turned towards his science officer and team.

The science officer looked at Klakin with a half puzzled frown knowing that his answer would not be a safe one. "Sir, there is no record of any weapon or natural entity which resembles those objects. I can however, confirm that they are not crafted by alien hands. They seem to be biological creatures, but I cannot be certain without a closer examination of their makeup. I need a sample."

"What you ask for is hard to do at the moment. But I will see what can be done. Lady Cerimon. Have you made contact with Lord Medroc?" Klakin replied and pushed a button on his comlink which was relayed through the communication console.

"That's affirmative Lord Klakin. Sedric is with him and they are heading back to your location. Medroc says that an object ten times the size of those you just encountered is in the nebula now."

"Tell the rescue teams to hurry up and get out of there. All other ships; move your ships two light years away from the nebula borders.

Klakin's intuition was confirmed as several hundred spherical bodies emerged out of the Zymas Nebula over a two light year span. Four alien objects were the size of Earth, but it wasn't a fact to dwell on as the very dark living planetoids warped several times the speed of light towards the Argonian ships which were scattered all over the sector. Prior to the aliens warping there was a burst of light which seemed to have indicated they had warped, but it wasn't. The communications officer reported that all communications was being jammed and engineering reported that their energy output was decreasing rapidly.

The Argonian ships were barely a light year away when the alien creatures started to attack them. The ships could probably out run the creatures, but engineering was reporting FTL capability was disabled.

Klakin sat in the captain's chair. "Navigation: face the enemy full speed ahead. Weapons at max. Pick the closest targets and fire at will."

The Hydrex main and secondary weapons opened up with fifty ports. The Argonian ships within sensor range followed Klakin's example and turned to fight. It was a fireworks display only surpassed by Quatris' annihilation of the Sitherians in the Void.

Sedric and Medroc were half a light year away when they saw the Seer spirits come out of the nebula. They knew that Klakin's ships had killed four of them, so it was probable that it stirred up the rest to come out of hiding. Medroc was almost fully recovered from his weaken state as Sedric was the one propelling them towards the Hydrex. "You said they drained your energy?" Sedric questioned Medroc to be sure it was what he meant.

"They dulled my energy is more like it." Medroc replied on his mouth piece.

"Okay, let's see what they think of me." Sedric answered and let go of Medroc, then warped towards one of the spheres closest to the nebula and trailing in the attack.

Sedric approached the unsuspecting Seer spirit from behind. He was several miles from the creature's rear, before it sensed an intense surge of energy from Sedric's body. The planetoid size Seer spirit was large indeed, but to Sedric is was like a target dummy he had used in deep space in preparation for the tournament. Quatris had taught him a valuable lesson in expending and regenerating energy. He didn't hold back as before with the Gillithe battle fortresses. He stayed close to the creature as he would absorb a portion of the energy released in the atomic reaction back to rejuvenate his energy levels. The quantum sable rounds were impressive, but Sedric's quantum blast was similar, except much stronger and acted like a cluster bomb. The area he attacked was several thousand miles in diameter and coned out into the Seer spirit's body without mercy. Sedric could hear the creature call out in pain as the sound waves Medroc had talked about went out in all directions. This didn't happen when the

Argonian ships killed four of them, or maybe he wasn't close enough to sense them, or maybe he had hit a nerve? It didn't matter to him. The sound waves which had weaken Medroc didn't seem to affect him. The creature was turning into an exploding planet as he flew off towards his next target.

Medroc saw Sedric's strategy and was impressed, but instead of following suit he looked carefully for the Hydrex. The ships were vulnerable to the creature's main weapon and he wanted to see if he could protect them. The Hydrex and forty eight surrounding ships were holding their own but it would not last for long as the main group of creatures would in time respond to Klakin's bold attack with lethal results. He thought as he flew within blasting range which for him was a quarter of a light year. His light energy powers worked similar to a star, but it was intentionally controlled and directed as he willed. He would have to keep from being weaken again, so maybe distance was the answer. As long as he could stay away from the sound/energy emissions, he could pick them off from a distance. He was at full strength now, and didn't have to worry about destroying a planet full of living beings. He concentrated on the second wave of creatures behind the targets the Hydrex was attacking and killing. An extremely large bright beam of light left Medroc's hands. The dozen light pulses hit four planetoids. A one mile by several hundred miles of creature was vaporized almost through the creature's entire body. The Seer spirits didn't explode, but they seemed to have been killed as they rotated uncontrollably and stayed moving in one direction and speed.

"There are more of those creatures coming out of the other three nebulas." Cerimon reported into all the Guardians' minds.

"Tell all the captains to attack them before they can neutralize our ships." Klakin ordered.

The Hydrex had killed six Seer spirits before a blast of energy vibrated through the ship. The ship went dead without power as if a lightning strike had hit the power company station. Backup power barely came up as even the battery cells were almost gone. "Divert all energy to weapon systems! Tell the crew to secure for open space" Klakin ordered.

The few crew members not already wearing space gear to survive in open space immediately geared up, while other crew members were preparing for a breach of the hull, trying to get power back, and resolve many more crisis situations aboard a spaceship with no working electrical equipment.

"Target that large creature and fire everything we have." Klakin ordered as he pointed the target out to the weapons officer.

The weapons officer managed to fire at the intended target, but the lack of stabilized propulsion by the ship made it very difficult to get a high hit percentage.

Medroc witnessed three dozen Seer spirits fire their energy pulses at the Argonian ships. The attrition rate of Argonian ships to spirits was in the Argonian favor, but to Medroc's dismay, the Hydrex was hit. The ship practically broke in half and then into smaller pieces. It didn't explode as most ships would normally with such damage, but the lack of energy on the ship made it so the engines and other power sources didn't go into overload. The only explosions were from self contained chemicals in the ship which were very minor in comparison to the structural damage already sustained.

Medroc flew in closer this time, not worrying about being weakened, wanting to get a higher chance of hitting his targets. He let it all out sending several hundred laser pulses at the creatures scattered over a half light year span. "The Hydrex is hit badly." Medroc reported.

"On my way." were Sedric's and Morinar's replies.

"Come to me Morinar," Sedric said as he warped into the Hydrex's flight path.

Sedric spotted Klakin and a large portion of the crew as they were dispersed amount the debris caused by the energy attack the creatures had released. As he approached Klakin, he could tell that Klakin was not moving, perhaps he was unconscious. In an instant, Sedric was there with a force field around them both.

Klakin's space visor was broken and his left foot was gone. A very strong impact with something solid caused the breakage, but it was the creature's energy beam which had been the cause for Klakin's lost foot. The combat suit was very tough, but it was not created to withstand the amount of damage the energy pulses did to the ship without working energy deflectors and shields. Sedric could not tell for how long Klakin had been in space, but to his best guess it was maybe a minute at the most since Klakin was exposed. Sedric saw no sign of live in his heart, plus his lungs were ruptured and frozen. The problem was that the vacuum of space had already killed Klakin if he went unconscious from the start, which by the looks if it, he did. Morinar appeared next to Sedric. Sedric handed him Klakin's body. "Take him to a working medical lab now!"

Morinar grabbed Klakin and teleported out of sight. Sedric turned towards the remaining thirty or so Seer spirits. Anger built inside of him as he told Cerimon to order the ships to pick up survivors from the damaged ships and retreat from the creatures as he would take care of them.

Sedric warped towards the largest Seer spirit he saw and without stopping to admire the creature, he blasted into the creature several hundred miles deep and used his quantum field to protect himself along with a burst of energy in the general direction of the core. He absorbed power as he left the exploding planetoid to the next target at his full FTL speed. In less than a minute only three smaller Seer spirits remained with Medroc killing them off. There was no time for pleasantries as Sedric warped toward the other three nebulas where he destroyed the remains of over a hundred spirits. Sedric was exhausted in the end, but there was no one left for him to challenge.

The Argonian ships with power assisted in rescue operations as the ones without power slowly regained life support and normal operations. Urhimia had survived the destruction of the Hydrex and took charge of consolidating the crew and accounting for them. The guardians assembled aboard the Destroyer Gurgus. It was a time of mourning with great losses. They had lost 89 ships. Lord Klakin was dead which included 14,921 crew members in total. Quatris was recalled, and both

Sedric and Quatris scouted the nebulas to ensure no other creatures were hiding in them. If there were any surviving Seer spirits in the nebulas, they had retreated into deep space before half of their forces were wiped out.

Hebshilon and a fourth of her armada met them in the sector a few weeks later. The Queen herself along with a fleet of her imperial guards met them all in the star system of Ios. Hebshilon didn't like her home planet for many reasons, but she thought it would be only right to bury her son next to his father; her beloved husband. The entire royal family attended the funeral along with Hebshilon's armada in orbit around Ios. The Baxcion government were resistant at first to the spaceships, but the overwhelming presence of three Argonian fleets, the Queen, ambassadors and leaders from many races, the Argonian telepaths, and Guardians quickly convinced them that they would be better off honoring Lord Klakin's funeral and putting it in their historical teachings for many generations to come. The funeral was televised live only to the surrounding ships and on Argonia.

Queen Omia was deeply touched by Klakin's death as if he were her own son. Hebshilon and Klakin opened their minds to the Princess, but the Queen had naturally looked into both their souls. Hebshilon, Queen Omia, and Sedric spoke at the funeral, They were short speeches, but fitting to the occasion. Each Guardian had their own personal speeches toward Hebshilon and the group in a private setting. The Guardians had been together for almost ten months before Klakin's death. In such a short period Klakin and Hebshilon had given their race a place of honor among the Empire and the planets they protected.

Many questions were brought up with the examination of the Seer spirits. Hebshilon and the Guardians were in agreement to track down where these creatures came from and find out why they had destroyed the star systems in the Colax sector of space. The creatures were labeled 'Crestins' in the Argonian archives. Due to Medroc's method of attack, seven Crestins were left intact and examinable to great lengths. The Crestins had flaps surrounding a portion of their hemisphere which opened up. Energy emissions from these areas propelled them and gave them their ability to go FTL. The size of their body was linked to the amount of power they could store and use. It would take many years for scientists to figure details on the creatures, which posed several issues for the Guardians and the Queen. The soothsayers told the Queen that the creatures would not bother the empire for over a decade, and that they had time to examine the creatures and prepare. The Queen agreed, and ordered the Argonian Science Department and military to research and develop space vessels to be able to counter the Crestins' energy neutralizing abilities. It was clear that if their vessels had power, they would have more of a fighting chance and perhaps prevent another great lose which the Argonians were not accustomed to receiving.

Sedric was made leader of the Guardians after the funeral and in the interim of salvaging the remains of the Crestins and looking for signs of their origin, the group scattered to all parts of the galaxy. Hellfire stayed with Hebshilon as a personal escort wherever she went. Quatris, Medroc, and Sedric traveled across the stars ensuring law and order was maintained while at the same time looking for signs of the Crestins in nebulas, quasars, and around black holes. They found nothing of significance, except that ever since Klakin's death, over ninety percent of pirate activity, and enemy border activity came to a complete stop. The galaxy was in relative peace for many years but it made a few people anxious, knowing that it was a sign of evil things brewing up. Hebshilon's armada was reconstituted to its former strength. Sedric and Princess Navia's relationship blossomed, but their duties to the crown and galaxy kept them apart. It was very difficult to maintain a long distance relationship, but they knew what they wanted in life and were willing to make it work even if it took many decades.

Quatris, Hellfire, and Morinar went back to Earth, but would always be on call as Guardians should they be needed by Hebshilon, Princess Navia, or Queen Omia. In addition, Lord Axer, of Argonian origin, and Lady Kara from the planet Shimoor were appointed Galactic Guardians prior to the Earthlings' departure.

The lengthy investigation revealed very little as the Seer spirits gave Argonian space a very wide berth. Pylaxian hired Drakon spies had stopped operations and went into hiding. Even though the Guardians going back to Earth was an expected move, the fact that they were loyal to the Queen was a major factor in Seer and Pylaxian resolve.

Emperor Tiaxtee and Vox'wer were very patient as they planned the destruction of the Argonian Empire and the Guardians many years out. All of the strengths and weaknesses were taken into account when their plan was put into full swing. The failed attempt to destroy the empire by making them spread their military might across the galaxy was received with mixed emotions. Vox'wer wanted revenge for the death of his brothers and sisters, while the emperor saw it as an opportunity to get the Seer to fight the Argonians' strongest assets.

Drakon insurgents commenced stage one of the plan with increased activity. Hebshilon ordered Medroc to go dark and find out what the Drakon agenda was in the up rise of rebellions and conflict in four sectors of space. In a way, the Drakons were used by many races to instigate hostilities among planets and races, just like the CIA and KGB did with countries in the Cold War period. Sedric was too high of a profile being the leader of the Guardians to do undercover work. He also needed to represent the Guardians and Empire as an approachable spokesperson.

Sedric went about the star systems, even once traveling to Earth and seeing for himself the planet which was home to his friends. His movement in the galaxy was mostly dictated by the needs of the empire which fate would have him linked to a humanitarian mission with the Star Destroyer Huron. There was a secondary mission which was to look for pirate activity in the area, but it was over shadowed by the need to save the lives of forty thousand colonists. The evacuation of several colonies had to be performed with a short time table of less than an two Earth days. Sedric's ability to transport people and equipment through space without a need for a shuttle greatly sped up progress and allowed for a safer transport of personal to the Huron and space freighters. It was ironic that this task was more energy consuming than any other task Sedric had performed as a Guardian. There was no major energy source he could absorb and the constant use of his powers to move objects and people was relentless.

They were almost complete with their task, when an emergency call from the nearby spaceport Kyos caused Sedric to take the Huron to investigate.

Chapter Ten

--- ✳ ---

Queen Omia's Fate

Kyos, a port for thousands of planetary travelers, spun out of control as it plummeted toward Polare, the fourth moon of the planet Nakei. The four-mile-long cylindrical spaceport expended its remaining emergency boosters trying to re-establish its orbit around the icy satellite. Polare's gravitational hold seemed too strong as the station seemed to ease towards the large moon. The poly alloy silver-plating protecting Kyos' outer structure dulled as Polare hid the dwarf star's light rays of a new day on the space port. Large landing-bay doors opened at each end of the port to reveal empty internal docking platforms and railways.

The last seven of forty-two spaceships of various sizes and designs exited the port in hopes of escaping destruction as the Destroyer Huron, closed in on Kyos. The main propulsion system of the spaceport once again failed to activate, its engineering section having suffered a critical hit by a thermo plasma beam

242

shot from a Drakon mercenary cruiser. Kyos would break apart and fall through Polare's krypton-based atmosphere before hitting solid ice.

The Star Destroyer Huron came within 500 meters of Kyos, matching its speed and trajectory. It had destroyed the Drakon cruiser but had appeared on the scene too late to stop the Drakons from injuring Queen Omia. The queen's guards watched in frustration, as the Huron remained at a distance, unable to physically attach itself to the spaceport docking arms or enter the landing bay.

Sedric exited the Argonian destroyer's personnel chamber and flew into space. His body glowed yellowish-white as he came within fifty meters of Kyos' secondary transport landing bay. Sedric disappeared into nothingness, and reappeared inside the bay. One of the Imperial Guards, with four of his comrades surrounding him, held the queen's limp body in his arms.

"Lord Sedric," one of the guards said to Sedric, "the queen is dying!"

Although Sedric's body continued to glow, his heart sank upon hearing those words. He was almost unable to believe that the queen was physically here in the spaceport. He had known before leaving the destroyer that he was on a rescue mission. But now it seemed that he was too late to protect the queen.

The landing bay shook violently as a fusion reactor at the other end of Kyos exploded. Three of the Imperial Guards, who were unable to keep their footing, fell on the platform floor. Sedric floated above the floor and flew in between the guards, touching the queen's arm. The queen's skin, normally almost silver, was now dull, and a large dark blood spot appeared on the left side of her dress. Her beautiful face was pale and long blond hair was turning gray. The wound was deep, but it was not the cause of her deteriorating situation. She was not regenerating and no one there was knowledgeable enough to know why.

Sedric extended his free hand toward the guard nearest him. "Take my hand. The rest of you join hands and make a chain around the queen."

Sedric spread his yellowish spherical force field around the group and lifted all of them from the floor of the landing bay. As they moved toward the barrier that sustained the atmosphere within the spaceport, the barrier collapsed. The emptiness of space sucked the air out of the bay along with Sedric and his group. Pieces of machinery, scrap metal, tools, and other equipment burst from the port and flew out with them toward the Huron. Sedric, although he was worried, betrayed no signs of fear. He knew that the Imperial Guards needed his reassurance.

The destroyer quickly moved away in self-defense as the last six reactors on Kyos exploded, shattering the spaceport so that debris flew in all directions. Twisted and scorched pieces of the structure, some of them ten to thirty meters long, streaked past Sedric's force field, spinning and striking one another in mid-space.

"Lord Sedric," one of the guards screamed, "we're not going to make it!"

Sedric looked back toward Kyos. Three large metal scraps were hurtling their way. He was uncertain whether he could destroy them without dropping his force field. The long fight against the Keedrin pirates left him below his prime strength. Alone he would have had little trouble getting to the Star Destroyer, but he wasn't alone.

"Hold each other tighter!" Sedric yelled as he focused his energy on the force field and himself. Using all of his willpower, he projected a bolt of energy that formed just outside the force field, launched itself toward the center object, and disintegrated it into a vaporous cloud. The other two objects splintered and veered from the group.

Thousands of bits of debris continued twirling toward them. Sedric had used a great deal of power already and doubted that he could go on protecting himself, the guards, and the queen all the way to the destroyer. He had been in worse situations before, but this time his fellow guardians were not there to aid him. This time it was up to him and him alone to determine a course of action and see it through.

Sedric decided to warp himself and his group through space toward the Huron and hope that they could outrun the debris or avoid being hit if they were overtaken. In a split second, they were traveling 3,000 miles per hour toward the retreating destroyer. Small pieces of debris, in the two-ton to three-ton range, struck Sedric's force field, but inflicted little damage. Still, Sedric was taxed from using many of his special powers at the same time. Although he was closing the distance between himself and the Huron, debris was steadily trailing behind him. The destroyer slowed to near 2,000 miles per hour.

Sedric hoped that the destroyer wasn't slowing so that he

and his group could board it. If he slowed, the debris was likely to rupture his force field and kill the guards and queen, who couldn't survive in a space environment with their present injuries. He maintained his speed and tried to fly over and around the Huron, placing the destroyer between the group and the debris. He strained with all his might only to slow down as his energy started to quickly fade. The Huron was within several thousand meters, but the debris was now almost on top of them.

At that moment, a blast of plasma energy streaked pass the group as the Huron fired its main guns at the debris and Kyos. Large sections of wreckage evaporated, and what remained of Kyos was cut in half as if a miniature nuclear bomb had hit its main structure. Debris scattered in all directions, a few pieces still heading toward Sedric's group. Sedric had to let the momentum in zero gravity take control as he conserved his energy to maintain the force field. The guards looked at Sedric, wondering why he had slowed down.

The Huron could not fire its guns again with the debris so close to the group. Besides, it was at the wrong angle to get a clear shot. The guards held each other tighter, hoping for another miracle. Sedric looked at the queen. He wished only to be forgiven for failing to save her and the guards. He might have a chance of protecting only her and leaving the guards to their fate, but it was wrong to leave them to die for the sake of even her. She would have told Sedric to save the guards had she been conscious and able to communicate.

Sedric looked up to see a piece of debris that seemed to increase in size as it approached them. But out of the corner of his eye he saw a beam of light shoot past their front and destroy it instantly.

"What was that?" one of guards said as they looked out into space.

Ship's blue and white skin showed as it decloaked, moving incredibly fast almost next to them.

"It's my ship!" Sedric said with relief.

Three of the Imperial Guards were in complete awe seeing the one-of-a-kind stealth scout ship. It was in this ship that the Galactic Guardians were said to have started their appointment as the queen's personal elite guards enforcing the queen's rule over the empire. This was the first time they saw the ship so close and decloaked.

The Huron moved around next to the group and scout ship. Sedric regained his strength as the destroyer opened its landing-bay doors on the port side. He flew into the bay next to a standby emergency medical team.

Sedric removed the force field and the yellowish aura around him. The guards spread out and allowed the ship's surgeon to treat the queen as she was placed on a floating white bed no more than six inches thick. Sedric called the Captain of the Imperial Guards. He noticed black burns on the guards' suits and knew that they had recently been in a firefight. The suits were strong enough to protect them and the queen, but something must have gone wrong. The Captain of the Guards stood at attention before Sedric as everyone else left the bay and moved toward the medical center.

"Tell me what happened in Kyos."

"My Lord, we were on a diplomatic mission to meet the chancellor of Nakei. The queen's mission was supposed to be a secret even to us until we were informed prior to entering Kyos. I protested because this was completely out of procedure, but the queen wouldn't hear of it. Four of my guards and I escorted the queen into Kyos, waiting for the chancellor's envoy. We didn't know we had walked into a trap until a sniper shot the queen with a phase rifle. We surrounded her, but it was too late. There was an explosion on the bridge while we killed the assassin. Twenty men in the main transport chamber were strategically located around us and attacked us with plasma rifles. We fought our way back to our ship, but before we entered the main loading dock our ship was blown up. It was all planned out, and we didn't see it coming."

"Did the queen tell you why she was meeting with the chancellor?"

"No, my Lord, she didn't seem too concerned about meeting him."

"Do you know who these assassins were?"

The one assassin we could get a hold of before he died was a Drakon spy. We made it back through the port to the landing bay you found us in. It was a miracle you showed up, my Lord."

Sedric thought carefully about what the captain had reported.

"Yes, well...that's all for now. Go and take care of your men and get the ship's guards to relieve you and your men for a few hours."

"Yes, my Lord!" The Imperial Guard said and bowed.

Sedric bowed his head and turned toward the open landing-bay doors. The Imperial Guard quickly walked away as Sedric viewed his scout ship a short distance from the destroyer. A smile came over him as he saw Medroc wearing his guardian uniform, black with sliver gloves, boots, and belt. He flew through the bay's force barrier and landed in front of Sedric.

"It's good to see you, Medroc." Sedric reached out and shook hands down close to the elbow.

"We were in the area and responded to the distress call from Kyos, and then I heard you needed some help and had to come and save the day."

"Really, what took you so long?" Sedric asked, knowing it was a one-in-a-quintillion chance Medroc was there by accident.

Medroc grinned and felt good seeing his friend for the first time in more than six months.

"Princess Navia will be here shortly. She's about ten minutes away."

"What?" Sedric asked. "How? Why?"

"We are her invisible escort. But the little bird that came to me didn't tell me the queen was here until we spotted you trying to dodge those bullets."

Sedric was used to hearing Medroc use English

metaphors, but his slang caught him off guard this time.

"What little bird?" Sedric asked all confused.

"I'll explain it to you later." Medroc laughed.

"Right. Come; let's go see how the queen is doing."

They ran to medical center only to find the queen being moved back out to the loading dock. Sedric stopped the captain of the Imperial Guards and demanded an explanation.

"My Lord, Princess Navia demands that the queen be present when she boards this ship."

Sedric knew that something was going on with the state of the empire and royal house, but what?

"What else did the princess demand?"

"My Lord, she demanded yours and Lord Medroc's presence."

Sedric allowed the crowd to continue moving the queen to the loading dock and pulled the chief surgeon aside to get the queen's diagnosis.

The royal shuttle wasted no time entering and landing in the dock. There were more than forty people waiting for the princess to emerge from the shuttle as a ramp extended from its side. The metal door slid open to reveal the Princess of Dothoria.

Princess Navia stepped onto the ramp wearing a green gown draped to her feet and extending several feet behind her like a wedding dress. The dress seemed to shift from emerald green to a shiny silvery green and was trimmed in light blue from chest to waistline. An emerald rested on a chain about her neck. Her silky silver hair flowed down to mid back, and her tan complexion brought out her cheekbones and rose-colored lips. Her beautiful green eyes normally brought happiness and comfort at a glance, but timing was everything, and they now showed only distress. Her aunt was dying. The only way to save her, Navia knew, was to become a living host.

Sedric and Medroc stood next to the queen as Princess Navia quickly, but majestically, walked toward them. Although Queen Omia was present, everyone in the dock knelt before the princess. She reigned as long as Queen Omia was incapacitated.

"Your Eminence, the surgeons cannot stop the queen's body from deteriorating," Sedric reported in perfect English. "They say she has less than one hour to live."

All stood up as Sedric informed the princess of Queen Omia's fate. A glimmer of hope came back to Princess Navia's eyes as she placed her hands on the queen's head.

"Then it is not too late," the princess said in a soothing voice. "There is no time to lose. I will absorb her essence now."

Sedric and Medroc stepped away from the princess and queen. Princess Navia's entourage of personal guards and advisers began walking down the fifteen-meter ramp, but stopped halfway. Everyone stood silently waiting to see if the princess could save the queen's life force.

The dock was silent except for the faint humming of the floating magnetic bed where the queen lay. Princess Navia's hands started to glow with a pure white light as she bowed at the waist and placed her forehead on the queen's forehead. It was a tense moment for everyone except the princess' soothsayer.

Sedric looked at Princess Navia's advisers and stopped his gaze on Navia's soothsayer. Now he understood how it was that he, Medroc, and the princess were all here at the same time. It couldn't have been coincidence. The royal family did not normally venture into deep space as a group. Kyos was in the far corner of the empire's realm, and he had been given instructions to take the Huron, to this sector in search of pirates. He was specially selected for missions by the Queen herself and had not seen Ship for the past six months. Princess Navia was also probably in the area, but for a different reason judging by the formal dress she wore. What he couldn't understand was why the queen had come to Kyos without his knowledge. The soothsayers were masters of predicting the future and had a good reputation with the royal family, but he knew they advised only on what needed to be heard by their distinguished audience. Klakin had warned him about the fortune tellers, and he half ignored him, but he wasn't going to make the same mistake twice.

Princess Navia broke the mental bond after several minutes.

"It is done," she said.

The queen's entire body turned a bright reddish color as her cosmic energy dispersed with the collision of energy particles moving through the space of the universe. Soon only her clothes remained on the bed. Princess Navia carefully took the queen's necklace and coiled it in her hand.

The five nurses and three doctors were unsure, hesitant to move the empty bed. But Sedric stepped up and grabbed the bed with one hand and flung it aside for them to take away.

Princess Navia stepped forward, giving the group on the ramp enough room to come down and join her. The others stepped away, maintaining their distance from the princess as she moved out into the middle of her people.

Sedric and Medroc, quickly assuming their duty of protecting the queen, stayed close to the princess. Princess Navia turned to face the group coming off the shuttle ramp. She stood gazing into space as if in deep thought. She didn't wait for everyone to get off the ramp but slowly approached Filia, her personal soothsayer.

Everyone in front of her bowed.

"Think carefully before you speak," said Princess Navia in a threatening tone of voice. "I will tolerate no deception. You will tell me everything of my task ahead in front of everyone here as witnesses."

Filia had kept the queen's fate hidden from her until the last minute, which made the princess very angry. The soothsayers had been playing with the royal family's destiny, and she hated knowing that they were the ones really in control of the future, even though she had limited powers to see into the future herself. She had no choice but to use them to restore the queen to the throne.

Filia spoke boldly. "Your Highness, the queen's life force must be fused with the Chosen. You must travel to a planet called

Earth in the thirty-fourth quadrant of the empire. Once the queen is in the Chosen, she will stabilize the empire and rule for thousands of years to come."

Princess Navia was learned in ancient history and remembered the prophecy about the Chosen, the queen who would bring lasting peace through a reign that would last almost an eternity. Princess Navia half doubted the prophecy, but Filia's demeanor was serious and strong. The princess also knew that very strong superhumans inhabited Earth being four of the first Guardians were Earthlings.

Medroc's eyes fixed on Filia as she spoke about Earth. He thought about Quatris, Hellfire, and Morinar who returned there after completing their five-year quest. He had not been to Earth in more than six years and wished he could visit his home planet and the state of Washington, but he knew that his duty right now was to protect the empire and inadvertently Earth as well.

Sedric recalled the blue planet and how many superhumans lived there. The queen's cosmic powers were close to being omnipotent and would require a special body that could manipulate the energy. Aside from Tir Goth, Earth was a perfect choice since it held rare and unique humans who might be able to do just that.

Princess Navia turned to Sedric.

"You and Lord Medroc will hunt down and find these murderers. You will find the traitors who dared to take the throne away from our queen. I do not care if royal blood is spilled. I want all of them found and executed."

"Princess," replied Sedric, "please let Lord Medroc go with you to Earth. He knows Earth better than anyone here."

"No, I need you and Lord Medroc to take the fleet and find the traitors. I know the royal family is involved, and you will need Lord Medroc to keep the empire from civil war. I will go to Earth, and Queen Omia will reign again." Navia mentally spoke to them.

Sedric and Medroc bowed at the waist, both feeling a sense of anger, desire for vengeance, but most importantly a desire for justice.

"It will be done as you command, my princess," Sedric said with certainty. Sedric wanted so much to hug and comfort Princess Navia, but his place was to obey her wishes and uphold the image of the royal family. He would have time later to comfort her and hopefully after the Queen was placed back on the throne, he would be able to ask Navia for her hand in marriage. It was a long shot, but the Queen's fate only made Sedric realize that he didn't want to waste time should Navia's and his relationship be made short in the future.

The princess and her crew departed the landing bay immediately making their way towards Earth, while Sedric and Medroc made preparations for finding and destroying the traitors with a vengeance the galaxy was yet to witness. The lack of progress in finding the creatures that killed an eighth of the armada to include Klakin was a constant motivation to execute a master plan to bait and trap the enemy.

Chapter Eleven

--- ❁ ---

Traitors, Spies, and Lies

Medroc read intelligence reports on the Sitherian movements outside of the spiral. The spiral was the one convergence of boundaries for the three races. It seemed they were maneuvering outside of the Pylaxian outer markers which made scanning in the area practically impossible without entering Pylaxian or Sitherian space and starting another war. Whatever the secret was, it had to wait because his focus was not on Sitherian or Pylaxian military activity; it was internal activity. The reports he requested were a smoke screen in case there was a spy among them. Sedric made sure that none of the classified information made it to the databases with Ship's help of course. Both men were saddened, but they were determined out of love and not revenge to get justice by finding the traitors. A communiqué was sent to Cerimon, and Hebshilon on the other side of the galaxy. Sedric had requested they activate the other two guardians which only Cerimon, he, Sedric, and Princess Navia knew about. Lord Paldez and Lady Sinop were new Guardians waiting for their next mission.

It was part of Sedric's master plan, knowing exactly what they would be doing since they were ideal for getting a strong foothold in the empire's political arena without raising many eyebrows. In the wake of secrets, the new Guardians were recruited covertly and in like manner they would infiltrate royal family ties. Lord Paldez was Argonian by birth and also of royal blood. He was fifty-eighth in line for the throne, but it was his blood line and his so far removed linage which made him a perfect insurgent into the political and royal environment without causing suspicion for any movement he made. His loyalty to the Queen was extremely strong due to his parent's display of loyalty, but it was not his ability to pretend to be someone else which gave him an advantage to complete his mission.

Lord Paldez was over six feet tall with silver hair down to his collar bones. His skin was also silver similar to the queen's, but his eyes were bright red. An uncanny characteristic for a royal, but it was his father's trademark as an elementalist. He was an expert Soldier and well educated in five higher learning institutions on five different planets. The fact that he spent most of his upbringing outside of Argonia was a plus, having very little exposure to other royals. He was an accomplished mentalist with regeneration powers by use of elemental controls. None of the soothsayers and telepaths knew he could instantly read minds and emotions around him. It was this main ability coupled with his loyalty to the Queen which Cerimon used as the basis for recruiting him as a Guardian. Queen Omia appointed him as special envoy and commander of the imperial guard force for all royals living in the palace and passing through the palace. It would be certain no spies or traitors would confide in him or try to recruit Paldez, but that was not the intent for him having access to everyone. Sedric knew that if Paldez were to come in close proximity to any spy or traitor on palace grounds, that person would give up their true intentions. Lord Paldez would keep an eye out for others linking to the traitor or spy, and then it would be up to Lady Sinop to go deeper.

Lady Sinop was also a covert recruit, unlike Lord Axer and Lady Kara who were publicly appointed Guardians; her recruitment was handled with extreme secrecy. Sinop was a shape shifter with unmatched abilities to take on any biological, non-biological, or energy forms. Her limit was only due to her personal energy storage and up to a thousand times her mass. She could turn into a small spaceship or even another Guardian, but would not be able to imitate the full magnitude of their powers, like that of Sedric or Quatris. Cerimon and Ship had personally trained and educated her in the intricate workings of Argonia, all known races, and boosted her capacity to defeat all known biological and mental scanners. She was for all intensive purposes the perfect copying machine which allowed her to take on powers she had never been able to have unless she came within twenty feet of the object in question.

Sedric was hoping that her abilities would allow her to spy on the traitors and/or spies that Paldez would find. The problem he wasn't satisfied with was that time would be a factor if the spies or traitors were not on the palace grounds. Telepaths were used constantly, and the Queen's fate was still in question. But the fact that an assassination attempt had occurred would only put the spies or traitors on their best behavior. The people he was hunting had to have some method of getting by the telepaths who scanned people around palace grounds. By law, the royals were never scanned without their knowledge, and this was one main reason Princess Navia thought a royal or royals were involved. There was either an invisible spy roaming the palace, or a royal was spilling information to the enemy once off palace grounds. There was a very small possibility that a royal was unaware he or she was giving information to the enemy, but that person would not have a lot of access to top secret information or critical information on activity by the queen or other high officials. Mental scans were performed on royals as routine security measures with consent, to ensure none were violated sort of speaking, but the ones with very high access were scanned deeper than usual. If there was a traitor, he or she would have to be willing to be scanned and mask that information; otherwise there was no way the person would give up information unknowingly. The last possible method of information gathering was that there was a very powerful telepath hiding among the telepaths or soothsayers. If that were the case, then there was a chance that Paldez or Sinop would be found out. Sedric trusted Cerimon's judgment and hoped that they would be able to keep such a telepath from ruining the investigation.

Both new Guardians were already strong with mental abilities, but Cerimon strengthen and helped them become very adaptive. It was easier for Sinop of course, since she was able to duplicate Cerimon's abilities and was able to assimilate an arsenal of mental weapons. When she assumed the form of inanimate objects it was her ability to sense her environment which was improved by her new and practiced mental clear voidance.

Sinop was five feet two inches tall in her true form with a stocky body. Her hair was purple and eyes pure gold, but her ability to alter characteristic colors kept her from being singled out as a mutant or attract attention to her special condition. She was an orphan, and never bothered trying to find her natural parents, being they probably abandoned her due to her weirdness, and not wanting to commit murder of an infant. At least that was what Sinop thought of her parents. She also didn't have an allegiance to her world, traveling to many planets using her abilities. She thought she was not known, but word of her actions was brought to Cerimon's attention by Feesel. It took Cerimon several months to find Sinop, but recruitment was quite easy since being a Galactic Guardian presented a completely different world and life to Sinop for as long as she lived. It also gave her an opportunity to meet these famous people who had already changed the galaxy.

Sinop and Paldez met a few days after the assassination attempt on the queen. The meeting inside Ship was somewhat compartmented by Cerimon. They knew they were Guardians, and their part in the plan, but they didn't know each other's full abilities. This would keep both of them from being used against each other should one of them be found out through a very strong mentalist. It wasn't likely, but Sedric didn't want that kind of risk in the plan, so he instructed Cerimon to make sure they knew only what they needed to know.

Lady Sinop took the form of one of Princess Navia's new special projects aide. The princess was gone, but a position was open that required attention since no one would know the fate of the queen for at least several months before the successfulness of

Princess Navia's quest would be revealed. It was this time period Sedric wished to use to get Sinop introduced to all the key personnel in the palace and other realms. Her access would be limited and times of travel, but that didn't really matter, because she could work her way into any area of the palace with her abilities to include the Queen's quarters and no one would know she was there.

The Argonian star shone clear rays into the main palace center tiled floor. The dark green and white marble design was slightly warm to the touch, being regulated by air conditioning and heat reducing window materials. The large throne room was practically empty due to the Queen's absence, but there were always imperial guards in the room. They were there as live witnesses to the events which occurred in the room. Day and night, at a minimum two guards stood watch inside being relieved by their counterparts every four hours on four eight hour shifts. Many other sections of the palace were also watched over. The two thousand four hundred Soldier guard force was not a waste of manpower, but in fact it was a security measure which guaranteed constant live surveillance and quick reactionary responses to security breaches or medical crises.

Captain Paldez walked to the throne room on his spot checking duties towards the parliament reception offices. Silver and gold metal as transparent and colorful as glass lined the corridors, doors, and ceilings of the smaller rooms. Each room was unique in the palace to include the offices which parliament administrators used to manage the planet and galaxy. The offices were basically a room full of communication systems that met the needs of a total digital environment. Hard copy information was maintained, but at the server level information was supplied directly to hard copy storage areas, and not in the offices. Hard copy meaning microscopic engravings into metal alloy rolled drums instead of ink and paper. Classified information was handled through secure parsers and network managers. Telepaths were used to scan workers as they came in and out of work at all hours of the day as not to allow unauthorized classified information from escaping through the memory of a worker or parliament members.

Paldez knew the people in the areas he was walking through would be scanned or had already been scanned to some degree but he was more interested in the royals and soothsayers who roamed the same office areas. Soothsayers followed the royals or were in training as were many royals who learned the political and legal realm of their positions for managing a planet within the palace grounds. His unannounced walkthroughs would hopefully produce some results, but it didn't. He had walked through the palace grounds for a week, and was sure he had covered all the areas being constantly walking and chatting with everyone he could as the Captain of the Guards. After another week of reading minds and sensing empathic emotions, he had not found any spies, but he had come to know so many people in a personal way even though they had no idea he knew their deep secrets.

It was a blessing and a curse to Paldez as he knew of some illegal and immoral things about several people in the palace which were for some reason not picked up by the telepaths, but there was very little he could do at the moment. If he raised any suspicion that he knew things which were impossible to find out without the use of telepathy, then his cover could be blown. He considered getting a telepath to see the things he saw as a third person, but even that might alert the telepath force that he was telepathic. For all he knew, the telepaths might all be in a conspiracy along with the royals and soothsayers. It might have been an exaggeration of the situation, but Paldez wouldn't take the chance that as farfetched as it seemed, it might be true.

A month passed and word that Princess Navia was still on Earth made him think that maybe if there was a traitor; that person was either still somewhere else on the planet or just maybe with the Princess. He knew his cousin was a powerful telepath, to include his Great Great Grandmother, Queen Omia, but it was not uncommon to be able to defend against a telepathic mind if given time, practice, and a baseline. The baseline to defend against Princess Navia or the Queen was very high, but the enemy would know what to act against. Lady Cerimon was an extremely powerful telepath and could easily learn to defend herself from mental scans, but Paldez was different. His mental scans were not totally active scans and his empathic abilities allowed him to see inside an emotion and use it like a back door into the person's mind. If a person were happy or angry, Paldez could sense it, focus on it, and then the mind of that person would automatically open up to him without them realizing it. He could also manipulate it to the point where if a telepath was scanning his mind he would show they what they wanted to see, but instead they were looking at themselves with Paldez dictating their own ideas of who and what he was thinking about or knew.

Lady Cerimon saw a reflection of her mental scan when she approached him to present him with the opportunity to be a

Guardian, but that was only because Paldez allowed her to. If he had not allowed her to, she could have walked right by him, and she would not have known he was telepathic. It was Queen Omia who alerted her to his abilities. Queen Omia would have also walked by Paldez without a second thought, but it was her precognition abilities which pointed her into Paldez's future as a Guardian. Cerimon had thought about how other soothsayers had not seen the two new Guardians, but realized that maybe the Queen had more powers than most people thought when it came to telling and changing the future.

Another two months passing by, but it allowed Paldez to see Lady Sinop a few times and it was helpful in that she copied his ability to also read minds and empathic impulses. Now there were two people roaming the palace grounds looking for any spies or traitors. Word came to the palace that Queen Omia was dead, but the Chosen had been found in the process. Elexsuia Peli Lanta, Navia's flagship commander, was also in the brig for treason. Orders were given to stay silent and the public would not be told about what had happened to the queen until the Princess returned to Argonia.

Cerimon informed Paldez to focus his efforts in finding a link by examining Elexsuia's activity before she left the planet. There was a lot of data to include inferred movement which Ship analyzed, but nothing seemed to show any red flags. Paldez told Sinop to take a trip with him to Princess Navia's palace which was twenty miles from the Queen Omia's palace. The imperial guards in Navia's palace were receptive to Captain Paldez's presence and his team which included Sinop as one of the guards. The four real guards didn't question Paldez's acceptance of a guard they never met, but it was not too uncommon since the queen's guard force was large and many guards changed duties every ten or so years. Paldez would also not allow a rookie to watch his back unless the rookie was far beyond exceptional. The guards wore body armor, six weapons to include long distance and close quarter high impact arsenal devices and rifles. Princess Navia's guards welcomed the team and a two guard escort was provided to ensure they had access to any location or people.

Lord Paldez was very forthcoming in telling Navia's Captain of the Guard in the palace that they were there to investigate Commander Elexsuia's whereabouts and activities prior to her trip with the princess. The Queen's Captain of the Guard had jurisdiction and prerogative to personally conduct investigations internal and external to any connection with the Queen's station. The guards' suits and helmets had sufficient digital gathering capabilities, but it was not a crime scene which they were looking for, they were looking for people to screen and interrogate. If they needed to analyze items for DNA or similar types of information, they had access to a forensics team on call from the Queen's palace.

They walked the palace grounds as if on a shift change. Princess Navia's palace was magnificent in its own ways. It was smaller than the Queen's palace, but its theme of white, topaz, onyx, and emerald floor plan was breathtaking. Many rooms were decorated in accordance with several planets and races across the galaxy. There was a room dedicated to the earth tone eclectic style in the late 1990s, which they would not have known except that Cerimon's knowledge base was now part of Paldez and Sinop. Ship had correlated Elexsuia's movements in the palace with people she met as part of her job and off the job. There was a long list of people they had to interrogate, but Paldez made it easier by just making sure they got close to the people so he and Sinop would do the rest. At times the guards that were escorting him wondered if they were going to actually interrogate anyone for any length of time, instead of asking simple biographical information, and what they were doing and talking about with Commander Elexsuia. But Paldez had a long list and many people to filter out as quickly as possible before any spy would catch on and leave the area.

Paldez ordered the group to split up and made Sinop leader of the second group. Paldez took the upper levels of the palace while Sinop took the lower levels without really asking any questions. The group she led was slightly confused but they automatically assumed the male guard they were being led by was telepathic. Sinop passed by people on the list with only a greeting and question as to whether they feel safe with them patrolling the palace. It was an odd question, but the response was one of emotion which was many a times very small, mainly thinking the question was weird. The empathic impulses Sinop received were enough for her to enter their mind and immediately know what they remembered about Commander Elexsuia.

The hunt turned out two leads which both pointed to the house of Cammeth. Her Royal Highness Toluvis, mother of Prince Hethos, was ruler of the Bursue Realm to the south. The group left the leads unaware of their un-consented mental scans, but Paldez ordered he get a direct feed of all cameras on and off the palace grounds for the next two months.

Lord Paldez returned to the new Queen's palace, and made preparations for Princess Navia's return. She would be occupying the throne for now and he had to make sure she didn't become a victim like Queen Omia while he was Captain of the Guards for the palace.

Her Royal Highness Toluvis was the late king's sister, who was always very aspiring for power and status. At least that was her reputation, but things didn't add up. She was not in line for the throne and things would not get better if she were linked to the assassination of the queen, princess, or the Chosen. Sinop stayed in Navia's palace instantly changing into several different people keeping an eye on the two leads, one of which was HRH Toluvis' royal soothsayer, Loar Crom, who was there as an exchange mentor for two apprentice soothsayers. His skinny tall body reflected his long service as a soothsayer who mediated and fasted for many days out of the year. His eyes were black with streaks of silver. His skin was dark tan and his dark gray hair was very short. It was not age that gave him his gray hair, but was his natural genetic makeup from the Hutor bloodline.

Commander Elexsuia believed that Queen Omia and Princess Navia were taking the empire into complete ruin. The Pylaxian and Sitherian races were threatening the empire, and they were not doing anything effective to stop their slow invasion of surrounding territories. The Galactic Guardians had apparently made things worse by causing the enemy to elevate hostilities to higher levels. She spoke her thoughts, but the two other conspirators also agreed that the enemy had to all be exterminated, and the queen's regime was preventing it from happening. Prince Hethos was third in line for the throne and with him as king, the empire could be swayed to go into full out war and kill all Pylaxian and Sitherian.

Lady Sinop wasn't convinced that the conspiracy had a strong leg to stand on. If anything was linked to Prince Hethos' mother, he would not be allowed to take the throne. In addition, a very extensive barrage of telepathic scans and conversations would be used to determine the next in line if Queen Neeva and Princess Navia were to die as part of the conspiracy. She was not an expert in strategy, but her gut told her that all of this drama was probably only going to cost more lives, time, money, and turmoil within the empire's leadership. She went to Loar's temporary quarters.

The palace cameras were all active and she could have used the powers she absorbed from Cerimon to alter the area they covered long enough for her to enter the room, but she had something else in mind. Before turning the corner towards Loar's door, she transformed into a stream of cold air particles. She seemed to just vaporize in a matter of two seconds. She repeatedly shifted her physical form from cold to hot and back so as to propel herself towards the door. Once she was at the door she used Cerimon's ability to phase through objects and entered without difficulty. She sensed her way around the room, making sure there were no alarms or devices which would tell security there was an unauthorized person in a room which was locked from the outside.

The room was small covering a twenty by twenty foot area. There were standard decorations and furnishings for temporary quarters, but she was looking for something unique.

Loar brought some personal items as expected, but soothsayers were very much minimalists and had very little personal possessions. Most of Loar's personal possessions were given him by the Council of Soothsayers which represented the collective of royal soothsayers who were acknowledged as bringers of truth and life for the royal family.

Lady Sinop was well versed in the culture due to Cerimon's teachings, but what helped most was her vision into the minds of all the soothsayers and telepaths she came across while roaming the two palaces in the past several months. She turned into Loar and opened an opal covered chest the size of small briefcase. It was placed on top of a side table by the bed. She made sure she didn't change anything in the room to include the exact position of the chest on the table. She knew that Loar was currently wearing a sapphire necklace which was the symbol of the third order within the council, and there was a space for it in the chest. She closed the chest and melted away like a thick gray liquid underneath the bed turning into a rubber floor mat.

Sinop could maintain simple forms for months, more complex forms for weeks, and very complicated energy forms for several days. It was a matter of time for her, so she waited patiently for Loar to return and retire for the day. Loar did retire for the day and placed his necklace in the chest before he bathed. It was during this time when Sinop took the necklace and using her phasing ability buried it six inched underneath the floor underneath the bed. She transformed into a flying insect and phased inside the chest, then transformed into the necklace.

The next ensuing days involved Loar performing his

duties as a soothsayer while wearing Sinop around his neck. Sinop could see all of the daily thoughts and emotions. Loar was indeed well educated in the law, politics, and the royal court. The two students he was training were naïve, but true to their calling. She slowly read their minds to include Loar's deep thoughts and memories. The students were very interested in what Loar had to teach, but Loar was more concerned with matters back in his palace. He had a strong sense of loyalty to HRH Toluvis which was natural since his was raised from birth to serve her. The more Sinop saw into Loar's mind the more she understood how the soothsayers interpreted the future. It was illegal for telepaths to look into a person's mind to the depths she had done, especially to another telepath or soothsayer; but as she vividly understood it, Princess Navia gave her that authority, since it also came from Lord Sedric who was officially the commander and enforcer of the queen's will and law.

The soothsayers didn't really know the future as many people thought. They saw visions of things which seemed like an alternate reality. Almost as if a person were dreaming, but it was very difficult to tell what was real, partially real, fake, past, present, or future. The visions Loar had were better organized if Sinop could explain it, compared to the two students. It was an organized mess of visions with no real anchor to reality except their own personal experiences. The soothsayers mediated most of the day which helped them keep their experiences and views of current events simple and plain. The less distractions and experiences in their lives; the easier it was to make sense of the visions. She did not read Joldar's mind, but Paldez had, and she was convinced that Joldar's mind must be very confusing considering that he was known for having many visions constantly requiring telepathic blocks.

Lady Sinop knew that in the arrival of Princess Navia, it was likely that Loar would return to his palace. It was also confirmed when a request for Loar's return by HRH Toluvis came to him on the fifth day of her surveillance.

The second conspirator was a telepath named Rudez, but she was a small pawn, used by Loar. She too was from the House of Cammeth. Her presence in Navia's palace was by accident, as she was escorting a courier when Paldez met her in the hallway. Rudez returned to the south, but Sinop knew she would find more conspirators once Loar returned to serve his royal highness.

The next day, Loar left the palace excited and relieved that he was making distance away from Princess Navia's realm. Sinop could tell that he was always trying not to focus on visions and kept them from materializing. He was probably keeping visions from materializing as not to have evidence or an overflow of information for telepaths to use in his conviction should he be found out. At least that was what Sinop concluded, being able to see into his mind with great ease now that he had been constantly exposed to her.

The shuttle landed in the palace shuttle pad. The grounds were elegantly designed to show off the wealth of the land. The palace itself was marked by amber and crystal quartz themes. Sinop liked this look very much with many different colorful plants and furnishings throughout the gardens and rooms. Loar was greeted by two soothsayers and three palace guards. Once he stepped on the ground, he asked for the whereabouts of HRH

Toluvis and Prince Hethos. It was an innocent question which the elder soothsayer replied to, but Sinop knew that all he really wanted to know was where Toluvis was so he could report to her without the prince being present.

"Her Royal Highness is in the bath chamber, and the prince is surveying the city of Yardim," the soothsayer answered.

"When did Her Royal Highness want me to see her?"

"Sir, Her Royal Highness stated she wanted you to eat with her after her bath." The soothsayer replied.

Loar nodded approval. "Very well, I will wait for her summons in the north wing conference room. Can you take my things to my room?"

"Certainly Sir." The younger soothsayer took Loar's one small bag and chest, as the elder soothsayer bid Loar a farewell bow.

Loar quickly walked off to the conference room with one guard as an escort but once he was indoors the escort peeled off and went back to his normal assignment guarding the shuttle pad area.

Sinop kept scanning anyone that crossed Loar's path. So far all the people he came close to didn't have any memories of an assassination or conspiracy. Loar waited patiently for thirty minutes, before he was summoned to one of many patios Toluvis used to eat her meals while enjoying the scenery.

HRH Toluvis sat at a medium sized oval blue quartz table. The table was very sleek being only an inch thick, but was as strong as two inches of solid metal. Three equally spaced out empty rolling cushioned chairs surrounded the table. Loar approached her from the side and moved to her front as he greeted her, almost as if reporting to a superior officer, even though he was not in the military. Toluvis was over six feet tall and medium stature of that of a female body builder or professional wrestler. Her beauty was not as it was in her prime several hundred years ago, but there was a brilliance of beauty which she radiated from her eyes and smile. Her skin was pinkish tan and very smooth. She wore a one piece thin black and white dress with short sleeves exposing her well defined muscles. Her eyes glistened with topaz and violet alternating slow changes in color. Her hair was covered with a shiny gold mesh, but strands of ebony black hair could be noticed through gaps where the mesh met her skin.

She looked around with her clear voidance being interested if anyone else was in the area. All was clear and the nearest people to them were guards fifty meters in the distance indoors and out.

"Come sit Loar and eat." Her Royal Highness replied to Loar's greeting.

Loar respectfully bowed and sat in front of her across the table. The mid day was bright on the patio, but an aerial tinted silk like canvas floated ten feet above the table providing shade. The patio was on the fourth level of the palace and had an elevated over watch view of the city, countryside, and mountains beyond the palace grounds.

"What news do I need to be aware of, or was your stay at Navia's home a vacation for you?" Toluvis asked as she started her lunch meal of fresh fruits. Her very clear soprano voice carried well as she spoke softly.

Loar was used to her forwardness and released several mental blocks in his mind. Sinop could sense the release of mental memories as if there was a secret door in his mind that just opened up. Cerimon had taught her to scan for telepathic blocks or memories that were camouflaged, but she didn't expect what was going on in Loar's mind. She could also see what Toluvis thought, but her mind was obviously blocking many areas of her memory.

Her Highness was a royal and having mental blocks was not uncommon since it was very rude to invade a royal's mind, hence telepathic blocks were legally and extensively used by them. Loar was another matter since he wasn't a royal and he was expected not to have mental blocks against mental scans. His mental blocks were not mental blocks as Sinop examined them carefully while paying attention to the discussion and thoughts Loar was having. They were very deep memories embedded inside a memory that was connected to a subject. In essence, when Loar was taught what an assassination was, murder, and conspiracy, the plan that had occurred in Kyos and in Princess Navia's flagship on Earth, was embedded into that memory of conspiracy being taught by the teacher. It was a sort of camouflage, but it was in the open, just very deep to get to unless it was brought up with telepathic help. Sinop peered into Toluvis' mind bypassing the blocks and going deeper into the areas Loar had used to screen his thoughts. To her surprise, Toluvis was in the middle of the conspiracy.

Loar was the one who gave her the idea of getting her son to take the throne and allow him to rule the way she envisioned the empire to be led. Toluvis was very ambitious and wanted the best for her son. Five of her grandchildren were killed in the Colax sector, and illogically she blamed the guardians and the queen for their deaths. Loar had suggested the idea and allowed her to enter his mind. Toluvis was telepathic, enough for her to see what Loar wanted her to see. Sinop on the other hand saw deeper into Loar's hidden memories and ideology.

An unnamed Argonian telepath was Loar's link to the conspiracy going beyond the House of Cammeth. Toluvis was part of it and at this point a leader of the conspiracy since she provided the fuel to the evil plot.

The two conspirators at the table were very concerned about what Elexsuia would reveal or had already revealed to Princess Navia. The possibility of one of them being exposed was always covered with a contingency. There was only one telepath strong enough to break the passive mental implants that they knew, which was Lady Cerimon. The thing was she didn't know about the implants and would not be searching for them and only get the surface thoughts which Elexsuia knew to allow.

They didn't expect Sinop or Paldez to be able to break the mental embedded memories. It was clear to Sinop that the unnamed Argonian who trained and gave Loar the conspiracy idea was a rogue or maybe something more. She was a super powered alien, and wasn't the only one in the galaxy, so this mystery man was maybe not Argonian. But that didn't really concern her at this point. She thought carefully, and then probed deeply into Her Highness' memories. She could see the four conspirators, plus the unknown messenger, nothing more. Prince Hethos and all the other people in the palace were unaware to their leader's disloyal inequities. Rudez was the conduit between HRH Toluvis and Elexsuia. Loar was the link between the mystery man, Toluvis, and Rudez. Apparently, Rudez's telepathic powers were much stronger than everyone credited her for, which the mystery man alluded to. Rudez was young and also lost her one love in the fight against the Crestin *(Seer spirits)*.

Sinop eased out of Toluvis' mind, but to her surprise, Toluvis sensed something was wrong and elegantly stopped eating. "When did you acquire your Allegiance Medallion?" Toluvis asked.

Loar was caught off guard. He was given the necklace by the Soothsayer Council when he took his office serving Her Highness, when she was three years old. She knew this, but it crossed his mind for a second that she had forgotten due to the stress or an illness. He quickly corrected himself and eyed her carefully. "Your highness, I was given the medallion on your third birthday." He answered and began to take it off his neck.

Sinop focused on her training and closed all contact with mental energy waves, then quickly finished getting out of Toluvis' mind. She thought only of being the medallion and pretended she was being scanned as a shape shifter or an electronic listening/tracking device.

"May I examine it?" Toluvis asked seeing that Loar understood her demeanor and held out her hand towards him.

Loar handed her the necklace and sat back on the cushions waiting to see what she was looking for on the necklace.

HRH Toluvis draped the necklace on top of both her palms facing the sky. Her mind probed the necklace looking for intelligence or anything that was not part of its makeup.

Sinop's powers were magnificent to the point of duplicating the imperfections of the silver, gems, and setting materials.

Toluvis saw and sensed nothing, but she was weary having sensed the source of a subtle telepathic probe from Loar's neck. She increased the area of her scan past the nearest guards. "Have you left the medallion alone while you were in Navia's palace?"

Loar thought about the question. "No your Highness, it has always been on my person or next to me for many years."

Toluvis placed the necklace on the table and allowed Loar to retrieve it. "I'm going to need you to talk with Rudez, and have her gather all the admirals and Soldiers that will follow me to take over the throne."

Loar was completely taken by surprise. "Your Highness, there has to be an easier way. As long a Princess Navia and this Chosen are alive, we can't take the throne over by force. The Guardians will not allow it."

"Drastic measures must be taken now. I need several ships to destroy Navia's flagship before she returns. I also need another small fleet of ships to find and kill the Chosen."

"Your highness." Loar paused. He was in accord with the

assassination of Queen Omia, but now it involved killing several hundred citizens, to include fellow soothsayers. The backlash of it all also made him sadly ponder the future, because even if both were killed, Lady Hebshilon and the Guardians would not sit idle and just serve the new master. The empire would go into civil war and everything he wanted to protect and loved would be destroyed. His love for Toluvis was at the top of his list and out of it he honored her wishes. "I will contact Rudez. She will need a few days to assemble everyone needed."

Sinop went back to passively sensing thoughts and emotions. She felt the sadness in Loar and used it to stay in tuned with him.

The lunch lasted only long enough for them to discuss about specific people that would greatly increase their chance of success.

Sinop thought carefully about her next move while Loar went to personally talk to Rudez. She could neutralize Loar, and report her findings to Sedric. It would keep many people from going into a situation where their loyalty would cause them to become traitors, but there was a problem. HRH Toluvis was a capable telepath and she could gather the forces she needed very easily, since in a way she already had over a long century of making sure she was surrounded by very loyal followers. Prince Hethos would also try to side with his mother and this act might cause him to take actions which could cause a civil war even if not intended.

She finally decided to rely on her in-depth knowledge of who was at fault and the circumstances of admirals and Soldiers to fight for their royal leader would be used heavily in Queen Neeva's or Princess Navia's final judgment when the dust settled and all criminals were brought before the new queen. She also needed to find this mystery man, and taking direct action right now would not allow her to do so.

Sinop allowed Loar to speak with Rudez within the hour. When reports of her progress were delivered to him; he notified Toluvis in person on the time and place for the meeting. Sinop carefully went over the historical events when Loar met the mystery man. The mystery man met him outside of the palace grounds, which seemed odd to her. Loar was a soothsayer and always had someone with him when off palace grounds, simply because soothsayers were always protected and always needed an escort off the grounds.

She dug deeper and realized that Loar had a feeling that something he should see was beyond the palace grounds. The feeling was very subtle, but in time he did leave the grounds without an escort. That was when the mystery man showed up, almost like if it were a dream.

After Toluvis talked with fifty of her officers, she spoke to an audience of four hundred people who all were completely loyal to her. The full extent of the planned attack on the Princess and the Chosen was sprinkled with deception. They thought they were on a mission to save the galaxy by destroying two imposters. The officers did know the truth and it was by their lead that the rest of the Soldiers followed orders as directed.

Sinop waited patiently and when Loar was alone with no scheduled tasks for the rest of the day, she used Cerimon's ability to control his mind. It wasn't very hard for her since she was so familiar with his mental patterns. She commanded him to go outside of the palace grounds to where he had met the mystery man in the past. It was night already, but there was ample lighting in the city, as Loar roamed the streets on a hover scooter.

Sinop knew she was shooting in the dark. The mystery man would not stick around and may not even be on the planet, but there was one thing she could do. She commanded Loar to go to the nearest local law enforcement station. The station was not very busy; in fact most of the routine cases that crossed their path were traffic violations, minor civil disturbances, and petty crimes. It was very rare to have homicides and major thefts. Telepaths ensured many major criminal activities were revealed or addressed in upbringing of citizens. But Sinop wasn't concerned about crimes, she was sure Ship would have correlated any criminal activity with the conspiracy if there were any that did link to it.

Sinop commanded Loar to order a digital facial recognition search for the mystery man. The on duty investigative officer relented to the order once Loar identified himself with a simple eye and palm scan. A telepath sketch artist took the images of the mystery man and in less than a few minutes; they had a digital 3D head and face of the mystery man going through their database. Sinop waited patiently making sure Loar rested his body, drank fluids, and performed body maintenance. A match came up on the person an hour later. The name that came up was Kilor Dax, a librarian who lived in a small town of Ismath, seventy three miles from their location.

Sinop was sure of two things. Kilor Dax was a fake person and it was an alien, or Kilor Dax was a real person who was being used by someone else. The chances of Kilor being a super telepath was unlikely since all babies and children during their early and late years went through telepathic tests and scans. It would have been found out that this person was as powerful as Cerimon or others at her level. Lord Paldez was a royal and his parents were the ones who hid his early age abilities. Kilor was a commoner and his abilities would have been almost impossible to hide. Whoever it was, she had an address and the means to investigate.

Through Sinop's mental control, Loar requested a vehicle transport. Sinop was constantly trying to find other hidden memories Loar might have while he drove to Ismath. A communiqué came into the electric fission powered car's communication dashboard. Sinop didn't know who was calling him, but it was probably someone in the palace who was alerted to his activities.

The communiqué was from the local police station in Ismath. The law enforcement office requested further information and the local station replied to the request. Kilor Dax was dead and an investigation was underway to find the cause of death. The soothsayer was not the perfect person to go around asking questions, but Sinop was counting on the fact that Loar was known to whoever started this conspiracy.

They arrived to the local station in Ismath under an hour. It was late at night and the investigators on the case had long since gone home for the day. Sinop scanned everyone still working in the station. She was able to see the investigating officers and commanded Loar to go to Kilor Dax's residence. As Loar was driving Sinop transformed into a serpent, and got on the passenger seat. She immediately transformed into the lead investigator, Lieutenant Olesse. Olesse was a female veteran Soldier with a very stern character. That would make it easy for her to ask very blunt questions. Sinop knew all this by the interactions her fellow officers had with Olesse while on and off the job. She wasn't able to copy her DNA, but she was able to copy her physical appearance, voice, smell, and mannerisms from the memories of the people still on duty.

Loar stopped the car in front of Kilor Dax's home. The house was a two story structure made of primarily granite with many quartz windows. The property was marked off with police tape to include a proximity sensor. If anyone trespassed, the sensor would record information and send real time alerts to the station. Sinop wasn't worried though because they would see Officer Olesse and Loar entering the property.

Sinop led the way to the front door, and scanned for people in the area. Kilor lived alone, but she sensed upon opening the door, there were signs of two other people who had been in the house. She told Loar to keep a lookout for anyone approaching the house. She left the light off and walked around the rooms looking to identify the two people who had signs of frequently being in the house. Both were females, possibly a maid and the other a girlfriend or relative. She examined where Kilor apparently fell down the stairs and broke his neck. It seemed like an accident, but it was too convenient with him being a link to the conspiracy; plus, it seemed Officer Olesse wasn't convinced it was an accident either.

The house was a standard home which all citizens had to some degree of size and luxury. The Argonian Empire was vast and the society on Argonia was practically a utopia. Working as a librarian was an occupation of choice. Money was not needed on Argonia, and if anyone left the planet, they would be given credits to fulfill their needs on a vacation, or get authority for something of more value depending on what it was, like helping out a relative or friend outside of the Argonian star system. Shelter, food, clothing, transportation, even entertainment was provided based on what the person requested. There were limits, like wanting to be a royal or being in charge of a high position without working for it, but for the most part, vacations, short work hours, and any entertainment venues were free to all citizens. Sinop had lived on other planets, and lived in the middle of poverty even though she herself had never really lacked anything. There was no monetary poverty on Argonia, but she knew that contentment in life was not solely based on having money or power. Many Argonians liked adventures which is why many didn't mind leaving Argonia to live in space or serve the empire in space for a time period. If there were Argonians who weren't content with their life, it was highly likely it was from an emotional state of boredom, envy, or unaddressed grief from a great lost or betrayal. Sinop tried to reason why Kilor would be mixed in this conspiracy, and in the end she concluded he was an expendable pawn. She continued to search inside the structure of the house for surveillance devices, but found none.

Kilor had a sister and so maybe it was his sister and a girlfriend that had lived there with him. She searched for information of the two females. After an hour of searching, she was able to get a number and address of Kilor's sister, but she lived on another continent. The girlfriend angle turned up better results. Kilor had two girlfriends and it seemed that he was in between relationships, but Sinop couldn't find much information since his personal computer and data devices he owned were taken to the station for the investigation.

Sinop was running out of time. She couldn't take Loar around everywhere looking for answers. The palace would find out where he was and things could get complicated in the next 24 hours. She decided to alert Cerimon of her findings and take Loar to Princess Navia's palace where he could be detained while she went around alone looking for more information. She and Loar left Kilor's home and drove towards a shuttleport. She transformed into HRH Toluvis' Captain of the Guard before they arrived to the main shuttleport entrance.

All seemed normal as they exited the car, and turned it over to the car rental valet. Loar was waiting for Sinop to come to his side as she was driving and the passenger side was closest to the shuttleport entrance, similar to the off loading area at an airport. It was past midnight, but many people were using the shuttleport as any busy international airport is in the normal vacation traveling season.

Before Sinop could react, a plasma bolt ripped through Loar's entire chest area leaving his head, lower body, and two forearms with hands falling to the ground. Sinop looked in the direction of the bolt only to see another one come at her. She focused on the origin of the bolt instead of trying to dodge it. The plasma bolt hit her square in the chest, but her imperial body armor took the energy damage. In the process it pushed Sinop six feet backwards on her back. The body armor would normally not be able to withstand the energy as well as it did, but Sinop's reflexive nature kept her from being physically damaged. If Toluvis had tried to break her while she was the necklace, she would have found out that the necklace was definitely not made of what it was supposed to be made of. In fact the necklace's makeup was perfect, but once Sinop's body would have felt instant unexpected damage, her reflexes would have protected her, and the necklace wouldn't have broken.

Sinop laid there playing dead for a few seconds. She had seen a sniper a mile away in an aerial vehicle. She turned into Lady Cerimon and flew out of sight from the sniper, which should have already confirmed the kill shot. She then flew at Cerimon's top speed towards the small twenty foot long shuttle. She could see through the buildings and made sure they were in the way as she closed in on the shuttle which was high tailing it out of the area.

Sinop could see inside the shuttle now that she was less than two hundred meters from it. There was one occupant whom was also the sniper assassin. She flew so fast it seemed like she teleported inside the shuttle as she also phased her body through the hull without damaging the vehicle. The craft was rectangular in shape with big windshields in the front. Two cylinder like fuselages were connected underneath its body. This shuttle was not suited for space travel, but she understood why the sniper used it since the doors were wide and allowed him to shoot from deep within the vehicle minimizing the weapon's signature and hiding his identity at the same time.

The assassin didn't notice Sinop next to him as she mind controlled him. She commanded him to fly to Princess Navia's palace at maximum speed. It was a forty minute flight at over mach three, and she could have flown them both alone there a lot faster; but the shuttle was now evidence. Sinop in the meantime contacted lord Paldez and got clearance to land in a secure shuttle pad.

Sinop scanned the assassin's memories and asked him questions at the same time. He was not Argonian, he was Hemilian, and was contracted to kill anyone linked to Kilor Dax. He knew Loar was one of those links so when he spotted Loar and Officer Olesse enter the house; he followed established orders and killed whoever came out of the car at the shuttleport. Sinop saw the vision she didn't want to see. Cerimon's memories made it seem very familiar. A Drakon contact had hired the Hemilian assassin. Once again, the Drakon underworld was involved.

The shuttle landed without incident. Lord Paldez and five of his most trusted guards met them at the base of the shuttle's opened doors. The assassin was not worth any more information than what Sinop had extracted, but his existence might be useful in the future. The guards took the assassin away and practically threw away the key in their maximum secure prisoner cells. Sinop mentally reported everything to Lord Paldez, and requested she be able to prevent the House of Cammeth from totally being dishonored and destroyed. Paldez understood her desire to save innocents, so he told her to go ahead with her plan, while he informed the other Guardians of the conspiracy and what was about to happen. The imperial fleet was mobilized, while Sinop took the queen's shuttle to HRH Toluvis' palace.

It wasn't long before HRH Toluvis' forces left Argonia for their secret mission. In the wake of secrecy, Lord Paldez waited patiently to infiltrate the palace and place the conspirators who had not left into outer space under arrest. He was sure that many other houses and realms would petition against his actions and want proof of the conspiracy itself, but he knew he was in the right. The truth to him would prevail, and there was no one to tell him he wasn't doing his duty for the throne and the people.

Sinop's plan was simple. She transformed into Queen Omia's hand maiden. A person Prince Hethos completely trusted, as she raised him for most of his early upbringing. It was easy for her to meet with the prince, give him a navigation strip, and tell him the story that he had to flee, because the imperial guards were going to take over the palace, and place him and his mother under arrest for treason. He didn't want to flee as would have been a noble response to the situation, but Sinop entered his mind to convince him that the navigation strip was going to take him to a place where he could prove his innocence and keep his mother from being put to death, because the new queen, Queen Neeva had made the arrangements. Sinop left the palace once she confirmed that the Prince had left not only the palace, but the planet. It was on her queue that Paldez ordered the imperial guards to invade the palace and surrounding area.

Chapter Twelve

--- ❋ ---

A Divided Royal Family

T he house of Cammeth was in great disorder. The royal soothsayer was dead, and the prince was under suspicion of treason. Prince Hethos sat in the captain's chair of his admiral's flagship. The ship was streaking through space at maximum speed. Its destination was unknown even to the prince as the navigation computer was taking orders from the AI strip given to him by Queen Omia's, and now Queen Neeva's hand maiden. He was eldest nephew to Omia, and had learned much from his grandmother and cousin. His heart was in the right place, but the situation made him the prime suspect in the death of royal blood. His mother was nowhere to be found, and his last hope was to trust Queen Neeva's hand maiden. Lord Paldez's imperial army invaded the palace shortly after the prince left Argonia, which caused parliament to have an emergency meeting.

Prince Hethos received reports of what was going on Argonia, but there was not as much information as expected. The imperial forces were censoring all out going transmissions. The bits of information he did get pointed to several supposedly facts. The assassination of Queen Omia was a conspiracy led by the House of Cammeth. He knew he had nothing to do with it, and the only other royal person to blame was his mother. He found it very hard to believe that his mother was involved, especially since he knew he was innocent and yet he was being accused of treason like his mother. Many thoughts and emotions came to him in the long weeks of space travel. The ship was not fully manned and the admiral was left on Argonia as the Prince gave them almost no prep time or notice that they were leaving into space.

Due to Prince Hethos' status he was able to get away with personally taking a flagship into space without notice or reason. Any other prince would require authority from higher levels before he would be allowed to do such an action. The flagship was left behind as not to alert any suspicious activity by the space fleet Toluvis was using to execute her plan to kill Princess Navia and Queen Neeva. Sinop knew this and to her credit, she had taken Prince Hethos out of the picture, at least until the conspiracy was completely stopped and all the culprits were captured or killed.

It would take several months for the spaceships to find and intercept Princess Navia's ship. It would also take about the same amount of time for Toluvis' ships to reach Earth and kill the queen. Sinop was sure Sedric and Medroc would get directly involved with Ship to stop the attack on Princess Navia. She wasn't too sure how the queen would be protected but it was likely the queen was safe with three Guardians already living on the planet.

Sinop made preparations to travel into the sector of space the assassin made contact with the Drakon male. It would take some time for word to get out on exactly what happened on Argonia, but as long as the assassin was not reported dead or captured, there was a lead she could use to find out the whole truth.

Argonian Parliament Chamber, Queen Neeva's Palace

Lord Paldez brought parliament to order under closed doors and secure electronic monitoring. All non royal telepaths were gathered outside and held in the main courtyard during the assembly. Lord Paldez introduced himself to the 649 parliament members as a Galactic Guardian, which was confirmed by lady Cerimon's presence and speech that everyone in the room would hear the evidence presented against the House of Cammeth; but that it was only preliminary for action to keep other realms from reacting harshly and recklessly.

Cerimon knew that her presence would make anyone involved with the conspiracy to be on the defensive, but they were not expecting her and Lord Paldez to be able to probe minds and bypass the mental camouflage implants. The House of Cammeth was clearly involved, but they still didn't know the extent of the treachery for all the realms. Cerimon stayed seated in the center of the semicircular auditorium while Lord Paldez walked from one end to the other, going up and down to the upper seats.

The evidence was presented in a chronological order with great detail as to who did what except for Sinop's existence and how the information was gathered. Word for word conversations were revealed, which was contrary to standard legal procedures since legal evidence was now possibly being contaminated. The queen or authorized magistrate would be making a judgment on the evidence, which was why Lady Cerimon was there. She was the appointed magistrate until the princess or queen returned to the palace.

Paldez had his work cut out for him. He had to speak the evidence since it was all in his head, while at the same time scan people as he got several meters near them. Cerimon was helping out by getting the people farthest from the center, but people would be focusing on her to scan them if they were involved. Cerimon was the strongest telepath there, but Paldez was the most subtle and didn't require for him to get a deep probe by force in order to get the information he wanted. The presentation of evidence helped him out because details were being said of what people spoke in secrecy, and it brought up a great number of mixed emotions. Most were of disbelief that HRH Toluvis would even entertain such an idea of killing the queen and princess. There was digital evidence from cameras, Loar's body parts, the queen's medical data, and testimonial recordings of the imperial guards with Queen Omia at the time of the assassination attempt.

Lord Paldez was wearing the Galactic Guardian uniform and it also invoked emotions in members as they remembered their legacy. Most accepted Paldez as a Guardian, but there were a few that questioned whether he was qualified for the position. The members thought of many things and as expected they came to their own conclusions, ideas streamed in about what they should believe, what they should do, what were they expected to do once Lord Paldez had presented all the evidence; and many more ideas of what was going to happen to the House of Cammeth, and everyone else when Paldez brought up the fact that high ranking officers were part of what was now a rebellion. Paldez couldn't find anything linking any member to the conspiracy which was very good, but the different views and emotions that he felt were almost overwhelming. Many members were loyal to the new queen, or if anything, loyal to Princess Navia who supported the new queen. There were very deep roots in the House of Cammeth, and disbelief was the major problem which Paldez finally sensed as he was making his last remarks on the evidence. Ninety-two members didn't think the information was true, and that the proceedings to this emergency assembly was in violation of legal rights protecting HRH Toluvis and her family name.

"Your Royal Highnesses; Lords; Ladies; and esteemed members. The telepaths were not allowed to be here because the truthfulness and legitimacy of this assembly is and would be in question. You all know that I am telepathic, beyond that of our late queen and the strongest telepath on the planet; however, I will prove the legitimacy of the actions taken today without the use of my powers." Cerimon announced once Paldez finished his presentation.

There were seven chairs and a long table at the center of the semicircular setup of seats, similar to the setup in the US Supreme Court room. The center chair however was distinguishably taller and wider than all the rest. It was the queen's chair, but it was used for the person leading full assemblies when the queen was not present. Cerimon sat on that chair. There was a live video feed going to two fifteen meter screens to the top left and right of the sixty-five foot tall wall behind the chairs.

"Zoom in on the chair's panel." Cerimon commanded, and the camera angle was changed and zoomed in on top of the chair panel. Cerimon touched the small display indicating a secure message being accessed.

"Computer, authorize release of message Princess Navia." Cerimon commanded. AIs or computers were not allowed to act in the parliament chamber without authority by the queen.

Princess Navia appeared on both screens. She sat in the captain's chair of her flagship. She was wearing her combat suit which was totally black, but her helmet was by her side so everyone could see it was her who was speaking.

"My fellow royals. Lords and Ladies. Parliament members. This message is to inform you what will happen in the next few months. Queen Neeva has placed me over all the empire until she leaves Earth to assume the throne. I do not know at which time she will do this; however, the imperial fleet is on its way to intercept the starships that have taken treacherous action against myself, the queen, and the empire. The Galactic Guardians have my full support in their investigation on this matter. Prince Hethos is not part of this conspiracy and the House of Cammeth will not be dishonored. I have ordered all conspirators to be taken alive, and I will personally preside over all their trials. For the next few months, all of you are restricted to the palace grounds. It is not a measure of distrust in your ability to keep this matter quite, it is a security and safety measure for all of you so you're not targets of the media, telepaths, and other enemies which we are still investigating. There will be order and you will comply. As you know by Lord Paldez's presentation, many people think they are doing the right thing by killing others, but I will not allow the empire's leadership to plummet us into civil war or worse. This is not a time to fight among ourselves. A dark enemy is approaching and we need to be ready for them. I thank you all for your understanding and cooperation." Princess Navia said with a very calm and confident demeanor.

Paldez could feel favorable changes of emotions and thoughts among most of the skeptical members. Either way, he could feel that Navia's speech was good enough to convince them that the actions of the guardians and queen were real and truthful. He knew that not everyone would agree, but it was okay with him. In time, they would either support the queen, or he hoped at least support the fight for peace.

Lord Paldez gave the members specific instructions on what they couldn't do, which was very simple. They couldn't communicate with the outside or go out of the palace ground. The realms would be temporarily managed by the highest ranking person of each realm outside of the palace. Telepathic interaction between members was allowed; however, it was highly recommended that personal thoughts not be shared on the matter until it was all cleared.

Princess Navia's video message faded away while Paldez gave his instructions. Lady Cerimon called forward the ten Lords and Ladies who ruled the remaining realms. They were all seated in the front row, and four of them usually sat at the table.

Cerimon asked them to open their minds so she could show them what the investigators had found out as to date.

Cerimon didn't like giving them telepathic proof of what Paldez said was true because it could be called questionable being she could alter reality if she wished, but she felt she owed it to them to see the evidence first hand, since they were not linked to the conspiracy. Cerimon didn't reveal Sinop's existence, but the rulers were able to see, feel, smell, and hear all the conversations, thoughts of why they did what they did, killing of Loar, and the capture of the assassin, which was not presented by Paldez. She also revealed to them the general actions which the other Guardians were taking to save the princess and queen. It was a gamble on her part that information wouldn't leak out to the enemy, but having the trust of the royal families was more important to her in the long run. She was confident that both the queen and princess were safe with the Guardians to guarantee success even if the enemy generally knew what they were doing. If they failed to carry out the assassination by aborting, they would not have a place to return and try again.

4,000 light years from Argonia

Admiral Silus ordered the task force to get into position after two weeks of waiting. A six prong ambush was devised to channel Princess Navia's flagship into their kill zones. Navia's flagship was cloaked and extremely hard to find if not impossible; but they were friendly ships and decloaking to a friendly ship was common. The cloaked flagship was also not always cloaked and the last known position of the flagship was 200 light years away. A destroyer was intentionally sabotaged to act as bait. They sent out a distress call fully knowing that no other Argonian ship should have been within 400 light years of the projected path of travel.

The cloaked ships didn't have to wait long, when the distress call was answered by Navia's ship. The flagship didn't come out of cloak, but it was tractable by the communication emissions it created by responding to the ship in distress. It was standard procedure for the flagship to stay cloaked until it had to de-cloak to provide shuttle assistance or perform a physical docking operation.

"Admiral, there is a very large number of displaced particles in quadrant 34, bearing 24, alt 4 degrees!" The science officer anxiously reported.

The displaced area was to their front, little to the right and up as the ship was positioned. The admiral would have been pleased with the displacement report, but the number and amount of displacement of particles as they were ever so slightly altering the reception of energy from distance stars only meant that there was a whole lot more than one cloaked ship approaching.

The admiral had 110 ships ready to ambush the flagship, but his hope of success vanished as over three hundred ships from Hebshilon's fleet de-cloaked in attack formation.

Princess Navia's flagship didn't de-cloak, but her video message certainly was visible. "Soldiers of the House of Cammeth, you have been deceived to believe that killing me will bring the empire into new leadership and everlasting peace. The queen's imperial fleet is approaching from your rear. You will surrender immediately; all of your officers are relieved of command as of now. Prince Hethos is now sole ruler of the House of Cammeth. De-cloak, power down weapons and shields to acknowledge your surrender."

Admiral Silus placed both hands together in the shape of a fist under his chin in thought for a few seconds and then pushed an icon on his chair communication console. "This is Admiral Silus, all ships comply with surrender."

The admiral knew that the coup had failed. If Princess Navia knew about the ambush, then the assassination attempt on Queen Neeva was also being foiled or had already been stopped. He would face trial and possible death if not exile; but Prince Hethos was still in power, and knowing HRH Toluvis' wishes, that was good enough for him and her if she couldn't pull off the coup she started.

The imperial fleet met Hebshilon's fleet and captured vessels without incident. All outgoing communication transmissions of the event were jammed, and the fleets headed back toward Argonia.

30,000 light years from Pylaxian border near Worhim Star System

Prince Hethos' ship stopped in the middle of open space. It was clear that they were not alone, as forty Argonian ships came into sensor range immediately after the navigation AI strip reported destination complete.

The science officer reported the specifics of the incoming vessels. The ships were from Lady Hebshilon's fleet; with one ship transmitting Sedric's hailing identifier. Prince Hethos didn't know what to think; they could be there to arrest him as a traitor and now a coward, or even kill him. But his fears vanished once he heard Lord Sedric speak to him on the ship's main screen.

"Prince Hethos, I am here on behave of Queen Neeva, Princess Navia, and myself. Your mother has committed treason against the throne along with many of your military leaders; however, you have not and it is through you that the House of Cammeth will be spared. Your personnel will be screened to ensure any traitors are arrested and no further harmful incidents occur. I request permission to come aboard and speak to you about many things." Sedric said as he stood beside the ship's captain wearing his Galactic Guardian uniform.

Prince Hethos' heart was calmed to a point, but he still worried about his mother. "Permission granted."

It wasn't very long before Sedric stood inside the bridge, having flew through the hulls of both ships and empty space without damaging anything in the process.

"I wish our meeting were under better circumstances, but welcome aboard Lord Sedric." Princess Hethos was the first to speak once Sedric's energy bubble disappeared around him.

"I agree wholeheartedly Prince. Please excuse me for a second. Navigator, set a course back to Argonia. Wait until you are cleared to engage by Commander Sorthan." Sedric instructed the navigator before attending to the prince.

"Your Highness, can we go talk in the captain's room?"

Prince Hethos had met the Guardians in the past and to him, Sedric hadn't changed at all. Sedric was always polite and respected the royals and everyone else for that matter, but it was more than that. There was always a strong confidence that demanded his attention and brought out a sense of humility out of a person when talking to him. Lord Sedric was known for his commitment to serving the Queen, which came from an upbringing in Tir Goth where the word of a Goth was his or her bond of certainty and truth. The Goth lived through a sense of honor and loyalty to someone they said they would follow or lead. Lord Sedric was made leader of the Guardians for a reason, and Hethos knew this very well, but he also knew Princess Navia trusted him with her life. Princess Navia was his close cousin and a true friend. Navia had a secret relationship with Sedric , but it was not a secret to him. He had known Navia for over 400 years, and knew that she was in love when the Galactic Guardians were appointed, but couldn't figure out with who until Lord Klakin's funeral. He asked Navia, and she confirmed his suspicions; but he kept it to himself only because of his friendship to her and because it was not his secret to reveal.

The two men went to the captain's quarters, while twelve Argonian shuttles with Soldiers boarded the flagship to ensure there were no enemy surprises in the works.

One light year from Pluto's orbital path, Solar System

Subspace communications was being jammed at the source as the Argonian scout ship tried to hail the incoming vessels.

HRH Toluvis' fleet was at maximum speed upon approach which was one reason they were not fully cloaked. The outer most markers surrounding the Solar System had been triggered. The Argonian scout ships would have instantly alerted Queen Neeva and the three Guardians on Earth that there was an alien attack approaching if her fleet had not decloaked. One or two cloaked ships wouldn't have been a major problem, but a hundred cloaked ships was an issue the scout ships were not going to try to resolve on their own. In addition, one or two cloaked ships would not have triggered the outer markers which were placed there centuries ago to prevent such an alien invasion. The Argonian vessels in the nearby star systems which normally patrolled the area were relocated ever since Quatris and Hellfire returned to Earth. Earth's defense system were the Guardians, and just like Tir Goth was left alone from would be conquering planets or races; so was Earth.

Toluvis knew that this might have happened, so her fleet decloaked and was able to get close enough to the solar system to jam communications. She hoped that her fleet could get close enough, find the queen, and blast her from a distance before Quatris or Hellfire could respond. The consequence to this tactic was of course her own destruction by the Guardians she hated; the same Guardians which her son was going to rule over if she succeeded. The fleet didn't know the extent of how far she was willing to go, even to sacrifice her own people. If any of the officers knew, they kept it to themselves in acceptance of her plan or were in denial of the fact. Either way, the Argonian ships approached quickly as one of three scout ships passed within

800,000 miles from Uranus, trying to penetrate the jamming signals.

"Your Highness, the Kolasus has stopped hailing and is warping into deep space. Should we send someone to pursue them" The science officer reported after receiving automatic telemetry information from the weapons and navigation officers.

HRH Toluvis understood that the captain of the scout ship must have figured out that they were hostile and was trying to escape the jamming area to get help from any friendly vessels in the area, or at least send out a message to Princess Navia or Argonia.

"Let them go. Focus on the other scouts ships and find me the queen."

The fleet continued its course, but now they slowed down and all ships cloaked.

Octavian Horse Farm, Fort Lauderdale, Florida

Richard sat on his favorite work chair trying to fabricate a small magnetic hover plate. Thousands of mixed materials lay on the ten by fifteen foot work table. His ebony black hair was cut short and stylish like a GQ magazine. His eyeballs however were onyx black and his pointed ears made him look like an alien or a dark Elf lord in a game. He was very muscular, but it didn't matter how he looked, because he was a shape shifter and could look like a twig of a human and still be able to pick up a hundred tons above his head without breaking a sweat.

"Richard, the Argonians are saying the Earth is under attack, I am speaking to the team as we speak. The battle room is ready for use." A seductive female voice and a one foot three dimensional figure hologram said a few inches above the work table in front of him.

"On my way." Richard replied and dropped everything.

Susan and John were all in the battle room once Richard arrived through one of three access elevators into the room. Larcis was in class, but would be notified if needed. Elizabeth, Richard's wife, arrived to the spacious room where many of their superhero plans were devised. She looked fantastic being six months pregnant. Susan and John had been married for ten months now, and it was clear that they were still not over their honeymoon by the way they held hands on a black leather sofa in front of the 90 inch main screen.

John's sandy brown hair complimented his green eyes which changed colors to pure white the more he used his powers. He stood tall as Richard, with a muscular figure, but not bulky or bulging. His slightly tanned skin was a result of the nuclear explosion he had survived a month ago, but anyone would assume he had laid out in the sun for a few days. Susan's skin in contrast was a vanilla brownish color which was due to her interaction with John and the cosmic energies they continually used and exchanged. Her ebony black hair was silky and long down to her mid waist.

"Erica, status on the Argonian report?" Richard said into the air knowing Erica heard, smelled and saw all that happened in the entire property.

"Captain Allina, says a fleet of Argonians ships are on their way here. She is sure they are not here to say hello. The scout ship Kolasus went to investigate and is currently heading out of the solar system to get help as per Argonian protocol. The fleet went into cloak seven minutes ago and is expected to be here no later than ten minutes. All communications is being jammed by the fleet." Erica reported as her normal full size two foot tall hologram stood in mid air in front of the main screen.

"If comms are being jammed, how did the captain tell you this?" Richard asked thinking logically.

"The scout ship Teldious is hovering above the farm right now. Their proximity to use cannot be jammed."

"What?" Richard replied.

"The scout ship Teldious is hovering..." Erica repeated before Richard cut her off.

"Yes, yes I heard you correctly." Richard signed. "Okay, Liz, stay here and hold the fort. The three of us will go with the Argonians and find out what we can do. Erica, contact EFL and tell them what is going on. I'm sure Quatris and Hellfire can help on this one." Richard instructed.

"What about Larcis?" John asked.

"Erica, you can text him, but I don't think he will mind sitting this one out." Richard replied, knowing Larcis was down to his last two weeks of courses for his Bachelor's in Criminal Science.

Elizabeth kissed Richard and whispered in his ear. "Don't

try to save the world all by yourself."

"If I do, it will be the first." Richard smiled and turned into his costume appearance of Creator.

"Okay hold on to my hands." John stood between Susan and Richard.

"I just hope the horses don't freak out from the ship being outside." Richard said as John saw the cloaked scout ship in his mind and teleported them into the bridge, in front of Captain Allina.

Captain Allina stood up from her captain's chair and bowed in surprise "Your Majesties."

The five bridge crew members also bowed in surprise, not expecting the king and queen to appear out of nowhere inside the cloaked spacecraft.

"Erica informed us that an Argonian fleet should be here in a few minutes. Do we know who they are?" John asked personally knowing Captain Allina and the other two scout ship commanders in the past six months.

"We have been able to identify them as being from the House of Cammeth."

"Her Royal Highness Toluvis' ships?" Susan interjected as a question and knowledge bit.

"Yes, your Highness."

"Get us out of the atmosphere and as far away from Earth as possible. Set a course directly in their path." John ordered.

"Your Majesty, this ship doesn't have the power to withstand their firepower.

"It's alright Captain. We will protect the crew and ship." John confidently replied.

The scout ship was seventy meters in length, and forty-five meters wide. It was twenty meters in height not including the few protruding stabilizing wings and weapon pods used in thick atmospheres and for increased firepower. It was almost mirror like on top and black underneath. It didn't have many windows as did many commercial spacecrafts, but that was to make it more durable in space and easier for it to use less energy when cloaked.

The two hybrid fission engines propelled the ship up and away from Earth at over 30 miles per second. There was a slight increase in gravity as all occupants of the ship were strapped in and seated, except for John.

Richard had kept quiet, not really needing to say anything since it was John and Susan's duty as king and queen to fix this Argonian situation. He also was waiting for the moment he would be needed. He couldn't fly at light speeds in space, and even though he had never seen Susan or John travel through space, he was sure they could; having obtained a big boost in power since the incident with Ego, a multidimensional creature who almost destroyed all life on Earth a few months ago.

Susan took Captain Allina's chair while John stood next to her as if he were planning to move around the bridge.

"Captain, can you see where these ships are located at this time?" John asked.

"Your Majesty. Since they are cloaked, the only thing our computer can do is plot their location in accordance to their last known location, path of travel, and speed."

"In other words, No." John smiled, but the Earth humor completely baffled the crew.

"Your Majesty?" Captain Allina replied thinking she had missed something, truly thinking that a computer plot was sufficient to find the fleet.

"They could have changed course and speed while cloaked, so the computer plot is a poor educated guess." John explained.

"Yes Your Majesty, but the computer takes into account of the captain's and HRH Toluvis' battle experience, tactics, and historical reasoning, so there is a sixty percent chance it is correct."

Susan smiled. "Captain, you will have to excuse my husband, but a forty percent chance of being incorrect is not what we would call a good plot. However, to answer your question darling; the cloaked ships will be detectable if we get within a million miles, if they are running silent. Which gives us about two seconds to change course if they are heading into us."

"Of course, the computer that plotted the guessed location will automatically keep us from hitting each other, right?" John commented with a wide grin.

Susan smiled back with a glare of her beautiful light brown eyes. "Captain, how much time do the computers say we have?"

"Commander Hismod, put the time on screen." Captain Allina ordered the navigator.

The screen displayed 2:09 seconds and counting, along with open space and lit up ship trajectories in light green.

"Hmm, I will search for Toluvis, can you contact Quatris and Hellfire?" Susan asked John.

'Your Majesties. Captain Plooas was supposed to have made contact with Lord Quatris and Lord Hellfire by now." Captain Allina interrupted.

"Take the ship up a million miles and slow down to ten thousand miles per second." John ordered.

Susan scanned far beyond the ship's extreme sensor range four trillion miles in the line of the computer projected path. Queen Omia's memories were still a strong part of her and she knew Toluvis' mental wavelengths. She first started by detecting the minds of the crew in the hundred ship fleet. Her mind touched nothing while John spoke to the communications officer.

Thirty seconds were left on the screen, when Susan felt several thousand minds moving quickly, about 40 million miles away, not in the computer's plotted path. They could cloak the ships, but they couldn't cloak their minds. She quickly looked for Toluvis. There were many minds, but she was sure Toluvis would be in a flagship so see looked for her in the minds of the largest concentrations of moving ships. The flagship was in the center of the fleet which was expected as to keep the flagship protected from all directions.

"I found her. She intends to kill me, and place Prince

Hethos on the throne." Susan said while at the same time plotting their locations on the captain's console and going into Toluvis' mind, seeing what had happened in the past six months. "My dear Toluvis, why have you gone down this path?"

Toluvis was surprised that a telepathic message had been linked to her so easily and from such a long distance, thinking the closest telepath was near or on Earth. She didn't know it was Queen Neeva at first but Susan let her see that Queen Omia and Susan were one person now. Omia was dead, but her memories and experiences lived on in Susan. "You know why I have chosen this path." She replied without honoring her title.

"Your highness. Two energy anomalies are approaching from Earth." Toluvis' science officer reported.

"You know who that is. You cannot succeed, please dear Toluvis; surrender now before more people are hurt or killed."

Deep sadness and anger filled Toluvis' mind. She saw her son living a dishonored life or at the very least a life of a follower which to her was the same as a commoner. She envisioned her desires for retribution and dreams shattered into nothingness. It angered her that her mind was being invaded without her permission, and the new queen had no problem with taking her deep thoughts into her possession. "Get out of my head!" Toluvis loudly said in anger.

The bridge crew around her looked on with concern.

"Please sister, it's alright, I forgive you." Susan replied in her mind.

Toluvis concentrated harder and blocked out Susan's mental link. Anger filled her heart which fueled her actions. "All ships stop. Admiral, I want all telepaths on this ship to come to the bridge immediately."

"HRH Toluvis has stopped the fleet. I think she is trying to get telepaths to find us." Susan told John and Captain Allina.

"As long as communications is being jammed, Quatris and Hellfire will not be able to communicate their intentions to the fleet. The crew will follow the leaders and things will get ugly." Captain Allina said, having learned human jargon.

"So do we want them to decloak or should I disable their jamming capability?" John asked as if he was fulfilling a customer service order.

"Communicating is more important than seeing them." Susan replied.

"Okay, I'm going to need to sit for this one." John moved over to the life support technician's chair and occupied his seat.

"I will tell Quatris and Hellfire where the cloaked fleet is at." Susan said as John focused on all the cloaked ships.

"Come to a complete stop." Captain Allina ordered knowing that they didn't need to be moving, especially closer to the enemy.

Quatris and Hellfire warped into the area roughly the distance of the asteroid belt to Earth except it was perpendicular to the orbital paths of the planets. They knew the details of the events leading to this situation, and waited for communication to come online, but at the same time they made it clear they were there by emanating bursts of energy. It seemed like a small blue star was placed next to a small black hole within the solar system.

John was in a statue like trance as communication signals were permitted to travel without hindrance. The jammers on all ships were shorted out with telekinetic impulses inside the main and backup controllers. Unfortunately, half of the ships in the fleet also lost communication transmission capabilities.

"The telepaths on the flagship are starting to probe the area. I can screen the minds of the crew, but not for long." Susan stated.

"Transmit a video message to all the ships." John got out of his trance a little tired and moved next to Susan.

"Your Majesty, they will be able to find our location if we transmit." The communications officer politely informed him.

"It's okay. Darling, can you make the flagship come out of cloak?" John asked Susan.

Susan never thought about forcing only one ship to decloak. It was an easy task considering all she had to do was mentally control the chief engineer to disable the cloaking generator and lock the system out with a twenty six digit password. It would take them at least a few minutes for them to override the system, but a few minutes was an eternity in combat.

Susan focused on the engineer to mind control him, while John waited for the flagship to come out of cloak.

Toluvis and everyone in the bridge were taken aback, as the science officer reported the ship was no longer cloaked.

"Honey, can you change clothes?" Susan asked John, seeing that he was about to go on the air with a pair of faded black slacks, and a white short sleeve collared shirt.

"Oh, yeah, thank you darling." John smiled and instantly turned into his Mindseye costume. Their cosmic powers allowed them to manipulate matter around them which they were able to easily do with practice. His head was exposed instead of having a mask covering it. The rest of his body was covered with a tight black skin rubbery outfit. His hands and feet were red which faded into the blackness of the rest of the outfit. There was also a small engraving of an eye where his heart was located. Susan had changed into her Eternal Champions costume as well. She wore her red and black outfit with a black cape that extended to her ankles. The inside of the cape was dark red, which linked to her shoulders. She also didn't wear her mask which was used on Earth to maintain her secret identity. A red arrow like stripe went down the middle of her chest down to her waist line. The sides of her waist were two large six inch diamond designs exposing her skin. There was a small box engraved on the polysynthetic material to the left of her heart.

"Argonians of the House of Cammeth. I am King Etron, your new King; and this is Queen Neeva, your queen. Lord Quatris and Lord Hellfire are as you can see on standby should you decide to continue with your plan to kill my wife, and me of course. HRH Toluvis has deceived you to believe we are going to ruin the empire and have conspired to kill the royals. Do not fear. We mean you no harm, but you must turn around and return home before anyone gets hurt." John said as politically correct as possible, but his words weren't heard by welcomed thoughts.

"Fellow Argonians, Queen Omia's essence is inside of me, and I know your pain and history. I wish most of all for us to live without fighting each other. We implore that you return home. I have already instructed Princess Navia on what she should do, but I will personally ensure you are not dishonored or treated unkindly by going to Argonia after your surrender." Susan added.

Toluvis' telepaths located the scout ship Tedious, as did the communication and weapon systems on the flagship.

"Your Royal Highness, we have the target acquired." The Admire reported with mixed feelings.

Toluvis ignored the words said over the intercom and communications screen, to the right of the main/battle screen.

"Fire all weapons." Toluvis said as her heart burned with despair and hatred.

"Yes your Highness." The admiral reluctantly replied and motioned the weapons officer to fire all weapons.

Thirty bolts of quantum rounds streaked through space giving the scout ship two seconds to see incoming. Captain Allina and the rest of the Argonian crew in the bridge saw their lives flash before their eyes.

John's body glowed with an almost invisible aura of air around him shifting reality. The entire scout ship seemed to decloak half way as if it were a translucent ghost ship. All of the quantum rounds were dead on target, but half of the rounds passed through the ship and the other half hit what seemed to be a spherical force field which took the full damage of nuclear entropy. The admiral and weapons officer stared in disbelief knowing the scout ship didn't have the ability to withstand five rounds, let alone thirty.

Everyone aboard the scout ship except John and Susan were astonished. The crew on Toluvis' bridge were also awed, as well as all those people on other ships who saw the attack which did nothing to the standard military scout ship. "Shoot again!" Toluvis commanded.

"Your Highness?" The admiral replied as if he had heard incorrectly.

Before Toluvis could say another word, Susan appeared inside of the bridge, standing in front of the main screen. "Sister, please stop."

The telepaths in the bridge thought it was a mental projection of Queen Neeva, but it wasn't. Susan instantly broke all mental links that the telepaths and Toluvis had created to find the scout ship. Everyone was paralyzed except for Susan and Toluvis. The crew members could move their head side to side and their eyes, but the muscles that controlled limbs and body motions were frozen. Susan casually walked towards Toluvis who was now strongly griping the captain's chair arms as she tried to sit back down.

Toluvis' mouth dropped with thoughts of regret, shame and fear. She started to sob, as Susan stood in front of her extending her arms as if wanting to hug her. "Sister, don't be afraid, it's your sister. All is well." Susan hugged her step-sister and released everyone else from the paralytic hold she used to have their undivided attention and keep them from intervening.

The event was broadcasted to the other ships and the fleet decloaked shortly afterwards. Quatris and Hellfire boarded the flagship, while Medroc appeared with Ship a few minutes later. Medroc was not disappointed at all having been late to the party since everything turned out peacefully, but was more thrilled with the fact he was so close to Earth.

John decided to go with Susan to Argonia and take Hellfire. Medroc would stay to visit family and friends for many months to come. Once Susan and John settled things on Argonia, they would return with Hellfire and Ship.

Argonia, four months later

Susan and John introduced themselves to the Argonian parliament. HRH Toluvis was allowed to live with her son, but Prince Hethos was officially made ruler of the realm. Several Admirals and field officers were allowed to retire with honorable standing. Rudez was placed under the care of Lady Cerimon, but her status was that of an apprentice, until otherwise appointed to a fitting position as a telepath in the House of Cammeth. Many sessions of telepathic therapy was performed for many people so the pain which they had for the death of family and friends in the war would be healed. It took time but all took responsibility for their actions which was internalized in a good edifying way.

Princess Navia, asked Sedric to make sure Lady Sinop continued her investigation. John and Susan agreed that the root of the conspiracy was a priority, but they had to return to Earth in the meantime. Susan and John had cosmic powers which surpassed many people, perhaps even Quatris if they combined powers; but it was their ability to manipulate their powers into specific areas they desired that made them very versatile and powerful. Elizabeth had powers of precognition, not like the soothsayers who had visions with little control or insight. Elizabeth's powers worked in telling the future with clear visions, not in filtering possible future visions. The interpretation of the visions and the amount of information Elizabeth had was what limited her abilities. However, Susan with her powers to include Omia's insight mimicked Liz's powers and saw that they were needed on Earth. It was this future vision of Richard being in terrible trouble that they needed to head back to Earth, along with Hellfire.

John and Susan were crowned as King and Queen before the parliament and people through the media. The acceptance of John and Susan as King and Queen didn't set well with everyone however. Many months of ignoring things by parliament slowed progress in the empire, and caused half of the royal family to focus on their own realms instead of the empire's needs. This aggravated Princess Navia, but the only thing she could do was talk to people and try to get them to open up and agree to overall progress. She had authorized mind reading, but that was in connection to a royal conspiracy. Now that the threat was gone, she couldn't continue to use telepathy as a way to run the empire.

Instead she focused on helping Sedric with his efforts to defend the galaxy, and took their relationship to deeper levels. She had never had a strong desire of love towards any man except for Sedric. In many ways, she was always distracted inside herself wanting to know what Sedric was doing, where he was, and when would be the next time she could be with him.

Sedric knew that there was something brooding in Pylaxian space, and wherever the Crestins lived, but Princess Navia was also in his mind more and more. Every time he met her, they exchanged thoughts and it didn't help that they knew exactly how much they missed and loved each other. The threat to the royal family being erased was an opportunity for both of them to make their relationship known to the empire. They were betrothed with the blessing of Sedric's mother, Celes, and Queen Neeva who was technically Navia's grandmother.

While Sedric and Navia strengthen their open relationship, Sinop infiltrated the Drakon underworld like an unyielding epidemic. Unfortunately she went completely black after making contact with them; her last report indicating that the Crestins were somehow involved with the conspiracy. The few people who knew Sinop, had faith that she would be fine, but it didn't mean they didn't worry nonetheless.

Chapter Thirteen

--- ❧ ---

Under King and Queen

Susan and John lay in bed both staring at the ceiling but their minds were inescapably linked in an intense conversation. It had been over a year since Toluvis had tried to take the throne for her son. Richard was not on trial anymore, and the Eternal Champions were more famous now than ever. Elizabeth and Richard were successfully raising a future baby superhero. The time had come for them to join their destiny in space. Erica had compiled information which John requested over the past few years on the Argonian Empire. Susan had shown him everything Queen Omia knew, but that was not enough for him. The EFL AI, Bob, assisted greatly in this effort, but it wasn't until Lord Morinar came back to Earth when the Argonian scout vessels assigned to Earth were the major source of current information to them. The divided royal family needed to mend back into harmony. The Galactic Guardians had given the human race a good name in the empire; however, them being at the top of the throne may have pulled that name and honor too far. "Things are going to get worst the more time we spend here on Earth." Susan continued to state.

"Darling, I agree, but timing is everything and we need to go with a good plan. Prejudices are never something to take likely since it involves change which many people are afraid of. I also think we should unite the galaxy instead of managing it."

"Sedric's team and Navia uncovered the conspiracy to its origin. We also know that the Pylaxians are preparing to attack. The only problem I see is getting everyone in critical positions to accept us as king and queen." Susan replied.

John thought about all that they had mentally discussed and let Susan see his reasoning and plan. In a matter of a few minutes, Susan understood what John was most concerned with, but he as usual had a plan to solve it. They came to an agreement and both enjoyed each other's physical and emotionally sexual pleasures while they still could before they had to leave Earth to a new home.

The morning was gloomy with tropical storm Erin moving through the eastern shores of south Florida.

The entire superhero group was in the living room of the farm's main house/mansion. Most of the employees were present as they said their goodbyes to John and Susan. The employees who didn't know their true identities were told that Susan and John were going to travel the world and probably settle down in the Fiji Islands. Some of the employees thought it odd that they were leaving in the middle of a tropical storm, but they were known to do crazy travel plans like in the middle of hurricanes and worldwide computer virus attacks. In addition, the employees lived on the farm and were getting paid overtime for their time at the farm in case the horses needed attention during the storm. Richard and Larcis drove them to the airport which was in the middle of nowhere deep on an Everglades side trail. Captain Allina's scout ship awaited them while the four superheroes talked the entire way.

It was a sorrowful parting as Richard, Larcis, and Erica II watched the almost invisible blur of the Tedious' hull vanish as it moved towards outer space. The wind produced by the ship only complimented the tropical storm's wind currents, but the sound the ship made almost sounded like constant thunder which Larcis thought was cool. The two men and AI headed back with many ideas of the future, but the conversation quickly turned to past stories of their friends whom they already missed.

Argonia, four and a half months later

John and Susan stepped on his, King Etron's, palace shuttle pad. They could have flown down from the star destroyer transport in orbit, but they thought it in good form to arrive as other royals normally do to their new home.

The precession event was celebrated with the attendance of over two hundred thousand citizens. The sky was clear and temperature was a steady seventy-six degrees with a cool light breeze. The weather modulators were doing their job, but it could only be maintained for hours or a day at the most, before nature would try to fight back or ecosystems would begin to change with damaging results in some cases. Unlike HARP on Earth, the modulators were not sound energy driven, but worked on manipulating gravitational fields and ionized particles in areas of the atmosphere. The planet had undergone many centuries of weather control, but this event was especially controlled for John, Susan, and the people. A long purple carpet was laid out to the main courtyard and large stage with a podium, which was set up so the audience could see and listen to them speak.

John and Susan were aware of the celebration and the events which they would have to attend in the coming months and years. John was fluent in over a hundred languages which came from Omia's knowledge base, and was able to easily interact with his entourage of aides, advisors, and Soldiers. Both of them impressed many people on their four month trip as they were extremely knowledgeable, respectful, and quick to adapt. The crew of the Tedious had seen their powers and personalities first hand which won their absolute loyalty. The Argonians around them who didn't know what happened with HRH Toluvis or just heard of the events through the grapevine, were skeptical at first, but the more they interacted with the couple, the more they saw Queen Omia's personality and the persona of true leaders.

So when the entourage trailed behind the king and queen, they all smiled as John wanted them to, not just because he asked them to, but because they were all at ease and happy for their new leaders and future. The aura of peace which Queen Omia gave around her was part of Susan's aura, but the couple radiated energy of charisma that made people feel safe and empowered with confidence. John was not on Earth anymore and was able to allow his cosmic energies to be seen and felt. People on Earth would have noticed his power level without him intentionally dampening his powers, otherwise his secret identity on Earth would've been instantly revealed.

Prince Hethos would be introducing Queen Neeva and King Etron to the people, but only after a word from Lady Hebshilon. All the royal family heads and twenty key world leaders were in attendance behind the couple. A thousand world leaders and ambassadors were seated among the audience, but the event was really to honor the citizens of the empire who received a large section in front of the three person wide podium. It was normal protocol for the royal ambassador to introduce the new King and Queen, but instead, Lady Hebshilon was given the honor of addressing the people in honor of them and the couple.

The crowd welcomed Hebshilon's words with open arms. A 3D image of her upper body was projected over the crowd far in the distance so everyone could see from the rear and beyond. She was known to be very humble and during the time after Klakin's death, she made it a priority to personally meet and help out the family members of the people killed and injured in the Colax sector of space. Her armada gave more humanitarian aid to star systems than any other single military or commercial organization in one year than ten of the leading providers gave in ten years. It was largely due to her decision to commit her resources for caring for others, which Sedric and the other Guardians encouraged her to do. Sedric knew that it would give Hebshilon a worthwhile cause to pursue. In the meantime, he had her armada upgraded ten ships at a time every two weeks. He was sure the Guardians could keep the peace and her armada would be best used for open friendly events.

Hebshilon spoke of the great strides many races had endured since the passing of Queen Omia. A new age was at hand, and she thanked everyone for their support in allowing her to help many worlds. The audience roared with applauses and cheers. John and Susan looked on with great interest and happiness. They had seen President Dean get cheers as they were part of the audience, but this was far more awesome. Aliens of many races attended, almost as if they were in a science-fiction movie set with two hundred thousand extras. The media coverage was also literally out of this world.

Lord Sedric looked on with interest too. The media was something that helped his cause. His hope was that the enemy would think they were complacent and make mistakes. He was partly right; the conspiracy worked to a degree, but the soothsayers, in particular, Joldar, told him that whatever happened to Queen Omia was supposed to. In the end the galaxy would be blessed. He didn't make that connection until he saw Susan and John the day they came home with HRH Toluvis. He knew that John was as powerful as he and Quatris, but it wasn't just John, Susan had something inside of her that wreaked a majestic peace and power. It wasn't just Omia's essence; it was an added power which Susan naturally possessed.

Hebshilon's final words were a profound thank you to HRH Toluvis and Prince Hethos who helped her efforts with massive logistical assistance. Prince Hethos took the podium and thanked her for her kind words, then moved on to introduce the King and Queen.

Both of them walked up to the podium and John spoke first. He didn't have a rehearsed speech, but he knew all of the topics he wanted address. He introduced himself as John Goodman, an Earthling, but now he was part of something bigger and would be known as King Etron. The speech was thirty-nine minutes long, but everything he said was not how he was going to do things as if he were campaigning. He explained how things would happen in accordance to a plan developed by him, the queen, and parliament. The plan involved further expansion to educate worlds that were in stages of their existence which threaten themselves and other living things on the planet. It included integrating all races into the fold of peace and prosperity. Giving many races places to live they could call their own, and the institution of exploration to other galaxies. The audience was receptive to his speech, but not really to all he said. Both of them could sense this, but John knew not everyone would be motivated or happy to hear what he said. The plan called for sacrifice of time and effort. It involved having to put aside prejudice and work for the cause instead of focusing on their own immediate goals and dreams. Susan took over and spoke of many things from her knowledge of the races and history in front of her that pointed to a rich history of cooperation and achievements. But what took everyone by surprise was her statement that the Sitherians and Pylaxians would also to be integrated into this plan.

Many worlds would have openly challenged them had the empire not been so powerful which included the might of the Guardians, but it was a statement which met very mixed feelings and opinions. Susan tapered the mixed thoughts by pronouncing a meeting with Emperor Tiaxtee and Emperor Zuphra; however, if they were not willing to move forward with peace and expansion, the empire would consider forcing them to comply for the good of the galaxy. The couple left the podium with many cheers, but there were many people thinking the future was up in the air with possible war as it was a millennium ago.

John and Susan were in total agreement before they stepped onto Allina's scout ship back on Earth. The announcement was meant to get the Pylaxians and Sitherians to decide what their next move was going to be. The empire was prepared to go to war, but if there was a chance that the two races would work for peace, then the announcement was an open invitation for them to accept or reject. The Pylaxians were building up forces and the first sign of a Crestin was reported inside Pylaxian space. The Sitherians were acting as business as usual, but their military resources were severely reduced by Quatris years before, and if they were to fight the empire alone, it would be a very short losing war.

The news went out, with many critics stating their points of views and where they stood politically and economically, but the crown kept a tight lid on their movements and responses. Military ships had been maneuvered somewhat, but they had been out in space for many months. The imperial fleets associated with each realm did however move towards sectors of space normally occupied by deep space garrisons and regular military forces.

An Argonian month passed which equated to two Earth months. In that time the Pylaxian response to the meeting was a resounding no. The Pylaxians would not be subjugated to the Argonian Empire and would fight to their last breathe. Sitherians on the other hand didn't respond openly, but it wasn't clear if they were going to submit and accept the proposal. Queen Neeva sent Ship with Lord Axer and Lady Cerimon to speak with Emperor Zuphar in private. Lord Axer was a specialist in covert operations, having been partially responsible for the victory in the ancient wars and the development of the quantum rounds now being used in the upgraded military arsenal.

John and Susan stayed together everywhere they went. It wasn't the fact that they were a couple, but more out of habit. The habit was developed when Queen Omia entered their lives. Since that time until Ego's destruction, they had to stabilize their molecular structures by constantly exchanging cosmic energies; otherwise they would start to uncontrollably destroy everything around them to include themselves. They left Argonia under pretense, but it was no real mystery as only one imperial fleet protected Argonia. Twenty-six fleets were out there in space, with the whereabouts of four fleets known to the many intelligence platforms of many worlds monitoring Argonian activity. Argonian fleets being invisible was no major surprise as all military vessels had cloaking capabilities. If the fleets spread out enough, they could infiltrate many areas of space without detection from specialized energy scanners.

Pylaxian border

"Ma'am, there is a wave of energy drains along twelve outposts." The Pylaxian lead technician reported.

The sector commander looked at the readings on the prismatic display. "Could it be cloaked ships?"

"I don't know Ma'am. We have lost contact with the outposts."

The commander showed surprise in both her compound and double lid eyes. "Sound battle stations, alert headquarters of an invasion!" Her high pitched commands rang throughout the command center.

The power in the planet's military base flicked as a plasma explosion hit on the perimeter of the command center. It didn't miss by chance, it was a warning for personnel to stand down, as a broadcast came over all frequencies to surrender. "Ma'am all planetary defense systems have been disabled."

Commander Gysmak couldn't believe what she was hearing. The planetary defense system was not linked together, and worked on separate power sources with fail safes to prevent any computer hacking or energy impulses from disabling each satellite. She assumed that the Argonians were using a secret weapon. She was partially correct, because Susan and John had disabled all defense systems within a five light year channel of space.

The Argonian space fleets were exploiting the penetration and continued on towards their intended targets, leaving ships to jam communication and maintain the breach. "This is a declaration of war." Commander Gysmak said softly in wonder and disbelief.

The stealthy infiltration didn't keep the Pylaxians from mobilizing deep within the empire and Plax. It was normal protocol to respond to indicators of an invasion, one being the absence of live feed from border outpost, neighboring systems, and defense markers. The lead Argonian fleet started to meet opposition as cloaked Pylaxian destroyers met them near the star system of Kebulis. The technology on both sides made it possible to see each other, but being cloaked helped greatly in combat. Susan commanded the fleets to disperse and continue on to their respective objectives.

John and Susan were on separate Star Destroyers as John lead the attack aboard the Lardose. The loss of life and property was minimal in their pact of five fleets for the first two weeks, but the other fleets didn't fare as well. Reports of Seer Spirits came in as John's spearhead of five fleets got closer to Plax.

The surprise attack was not meant to win the war, it was meant to minimize deaths and cause the Seer Spirits to react. Sinop had done her job very well in finding out that the Crestins were called Seer Spirits and in league with the Pylaxians; who were allowing them to inhabit their space in preparation for an assault on Argonia.

John sat in the captain's chair scanning thousands of light years of space. Lady Sinop's last report to him was faint and short, but he knew they were heading in the right direction. "Order the fleets to disperse into a column formation." John instructed the communication's officer to relay the command.

Susan trailed in the last fleet, but it didn't matter, because she could teleport into any ship she wished if need be as long as she knew where the ship was within a ten light year range. "Your Majesty, Admiral Blac's fleet has encountered a large mass of Seer Spirits in Delax sector 903."

"Susan, I got this. This is what we were looking for. Take four of the fleets to Plax." John mentally spoke to her.

"Fleet Lardose, change course heading Delax sector 903." John said on general broadcast for all five fleets.

John's fleet peeled off towards the reported mass of Seer Spirits.

Admiral Blac's fleet was in full retreat as fleet Lardose arrived on the scene two days later. The upgrades to the Argonian ships helped greatly, but they still were unable to completely defend against the Seer Spirit's energy neutralizing attacks. The remains of sixty-one ships at maximum FTL passed the Lardose.

"Your Majesty, there are two-thousand twelve Seer Spirit scanner hits coming fast, ten light years out." The science officer reported with a hint of concern.

"All ships stop." John commanded and started to input information in his captain's arm console. "Commander Jin, forward at half FTL. Let the fleet get some distance behind us before we stop."

The navigation officer's fourteen fingers carefully maintained contact with the console. It wasn't really necessary to constantly touch the controls, but it made him feel like if he were more in control. His brain waves were linked to the console through his battle suit head band, and his fingers were an extension of his reflexes and actions. He could be ten meters away from the console and it would react to his finger movements and wishes as long as he authorized commands, like pressing the enter key on a computer. If he was injured or killed, the default controls would go to the science officer, captain, or whoever the computer recognized as being in command at the time, if the console was not manually occupied by another crewmember. The other station systems also worked in like fashion, which made the bridge crew very efficient.

"Your Majesty! It's confirmed, there is a Seer Spirit two million miles in diameter, to the rear of the mass." The science officer reported.

Admiral Blac's ships reported the same, but there was no scanning data to confirm it, or maybe no one really wanted to believe it.

"General broadcast." John instructed the communications officer. "Seer Spirits, you will cease all hostilities immediately and return to your galaxy. Resistance will be your doom. You have ten seconds to comply." John said as he scanned the area. The Seer Spirits were dispersed within a forty light year surface area thirty light years deep. The broadcast wouldn't get to all of them for a least a few minutes, but if the spirits closest to him didn't comply he would unleash his trump card.

"You two are up." John said as he touched an icon on the arm console.

Lord Quatris and Sedric flew out of the Lardose's upper deck and almost instantly flew two light years in front of the ship. Quatris was glowing white as was Sedric who was feeding off of Quatris's energy. Very strong invisible energy sound waves passed through space hitting the Lardose and extended to the fleet three lights years to the rear. Quatris and Sedric felt nothing. The Lardose was equipped with four backups to include many alternating quantum generators. The first and second backups failed, but the third didn't, and maintained energy to shields and weapon systems. The answer was clear and both Guardians systematically went all out attacking Seer spirits.

The energy wave neutralized Quatris' and Sedric's space comlinks, but they seemed to be attacking targets in perfect unison without leaving any pockets of spirits on the surrounding area.

Lady Kara entered the Lardose's bridge and sat next to the John where a spot was saved just for her. "Tell them to focus on the larger spirits. The fleet can handle the smaller ones if they try to escape." John said while Kara was sitting down.

"Yes, your Majesty." Kara replied and mentally told Quatris and Sedric what John wanted them to do. John had scanned space to locate the Seer Spirits, and then transferred the information to Lady Kara who was keeping Quatris' energy level from being seen while they were on board of the Lardose.

Lady Kara was as tall as Princess Navia and resembled her except for a slender cheekbone, topaz eyeballs and dyed red hair. Her voice was slightly higher pitched, but very mature and sensual if she wanted it to be. The appointment of Lady Kara as a Guardian was no surprise to anyone, She was extremely loyal to the crown, and had energy manipulation powers that could alter her surroundings. In essence, she could cloak a ship which didn't have cloaking capabilities or make it so a cloaked ship was harder to find, even with telepathy. Her ability to mask energy was part of Susan's plan when they left Earth. Quatris and Hellfire were brought to Argonia inside Ship with Lady Kara at the helm. No one really knew what Lady Kara was doing during the arrival of John and Susan to Argonia; people just assumed she was on a mission; the mission being inside of Ship, watching the precession on video with the two Earthlings in Argonia's orbit.

Now Lady Kara was helping direct Quatris and Sedric to their targets. The Seer Spirits bolted around trying to hit the two Guardians with their energy beams. Quatris and Sedric were hit several times, but the energy which normally destroyed planetary matter only delayed them from flying around faster.

Quatris didn't really care too much about their attacks, being stronger than that of an Argonian starship, but he thought he was invincible, so why care? Sedric on the other hand kept the larger spirits from hitting him with their energy beams which was probably why he wasn't hurt. Either way, Sedric wasn't going to find out. The beams had no problem eating through non-shielded starships, and the less he got hit, the more he could focus on attacking, instead of defending.

John could now sense another mental presence. It had not been there earlier, and it was getting stronger by the second. He paid closer attention to the source and found it was the largest Seer Spirit in the rear. "You cannot win this battle. Return home now, or you will never return." John mentally projected his thoughts.

Very heavy mental impulses replied. "I am Vox'wer. We did not come here to return. I will eat you soon."

John could sense the message was personal, directed specifically at him. "You really want to eat me. Hmm, Richard would be laughing by now, because I'm pretty sure I don't taste well at all."

"Your Majesty?" Commander Jin asked, not knowing who he was speaking to.

John looked at the navigator. "Oh, I wasn't talking to you. I was having a conversation with Jaws."

Commander Jin didn't know what to say except, "Yes, your Majesty."

"Lady Kara, tell them to kill the big guy in the rear." John said, and then told Commander Jin to pull back towards the fleet, hoping that his retreat would pull the smaller Seer spirits away from Vox'wer.

"Tell the fleet to retreat, now."

Quatris and Sedric paused their attacks and went straight for Vox'wer. The mammoth Seer Spirit was different than most of his brothers and sisters. Vox'wer seemed to have four large jelly-like wings, and his core was a lot bigger in proportion to its body. An energy beam blasted out of its half a million mile diameter core. The enormous beam would have engulfed the Sun without a doubt, and probably caused it to super nova if it did hit it.

A dozen Seer Spirits caught in the blast were atomized but Quatris was also caught inside of it. Lady Kara almost jumped out her seat, realizing that the blast had hit Quatris. She could every now and then see what the two Guardians were seeing and feeling. She saw the extreme light, but then every signal Quatris was mentally giving her went black.

Sedric was also linked to Kara, and instantly went to Quatris' aid. He scanned for his energy signature and got a visual confirmation. Sedric warped next to him, remembering the same feelings he had when he came upon Klakin. Quatris was unconscious, his superhero costume practically disintegrated. He was soaring through space naked, but alive. 'Kara, can you wake him up!' Sedric asked her, sensing Vox'wer was about to fire again. Time was running out, but he noticed that Vox'wer was very fast in changing his direction of travel and aiming at his targets for such a large creature; but there was a chance he could use that to his advantage.

Kara with John's help mentally probed deep into Quatris' mind. Quatris woke up as Sedric was warping him around to the opposite side of where the Lardose was moving. Sedric made sure Quatris was looking at his face. The darkness of space didn't keep them from seeing in other light wave lengths and forms, "Put on your clothes and get the large guy to shoot at us while we fly by the other big guys."

Quatris was quite awake, probably due to John and Kara's mental caffeinated adrenaline boost. He understood Sedric's mouth movements and the telepathic link which was reestablished. They split up and warped around the Seer Spirits measuring half a million miles in diameter. Quatris felt very refreshed as if he got energized by a super TAZOR. It would have been very painful to a normal person, but he was a superhuman who was constantly keeping his antimatter energies from coming out uncontrollably. New costume attire instantly appeared on his skin, this one had his mask, being an older version of his superhero costume.

Kara was relieved that Quatris was not hurt, believing he was indeed impossible to kill. The fact that the energy pulse from

Vox'wer didn't kill or hurt him too bad was a testament as to his super abilities and invulnerability. The energy pulse would have killed everyone on Argonia. Perhaps if Quatris were hit more than once he might meet his doom; but the Guardians were not about to test that theory out.

Sedric used his last strategy when fighting the Gillithe battle fortresses. He hugged the larger Seer Spirits while attacking them. There was a faint spike of energy before they used their energy beams which he paid close attention to. Vox'wer attempted to shoot at him and Quatris, but he stopped once two of his larger brothers were killed by his own attacks.

The tactics partially worked in Quatris' eyes, but the rest of the spirits were now getting closer to the fleet. They needed to attack Vox'wer directly and ignore the spirits around them in the process. Quatris warped at Vox'wer. Sedric saw him and likewise followed his lead. They kept separated enough so Vox'wer would not be able to shoot them both with one beam.

The four drape like ground covered finlike wings on Vox'wer lit up and the creature quickly moved away from everyone but was still in the general direction of John's fleet. Vox'wer was moving several times the speed of light which was magnificent to behold as an object so big was intentionally changing direction at such speeds.

Quatris quickly closed in on Vox'wer and knew that he was trying to bait them to move in the open. Vox'wer wouldn't have to worry about committing more fratricide, and would be able to target the guardians better. Quatris turned on the afterburners and came from behind Vox'wer shooting a gigantic ball of antimatter. The ball hit Vox'wer's outer membrane and disintegrated a very large portion of his skin creating a twenty thousand mile crater. Vox'wer twirled around instantly and shot his energy beam, but Quatris had already moved out of the way. Sedric showed up behind Vox'wer and also shot a quantum blast where Quatris had injured the creature. The crater enlarged a little, but it was the depth which made Vox'wer roar in pain. The strange sound waves could be felt by the two Guardians, and all the telepaths in the area.

"Tell the rest to go back home to your galaxy, it will be your gift to them, otherwise you and they will die right now." John gave Vox'wer a way out for his brothers and sisters.

There were still less than a thousand Seer Spirits moving around and now engaging John's fleet. John could sense anger and pain coming from Vox'wer, but there was something else. It was like desperation, or a sense of dying by taking someone with him. Vox'wer generated a large energy spike and instantly turned towards the Lardose. John wasn't sure how the creature's targeting system worked, but it seemed they were aware of their surrounding like Sedric and Quatris were aware of energy levels and directions.

A massive energy beam came out of Vox'wer a little more than a million miles in diameter. The Lardose was a little more than a light year away, but the beam was moving a lot faster than any other blast. They had a few seconds to react which meant that they couldn't move out of the way from beam even at FTL. John relaxed as he focused his cosmic energies. The three mile long Lardose didn't turn ghost like, but it did seem to stop in time as a red energy shield surrounded it. Three Argonian ships in the path of the beam behind them seemed be able to move out of the way, but they too were engulfed with the red energy shields. Everyone in the bridge crewmembers braced themselves as if they were going to get hit with a physical force, but it was more out of reflex knowing that what was coming at them was massive and deadly.

The energy beam lasted three seconds, and there was so much energy being moved through space that the Lardose did indeed feel a physical force hit them hard. Crew members not prepared or strapped down all throughout the ship were flung around like toy in a dog's mouth.

The Lardose's hull was breached with surface thermo and ionized damage, but they were intact and alive. John looked as if someone had given him a beating while in his chair. His entire body muscles ached, and his head was slightly dazed. Kara could feel the pain he was in and severe concern set in.

"We can't survive another attack like that!" She mentally screamed into Quatris and Sedric's minds.

"Link us together." Quatris commanded Kara.

"Sedric, follow my lead, you take the opposite side and don't stopping shooting until that thing is dead." Quatris said after Kara linked him to Sedric's mind.

Quatris flew behind Vox'wer once again, but he knew Vox'wer would try to turn and face him. Sedric flew in on the exposed crater, and both Guardians blasted away. Vox'wer fired point blank at Quatris with his energy beam. Quatris was expecting it and put all he had into a continuous beam of antimatter into the heart of Vox'wer's core. Sedric's quantum blasts dug deeper into the Seer Spirit's body but it wasn't straight. Sedric angled his blasts so that it was like digging a knife and scrambling the insides of body. Quatris was just as effective, countering the energy beam around him and collapsing half of the core energy projector. Hundreds of nuclear explosions erupted from inside of Vox'wer's body, and the creature aimlessly thrilled and released energy and debris in all directions.

The Seer Spirits still alive went into a frenzy of rage or fear. It was hard to tell but all of them went to attack the nearest enemy target. Cooperation went out the window as it was obvious they were going to each do it on their own and get payback.

The fleet stopped their retreat and turned back to protect the Lardose and their king. Quatris and Sedric separated themselves away from the exploding leading Seer Spirit. It was the first spirit to explode like a super nova. The two Guardians lost mental contact with each other, but it didn't matter too much at this point, They both could see that the Seer Spirits were all out of control. Vox'wer was either maintaining a sense of organization and control of them or they just went crazy as if the Queen Bee had died and they were out for blood.

Quatris focused on the larger spirits attacking him. He was getting tired, but he noticed that the energy generated inside of them could be absorbed to a point. He attacked the creatures same as Sedric, by burying himself inside the creature and exploding outward. It kept other spirits from attacking him and seemed to work better than he thought. Sedric wasn't getting tired because of his method of attack, which Quatris now implemented.

"Damage report!" John asked still straining from the many muscle cramps he was having.

Kara touched him and energy moved around his body, relaxing his muscles, taking away the cramps.

"Your Majesty, we have lost FTL power, aft and stern shielding is gone, other shielding is at four percent, and backup power is barely keeping life support and propulsion systems active." The science officer reported.

"Divert all power to weapon systems and fire at any Seer Spirit within range." John commanded.

"Diverting power." The science officer replied, knowing it was their last effort to stay alive.

Twenty Seer Spirits approached the Lardose. Several hundred Argonian ships came out of cloak and warped within range, firing a massive barrage of quantum rounds all over the approaching creatures.

Many Seer Spirits were killed or crippled, but the barrage caused the surrounding spirits to change targets and attack the de-cloaked ships. The last Seer Spirit was killed by Quatris; but the fleet had lost thirty four ships. Crippled spirits were put out of their misery quickly. It was a heavy decision John came to, but they were not knowledgeable or able in helping the creatures. In addition, the spirits were hostile in all respects. They seemed to act like wild animals with no form of coherent reasoning now that their leader or perhaps mother was dead. It left many questions open for interpretation, but John was not going to just leave the area with dying creatures. He ordered half of the capable fleet to salvage ships, find and rescue survivors, and destroy all evidence of the Seer Spirits.

Lady Hebshilon and Princess Navia stayed with the imperial fleet defending Argonia. Her flagship – the Lardose, other damaged ships, and escort headed back to Argonia, the same way they came into Pylaxian space. John transferred to the Star Destroyer Volatis and the left over fleet of a hundred ships continued to Plax.

Susan's armada, along with Hellfire and Medroc, had a week head start. John knew that they would get there long after Plax would be taken over by force. John changed their destination and went deeper into Pylaxian space instead of going parallel towards Plax. Kara and Quatris asked him what he had in mind. John's reply was simple. "If I wanted to keep top secret military information a secret, I would conduct research and development as far away from the Argonian borders as possible. The Pylaxian realm is on the edge of the galaxy which allowed them to get Seer Spirits in their space without anyone knowing. At least that's what Richard would say."

"So we are going to find out, what exactly?" Quatris asked and smiled knowing Richard was an expert tactician.

"My gut says something important." John replied and commanded the ships to spread out and gather as much information they could concerning research and development, and military installations.

The three Guardians sat in the bridge with their king,

wondering about the future, knowing that this decision to invade and conquer the Pylaxian Empire had already changed the galaxy forever.

Chapter Fourteen

--- ⚜ ---

The End to Galactic War

Lady Sinop quickly wrote commands into the weapons console. Her Pylaxian body was perfect, down to the DNA. The computer recognized the DNA of the station commander and instantly complied with the commands. She wasn't doing any overriding which required override input and would be detected by other consoles aboard the station. She searched the database for information on the weapon systems to include command protocols which instructed weapons to be fired, modified, or in some cases munitions delivery systems to be aborted. Plax was defended similar to Argonia, but there was a major difference on the extreme limits of the surrounding star systems. Plax was surrounded by ten star systems within a four to seven light year spherical area. An array of defense markers and automated weapon systems prevented any fleet from infiltrating undetected. There would be heavy resistance with Pylaxian forces knowing where military vessels were trying to fly through. The fortified areas would cause the

Argonian forces to slow down or even stop which would make them vulnerable to attack since they would be very close to each other. If the Argonian forces dispersed evenly to keep from bottlenecking, there firepower and effectiveness on the fortified star systems would be greatly diminished. Further out, the defense systems were in the form of mobile mines that were packed with fusion bombs capable to disabling the strongest Argonian ships if they got close enough.

Susan was aware of most of the defenses, but as they got closer Sinop was able to mentally report all of the final data bits she needed to prevent mass losses on both sides. The advantage always went to the defender, especially one that had comparable technology and the home advantage. Susan told Sinop the timetable of their arrival and intentionally broke mental connection.

Sinop moved to a latrine, where she changed form into one of the technician workers in the loading locks. She waited patiently for three hours, and even had to give off the odors associated with using the toilet so other crew members wouldn't get suspicious of someone staying in the stall for so long. When it was time for her to act, she transformed into a life support technician and entered the communication center. The class D battle station was in the Iqiris star system on the outer most planet. Reports had begun to come in that a very large number of Argonian ships were moving through the minefields ten light years from their location. The Pylaxian 7th fleet was mobilized to cover the defensive line in their area, which meant three fleets were left to defend Plax.

Sinop didn't probe the minds of the crew around her. The Pylaxians were very different than most alien life forms. Their mental thought patterns were slightly synchronized with their audio receptors and vibrators in their three vocal cords and ears. They were very sensitive to mental imbalances which meant they could sense a telepathic probe a lot easier than almost all the races she had encountered since she got the ability to read minds from other telepaths, to include Lady Cerimon.

Sinop could passively sense thoughts and emotions which was good enough for her. All she really needed to know was what their actions were at the time the queen's lead ships came in contact with the outer markers of the star system. Sinop had put the technician's information in the station's database, so the technician she was impersonating was partially nonexistent. However, his DNA was a replication of a common citizen several hundred light years away. Being a life support technician didn't require DNA access, and it really might not have mattered with the database information she put in the system, but she wasn't about to take a chance in someone finding out she was an imposter. The work station she was at required she be ready to fix things or reroute atmospheric actuators in the communication center should the station be damaged. She was the perfect ease dropping bug inside the command center.

Hellfire and Medroc were clearing the path by destroying mines with ease being more accurate and faster than the star destroyers. They were also able to get closer to the mines without triggering their mobile thrusters which shot them into the intended targets. The Pylaxians had taken this into anticipation knowing the Guardians might be attacking Plax in the future, and they modified them to react to any movement once the first three layers of mines had been destroyed or triggered. What they didn't expect was the ability for both Medroc and Hellfire to be able to maintain a steady stream of energy which extended almost a light year away. A clear path a light year wide was established within fifteen minutes through the entire array of mines and sensor markers. The outer markers were buoy sensors, but some were equipped with targeting markers. A neutron laser system radiated a ship and marked it for a few hours. The defense grid near the stations would automatically fire their missiles and plasma probes which would seek out the marked ships once they came within missile range.

Missile range was half a light year. The defensive grids of missile pods were concentrated between the star systems. The firepower in the star systems was greater than the concentration of pods, but it was only meant to hit incoming vessels with a high probability of damaging the ships' cloaking capabilities. Reactionary ships would also over watch the pods when activated. But Susan had a different plan. Sinop's intelligence was the key factor in the decision to attack the star system directly and use it as a staging point for a direct attack on Plax.

The Pylaxian battle station went on red alert as long range sensors picked up evidence of a penetration of cloaked ships in the mine field array, and the outer markers being triggered. The 7th Fleet was already entering the Iqiris star system when Sinop made her move. She went up to a communication console and touched the female Pylaxian at the controls. She entered her mind and paralyzed her limbs and vocal cords. Sinop changed her DNA on her hand to that of the commander. She input overriding commands for the markers to not mark all uncloaked known or unknown ships. Then she input a distress command to flood the command center with phasing paralyzing light. It was an anti-boarding measure in case the center was taken over by enemy invaders. The flashing light would penetrate the optical nerve and knockout most invaders. Robotic droids controlled by the center computer would wake up the commander and key personal in order to take back control of the station. It wasn't a good method of taking the station but it caused the station critical time which they didn't have to spare in combat. Sinop closed her eyes as she activated the program, instantly turned into Sedric and flew out of the station into space with a force bubble around her.

Susan sensed Sinop's actions as she was scanning for the mental impulses from the station which changed dramatically. "All ships decloak; maximum speed towards the station."

The fleets had gone this far with practically no major hindrance, and the crews owed it all to the king and queen's war plan. The science officer scanned the pods as they approached them and passed them. All ships were scanning to ensure they had not been marked. Not that they would know for sure not having the markers' exact frequencies and methods, but the inactivity of the scanning buoys and nearby missile pods was the scientific determining method they used to come to that conclusion. At least that's how John saw it when he suggested the maneuver back on Argonia.

Sixteen hundred Argonian starships raced to the station, dispersing within half a light year from the border of the star system. They held their position as a hundred ships attacked the command station and nearby satellite outposts. All ships re-cloaked as they attacked the station. Pinpoint plasma beams knocked out the shield generators which left the outposts open to boarding parties. They could have obliterated the station with a few dozen quantum rounds, but that was not what they wanted to accomplish.

Two hundred ships re-cloaked and moved in to intercept the 7th Pylaxian fleet. Thirteen hundred Argonian ships watched on as if they were an audience to a large fireworks celebration. Admiral Frouls Lek looked at the battle screen with great concern. They were outnumbered three to one. His fleet was augmented with planet destroyers, but even that seemed too little too late.

"Admiral, two Guardians are approaching, bearing 346." The intelligence officer reported.

"Employ four Drakes immediately." Admiral Lek commanded, referring to the planet destroyers.

Four ten mile long heptagon shaped ships warped ahead of the fleet. There was no distinct command center, main engine, or anything except a cluster of weapon and exhaust ports throughout the multiple surfaces.

Hellfire and Medroc could see the ships come at them, but they were very different than any ships they knew. Sinop's or other spies' intel didn't mention them, which would have worried most people, but this was Hellfire and Medroc. They both flew faster at the ships, which had spread out five trillion miles apart. They fired on the ships from over a light year away. The beams hit their intended targets, but the energy shields dispersed most of the attacks. If the shields had weakened, they couldn't tell being so far away. They both committed to a strafing run, but to their surprise two of the ships let loose with several thousand missiles and five to eight hundred electron particle beams the width of dump trucks. Both Guardians dodged many of the oncoming missiles and beams, but there were too many without stopping. The missiles had proximity settings so if they came close to them, they would explode. A massive streak of nuclear explosions trailed the two Guardians as they flew away from the ships on the other side. Medroc was hit several times by the particle beams which actually hurt him as if he were being burned by a glowing hot branding iron. The nuclear explosions didn't do that much, but he could see that these ships were made to exploit quantity over quality.

Hellfire fared much better, almost not feeling any damage, but he knew that if he were to slow down or stop, the constant attacks could potentially hurt or kill him. He could tell that the entire ship didn't rotate, all the surfaces of the ship were created with weapon ports, so if the ship wanted to, it could fire at any target all at one time within a three dimensional 360 degree area. Hellfire smiled. It was an impressive thing to see. He as a scientist knew it was some kind of planet destroyer by design and was now being used against the Guardians as a power balancer. He flew in for the kill and landed on the shield. It automatically tried to push him away and electrocute him at the same time. His fire shield came on and he fired directly between his feet. He entered the ship and saw that the shield went back to full power behind him. He put everything he had in blasting through the ship's interior.

The ship blew up from the inside; very large debris, light, and nuclear explosions marked the location of where the Drake was moving. Hellfire would have been unconscious, but Susan was keeping both Guardians from blacking out.

Medroc continued his same tactic, but this time he stayed between the Drakes and the Pylaxian fleet. He stayed out of missile range hoping the ship would move closer to him and commit fratricide. The firepower dished out by the Drake was almost that of an entire fleet. Medroc was wondering what power source was inside that thing, but realized that it didn't matter right now. Two Drakes moved in closer, but the amount of missiles decreased and beams increased. He blasted away and noticed that one Drake was damaged. A large section of the ship had broken off into space. What he didn't notice was the extreme amount of missiles which were converging on him. Fifty missiles practically bypassed him without exploding. He thought it was a malfunction, but when the particle beams sliced through and detonated the missiles all around him even though he was flying past the speed of light; the nuclear explosions overlapped each other. The radiation and gravitational energy waves caught him in the middle of multiple ground zeroes.

He felt extreme heat all around him, several abrupt pushes against his body and head. He knew that he should have gone unconscious but Susan was keeping him in the fight. The Guardian uniform was shredded with numerous burn spots. He flew in the middle of the Pylaxian fleet and fired at the damaged Drake from almost a light year away. The Pylaxian fleet took advantage of Medroc's distance to them and fired their plasma beams which were more powerful than the particle weapons.

Medroc was hoping they would use their plasma weapons, which is why he was in the middle of the fleet. The beams were more powerful, but they were slower. He dodged all the plasma beams and was able to hit the Drake at the same time which blew up into a ball of light.

Hellfire had no problem destroying the third Drake, but when four more Drakes were reported to have entered the Iqiris star system, Hellfire signed a breath of concern. He was getting tired, and was sure Medroc was too. Four more of those ships would make them too tired to help in defeating the Pylaxian fleet.

Susan was mentally talking to the two Guardians, and gave them good news. "Lady Sinop is on her way, let her help you out."

Hellfire knew Sinop was a shape shifter, and wondered how she would be able to help. Creator on Earth was also a shape shifter, but he didn't know the extent of her powers when compared to Creator.

A Drake trailing in the rear exploded in another ball of light to everyone's surprise. "Admiral, Lord Sedric is behind the fleet." The intelligence officer reported to Lek.

Sinop flew straight to the second Drake, turned into Lady Cerimon and bypassed the weapon tracking and shields like a ghost lightning bolt. She turned back into Sedric and blasted the inside of the planet destroyer without letting up until she could see the ship implode and explode. The amount of power she had as Sedric was not to the extent of Sedric himself, but it did the job since his energy was unique as was Cerimon's ability to phase through energy shields.

Medroc started fighting the fleet as Hellfire destroyed the last of the four initial Drakes. Susan ordered three fleets to bypass the station once word was given that the station was under their control.

Admiral Lek was stupefied in failure. The eight new planet destroyers assigned to him were almost gone. His fleet was under attack from one Guardian, and the Argonian armada was yet to be significantly challenged. Even though Pylaxian ships from neighboring star systems were being deployed to their location, it wouldn't be enough firepower to make a difference, and it would also take too long before the battle ended. An entire Argonian fleet stayed guarding the Iqiris command station and the cleared path towards the Plax star system. Susan's call for surrender was finally accepted once the 7th fleet was left with fifty-four ships. Admiral Lek's flagship was crippled and he himself had two broken legs, before he surrender's his fleet and command.

Susan sat in her chair and briefly read the Admiral's mind still in his ship and understood many of the Pylaxian customs and military ethics. She saw Emperor Tiaxtee and felt it would be very hard to convince him to surrender. She was prepared for this and on her command three fleets and her Guardians sped off towards Plax's defensive planetary satellites.

Plax was thirty-two thousand miles in circumference with a high rotation speed. It was the fourth planet of a Red Giant star system. Pylaxians were very rugged and took a lot of damage, but the loss of life was still great. Plax was full of citizens who would die rather than live under the rule of an alien. It was their upbringing and centuries of dictatorial control which gave them this strong sense of duty for their own people and hatred of the enemy. Sinop reported that three fleets surrounded the planet. They were stationary which allowed them to stay cloaked to targeting scanners; which meant that the Pylaxains would have first strike and surprise before Argonian ships would be able to effectively engage them.

Susan ordered Hellfire to penetrate the planet's defenses and take the palace. The odds of the emperor being in the palace was extremely low; less than one percent. But it was not about the emperor alone. Hellfire would fly down there and recon the palace which was a symbol for the people, and also conduct a recon. In addition, it might trigger an action plan for the emperor to act on; Susan was hoping it would make him move or give up his location.

Sinop and Medroc flew in first destroying any satellite missile pods and laser weapons. Hellfire trailed and entered Plax's atmosphere. Gravity was ten times that of Earth which may have been one reason Pylaxians evolved into being so strong, with four legs. As Hellfire torpedoed through the atmosphere, Sinop and Medroc went hunting for the Pylaxian cloaked ships.

Sinop mentally scanned the area around the planet, but the thoughts of the Pylaxians were hidden from her. Sinop was intimate with their thought patterns and knew she needed to be very close to any of them before she could sense their minds. However, Sedric never told her, but with his body she could sense energy levels. The cloaked ships were dampening their energy levels, but the energy levels of thousands of Pylaxian crew members was something different. She didn't sense anything in so much empty space but she was sure to sense the energy levels if she got close enough to a ship. She, as Sedric, warped through space at half the speed of light. Medroc followed her knowing she had the best chance of finding the invisible ships, plus he didn't want to accidentally run into a cloaked ship.

Sinop felt something 400,000 miles out from the planet surface. There were hundreds of very faint energy sources. She changed course and flew towards the sources. They very quickly got stronger, but faded away just as quickly. She came to a complete stop as did Medroc several hundred miles from her. She had just passed a ship or two. They had not engaged her or Medroc, probably hoping an all clear would be given and the Argonian fleets would move in. Sinop thought about what one of the Argonian scientists had mentioned. Each cloaked ship had to have a way to know or see where the other cloaked ships were. The Argonian ships knew where they were at due to specific energy vibrations which mirrored normal cosmic energy waves. It was not a full proof method because the vibrations were not constant and there was interference from stars or other energy sources. Argonians used telepathic cloak navigators that kept the ship's primary helmsman up to date on friendly locations. The Pylaxians had moved to known locations and stopped transmitting their locations to friendly targets, they were on wavebands that were too subtle to distinguish, or they had telepathic knowledge on locations. What Sinop wanted to do was get inside one ship and read the mind of the navigator. Perhaps she could find out where the rest were and get that information to Susan. She flew back to where she felt the energy sources. Then she turned into Susan. She had not changed into Susan in the past because she had never been close enough to copy her, but after Admiral Lek's surrender, she had the opportunity to meet with her queen, even though it was only for a minute.

The cosmic energies which she was now absorbing was almost too much for her to control. She concentrated and amplified her senses to the way Sedric's powers worked. She could sense the energy levels a lot clearer now with the help of Susan's abilities. She warped inside a Pylaxian ship bypassing the shields and hull. Medroc saw her vanish, and decided to fly back to Plax. If anyone needed him later, he could always fly back in time to fight, but staying out in the open was not a safe thing to do.

Sinop found herself inside an accelerator chamber. Engineers and workers seemed to be attending to their stations as if in preparation for battle. The alarm went out once one of them saw Sinop in the form of Lady Cerimon mentally scanning a paralyzed engineer. Security guards stormed in, but they had no target as Sinop changed into Susan and teleported through the ship into the main bridge. The captain of the cruiser was unable to blurt out orders as all the Pylaxians were being relentlessly tossed around from ceiling to floor except over the navigation computer console. Sinop cloned the navigator's DNA and asked for the location of all the other ships. She mentally told Susan the coordinates of a thousand ships and then moved to weapons control. In less than a few seconds, she auto-programmed the cruiser to fire everything it had at the nearest flagship. She released the captain from bouncing around. "Your ship is going to fire on your flagship. I can save your crew and your life if you surrender to me right now." Sinop plainly put it.

The captain was contemplating other options, but Sinop added some incentive. "We are not the murders you have been told we were; this is war, but in war there is honor and life, just as there is dishonor and death. You choose which one you want now." Sinop was in the form of Susan while speaking in perfect Kiex, the Pylaxian language.

Sinop stopped abusing the rest of the crew giving the captain no reason to change the subject. Half of the bridge crew were temporarily knocked out and would recover in a minute or two. One member had a broken arm which was not easy to do on such a strong bone structure. Two Pylaxians were about to jump Sinop, but the captain ordered them to stand down. "We surrender. Commander, order the rest of the crew to secure from quarters. No one is to take offensive actions against the Argonians. Navigator move the ship toward the Argonian fleet at one half light speed."

"Negative, move the ship at maximum speed. If your comrades see you moving slowly towards the Argonians, they will destroy the ship. In addition, your navigator can't do anything without my override command." Sinop interrupted.

"What will keep the Argonians from destroying us?" The captain asked thinking that movement at max speed would be taken as a hostile act toward them.

"I will keep them from killing us." Sinop said.

Susan gave the order once locations were determined and targets assigned. The Argonian fleets all cloaked and warped as fast as they could to point blank range and fired on the cloaked Pylaxian ships. Each ship had one separate target and it seemed as if all of the Pylaxian ships had been lit up with a flare in the pitch of black on a flat piece of white concrete. The cruiser Sinop was in was not targeted and allowed to cross into enemy territory without harm. Susan had input all the target information into the targeting system of the flagship which in turn assigned targets to all the other ships.

The Pylaxian fleets were not prepared for such a ferocious, synchronized, and accurate assault. They did have twelve seconds to react by seeing the fleets go into cloak. Fifteen hundred Pylaxian ships were neutralized, some destroyed to the point of exploding. A handful of the ships were combat effective, but they were the smaller cruiser class with little chance of winning a victory over five hundred star destroyers. Argonian ships received minimal damage, but a few were crippled. Any Pylaxian ship that continued to fight was quickly shot at by the nearest Argonian ships. "Pylaxians, you will surrender now; power down your shields, weapons, and start rescue operations of your comrades." Susan broadcasted the message in Kiex and Du Los languages.

Hellfire stood in the middle of the throne room while imperial guards surrounded him. They had been firing plasma rifles at him while he entered the palace, but he completely ignored them. Hellfire smiled thinking of the police and armies on Earth that actually thought they could hurt him with bullets or even A-10 tank destroyer mini-guns. The plasma guns were easier to ignore since they had almost no knockback, unlike a tank round from an M1 Abrams. "So you guys aren't going to tell me where Emperor Tiaxtee is right now?" Hellfire said in Du Los.

Chances were that they understood what he was saying, but they were not going to answer his question. Hellfire looked around through the palace walls, focusing on any underground passages or complex. There was a complex, but it seemed occupied by people seeking shelter. He knew what Tiaxtee looked like, but the Pylaxians all looked very similar to him and it would be easy for him to incorrectly identify the emperor's face. There was also a high probability the emperor had a double. He flew around through the hallways above everyone's heads and searched the underground complex.

Medroc landed on top of a very tall building. He looked at the capitol city with interest. The city was humongous, maybe twice the size of Tokyo. It was constructed out of heavy duty materials specifically made to withstand the harsh weather and rays from the Red Giant star. He looked up and scanned space. The flashes of light which came to him allowed him to zoom in and see the battle between five fleets of ships, He was about to fly up there and help, but noticed that the Pylaxians had already been neutralized. He signed, wondering if there was anything he could do in such an important occasion in history. Thoughts ran quickly through his brain. If I were a ruler of a galactic empire which was going down the drain very quickly, where would I go? He scanned the skies, but this time he looked for the star system on the opposite side of the Iqiris star system. "I would run away." Medroc said, thinking of the movie 'Monty Python and the Holy Grail'.

Medroc blasted off into space and headed straight for the Virquis star system. 'My Queen, if you can hear me, I think the emperor is trying to escape through the Virquis star system.'

Susan sensed Medroc's message, but had her doubts. "All fleets. Separate you forces and block all ship travel from all the star systems surrounding Plax. Emperor Tiaxtee is believed to be fleeing through one of these star systems. Disperse your forces as directed by Commander Cras." Susan motioned her navigator to evenly disperse the ships to the star systems and direct small task forces to patrol the space between the star systems.

Susan turned to the communications officer. "Recall Hellfire and tell him to start disabling the station centers in the remaining star systems."

"Commander Cras, circle the planet so I can look for the Emperor and make sure he's not still there."

Susan scanned the planet for thoughts of the emperor. It took all her attention and power, but she had a pretty good idea that the emperor was in fact not on the planet anymore. He had to be found and captured; otherwise, he could start an underground resistance which was not something they needed if peace was the end goal. Susan ordered the ship towards the Virquis star system once she was sure of her findings.

Medroc warped next to the largest command station on the fourth planet. He ignored their attempts to shoot him out of the sky, and landed on top of the station itself. He looked for the main control room, and burned a hole into the complex. He quickly flew into the command center. "Plax has fallen to the

Argonian Empire. You will surrender yourself and your emperor to me now, or I will ensure you rot in a prison cell for the rest of your lives." Medroc threaten in the Vorlin language.

Half of the Soldiers were uncertain as to what to do. They either knew Lord Medroc as a Guardian and feared him, or were clueless as to how to hurt or capture the alien. The other half were confused as to why this alien hadn't already killed them since they were taught that the Argonians were killers and used Pylaxians as food for their livestock and pets. The majority of the Pylaxian race lived under the umbrella of suppression by dictated information and truths which included the default that the emperor was always right.

"Show me where the emperor is located." Medroc stood in front of what he assumed was the commander of the center.

"My emperor is on his way out of the sector. You will never find him." The Pylaxian replied with a hint of a laugh in the form of a very high pitched whining sound as if there was nothing Medroc could do to prevent it.

"That is something I won't need to do my big friend.' Medroc said as he stood a foot shorter than the commander in front of him. 'My Queen, there is a Soldier here who knows where the emperor is. Can you get here and pick his brain before it's too late.' Medroc mentally reported.

'Is he standing in front of you?' Susan mentally asked Medroc.

Susan's flagship was within a light year of the station, but instead of waiting for them to get closer she teleported next to Medroc.

The Pylaxians in the command center to include the security guards which entered a few seconds ago, saw Susan appear inside the room as if she were a ghostly spirit turned to real life. "Medroc, take care of the weapons." Susan instructed as not to have to use her powers to paralyze or control other Pylaxians.

Medroc instantly moved next to the security guards and manhandled their weapons away from them as if they were offering free gifts. The four guards were speechless as the weapons exchanged hands without them being able to look down at their weapons; instead they looked down on empty hands.

Susan probed deep into the commander's mind and knew the authorized route the cloaked cruiser was taking through the outer markers beyond the missile pods. She put the information inside Medroc's head, and they both flew outside through the ceiling, the planet's atmosphere, and into space.

Medroc and Susan soared through space a dozen times the speed of light, while the Argonian ships and her flagship moved in on their projected trajectory.

Susan scanned for the area where the ship should be located. She was sure that they would have detected their approach and probably sped up the ship, so she scanned further out.

"Anything?" Medroc asked through his mouth piece while

looking as far as he could, trying to detect uncommon deviations in starlight background.

Susan ignored Medroc's question and concentrated harder. She felt a presence of mental activity ahead of her a quarter of a light year away. "There." Susan pointed as if Medroc could tell exactly where she was pointing. Susan flew faster and both their bodies phased into ghostly figures. Susan grabbed Medroc's arm and stopped him from flying further being they were inside the Pylaxian cruiser's mess area. The ship was on silent running and all crew members were in their respected battle stations, so the mess area was clear of any personnel.

Now that Susan was inside the ship without having to fly or phase the molecular makeup of her body, she focused solely on finding the emperor. She found him and teleported herself and Medroc in front of him.

Emperor Tiaxtee didn't say a word, but was waiting for the moment having seen that his empire was now destroyed, along with a future for his people. All of his allies were dead, or had abandoned him. Emperor Zuphra had surrendered the entire Sitherian Empire to Lord Axer and Lady Cerimon along with the four hundred Goth Soldiers accompanying them. He depressed an icon on his arm chair as if in triumph victory, and the ship's self destruct final sequence commenced at six seconds.

Susan paralyzed his body, but it was too late. She and Medroc looked at the countdown numbers with surprise. "Can you get us out of here?" Medroc asked, but Susan was more angered than anything else. This supposed great leader had decided the fate of the crew on the cruiser and billions of lives across the galaxy to death. The self destruct explosion would probably not do much damage or anything to her and Medroc, which she was sure the Emperor knew. She entered his mind for a fraction of a second to make sure it was him and not an imposter. She grabbed Medroc's arm again, and they both teleported half a light year away one second before the cruiser exploded into atomized particles. They returned to the flagship to assemble the fleets and organize a defensive perimeter from any remnant Pylaxian forces outside of the sector and also to keep military forces from leaving the sector. They had to bring peace and order back to the total chaos of post war consequences.

Chapter Fifteen

--- ⚜ ---

Planet Destroyers

Planet 5, outer most star system in Pylaxian space

Neutron beams penetrated the unknown planet's atmosphere. It didn't destroy living or non-living things, but it did mark them for destruction. The Star Destroyer Volatis scanned the planet's bio-domes. John's ships had already destroyed the garrison of two ships surrounding the planet who fought to the end. It was weird that the bio-domes were filled with every life form except for Pylaxians. Other than the domes, the rest of the planet was completely desolate of life. This also didn't add up since the planet was in perfect distance from an M-class star and water was present at one time or another. "Is your analysis complete?" John asked the team of science officers who were gathering information from several ships and other teams.

"Your Majesty, Planet 5 appears to be some kind of testing ground. The readings indicate many live forms and elements which could sustain life, existed several days ago." The science officer reported still frustrated that they were nowhere near to knowing what happened on the planet.

"What do you mean existed?" Quatris asked being seated next to the navigation console.

"My Lord, the live forms were scorched as if a solar flare destroyed the planet to include all liquids; however, there is still an atmosphere that is barely allowing for wind currents. The bio-domes are the only positive living proof that life ever existed on the planet."

"How do we know if they didn't transport the living things from another planet?" Quatris countered.

"We wouldn't normally know, but the microscopic organisms which are linked to the terrain cannot be duplicated on another planet." The science officer replied.

"So what is the mystery again?" Sedric asked, standing behind the captain's chair.

"Your Majesty, My Lords. A solar flare would have completely destroyed the atmosphere and the bio-domes."

"So, it's some kind of planet destroyer." Quatris said it as a fact, not as a question.

John paced the bridge floor. "Okay, can you scan deeper in the planet?"

"Your Majesty, we have scanned underneath the scorched surfaces down several miles."

"No, I mean under the bio-domes, and look for cloaked

technology."

"Yes, your Majesty." The science officer replied as his team initiated the scan.

The flagship and surrounding ships orbiting the planet lost power for a few seconds shortly after the scan started to return data. The last of the backup systems kicked in and the main screen on the ship showed a bright green opaque force field surrounding the entire planet.

"Your Majesty, our scanners can't penetrate the force field." The science officer reported.

"Maybe I should have gone to investigate?" Quatris smiled.

John grinned and turned his head to meet his eyes. "What's stopping you?"

"We'll find out when I hit that thing." Quatris said as a dark shadowy bubble surrounded him and he flew out of the ship through the ceiling without leaving a mark, and headed straight towards the green force field looking atmosphere. Sedric followed him wanting to get a closer look at this energy field.

Quatris abruptly slowed down once he was at the field and passed through it a few miles per hour. The energy felt like a heat blanket to him, but he knew it would have melted a car into liquid soup in a few seconds. There was no indication that the energy field was generating that much heat aside from reflecting the star's radiation, but it was more complicated than that. He sped up and flew down a mile where the surface of the planet was revealed. He was not able to see through the field completely which meant the field was interfering with his super vision abilities. In such a way that it manipulated energy on a constant basis, almost as if the energy field was alive.

"King Etron, can you hear me?" His comlink either died or the subspace transmission was being blocked by the field.

Sedric joined him but he was forty miles away. "I hear you, can you hear me." Sedric replied and flew next to him.

The planet's atmosphere was very warm, but it was nothing out of the ordinary to them. Sedric saw that a thin green beam came out of the top of a bio-dome four thousand miles away. "Well we might as well check what's underneath that bio-dome."

"Agreed, oh let me know if King Etron talks to you. I don't hear him in my head."

"Roger." Sedric replied and both men flew down to through the bio-dome which measured fifty miles in diameter. They both ignored the wildlife and stood on the ground peering into the planet's crust. The thin beam of energy seemed to be coming out of the bio-dome's shell on top, not in the center of the ground on the dome. The layers of rock and minerals didn't sync exactly with the surroundings.

"A cloaking machine in the rocks?" Sedric asked knowing Quatris saw the same thing.

"Yeah." Quatris said and without warning shot an antimatter ball into the ground in front of him.

The antimatter ball dug a cone shaped hole one mile deep

and almost half a mile in diameter at the other end. There was however, a very large metallic cylinder protruding through the area that was not cleared of earth. It was more than a cylinder, it resembled a section of a ship or battle station. The portion closer to the two heroes was half disintegrated and melted. They could see the entire apparatus or what would be called monstrous complex. Twenty miles deep in the shape of a metallic football with the points facing upward and downward, it was an impressive piece of weaponry.

Quatris and Sedric looked on trying to find the operators, but it seemed they were hidden in a back room at the other end in the deep end or there were no operators controlling the device. "Okay, let's go outside, destroy this thing, and see what happens." Quatris suggested.

Sedric smiled and flew up twenty miles. Quatris was next to him and both men fired at the dome. The combination of a quantum blot and antimatter ball created a low almost flat like mushroom of light and darkness instead of dark ground and light in a nuclear explosion. A wave of air moved in all directions out and back in. The lack of radiation was almost mind twisting, because the energy had to go somewhere, yet the destruction was similar to that of a megaton nuke. The entire dome and three quarters of the device was vaporized. The remains of the device was on fire, melting away with the crust and magma. An earthquake was triggered and the force of molted lava erupted out of the created crater to completely destroy what was left surrounding the bio-dome.

Sedric looked around and saw no change in the force field around the planet. "Nothing."

Quatris looked at Sedric. "What did you expect; a one point of failure?"

"Yeah, that would be too easy." Sedric looked around for more green beams.

"Let's split up and destroy all the beam generators." Quatris said.

"Roger."

Both men flew in opposite directions, destroying all the domes that emitted a green beam into the atmosphere.

"What's going on down here?" John mentally asked both men.

"There is some kind of beam generators under most of the domes. We think that is what is creating the force field." Quatris replied.

"Don't destroy them all. I'm going to get a research team to examine them." John ordered.

"How are we going to get the team through the force field?" Sedric asked, thinking he and Quatris would have to transport people and equipment.

"The same way I got through it. I wasn't able to mentally connect with you when you two entered so I came down to see for myself." John replied while floating eighty miles up in the atmosphere.

"We can leave the domes at the poles alone." Sedric suggested.

"Okay do that I will start moving people down to them now." John said.

"You might want to make it a small group. The depth of these machines is causing worldwide quakes and lava eruptions." Quatris added.

John reflected on what Quatris said as he returned to the Volatis and got a team of volunteers to examine the devices. It wasn't long before Quatris and Sedric came out into outer space. John created a force bubble around the team and flew them into the atmosphere and directly into the western bio-dome, being the poles were on the east and west.

Sedric and John stayed with the team of six crewmembers as they scanned and worked their way into the control centers of the machine. Quatris stayed in the flagship with Lady Kara making sure no Pylaxian spaceships would attack their partial fleet of ninety-four ships. The team spent several hours in the device before word came to the Star Destroyer Volatis that Plax had fallen to the Argonian Empire.

John and Sedric were informed by Quatris, who also joined the team. On his way through the atmosphere he saw that the condition of the planet had worsened. The lead science officer was able to get many questions answered before the planet became too unstable and dangerous for the Soldiers to stay on the planet. In addition, the surface of the planet was boiling due to a combination of the force field around the planet and geo quakes expelling heat and gases into the now very toxic atmosphere.

The research team was returned to the Volatis, and John ordered the two domes be destroyed. Both domes were destroyed almost simultaneously by the two guardians. The green force field faded away releasing an electrical reaction worldwide. The toxic neon and sulfur dioxide gases would have easily killed any life form on the planet had there been any left in the 300 plus degree Fahrenheit temperatures.

The planet was now a desolate wasteland of volcanoes and acid oceans or magma. The Guardians, King, and many crewmembers watched on from the Volatis, witnesses to the doomed planet. John ordered five ships to patrol the star system and stay hidden in case someone came to see the results of their experiment. The rest of the ships left the area and headed towards Plax.

A conference was held with head departments and a secure video broadcast to all the vessels in the task force. The video feed was also being sent to Queen Neeva, Lord Axer, and Prince Hethos on Argonia who would get it many minutes to hours after the fact.

The science officer started his report which was displayed at the center of the conference room along with a 3D hologram construction of the planet, zooming into the bio-dome, and then the force field generator. The briefing was very detailed and long. The force field generators were linked to the ground using thermo energy as their primary source of power. The devices were fully automated to the point where once started the device would only voluntarily stop until it was severed from the ground. Commander Fir asked questions to himself and answered them as he briefed the information. The devices were used prior to them arriving, and were set to stop, but the settings were changed. Someone triggered them remotely from a distance or they were set on a timer or event. He speculated that the scanning under the domes triggered one which also triggered the rest. The force field caused an accelerated furnace effect on the surface of the planet. The opaque aspect of the field was made on purpose so someone from outer space couldn't just destroy the devices from a distance.

He speculated that it was for other reasons, but couldn't determine what those reasons were. The field was highly resistant to physical matter which meant that if a starship were to attempt to enter the atmosphere it would tear it apart. A small shuttle could have entered the field when it was weakest since it would have taken less surface area to penetrate the field. The Guardians and king were able to enter because they occupied less physical surface mass than larger physical objects. The increase of the surface and atmospheric temperature was exponential which increased with the number of generators. All life forms on the planet had no chance of surviving without the generators being stopped before the first two to three hours. The commander concluded with a more terrible statement. It was a planet destroyer and was made so that if the devices were physically destroyed or disabled, they would trigger catastrophic damage to the crust of the planet and release massive magma to the surface. The devices had fail safes which only made things worse, but there was a way to neutralize the effects by dismantling the devices from the inside and replacing the crust which was excavated.

Commander Fir ended his presentation waiting for many questions, but there was only silence as if everyone was still synthesizing the flood of information.

"It's a good thing these things are big. But let me ask you this. How is someone going to get these things into the ground without the inhabitants knowing it?" Sedric asked, knowing that on Tir Goth, no one would allow the devices to be planted on his planet.

"My Lord, that's a logical question considering most of the planets with geo monitors, would indicate such activity and it would be stopped if it did get to the point of deploying the materials in proper locations inside the crust layer. However, I suspect that the devices can be launched from outer space and forced into a planet's crust within ten to thirty minutes."

"There are more efficient and faster ways of destroying a planet or employing a weapon. Why go through the trouble?" Lady Kara asked.

"It wasn't supposed to make the planet desolate like it did this one, which went too far. I think they would use it to the point of just killing the inhabitants and repopulate it later as they wished." Commander Fir stated.

"So are we going to go searching for the devices or the people that made them?" Sedric asked.

"For now, they are no threat to our objectives. The fleets will gather at Plax. A garrison needs to be set in place, and the border defenses need to be moved to protect against threats from outside of the galaxy boundaries. Drop off twenty ships half way between Plax and Planet 5 of Star System 92. Start coordinating a rotation schedule for the ships to be relieved. Once you receive the battle assessment from Queen Neeva's logistics center, incorporate the able ships to be included in the rotation. Contact Lord Axer and ask him if he can speak to the Goth, to see if any of them will volunteer to direct operations in Pylaxian space, the more the better. Ladies and Gentlemen, we have to be able to lead and protect the lives of everyone in the empire, now that everyone is under one empire." John stated as his final words of the conference.

Once the video transmission was ended, almost everyone left the conference room except for John and Lady Kara.

"Your Majesty. May I ask a question that has been bothering me for some time?" Lady Kara sat next to John.

John looked at the woman's honest looking face. "Do you know why I decided to accept the throne as king?"

"No, your Majesty, I don't believe you ever mentioned why exactly."

"It was because I knew people could always come to me and ask me what I thought." John grinned, waiting for the question.

Kara felt a little embarrassed and relieved that the king welcomed her with open arms. "Thank you your Majesty. I was wondering why all the soothsayers were quarantined under guard in the palaces before we started the war?"

John sat there in thought. "You probably thought that they would help the war effort or be used to keep people from dying?" John said as if he knew what Kara was thinking.

"They have been in the royal families for a millennium. They have saved my life more than once." Kara countered as if he was accusing them before actually considering the facts.

"Back on Earth there are many people called fortune tellers. Most are charlatans, but there are a few who tell people they should leave their families or spend their life savings into a business or investing in stocks. They become very rich; find a family they are happy with, or the complete opposite. The thing which I noticed was that these people based their decisions on what the witch doctor or fortune teller would say or not say. Good decisions are sometimes seen as good only because the end result was favorable. Your former Queen and my good friend Elizabeth can tell the future. I mean really tell the future; for the many years I have known Liz, she was never wrong. She could tell you what you will eat tomorrow and even though you know and try not to, you end up eating exactly what she said you would. It is not because you don't have a choice." John paused making sure Kara was following him.

"One thing Elizabeth never did was tell us exactly how something would happen, or events which were critical decision makers. I asked her why she never did that, and she told me that if she did, then it was her that would be dictating other people's future, not them dictating their own future. The soothsayers see a possible future. The decisions of the captains and royals all over the empire are affected by possible interpretations of what they say. Even if the visions were accurate, the decisions of the leaders are based on that information, which in essence means the soothsayers are deciding for us. That might not be enough reason for you or even me; but the decision to keep them out of the war was Joldar's recommendation. I entered his mind and saw what he saw. We, my wife, Joldar, and I agreed that they needed to be left out of the decision process. The only way to accomplish that was to make sure the captains and leaders of the fleets didn't have access to them."

Lady Kara was already amazed by the king and queen's persona and brilliance, but now it dawned on her that they were more than a king and queen, it was destiny that made them leaders of the entire galaxy. "Thank you your Majesty for answering my question."

"You're very welcome, Lady Kara. Now, I need to rest a little bit by helping out the engineers in constructing a more efficient medical center." John said and stood up, but waited for Lady Kara so he could escort her out of the conference room like a gentleman, even though he was king.

Three hours after the briefing, a message came into John's wristband. He looked at the hologram of a text message above his wrist. It was Susan. She had seen the video broadcast, but the message wasn't about the briefing. It simply said. "The galaxy is ours. Love, Susan." John smiled knowing that the prosperity of the empire meant prosperity and peace for all worlds, to include Earth.

Chapter Sixteen

--- ⚜ ---

Last Stop: Earth

Extreme orbit around the planet Plax, hours prior to Plant 27 Brief

Queen Neeva stood in front of the ship's panoramic main screen. "Your emperor is dead, and so is your world. I am not here to condemn you, but I ask that you accept our help to relocate you to a livable planet. You have lost much more than any other race and it is out of compassion that I ask you to accept life and surrender."

Due to Goth technology, Argonian upgraded weaponry and engines made them five times faster and deadly with quantum energy manipulation capabilities. But all the power and speed could not change the ideology of a people who thought the enemy was the source of all evil. The planetary ground particle beam batteries and missiles fired up at the starships in orbit. The attempt to damage the ships or hit the Queen's flagship was dismal. Their targeting system was not equipped to target cloaked ships, to include missiles leaving an atmosphere with great effectiveness. The arsenal was primarily made to combat close targets inside or near the atmosphere. They relied on spaceships and satellites to fight other spaceships out in outer space. The beam weapons did reach out to the extreme orbit of forty thousand miles, but without a strong targeting system, they were shooting blind.

"Your efforts to resist is counterproductive. Select a leader worthy of speaking for your race and reply with your terms of surrender. You have thirty minutes to respond before we start destroying all of your military installations." Susan announced and the broadcast was terminated.

"Your Majesty, the Pylaxians have only surrendered when they are down to a handful in numbers. According to these trends, they are not likely to surrender Plax until seventy-five percent of the population has died." Commander Vods, the political and economic expert reported.

"There was a reason I didn't want to hear your report." Susan joked, but the science officer looked at her with a blank gaze.

Susan stood up and walked around, then stopped behind the navigation officer. "Move the ship .2 light years away. Tell the other ships to do the same."

Susan turned to the communication officer. "Contact the other ships and find me the highest ranking prisoners and bring the top three to the bridge immediately."

The ships around Plax moved away from the home world passing the orbital path of the fifth planet. The Argonians were very efficient in identifying, segregating, and securing prisoners aboard their starships. It didn't take very long for the communication officer to task the prisoner ships to transport two surviving admirals and a battle fortress captain to the queen's flagship.

Susan instructed the ships in her sector to perform any required maintenance and be prepared to destroy all the defense grids. She had threaten the Pylaxians, but it was a bluff she was about to alter for the good of everyone.

It took almost forty minutes for the three prisoners to arrive to the bridge with an eight Soldier security escort. The escort was told to leave them. Lord Hellfire and Medroc were there but it wasn't for them to protect her. Susan wanted them close to her in case she had a mission for them, but it also ensured no one had any crazy idea of taking the bridge; that way she could focus on what she was about to do.

"Gentlemen and Lady, I brought you here because your honorable people want to fight to the death it seems. So I wish to speak to you as the new world leaders, since your emperor is dead."

"You killed the emperor?" Admiral Ortaxlith asked in an almost denial or accusation kind of high pitched screech.

"No, I did not, nor did any other Argonian. Your emperor pushed the self destruct button on the ship he was fleeing in and killed himself and the souls of the crew. People would say he was a coward or great leader for sacrificing himself and others; but that doesn't matter right now. I think he killed himself because he was hiding something." Susan watched the prisoners carefully, but she really didn't know what to look for if any of them betrayed themselves by their facial features or body language.

"But it is not about what he might have been hiding. I brought you here because it is about your families, and the children of your families, and the many generations to come. I am going to enter your minds, not to steal secrets or make you believe what I'm about to show you, but maybe it will help you understand why I'm not killing your race into extinction."

Susan concentrated on all three of their minds and with her knowledge of the Kiex language, she narrated the vivid visions of Japanese Soldiers who in WWII fought for their lives to the last man because they were taught that the Allies, in particular, the Marines would torture and kill them slowly to include even cannibalism. She showed them the damage Japanese Soldiers went through because they were so isolated that they lived in caves for years because they thought the war was still going on. Lives were ruined because of one person, the Japanese emperor decided to teach his people that everyone else was inferior or evil. She showed them the horrors of many leaders and countries that did the same which included Hitler, Genghis Khan, Basil II (the Bulgar Slayer), and Attila the Hun. She made it clear that she was not comparing these rulers with Emperor Tiaxtee; however, she was pointing to the fact that these rulers were from her planet and part of her history. Then she showed them visions of Martin Luther King Jr., Gandhi, and beautiful scenes of families at the beach, in a park, around a campfire singing, and the happiness of couples together in marriage, giving birth, giving a daughter away or a gift to a child. All these visions were understood by the Pylaxians even though they had not known about Earth and Earthling customs and history. It took a few minutes, but now they understood that Susan didn't want to hurt them, and all she wanted was for the Pylaxians to live a life of happiness.

"I know you feel like your resources are stretched too far and we are in the way of your survival. I would agree with you, but we live in this galaxy together and together will be how we survive. I ask that you help me by taking charge of your people and convince them to surrender the planet. We need to get rid of these weapons of mass destruction and figure out how we can help you live a free life without fearing we are the enemy and waiting to kill you."

"What makes you think they will listen to us? We are your prisoners." Admiral Lek asked.

'No, you're not. You are leaders who know the truth; you can go back to try to fight us, or you can stop the needless killing and fight to live a new way of life." Susan said and turned towards the communication officer.

"I can order my ships to take Plax by force, but to me the war is over. A new beginning has started. If you wish to help, give the locations of the ground defense command centers. My Guardians will go in and neutralize the centers without killing anyone. Once the missiles and beam weapons are disabled, one or both of you two admirals can talk to your people and tell them what is expected of them."

"What is expected?" Admiral Ortaxlith asked a lot claimer

than before.

"They are expected to put down their arms, and start to rebuild, focus on burying the dead, healing the injured, and learning the truth about the aliens everyone is hating or fearing." Susan solemnly replied.

"Can we talk in private?" Admiral Lek asked referring to the three Pylaxians.

Susan motioned to Hellfire. Hellfire led them to the conference room where Susan assured them audio privacy.

It was almost ten minutes later when the three leaders came back to the bridge and gave the location of the command centers to the science officer.

Sinop as Sedric, Hellfire, and Medroc flew down to Plax, and quickly disabled their capability to launch attacks into orbit. The leaders were given three Pylaxian cruisers with full crews to approach Plax and declare Admiral Frouls Lek new leader of the Pylaxian people.

The Argonian fleets retreated to the outer markers where they destroyed all missile pods and satellites. Hellfire and Sinop were the liaisons for the empire on Plax while everyone waited for King Etron to arrive in the sector.

A few days passed and John's partial fleet arrived.

The two royals, all the Guardians, and elected Pylaxian leaders met aboard the Volatis. Sinop took the form of Lady Cerimon as not to let anyone else know her true form. A peace treaty was agreed upon and signed, but shortly after the televised event, the Queen's intelligence analyst stormed in on Susan as she was taking in reports on Pylaxian activity while sitting on John's chair. The science officer stepped in and stopped the anxious female from interrupting the reporting session. But, it wasn't long before the science officer respectfully, interrupted.

"Your Majesty, Lieutenant Commander Hevos has analyzed the data sent on Planet 27 and Princess Dialara in sector 3026. There seems to be critical information which indicates the planet destroyer was never meant to destroy just any world, it was meant to destroy the planet Earth."

Susan showed surprise and deep concern for the first time she had become queen. "Lieutenant Commander Hevos, let me see your thoughts."

The commander bowled her head in consent. "Yes, your Majesty."

The data indicated that planet 5 was a duplicate size of Earth, in a star system with an M-class star, and was roughly the same distance from the star. The makeup of the planet was also similar except for the life forms which were close enough for their purposes. Earth didn't have geo monitors to detect the type of excavation used by the Pylaxians, and the materials of the devices were made mostly of elements on Earth, which meant they didn't need to sneak in large amounts of materials and equipment to Earth. The scout ships would be able to detect large amounts of movement from space, but all they needed was maybe one to three well placed spaceships to slip in. Princess Dialara was on the other side of Pylaxian space and the intel her fleet gathered mentioned heavy studies on Earth's cultures, and countries that would side with them. Susan thought about the events on Earth and now she understood that Australia had made a deal with the Pylaxians. Now she understood what the emperor was trying to protect by killing himself. Chances were that Admiral Lek didn't know about the covert planet destroyer, and if he did, he would have told them, or he was deceiving everyone, waiting for the Earth to die and continue a war maybe he thought was not over.

Susan concentrated and mentally contacted all the Guardians and John. In less than a minute, the decision was made for Quatris to fly ahead of everyone to see if he could save Earth before the generators activated.

Susan called Admiral Lek and asked him if he knew about the planet destroyer which was currently being used on Earth. He told her no, but she asked him for consent to read his mind. It was a courtesy which the Admiral Lek understood. The planet she grew up on was about to die as collateral damage in a war which was already won and lost. He let her see what he knew, which was mutually important to him, so she would be able to trust him in the future.

Before Quatris left the star system, Sedric poured as much power as he could give him for extra speed and make it back to Earth in record time.

Earths' Orbit, Observatory lounge area, UFF Andromeda

Quatris narrated the story to this point, but stopped, noticing the expression on their faces that the two astronauts were probably wondering why he had not stopped the planet destroyer from activating. "You're probably wondering why I didn't stop the field generators from working since I arrived on the scene two days ago."

"That crossed our minds." Colonel Cornelius replied for both of them.

"There are many superhumans on Earth. They are not as powerful as the Guardians, but the good ones fight for justice and all that is good. There are a few that have assembled superhumans to protect the Earth in this particular time of need. Creator is one of those superhumans who's leading the fight not just to destroy the force field generators, but the superhumans and aliens threatening the planet. There is also a very powerful superhuman down there somewhere who will protect all life forms. I was going to ignore the South American's invasion and find the generators two days ago, but this powerful superhuman told me not to. If I were to save Earth today, the people will never know how close they came to their own destruction. There was also a good chance that me destroying the generators would also destroy Earth in the process."

"So you and the other superhumans are teaching us humans a lesson? How crass can you be?" LTC Golubova said a little disgusted.

Quatris would have normally told him off, but he saw the anger and confusion in their minds and hearts. "Do you know how many times Hellfire and I have saved the Earth? Did you know that Creator and his team kept the Earth from total destruction less than three years ago? Yet, he was paraded into the court room being portrayed as evil, uncaring, and only out for himself. The people, humans, and superhumans saw nothing except what they were told, not what they experienced. The whole world will see and experience the fight for their lives, and everyone will save the Earth. All of us, together we will get through this." Quatris countered with a stern face, but his eyes showed compassion and confidence.

The two men kept quiet, trying to balance reason with personal feelings.

"Like I said, if I were to go down there and destroy the generators with my antimatter blasts, the devices will trigger super quakes and volcanoes which will kill more people than it will save. Creator and the South Americans have a plan to disable the devices and slowly take them apart once the Australian's are defeated. Relax, have some faith and hope for the best. I know I do and I have to so we all can see a brighter future." Quatris said, but in the back of his mind, he wondered what was going on in space.

His coming to Earth this early was not expected, and it worried him that Admiral Lek told everyone after seeing Lt. Commander Hevos' report, that the Seer Spirits were not all dead. It was probable that a hand full were going to Earth. He could kill them, but nothing hindered them from attacking Earth before he had a chance to stop them. The Argonian scout ships were on high alert out beyond the system, which would give him the needed time to react to multiple assaults. It wouldn't be long before Ship would be there, hopefully with his fellow Guardians. The South Americans had taken the initiative out of the Australian's hands. If they could distract them long enough, the superhumans could covertly disable the devices without triggering their secondary destructive effects. His family was down there in New York, and he knew they were safe, because he trusted his fellow Earthlings, and Joshua's promise that he would protect everyone on the planet.

Quatris and the two astronauts sat back on the long sofa staring at Earth and the Sun in the background wondering what the future held.

Author Notes

--- ❦ ---

This book starts the story of the Argonian Empire which is the salvation for Earth's future against alien invasion and total destruction. There are superhumans like Quatris, Hellfire, and Joshua who could defend Earth from the alien enemies; but who would protect other planets like Earth?

This book jumps into a space world of existence that spans about a decade and a half of story time. I didn't want to keep jumping in and out of space in the eight book series so I created one book to focus on the majority of the space adventure. It is also one of the middle books so as to place the overall context of what happened in space to warrant so much attention to Earth. Susan and John, becoming Queen and King of the Argonian Empire is part of that attraction, but in reality it was the Galactic Guardians who placed Earth as a prime target for destruction. The Pylaxians, Sitherians, and Seer couldn't fight the Guardians as a group, so they had to divide and not just conquer, but kill the guardians. The fact that four out of the seven initial Guardians came from Earth was enough for them to make a plan to destroy the planet from within and not just rely on a planet destroyer from space.

This storyline is very long and I know this book could have easily been written into two or three books total; however, I didn't want to put too many books into a series which is not supposed to be solely in space. I also wanted to weigh heavily on the lifestyles and actions of superheroes on Earth. There is a possibility I will write more books after the Superhero Epic series which compliment or are a spinoff of the storyline, but only time and how fans enjoy this current series will tell. If I do, it will more than likely be about the South American spies who infiltrate the countries, Joshua's future after Earth, a closer look at Lady Sinop's history and future as a Guardian, and Lord Axer's character who was a major factor in the victory of the empire in the ancient wars. I'm always open for suggestions and I'm sure someone will ask me to write about other superhero characters before EFL was established, and the time period after the timeline of the eighth book. I do plan to continue writing until I am well into my early hundreds, so I hope my writing is constantly improving, as it should be for all authors.

Once again there are many names being thrown out there for the reader, but it is inescapable for me to tell the story without all the different characters, so I ensured the reader didn't get more than one alias or name for each character, except for John and Susan. This list of characters, languages, names of spaceships, and races is by far the longest list I have created in the first four books of the series. Hopefully this list minimized the confusion as to who was who throughout the story. The list is included at the beginning and end of the book in such a way that the list starts on a back page allowing the reader to see two pages at a glance. My purpose was so the reader can track the story and action without worrying about forgetting a name and placing it with a face or description. Unfortunately, the story stops, timeline wise, in book seven of the series. I hope you have enjoyed this book and continue to read the Superhero Epic series.

Masterminds	-	book 5
Superhumans From the Past	-	book 6
Ultimate Assassins	-	book 7
Last Hope for Earth	-	book 8

List of Characters

Lord Klakin — Leader of the Galactic Guardians (born on the planet Ios)

Lady Cerimon — Galactic Guardian (born on the planet Jahnuny)

Lord Hellfire (Rick Alexander) — Galactic Guardian and Member of Energy, Fire and Light (EFL) superhero group in New York

Lord Medroc (Patrick Lawrence) — Galactic Guardian (born in Seattle, WA)

Lord Morinar (Fedar Emsky) — Galactic Guardian (born in Arsk, Russia)

Lord Sedric — Galactic Guardian (born on the planet Tir Goth)

Lord Quatris (Scott Emerson) — Galactic Guardian and Leader of EFL

Lord Axer — Galactic Guardian (born on the planet Argonia)

Lady Kara — Galactic Guardian (born on the planet Shimoor)

Lord Paldez — Galactic Guardian (born on the planet Argonia)

Lady Sinop — Galactic Guardian (born on the planet Rasdal)

Lady Hebshilon — Klakin's mother and Special Envoy for Queen Omia

Larissa Emsky — Fedar Emsky's mother (born in Perm, Russia)

Princess Navia Yalu — Princess of Dothoria, the largest realm in the Argonian Empire

Queen Omia — Sole ruler and queen of the Argonian Empire

Sorthan — Emissary for Queen Omia and Princess Navia, in Kron sector of the Argonian Empire

Urhimia — Emissary for Queen Omia and Princess Navia, in Rim sector of the Argonian Empire

Yohania — Emissary for Queen Omia and Princess Navia, in Hith sector of the Argonian Empire, second in command of the starship Lardose

Elexsuia Peli Lanta — Second in command of Princess Navia's flagship

Joldar Crom — Argonian Royal Soothsayer for the Queen

Loar Crom — Argonian Royal Soothsayer for HRH Toluvis

Lieutenant Rudez — Argonian telepath of the House of Cammeth

Prince Hethos — Argonian Prince of the House of Cammeth

Her Royal Highness Toluvis Cammeth — Ruler of the House of Cammeth

Queen Neeva / Susan M. Goodman / Pandora — New Queen of the Argonian Empire and member of the Eternal Champions

King Etron / John Goodman / Mindseye — New King of the Argonian Empire and member of the Eternal Champions

Captain Allina — Captain of the lead scout ship Teldious

Admiral Frouls Lek — Admiral of the Royal 7th Pylaxian Space Fleet

Feesel — Drakon, mercenary

Hamiftar — Drakon, space suit engineer

Kormath Sittar — Faction Leader of Drakon spies

Emperor Tiaxtee — Ruler of the Pylaxian Empire

Emperor Zuphra — Ruler of the Sitherian Empire

Vox'wer — Celestial Seer spirit, planet destroyer

Colonel Peter Cornelius — US Astronaut and ISS commander

Lieutenant Colonel Milan Golubova — Russian Cosmonaut and communications specialist on the ISS

Joshua Marks — All powerful superhuman

Richard Octavian / Creator — Leader of the Eternal Champions

Elizabeth A. Octavian / Isis — Member of the Eternal Champions

Larcis G. Draven / Night — Member of the Eternal Champions

Erica — Member of the Eternal Champions (Super Artificial Intelligence computer)

Battle Fortress Lardose — Lady Hebshilon's flagship

Star Destroyer Darhim — Commander Sorthan's scout ship

Star Destroyer Gurgus — Cerimon's flagship in the Colax sector of space

Star Destroyer Hydrex — Commander Urhimia's scout ship

Star Destroyer Volatis — King Etron's secondary flagship

UFF Andromeda –South American Space Fleet Flagship

UFC Antares – South American Space Cruiser, Battleship class

Kiex – Pylaxian language

Vorlin, or Du Los – Universal languages used in the Milky Way Galaxy

Races

Argonian — Origin – Argonia   **Kelos** — Origin – Kel

Baxcion — Origin – Ios   **Moridanian** — Origin – Moridan

Drakon — Origin – Lyra sector of space

Earthling — Origin – Earth   **Pylaxian** — Origin – Plax

Gillithe — Origin – Tarthillia   **Seer** (Crestin) — from dwarf galaxy

Goth — Origin – Tir Goth   **Sitherian** — Origin – Cros Asviel

Keelin — Origin – Jahnuny   **Wordian** — Origin – Cameil

Hutor, Quilar, and Morthemar — Argonian bloodlines, most royal bloodline traits come from the Quilar.

www.ingramcontent.com/pod-product-compliance
Lightning Source LLC
Chambersburg PA
CBHW02025303726
47499CB00001B/191